"The old advice has it that great novelists sl[...] then Thomas Reed is of the first rank. *Pocket[...] warp and weft of the contemporary, often with a comic awareness of how these fabrics are woven in. But for me it is the outbursts of wisdom and poignancy, often completely unexpected in his dramatic scenes, that are the even greater achievement. us, maybe the thing Reed notices best, when one comes to the end, is how family is always forged in change. To read *Pocketful of Poseys* is to experience this startling thought, so relevant to what makes fiction meaningful, anew."

–RICK MOODY, AUTHOR OF *THE ICE STORM* AND *HOTELS OF NORTH AMERICA*

"Grippingly poignant and elegantly profound, *Pocketful of Poseys* will have you laughing in one moment and crying in the next as you journey with the adult children of the Posey family to scatter their parents' ashes across the globe. A must read for anyone who has ever experienced life."

–LIZ MACCIE, AUTHOR OF *LESSONS I NEVER LEARNED AT MEADOWBROOK ACADEMY* AND FILM PRODUCER

"Tom Reed is a raconteur of the best and rarest kind: a spell-binding, curl-up-in-your-armchair-and-let-the-afternoon-slip-away storyteller. Turn the wi-fi off, put the kettle on, and let his storytelling carry you into the past, around the world, and down every channel of human experience from the heartbreakingly sad to the side-splittingly funny."

–SUSAN CHOI, AUTHOR OF *TRUST EXERCISE*

"*Pocketful of Poseys* is a clever dark comedy that mines heavy topics with a light touch. Reed takes us on a hilarious family trip, rife with sibling rivalry and generational conflict, to four continents, all to unearth long held family secrets one envelope at a time. Enjoy the ride!"

"We have the Durrells of Corfu, the Wapshots of St. Botolphs, and now the Poseys of New Hampshire—the rockbound land of Live Free or Die. Witty, dark, picaresque, and joyously contrarian, the saga of the Poseys family will warm your heart, make you cringe, and ultimately lift your spirit. Another outstanding novel from Thomas Reed."

"A poignant and entertaining family odyssey that takes the reader all across the globe with the grown children and grandchildren of Cinny Posey and her husband Frank as they scatter the couple's ashes, fulfilling Cinny's wishes and revealing the secrets she couldn't share in her lifetime."

"*Pocketful of Poseys* is a tour de force and a tour of the world that takes you out of your comfort zone and into the shadowy secret life of a mother who sacrificed again and again."

"A funny, authentic, and contemporary story of the shifting dynamics between two adult siblings and their families in the wake of their mother's death. A trip around the world turns into a journey into the past as secrets are revealed and new connections are forged. Reed's dialogue sparkles."

–SUSAN PERABO, AUTHOR OF *THE FALL OF LISA BELLOW*

"Buckle up and circle the globe with the Poseys' six surviving family members as they sprinkle Cinny and Frank's ashes everywhere from a remote Thai island to St. Peter's piazza in Rome to a rest stop on the New Jersey Turnpike. Thomas Reed's delightful *Pocketful of Poseys* will have you laughing and crying from the very first chapter."

–TULLAN HOLMQVIST, CO-AUTHOR,
THE WOMAN IN THE PARK AND *LACIE'S SECRETS*

POCKETFUL OF POSEYS

THOMAS REED

BEAUFORT BOOKS

Poem on page 167
Clare Harner, 1934, "Do Not Stand At My Grave And Weep," *The Gypsy*.

Paperback: 9780825310263
Ebook: 9780825309014

For inquiries about volume orders, please contact:
Beaufort Books, sales@beaufortbooks.com

Published in the United States by Beaufort Books
www.beaufortbooks.com

Distributed by Midpoint Trade Books
a division of Independent Publisher Group
https://www.ipgbook.com/

Book designed by Mark Karis
Printed in the United States of America

TO DOTTIE

My soul and travel mate through tears and laughter alike.

HANOVER

Grace Tingley always struggled letting herself into her mother's cottage, especially when her arms were full. Cinny Posey's front door had a handle as quirky as its owner. Unless you pressed the latch down with one hand, just so, while you twisted the key with the other, you might as well have been trying to husk a coconut with a plastic spoon.

Grace huffed in exasperation, dropped the bundle of clothing onto the brick stoop, and did it the only way that worked. It had been raining for twenty-four hours, but the door swung open with its usual dry squeak. Grace took a deep breath and bent down for the things her mother had portentously announced she wouldn't be needing any more.

"Shit!" Grace muttered as she straightened up.

The puddle on the stoop hadn't looked deep, but an added weight to the clothes and a chill seep of water through her sleeve told Grace otherwise. She stepped into the narrow entryway, wiped her feet half-heartedly on the mat, and nudged the door closed with her butt. Her mother's things were still dripping when she reached the laundry room and dumped the pile on top of the washer. She had plenty of time to deal with them. Plenty of time, too, to grab a mop and soak up her wet footprints and the trail of rainwater from Lucinda Maynard Posey's last load of everyday wash.

Grace eyed the rain-pocked sweater she'd draped over her mother's undergarments so they wouldn't be on display if anyone spied her scurrying through the lingering March showers back to the "Level Three Deluxe" she'd talked her parents into taking years back. "We don't need that much space anymore," her mother had protested. "I'd be happy in a tent."

"Do you think you might possibly have visitors?" Grace had retorted. "Like maybe children who love you?"

The dampened red woolen cardigan was classic Talbots. Cinny Posey had a weakness for Italian lingerie, but she'd always been a Bean or Patagonia girl—far more Hanover-Norwich than Greenwich-Darien. Still, a few years back she'd evinced a fair semblance of gratitude when Grace's well of Christmas-gifting ideas had run dry and she'd settled, glumly, for a $200 gift certificate from the classic purveyor to preppy matrons. That, and a professional photograph of Cinny's Maine Coon cat, Jimi.

So much depends upon a red sweater, thought Grace, *glazed with rainwater…beside the white chemise.*

It must have been the endless showers that reminded her of the Williams poem, lurking there in her memory like attic dust. She was tempted to pick the sweater up and press it to her face, just to take in the scent. Just to see how it made her feel. Her mother had been living at Hanover Hills for three years now, alone (excepting Jimi) for all but a few months. Still, the cottage hadn't taken on any distinctive aura besides that of generic cleansers with a hint of used kitty litter. Maybe the old, unmistakable, comforting-yet-consternating scent of the historic Posey household had depended more on Grace's father than on her mother.

Grace walked back to the kitchen, tossed her coat onto the counter, and tugged open the refrigerator. The cold air flowed down and around her bare ankles like invisible liquid. The fridge was still depressingly empty, mute testimony to her mother's dwindled appetite and Grace's own disinclination, honestly, to settle into her current familial role. Lowfat milk. Lowfat yogurt. Some celery and carrots in the veggie drawer. A squeeze bottle of Grey Poupon. A jar of Hellmann's Light. Three half-empty cans of Jimi's wet food: Chicken Choice, Tuna Treat, and Tasty Turkey. Grace hadn't touched any of them, dreading the musty stench she knew they'd exude at room temperature. Jimi seemed to be doing just fine on dry Friskies anyway.

Grace grabbed one of the bottles of sauvignon blanc she'd slotted into the bottom rack, swept the door shut with her knee, and walked over to the island. Yesterday's unwashed stem glass looked totally reusable. She twisted off the cap, poured a healthy measure, and trudged over to the couch. The sigh that escaped her as she sank into the deep cushions would have passed muster in the House of Usher.

"Hang in there, Gracie," she said as she tipped back a hearty gulp.

Jimi materialized out of nowhere and leaped up beside her. He stared at her briefly—his eyes saucer-wide and his marbled nose flaring with the smells she'd brought in from outside—then curled up to lick his luxuriant tail.

Grace reached for her phone. She'd switched it off that morning—not her habit, but there'd been some big items on the day's docket. The screen lit to the press of her thumb. It was a relief to see nothing more than a "3" in the red ball above the WhatsApp icon. The first message was from her husband Jack, back in Connecticut. *Been thinking about you a bunch, Honey Pot. Call me after a glass or two. Miss and love you.*

Grace grinned and hit "Chelsea," next to a tiny picture of a smiling blond twenty-something woman, sporting trendy sunglasses on the beach in Aruba—or had it been Antigua? *Wish I could be there, Mom. Give Nana my love and give me a call after you've had something to eat. Only if you want to. You're the best daughter ever! And the best mom! [Heart emoji]. Chel.*

Grace kicked off her shoes, crossed her ankles on the coffee table, and took another serious pull. The next line read, "Brian." Smirking amiably out from the image ball was a handsome forty-plus man with a trim, brown beard and a baseball cap that read, *Life Is Good.* A snow-capped volcano loomed in the background. If the picture were bigger, you might have seen that his eyes were Grace's eyes, too. Wide set. Direct. Blue. She pressed to see what her fraternal twin and sole sibling had to say.

What the hell, Grace? The Director of Nursing called to say you're not letting Mom eat. What the fuck is going on?

"Bloody hell!" she said.

Despite her indulgent embracing of the red Talbots cardigan, Lucinda Posey was a child of the Sixties. Her countercultural birthright had served her well when Frank landed his lifelong job at Dartmouth. Instantly pegged as "the young Shelley guy and his Joni Mitchell wife," the couple settled into the casually hip enclave of Hanover as easily as sun-bronzed feet slide into a seasoned pair of huaraches. It helped that they'd met at Oberlin, he as an English major, she as a budding art historian with a minor in Studio Art. Nor did it hurt that they'd helped found a co-op rumored to put on two "naturist" banquets a year—one on Halloween and the other on Valentine's Day—both reportedly climaxing with hosts and guests eating dessert off each other's naked abs. On more than one evening around the Posey dinner table after Grace and Brian had reached their teens, Brian pressed his parents hard to confirm the alleged postprandial rite. Every time, Grace—whose early traumas included walking into her parents' bedroom in search of midnight comfort only to find the two deep in the primal act—leered at her rashly curious brother with equal rage and dread. Frank had always lowered his head in what could have been either shame or remorse. Cinny's eyes had always sparkled.

Grace's mother had made it to Woodstock for that celebrated August weekend. Frank had been caught up in his parents' grand thirtieth-anniversary celebration on the Jersey Shore, but Lucinda had grabbed a couple of girlfriends and hitched on up, macramé totes flung over their shoulders and sleeping bags under their arms. She was never the type to gloat or put on airs, but the fact that she'd been a cog in that wondrous "something turning" all the way from Richie Havens on Friday to Jimi Hendrix on Monday gave her a sense of spiritual worth that buoyed her mightily any of the rare times she and Frank fell into conflict or competition. She was never without a cat—sometimes multiple cats—and she endowed a long line of them with names straight out of the fabled lineup: Arlo; Janis; Ravi; Country Joe; Crosby, Stills, Nash, and Young (all from one litter); and now, likely the last but arguably the most splendiferous, Jimi. Her mother never confirmed it, but Grace knew in her bones that she'd been named after Gracie Slick, the stoned chanteuse of Jefferson Airplane. Meanwhile, Brian's one real gripe against the parent he otherwise adored was that she hadn't favored him with an equally luminary moniker—say Santana or Sly.

As for Mother Posey herself, although she flagged her rides up to Yasgur's Farm as Lucinda Billings Maynard, she was curiously but insistently "Cinny" by the time she hitched back south to Frank. Exactly why the change, she never let on. When she was asked—as she was now and again—she'd respond as coyly as she did when people asked her about per-capita whipped-cream consumption rates in Oberlin, Ohio.

Frank Posey's college professors fired him up with much the same passion as the thought of strawberry shortcake dished up in his girl-friend's navel. The September after graduation, he'd driven his jet-black Karmann Ghia down to Charlottesville to begin his graduate studies at UVA. His family was rich enough that living on a professor's salary was a plausible option, and once he'd convinced Cinny that legal wedlock wasn't just an oppressive remnant of the Middle Ages, she'd agreed to marry him. There was a bit of a flap over the vows at the ceremony—the temperamentally anti-Jesuit groom insisted on taking Cinny as "Frank" rather than as Francis Xavier Posey—but once Frank promised a pair of very determined grandmothers that he and Cinny would raise all of their offspring in the True Faith, he quashed enough familial anxiety that most of the tears shed at the ceremony were happy ones.

As for that promise to his grandmothers, Frank's family had always been so relentlessly dysfunctional that he'd vowed since adolescence that he'd absolutely, positively, never become a father. His mother, for example, had gleefully blown the whistle on her own brother-in-law for serial tax fraud. In return, when she came down with acute appendicitis, her sister reportedly offered her surgeon ten thousand dollars to remove her uterus along with the infected organ. For her part, the hyper-skeptical Cinny barely acquiesced to enter a church, let alone wear a white gown. (That, however, hadn't kept her from cheerfully accepting her in-laws' wedding gift of an extended honeymoon in Australasia.) As for ever having children, she was as indifferent to the prospect as she was to rodeos and frozen TV dinners. When Grace and Brian finally came along, the couple quickly agreed that theirs would be a militantly agnostic household.

Frank arrived at UVA just after a legendary chairman of the English Department had finished raiding the best universities in the country to assemble a world-beating team of literary scholars. Frank caught the ensuing wave of academic momentum with the verve and daring of a Waimea nose rider, publishing three articles in distinguished literary journals before the end of his second year. In his fourth year, he landed a Fulbright Fellowship and spent ten months at University College, Oxford, doing research for a dissertation on Percy Shelley—specifically the impact on the poet of his marriage to Mary Wollstonecraft Godwin. Frank would probably have said it was a productive year *despite* his own marriage, with Cinny constantly declaring, say, that it would be much more fun to go punting on the Cherwell, or lunching at the potato pub up in Woodstock, than for him to spend another dreary day poring over musty volumes in the Bodleian's Upper Reading Room. The end result, though, was a dissertation that was published by Cornell with only minimal revisions—and which secured Frank that consequential job offer from Dartmouth. He remained in Hanover for his whole career, moving on only when he ended his earthly days at the age of seventy-one.

Even though Cinny never tired of tempting Frank to duck his professional responsibilities for a little casual hedonism, she was enduringly proud of her husband during his lifetime. When he'd inexplicably developed a fondness for pricey professorial sports coats after making it through graduate school in peasant shirts and a fringed leather hippie vest, she *did* roll her eyes each time he added another scratchy specimen to what became the biggest collection of Harris Tweed in the Upper Valley. Still, he always wore his herringbones with a pair of faded jeans and—weather permitting—Birkenstocks; and as for Cinny, she'd choked back her scorn for preppy clothing and clerked in James Campion Clothing's women's section to bolster the family finances until Frank earned tenure. Once he'd attained that scholarly beatitude, she moved on to volunteer at Planned Parenthood until an unplanned pregnancy—for her, gracefully, and for him, grudgingly accepted—led to the births of Grace and, fifteen minutes later, Brian.

A rip-roaring case of post-partum depression kept her housebound until the relentless visits from Frank's mother became more insupportable than any degree of lingering melancholy—at which point Cinny snapped out of her funk with a speed that took Frank's breath away. For a while, she arranged for one of Frank's students to look after the children one day a week while she resumed her volunteer work at Planned Parenthood. Then an art class Frank lined up for her re-ignited an old Oberlin passion, and she began to draft and illustrate her own children's books—books, at least, that *featured* children.

Frank hadn't been sure whether his wife's prime creative goal was parental nurturance or progressive satire; to him it was as though Jonathan Swift had decided to rewrite *Mother Goose*. *Where Sausages Come From* seemed meant to do for the under-eight set what *The Jungle* had done for the adult reading public many decades earlier. *The Unkindest Cut* shone a critical spotlight on the questionable practice of tail-docking and ear-clipping with select breeds of dogs (Frank having successfully diverted her from an earlier focus on various forms of human genital mutilation). And *Say Goodbye to Bessie* told the moving story of a Nebraska farm girl who learns of the passing of her pet calf over a plate of home-made veal piccata. With this last especially, Frank secretly wondered if his wife's post-partum woes hadn't been supplanted by something demonic.

Frustratingly, Cinny's efforts to find either agent or publisher met with little success. One editor tactfully wrote, "What is it, basically, with your meat obsession?" and suggested she consider a story about root vegetables. It wasn't until she dialed back on her drive to be truly innovative that she'd managed to place and publish *Markie Has an Accident*. Luckily, the critics were more favorably disposed than Frank to Cinny's eccentric parental vision, lauding her book as "a disarmingly honest foray into childhood leakage of all sorts" with illustrations that "playfully evoke all of the requisite messy realities—yet with a palette and a style that recall the French pointillists." Her children, young as they were, remained less sure of the book's excellence: Brian had worried that Markie's dimpled, vomiting cheeks looked suspiciously like his own, while Grace was certain the book was really about her own admittedly erratic progress toward evacuative control.

Frank's career had unfolded with more comfortable predictability. His Shelley book was followed by a brilliantly innovative study of Romantic treatments of flowing water (not at all indebted, he wittily declared in the volume's back matter, to his wife's *Markie* volume). Sabbaticals came every seven years, the most memorable of them being the nine months the family had spent in Christchurch, New Zealand, while Frank shifted gears and researched the voyages of Captain Cook and their impact on British representations of the female body. (Cinny cynically dubbed the resulting study "Frank's Tit Book.") His sentence to chair the English Department came right when anyone might have expected—likewise his promotion to full professor. His last big project was a magisterial biography of Shelley that, among other novel revelations, reported for the first time that the famous poet had drowned off the coast of Livorno during a daft, opium-induced search for a mermaid that local fishermen swore frequented the area. Reviewers deemed Frank's effort less magisterial than he'd hoped, largely because the explosive letter about the northern Italian mermaid, "discovered" by Frank in the University College library, turned out to be a sophisticated fake produced by a notorious undergraduate prankster. To say that the borderline-scathing critical response took some of the luster off of Frank's final years at Dartmouth would be an understatement—and for the first time in his life, Frank had grown a full beard and started sporting sunglasses, even on cloudy days.

Cinny, meanwhile, continued to balance running the Posey household with her work at Planned Parenthood and her writing career. *Markie Has an Accident* was followed by *Chicken Pox Are Coming to Town, Gamma Isn't Crazy—She's Just Old*, and *Hooray! Your First Kiss!* She secretly hoped the Caldecott people would eventually single her out for their fame-assuring honors, but she contented herself with the royalties that, more and more dependably, bolstered the family coffers.

The children progressed through primary, middle, and high school. Grace excelled in every realm imaginable. Brian in turn accepted, with annoyance and cynical resignation, his identity as "Grace Posey's twin brother." She garnered countless academic awards at Hanover High, starred on the girls' soccer team (repeat State champs!), served as Homecoming Queen (with the appropriate sarcasm), and earned herself a scholarship at Princeton. Dropping soccer her junior year to concentrate on academics, she followed in her father's footsteps with a prize-winning senior thesis on gender ambiguity in the novels of D. H. Lawrence—which (for reasons that weren't immediately clear to everyone who knew her) she dedicated to her brother. Her impressive mix of talents and commitments made her a natural for a Rhodes Scholarship, and she made it all the way to a face-to-face interview with the regional Rhodes committee before she lost out to the son of a United States senator. Meanwhile, Brian repeated Introductory Spanish (twice), played three years on the Ultimate Frisbee team (but never lettered), totaled a dirt bike he'd borrowed from a classmate (without asking), and managed, over his four high-school years, to hike every mile of the Appalachian Trail between Massachusetts and Maine. Littleton State took a little longer, but he capped off six years of sporadic attendance with a degree in Recreation Management. Several years after graduation, he admitted to himself that he would have majored in film studies if it hadn't seemed like something Grace would do.

Cinny and Frank had stayed in their big house near the college for a half-dozen years after he retired. Cinny encouraged him to offer a course at Dartmouth every once in a while—dust off his old Shelley text and introduce a few more youths to "Ozymandias"—but he showed no interest. "I'm done with them," he muttered resolutely, "and they're done with me." After a few tries, Cinny gave up pushing.

Every time Grace visited Hanover, she'd pointed out that the old family house was getting too big for the two of them. The day was surely coming when negotiating the long staircase up to and down from their bedroom would be more a peril than a useful exercise. They finally moved, at her insistence, to Hanover Hills, but they'd only been there a little over three months when, on a frosty January evening, driving to visit a friend at the VA Hospital, Frank had swerved off I-91 at the sharp curve just short of the White River Bridge. The car had flown through the high snowbank, slammed into the granite wall behind it, and exploded into flames.

The police assured Cinny that her husband had died instantly. She found that to be small consolation for losing her partner of fifty years.

That spring, Cinny had begun to notice a tremor in her right hand. She thought at first that it might be the by-product of some exercise classes she'd been taking. But weeks and then months passed, with no improvement.

Grace had tried to reassure her. Neurological ructions were par for the course as one matured, she insisted.

"And what's the difference," Cinny asked, "between 'maturing' and 'withering'?"

Grace said she should be glad she still turned heads at the co-op every time she went grocery shopping. "Great!" Cinny replied. "Now I'm the hot granny who can't stop *twerking*!"

True to form, Cinny kept on joking about her condition, making no effort to hide it from anyone. One of the more memorable blushes she ever drew from her daughter was on the Thanksgiving when Grace and Jack and Chelsea had driven up from Westport and Brian bused up from Boston. They'd all been sitting around the dinner table after a gargantuan turkey course when Cinny power-trembled a slice of pumpkin pie right off the pie server and onto the tablecloth. Shaking her head, she tittered, "It's such a pity Frank's gone. Can you imagine the hand jobs I could be giving him?"

Brian laughed so hard he'd thrown up in his mouth. Grace reddened mightily and left the room.

As bravely as she'd carried on, Cinny was secretly terrified. Her own mother had died of Parkinson's disease when she just a little older than Cinny—after years of being cared for in her sister's home while she slid deeper and deeper into motor incompetence and dementia. At first, Cinny refused to seek medical advice, dreading what might be confirmed. The tremor grew worse, though, and it cropped up on her left side too. Grace and Brian finally convinced her to see a specialist. One of New England's most celebrated neurologists was based at Dartmouth Hitchcock Medical Center, and Cinny agreed to meet with him as soon as it could be arranged. A month later, she dutifully kept her word, only to be told that the only way to diagnose her condition (short of an autopsy, which she said she wasn't quite ready for) was to put her on a Parkinson's medication and see if the symptoms diminished. If they did, she probably had the disease. If they didn't, it had to be something else.

"That's about as sensible as throwing me off the roof of the hospital," Cinny argued. "If I glide down, I'm a flying squirrel. If I'm killed, I was something else."

She told Grace that evening that she must have wandered by mistake into the Proctology Department: all she'd seen at the hospital was a huge asshole.

Before long, the falls started. The first time, after she'd gotten up in the middle of the night to pee, Cinny managed to get back on her feet and stagger back to bed, where she lay until dawn, staring grimly at the spinning ceiling fan. The second time, though, she couldn't for the life of her get off the floor and had to crawl to the den to find a phone low enough to reach to call the main desk for help. The talk at their regular care-plan consults had turned to the advisability of assisted living.

Cinny had spent a lifetime flitting from one enthusiasm to the next and, when she wasn't flitting, throwing herself body and soul into helping others. The prospect of assisted living was as appealing to her as double amputations at the knee. Since the neurologist's proposed "diagnostic leap" seemed almost sensible in comparison, she agreed to give it a try.

Unfortunately, she'd always been hypersensitive to drugs of any kind. For Cinny, a standard-strength Tylenol was like a triple dose of Nembutal. As a result, whenever she'd suffered from one of her rare headaches, she'd enlisted Frank or, later, Brian to rub her temples until the pain subsided. It might have been inevitable, then, that the trial run of Levodopa wasn't very successful. The pills reduced her tremor, but only by suppressing almost every other sign of life as well. She tolerated Sinemet no better. A woman who'd always sparkled like a burning fuse now plodded through the days of her trial with an affect as flat as month-old roadkill.

Grace had driven up from Westport to take stock of things, and phoned Brian to say their mother had turned into a zombie. He'd quipped nervously that Grace should lock her bedroom door at night so Cinny couldn't sneak in and eat her brain.

"Mom's not eating *anything*," Grace replied.

That same night, Cinny fell again. She hit her head on her bathtub going down, and even though she swore over and over in a lifelessly chilly voice that she hadn't passed out, Grace called the EMTs. The ambulance sped her mother to Hitchcock, where a CAT scan detected no intracranial bleeding. Hanover Hills insisted, however, that she move into their special care unit for several days to be observed and "assessed for placement." Meanwhile, they discontinued all pharmaceutical experiments.

As for residential placement, although Cinny had insisted on going back to her cottage and cat posthaste, Grace had to agree with the chief staff physician and Director of Nursing that the time for assisted living had sadly arrived. When she shared the news with her mother, Cinny raised herself bolt upright in bed and declared, in a voice that shook the room like a subway train rumbling into the station, "I'll be goddamned if I'm going to have you wiping my ass, Gracie Posey—you or anyone else. If I can't wipe my own ass, I just want to get the hell out of here like your dad did."

If Grace hadn't been stunned by the bellow her ailing mother managed to produce—and even more, by the stark practical implications of her nixing any change in her level of care—she might have asked what Cinny had meant by that cryptic *like your dad did.* As it was, she called the medical office and, as calmly as she could manage, suggested that she and her mother might be able to discuss the options the following morning.

Grace slept miserably that night, anticipating a daunting conversation come sunrise. As long as she remained within earshot, Cinny had fumed continuously, claiming that an unholy alliance between her own daughter and a place that was bilking her for eighty grand a year was plotting to lock her up in diapers and set her in front of the Shopping Channel for twelve hours a day. Following that, it hadn't helped Grace's quest for sleep that Jimi kept coming into the guest bedroom, jumping up onto her pillow, and muffling her like a furry CPAP. She toyed with calling Brian as soon as she got back to the cottage to bring him up to speed, but there would be more to talk about tomorrow; besides, he was so prickly lately about Matters of Mom that she hadn't wanted to put herself through an unnecessary call. Still, she worried now that she should have.

In the morning, Cinny claimed to have slept like a baby. She remained adamantly against any move into assisted living "But to be honest," she allowed, "I *have* been thinking about assisted dying."

Grace's mouth had fallen open.

"Seriously!" Cinny said.

"Mom!" Grace gasped. "What are you talking about?"

"Look at me, Gracie! I don't eat. I can't walk ten feet without taking a digger. I shake as bad as your dad the first time he tried to have sex with me."

"Mom!"

"He *did!* You should have seen him. He was petrified. Of course, it *was* kind of cold out there on the golf course."

"Mom!" Grace said again, blushing. "We have some serious decisions to make."

"Tell me about it."

"Really!"

"Really. Nobody knows that better than I do. I'm serious, though."

"About what?" asked Grace, as though the question might shunt them off onto an entirely different conversational track—about Tom Brady, maybe, or the future of Social Security.

"About dying," Cinny said simply. "About just calling it quits on all this nonsense and going to be with Frank." She coughed softly into a closed fist.

"Mom, you don't even believe in the afterlife."

"It sounds romantic, though, doesn't it?" Cinny grinned like a septuagenarian pixie. "And the doctors don't know I'm an agnostic."

Grace began to sense her mother was serious. "What have the doctors got to do with it?" she asked.

"They're the ones that can get me into a hospice program."

"Oh, God!" Grace shook her head vigorously.

"Oh, God, what?"

"Mom, you have so much to live for. There's Chelsea. She loves you so much. Your books are still selling incredibly well—"

Cinny flapped her hand dismissively.

"—and Brian just got married to a wonderful woman. You have a new step-granddaughter you barely even know yet. And there's Jimi!"

Cinny stared at her coolly. "Jimi's a sweetie," she said, "but am I supposed to want to keep living for a cat?"

Grace heaved a great sigh. "Hospice is for people who are already dying. We don't even know that you're dying."

"I do."

"So you're suddenly an effing doctor?" Grace asked, then cringed. She'd almost yelled. She was slipping back into a pattern she knew only too well. What was it with mothers and daughters? It was like the love came with strict instructions not to engage in it for more than twenty minutes without disassembling it for cleaning in an acid bath.

"Look at me!" Cinny croaked.

"I am looking at you, Mom."

"And?" Cinny's eyes probed her daughter's face. She looked like an early Christian, peering across the Colosseum toward the lion door. Her tremor only added to the effect.

Grace opened her mouth to speak and closed it again. It was true. For anyone who hadn't known Cinny in her prime, even three years earlier, she might have looked today like a reasonably healthy seventy-five-year-old—on the thin side, maybe, and slow-moving when she reached for things or tried to walk. And sure, she might need to use two hands to steady her coffee mug. But Grace still remembered her mother, as recently as the year her father died, looking and acting more like an Olympic decathlete with reading glasses than like any woman remotely her age.

Grace breathed in deeply, let the air out, and nodded.

Cinny had smiled. "Frank and I worked so hard to keep you and Brian from seeing how bad things got for your grandmother. At Aunt Ruth's. How she just went down and down, like a lead weight. Like a ..." She held her fist up to her mouth again, sniffed twice, and shook her head. "Maybe that was a mistake. Maybe we should have let you see what Mom was going through."

"We saw," said Grace, after a beat. "Both of us. And we talked about it. Then, and lately too." Cinny cocked an eyebrow at her skeptically, and Grace felt tears pushing up. "We don't want that for you, Mom."

"Oh, honey! Come over here." Cinny reached out, the short sleeves of her gown pulling back over the slack skin of her upper arms. Grace jumped up and rushed into her mother's embrace. The bed lurched and bumped into the nightstand, sending a plastic mug careening onto the floor, where it bounced in a spray of brown liquid. "That's okay, honey," Cinny said, squeezing her daughter then reaching up to stroke her hair. "Their coffee sucks. Eighty grand a year, and their coffee sucks."

Grace had burst out laughing, then sat up and swiped at her eyes with the backs of her fingers, gazing into her mother's face. She thought Cinny might be shaking in some new way, but no—she was just nodding. Now she was grinning.

"Oh, Mom," said Grace, the tears flowing again. "You're still so *here*. You're still so…Oh God! I don't know." She'd grabbed Cinny's hand and laughed again.

"I *am* still here, honey. I need you to know that. Brian, too. And I need you to hear me and help me slip away while I can still wear my fancy undies. Before these humorless bastards kit me out in dignity pants."

Grace had been slow to respond, caught in a Bermuda Triangle of admiration, resignation, and regret. There'd been times in the past when she *had* almost wished her mother were dead: provisionally, when Cinny had told her that the dress she'd chosen for the junior prom made her look like Shirley Temple fresh off a monthlong ice-cream bender; most definitely when she'd dragged Grace in for an HIV test after it emerged that her star-quarterback boyfriend at Hanover High was having sex with other boys. Now, though, the thought of her mother leaving this earth felt like it would end Time itself. How was she supposed to get back around to wishing her mother were dead—or at least helping her realize that wish for herself?

"Okay, Mom," she'd sighed, after what might have seemed a cruelly long pause. "How do you plan to do this?"

"I'll just stop eating," Cinny said.

"Can you really do that?"

"You mean, is it legal in the State of New Hampshire?"

"Not really," Grace smiled. "But is it?"

"It is. What's illegal is helping somebody else." Cinny leaned forward so Grace could adjust her pillows. "*Not*, you know, just by supporting somebody's decision." She said it with emphasis. "Or feeding them such shit meals they stop eating in self-defense. What you can't do is, say, slip them pills. Or give them a loaded gun."

"How do you know this?" asked Grace, struggling with the sudden urge to vomit. "Is this something you've, you know, been thinking about? For a while?"

"Not exactly, honey," Cinny grimaced. "Let's not get into it, okay?"

Grace stared at her mother; she looked like a withered wallflower hoping to be asked out onto the dance floor for one last time.

"Okay, so you wouldn't be facing a jail term. But not eating? At all? Do you really think you could manage that?"

"You've seen the fridge at the cottage," Cinny said, smiling. "I'm probably already halfway there."

If Grace had known in advance what she'd have to go through to get her mother into the hospice program at Hanover Hills—or, beyond that, how sketchy elements of the hospice experience at Hanover Hills would turn out to be—she might never have kept her appointment later that morning. She might have hopped on a plane to Seattle and spent the rest of her life hashing out old grievances with her brother.

Doctor Patel and Nurse Pease hadn't kept her waiting long, but they'd seemed genuinely shocked when Grace reported on her morning's conversation with her mother. "Voluntary self-starvation is a troublingly radical move to consider," the doctor had observed.

"If my mother proposing something radical surprises you," Grace had responded, "then you clearly haven't talked with her for more than five minutes."

When pressed, Nurse Pease confirmed that there was a "hospice option" at Hanover Hills. Yet she quickly added that, even if Cinny were somehow deemed to be suffering from a terminal condition, Grace herself would have to arrange for an independent hospice-care provider to send staff to the facility to tend to her mother. A far bigger logistical problem, she added, was that there was no official diagnosis in place. As things stood, Hanover Hills' prime legal obligation wasn't to let Mrs. Posey slip away to an ethereal reunion with her late husband (as romantic as they agreed that sounded), but rather to keep her as alive and healthy as she could possibly be. What if she were diagnosed as terminal? Grace had asked. Then they'd be able to respect the patient's and her family's wishes. Could anyone at Hanover Hills make that diagnosis? Not ordinarily, Dr. Patel replied. Then who could, ordinarily? Grace asked, anticipating the answer but about as eager to return with her mother to the neurologist's office as she would have been to undergo a pelvic exam on national television.

"That would be Mrs. Posey's specialist at Hitchcock," the doctor and nurse replied, in what struck Grace as calculatedly perverse unison.

Naturally, Grace went back to see Dr. Phillips. For years, she'd taken care of the bulk of Posey senior care, bearing front-seat witness to that strange but inevitable metamorphosis that occurs when people's parents become more and more like their children—only far less cuddly, far more susceptible to fatal illness, and annoyingly prone to resent their irksome new dependence on what had formerly been nothing more than helpless spawn. But that was only after she'd checked in with her brother.

Brian had lived in Seattle for nearly two decades, working in REI's Adventure Travel division. He'd made it back East at least once a year, but Grace was the designated sibling-on-call, living just five hours downriver from Hanover. She kept her brother posted about their mother's week-to-week condition, and he'd been East often enough to witness her steady decline; he'd even commented, lately, that her voice had gotten so tremulous she could have been taking his phone calls from the back seat of a 4x4 in the thick of the Baja 1000. Still, she suspected he'd be totally shocked by the most recent news. It was with some trepidation, then, that she'd rung him up.

"So, she's just going to stop eating?" he asked incredulously.

"That's her plan," said Grace.

"The food there must really suck."

"It doesn't. You've had it, remember?"

"Oh, yeah."

"Like, one of the two or three times you've bothered to come?"

There was silence at the other end.

"Are you still there?" Grace had asked.

"Where else would I be?"

"Okay. Sorry. I know how far it is."

"And expensive. It's not like I'm just driving up from Connecticut."

"*Just*? Just what?" Grace always hated it when this elevated pitch of aggravation came out of her mouth; it made her feel like she was turning into a crow. But her brother's dismissal enraged her. "The two, three times a month I'm doing, aside from emergencies?"

"Okay, Gracie. I'm sorry, too. I appreciate everything you've been doing." He paused. "So, what's next?"

"I've got to go back to that effing moron who put her on Levodopa and see if he'll give her a terminal diagnosis."

"Any chance of that?"

"If he's got any kind of heart under that pretentious white bath robe," Grace answered. "But I'm not holding my breath."

"And if he doesn't?"

"I don't know, Brian. Maybe there's some wiggle room at Hanover Hills. They know her. They like her."

"Yeah. How's she doing, anyway?"

"You know, except for the shakes and all, she's doing incredibly well. She looks ten years older, but there's so much of the old Mom there. Laughing. Joking. Giving me shit. I don't have a clue how she manages to keep it up. It's just that what she wants most in life now is to die."

"I know," Brian had said, after a beat. "God!"

Grace sniffed. "By the way, she asked me today to bring her a spiral notebook and some pens."

"Hmm. Maybe she's writing a journal."

"When has Mom ever kept a journal?"

"When has she ever decided to starve herself to death?"

Grace sighed. "I hope she's not writing a memoir. Some mortifying tell-all, you know?"

"One last chance to humiliate you?"

"I'm getting better, aren't I?" Grace asked. "Less prissy?"

"Maybe."

Maybe! she scoffed. *Caw!*

"*I* hope she's not writing another children's book," said Brian. "Like *Nana Pulls the Plug.*"

Grace giggled. "Or, maybe, *Markie's First Open-Casket Visitation.*

You should see her handwriting, by the way. It's atrocious."

There'd been another pause.

"Look," Brian said at last. "If you get her into hospice…"

"Yeah?"

"Let's make sure she really wants to go through with it."

"She really wants to go through with it, Brian. When did Mom ever start anything she didn't want to go through with?"

"Right. Well, maybe this isn't like anything else."

"Maybe."

For a moment, all Grace could hear was Brian breathing. "So," he said finally, "if she, like, starts to get close and she freaks out…"

"Yeah?"

"If she wants to change her mind, she can, right?"

"Of course, Brian. She's an adult."

"And you won't get on her case and tell her she's got to keep going?"

"Brian!"

"Or tell the doctors she's crazy and get them to sedate her and let her die?"

"Brian, what the fuck? Who do you think I am?"

"You know. You and her, you haven't always seen eye to eye on everything."

"That's 'You and *she*!' And fuck you, Brian—fuck you to hell! I ought to just hang up on you, you gay piece of shit." Grace heard a sigh, then the clicking thing her brother did with his tongue when he didn't know what to do or say. "Okay," she said. "Time out. I'm sorry. That was a shitty thing to say."

"It was." She could barely hear him.

"I was just so pissed that you could think…"

"I know," Brian said. "I was completely out of line. I just worry about her so much."

"Well, so do I."

"I know. It sounds like we have a plan, anyway."

"Yup."

"You'll keep me posted?"

"Of course."

"I wish I was there, babe."

"Yeah," she said. "So do I."

Grace had gone to Dr. Phillips's office at 6:30 the next morning to catch him before rounds. The Levodopa/Sinemet experiment had been inconclusive, he reminded her. The Levodopa/Sinemet experiment had been little beyond a hazing ritual for the sorority of the walking dead, she reminded him. It was unfortunate, he granted, that the side effects had proven too challenging for her mother to stay the course. It was unforgiveable, she retorted, that someone with a family history of Parkinson's disease showing Parkinson's-like symptoms that had clearly been diminished by bona fide Parkinson's drugs couldn't expect ethical treatment from the American healthcare industry. He'd reminded her that all physicians are bound by the Hippocratic Oath. She'd urged him, in that case, to go home that night and engage in repetitive self-penetration. Grace had left the office without the thing she'd come for—but with the certainty that she was an acorn fallen straight from the Cinny Posey tree.

Grace drove back to Hanover Hills, discouraged but not disheartened. She then laid siege to Doctor Patel and Nurse Pease, dragging them in on two separate occasions to sit with Cinny as she spun the moving tale of her long, long watch as her own mother went vegetable before her very eyes.

"I'm tired of trying new drugs," Cinny had sighed. "I'm tired," she'd added, with a pointed glance at Doctor Patel, "of listening to doctors. There's an inner voice telling me it's time to bow out. I want to honor that voice. Besides," she'd continued, with a meaningful glance at Grace, "I want so much to be with my husband. To be with my dear Frank in Heaven." Prepared for a conspiratorial wink, Grace had been very much relieved when it didn't come.

In the end, and despite Nurse Pease's poorly concealed reservations,

Doctor Patel had agreed to cross the final "T" and move Cinny to the ersatz hospice wing—provided the neurologist certified that her response to the trial medications was in line with Parkinson's. When Grace confessed, blushing, that her last exchange with Dr. Phillips hadn't ended well, Doctor Patel offered to float the proposal himself.

Within a day they had their certification, and Cinny had moved to a private room in the skilled-nursing wing.

Within another day, some significant challenges had emerged. The patient across the hall—an old fellow named Milt who was dying, quite painfully, of pancreatic cancer—had insisted on playing country-and-western music at ear-splitting volume. When Cinny sent word that she'd be grateful if he'd turn it down, he sent word back that he was surely entitled to spend his last, agonized hours listening to Merle Haggard at the volume Merle deserved. Always the optimist, Cinny assured Grace that the old S.O.B. was just going to motivate her to get through "all this shit" faster than she'd planned.

Ironically, the skilled-nursing staff had proven to be more of a challenge than Milt. As kind and dedicated as they clearly were, they were slow grasping the fact that Cinny wasn't in their care to get better. Her aim wasn't to stay in a medically facilitated holding pattern as long as she could, but rather to die as fast as she could reasonably manage. In contrast, the contracted visitors from Upper Valley Hospice had been wonderful. They got it to the soles of their Bean rubber duck boots. They'd washed her, helped her brush her teeth, talked to her, asked questions about the dozens of photographs Grace had pinned up next to Cinny's bed to remind her of her whole wonderful life, told her about their own families, and held her hand when Grace couldn't be there. One of them even played the harp for her when Milt was napping and the airwaves were temporarily free of nasal dirges bemoaning the death of a beloved coonhound or a man's singular misery when his teenage bride runs off with the Monsanto seed salesman.

But the regular skilled-nursing staff had been another story. Out of the salt-of-the-earth goodness of their hearts, no doubt, they couldn't serve breakfast to all the recuperating—or simply persisting—patients without dropping by to ask Cinny if she wouldn't enjoy a piece of smoked bacon, or a spoonful of scrambled eggs, or just the teeny-weeny corner of a cinnamon bun. At lunchtime—"Maybe just a sip of this yummy tomato soup?" At supper—"Everyone says these cute little potato buds are the best they've ever had. See? They look like little hearing aids!" They were, in their minds anyway, just being kind hosts to one more in an unending line of poor, suffering strangers entrusted to their care. *Whatsoever you do to the least of your kindred,* they may piously have reminded themselves, *that you do unto me!*

The part of Cinny that had always pulled for the Workers of the World had been powerfully tempted to say, "Well, just a spoonful of that yummy-looking tapioca you were *so* sweet to bring." And despite her grim determination to wing on, Cinny might just have conceded if Grace hadn't been there to nix an intake that would have jolted her metabolism out of its slow but steady dismantling of her being—that would have sent the counterproductive signal, *Hey! You're supposed to get going again!*—that would have extended for another day, or five, the whole exhausting business of Cinny's Final Escape.

"It's hard work, starving to death!" Cinny had confessed, a few days into the ordeal. "No little treats when you can't think of anything else to do. No Saltines. No peanut M&Ms. Not even a single solitary pomegranate seed!"

It was always clear that Grace's mother had spent her life with a man of letters.

Predictably, the misunderstanding over food intake between Grace and her brother had grown out of this tension between nursing Cinny's body and supporting her weary spirit. It came down to one incident in particular that took place when, after numerous awkward moments and conversations, Grace had assumed the regular staff had finally gotten the message.

She'd failed, as it turned out, to reckon on Meatloaf Night.

The food at Hanover Hills was deservedly famous among northern New England retirement communities. The home's executive chef had made his bones in Manhattan, and he'd assembled a staff that the two retirement communities north of town were constantly trying to poach. His menu was international, his nutritional savvy unparalleled, and his commitment to artful presentation astonishingly effective at luring diners poised on the doorstep of Eternity back to the Earthly Dining Room for at least one more tuck-in.

Despite his tony culinary chops, he was most famous for his home-style meatloaf. When the second Tuesday of each month rolled around, residents lined up at the doors of the main dining room right after their mid-afternoon naps, eager to get a seat near the buffet so they'd have a shot at seconds and thirds. Staff members who ordinarily rushed home right after work stuck around for dinner, sometimes inviting their spouses to join them. There was even a legend from a few years back about a woman who had slipped into a coma one Friday and seemed, through the weekend and the first of the week, to be steadily nearing the end. Come three o'clock the following Tuesday, however, she was seen to twitch modestly about the nose. At four o'clock, her eyes opened for the first time in a hundred hours; at 4:45, she was slipping into her tattered pair of pink plush mules; and at five o'clock, she was trundling down the corridor behind her walker, moving just as fast as her frail, resurrected body could carry her to be in good time for Meatloaf Night.

Small wonder, then, that on Cinny's first Tuesday in her hospice room, a nurse's aide had shown up at the door at 4:30 with a huge grin on her face and holding something behind her back as she leaned into the room.

"Helloooooooo, Mrs. Posey!" she said.

"Oh, hello dear," said Cinny.

"You know what night it is, don't you?"

"Christmas Eve?"

"Nooooo!"

"Walpurgisnacht?"

The girl looked mystified. "No, silly. It's Meatloaf Night."

"Oh, right. Tuesday."

"Yes, it is. And do you know what?"

"The chef forgot and made chow mein?"

The girl looked at Grace, who was in the habit of staying with Cinny until she put her to bed with a backrub at about eight o'clock. "Your mom's a real stitch," the aide said.

"Yes, she is," Grace agreed with a smile. "But what's that you've got there?"

The girl took a ten-ounce paper coffee cup out from behind her back. A straw stuck out of it, the kind with the corrugated section that you can bend to drink lying down. Looking at Cinny, she started to walk over to her bed. "I had the chef make it up special just for you," she said. "It's...puréed...MEAT LOAF!"

Grace sprang up faster than a nude picnicker who's just sat on fire ants. "Get that shit out of here!" she shouted.

The poor girl looked shocked. Remorse hit Grace as quickly as her rage.

"I'm sorry," she said. "That was awful. But Mom's not eating anything. And she hasn't had meat in months. Not that the food-group really matters." She felt herself flushing. "But you can't be feeding her, you know? Or else everything we're working so hard for, despite the assholes over at Hitchcock...well, please don't bring any more food in here. Ever."

The girl looked over at Cinny, who shrugged. "Okay," she said meekly. "Okay. Sorry."

She'd backed out of the room, her eyes on the floor. In another moment, Grace heard her running down the hall.

"So, Brian," Grace explained, having placed that dreaded return phone call the night of the drenched laundry, "I'm not keeping Mom from eating. I'm just protecting her from the kindness of idiots."

"You're not actually killing her, then. Just helping her commit suicide. Good to know."

"Actually, kiddo, I've thought about this," Grace replied pointedly. "We need to be careful about using any kind of 'helping' language here. Even when we're just talking to each other."

"Yeah," sighed her brother. "So, you haven't ordered Amazon's top-rated drug pump."

Grace snorted. "Not yet."

"And you think the Director of Nursing has it all straight now?"

"I do. Although I don't think she's ever been a big fan of the plan."

Brian was silent for a bit.

"You're okay with this, aren't you?" asked Grace.

"Well, yeah. I guess I have to be."

"It's what Mom wants."

"Not that Mom wanting it makes it any easier," said Brian.

"No," Grace agreed. "Not one effing bit."

"So. What kind of timeline are we looking at?"

"Hard to say," Grace sighed. "Ten days? Two weeks? Maybe longer. The doctor couldn't say."

"Has she stopped drinking?"

"She has. She was rinsing her mouth with water at first, but she said it was too tempting to swallow. She's got these glycerin mouth swabs… that I…" She choked up and couldn't speak.

"Geez, Gracie. It's gotta be so hard for you. When do you think I ought to come?"

Grace had to clear her throat twice before she could answer. "I don't know, kiddo. Don't wait long. Like more than a week."

"I'll get on it tomorrow."

There was a sudden thundering of cat feet as Jimi streaked out of the hallway and through the room, his tail fluffed up as fat as a swimming-pool noodle. A cloud of fur swirled in his wake. Grace giggled.

"What?" Brian asked.

"Jimi's on one of his manic tears. I can't seem to find his lithium." Brian chuckled. "So how's Ella?"

"Great! Ella's great."

"You guys doing all right?"

"Of course. Why wouldn't we be?"

"No reason—forget it."

"God, Gracie, you're so full of shit! I swear you think I'm only with Ella because I went through conversion therapy or something. Like it's a fake marriage, or—"

"No, no. Let's just cool it, okay?" Grace paused, thinking Brian might be clicking. "I'm asking because I love you. And I'm scared. And I guess I just need to know *you're* okay. Both of you."

"I get it, babe," said Brian after a moment. "Really. Look, I'll ring you up tomorrow, maybe. If I find a flight. I'll be calling Mom anyway."

"Okay. That'll be good."

"Hang in there, Tiger."

Every time he called her Tiger, Grace felt, Brian might just as well have been saying, *You were this close to Princeton sending you to Oxford. I was this close to Littleton State sending me home.* For the first nine months of their existence, the two of them had been obliged to share a space smaller than the inside of a basketball. Ever since, they'd continued to find ways to metaphorically elbow each other in the eye or kick each other in the groin. What never failed to amaze Grace was the way Brian could allude to any distinction she'd earned for herself—never, by the way, with anything less than stupendous effort—and still make her feel as though it was shrewdly calculated to throw mud in his eye. She had no idea how she'd managed to squeeze out of their mother's birth canal ahead of him, but Brian had clearly never forgiven her for showing him her heels as she broke out into the world of light and wonder.

Still, given that enduring undercurrent of resentment, Grace had been amazed when Brian became a pillar of strength for her during the most frightening time of her life.

It was in her third year at Yale, when she was in the graduate English program. She'd completed all her coursework and sailed through her orals with distinction (something she'd honestly considered keeping a secret from Brian) when she and Jack learned that they were going to be parents. They hadn't planned on it, but with only her dissertation to go and Jack's family eager to help with the expense of childcare, they'd come around to welcoming the joyous event.

Grace had always known to expect something in the way of morning sickness—something she imagined might be quelled by some light stretching and a glass of carrot juice. She was totally unprepared for the robust vomiting she experienced shortly into the first trimester and which carried on for weeks. *Hyperemesis*, they'd called it at Yale-New Haven—assuring her that, although it was something to monitor, she didn't need to be unduly concerned. Small consolation when, on two consecutive mornings, Grace didn't make it out of the Sterling Library stacks and into the restroom before she heaved up not only her meager breakfast but also, it felt like, the better part of her upper intestinal tract. It was bad enough that, on day two, as she crouched in the Romantic poetry section, eyes watering over a puddle of low-fat milk and soggy rice puffs, she suddenly flashed on the bizarre image of a walk home with a prolapsed esophagus dangling from her face like an elephant trunk.

A week later, she'd awoken to find blood—lots of it—on the bedsheets and in her underwear. She'd rushed to the emergency room, where an ultrasound revealed an enlarged uterus. Grace's OB/GYN ordered another round of testing, which led to the diagnosis of something called gestational trophoblastic disease—essentially a tumor of the placenta. Eighty percent of cases were benign, they told her, but it was rare for a fetus to develop normally in a woman with the condition. Against the odds, the tiny agglomeration of cells that would become Chelsea Marion Tingley was found to be perking along just fine. Grace, on tenterhooks, had asked her doctors whether it might be possible to take the baby to term. It was, they'd replied: a phenomenon known as "twin pregnancy." There was a forty percent chance of a successful birth.

"So," she'd said to Jack that evening as she drank a glass of water when she really wanted to be drinking a bottle or two of Pouilly-Fuissé, "the calculation here is whether the four-in-ten chance of our having a healthy baby is worth the one-in-five chance I develop cancer."

"Cancer," sighed Jack, who (at Grace's insistence) *was* in fact enjoying a nice French chardonnay.

"Choriocarcinoma, it's called," said Grace. "A nasty one. But also very susceptible to chemo, they say."

"*That*'s a mixed blessing," replied Jack, looking consummately dour.

"Hey! I'm already used to nausea and vomiting. But how would you feel about having a hairless wife?"

"Better than I would about having *no* wife, Honey Pot. I think we should just go ahead and have the whole mess scooped out."

Grace had sat speechless for a good minute, pondering the surreal implications of her life mate's lumping his own developing child together with a potentially lethal neoplasm under the simple phrase, *the whole mess*. "If I want to keep the baby," she'd asked at length, "could you support my decision?"

Jack had sighed, but soon nodded soberly.

"Okay," she said. "Let's do this. Only promise me one thing."

"What's that?"

"Don't ever tell Brian this is going to be something called a *twin pregnancy*."

"Because?"

"Because the baby will pop out first, the way I did. The bloody afterbirth—that'll be him. I'll never hear the end of it."

In the event, Brian came down to New Haven for the last month of Grace's pregnancy so Jack could study fourteen hours a day for the Connecticut bar exam. Cinny offered to help, but she and Frank were in the thick of major house renovations, and a lengthy visit would be hard to swing. Brian told her to stay put and just visit when the baby was born. He was sick of his retail job anyway. So it was Brian who cooked those weeks for the Tingleys, bought their groceries, lugged their laundry out to the laundromat, cleaned their house, and managed to get a Denver Boot slapped onto Jack's new BMW 2002 just nights after he'd brought it home from the dealership. As the days rolled by,

Grace came to feel closer to him than she could ever remember—even, she imagined, during all those months when they had floated in dark tandem at the end of their own individual umbilical cords: hers no better than his, no matter what he might have thought at the time. There had certainly been times, well beyond the normal antipathies of siblings, when she'd had reason to curse her brother. They'd suffered at least one major row that she thought, frankly, they might never work out. But once her ten-hour labor was past, seeing Brian press his nose up to Chelsea's little newborn snout and grin like a madman had given Grace a margin of hope that their relationship might not end in bloodshed.

So despite their ongoing gibes and jabs—always directed, in either direction, with the exquisite timing and lethal accuracy unique to those who know each other intimately—the thought of her twin brother getting to Hanover Hills was tearfully buoying to Grace. Cinny was thrilled as well. The week that ticked by between Brian's booking his ticket and his arrival felt to them both like the run-up to Christmas.

Grace met him at the Hopkins Center bus stop and drove him straight to the nursing facility. When he stuck his head inside the door, Cinny rose from bed, unassisted, for the last time she ever would and lurched barefoot across the cold floor to embrace him. Grace could see tears as Brian squinted above a bittersweet smile. Cinny held him tight for a good minute, eyes closed, head pressed against his chest.

Suddenly, from across the hall, came a plaintive, twanging whine. *When I tell you that I love you, you just whisper, "Go away!" All those kinky duds I bought you? Now—consarn it!—you won't play.*

Cinny pulled back from the clinch and looked Brian square in the eye. "You hear the shit I have to put up with?"

Although the tremor in her voice unsettled him, Brian laughed as he helped his mother turn back toward the bed. "That Milt?"

"How'd you know about Milt?"

"I guess Gracie mentioned him." Brian smiled.

"Milt's never going to die." Cinny cleared her throat with some effort. "He might as well be a vampire."

"So, Mom," said Brian, after he'd gotten her back into the bed and helped her pull up her covers, "what have you been up to?"

"Besides getting ready to check out of the Hotel California here?"

Brian looked at Grace with something between a grin and a grimace. "Well, sure."

"Thinking about you. And Gracie. How good you are to come all this way. To give up all this time for your mother."

"You've given up more than forty years for us, Mom," said Brian.

"They've been the best years of my life." Cinny beamed at the two until concern swept over her face. "Look at the pair of you now! I can't be saying sentimental shit like that. The last thing I want is a tear fest."

"What *do* you want, Mom?" asked Brian. "We're here to help. Whatever."

"Oh, you know. I want you and Grace to be happy. And Jack. And…"

"Ella?"

"Damn it! Yes. Ella. And Chelsea, of course. But to be honest," said Cinny, "I sort of wish you'd walked in and told me my eyes had rolled up into the back of my head. You know?"

Brian looked at Grace, who managed a smile. He reached out for Cinny's hand.

"Honestly," she said, "this is so damned long and drawn out. I don't have the faintest idea, really, how far along I am. Some nights I dream I'm dead. Then I wake up, and I'm not! It would have been easier to go out and get hit by a truck."

"Maybe," responded Brian through a nervous laugh. "I'm glad you didn't, though. At least before I made it back."

Cinny cleared her throat again. "Me, too."

"So, Mom," said Brian after a long pause. "Gracie says you've been writing something. Some journal or something."

"Not really," said Cinny. "I've just been jotting down a few notes."

"About…?"

"I'll tell you sometime. No hurry."

"Very mysterious, Mom. Very interesting." Brian reached out to brush a flake of dried skin off her lower lip. "That looks like a piece of steak. Are you living a secret life in the middle of the night?"

"The janitor and I are having a ball," said Cinny. "Your dad would have wanted that for me."

Grace and Brian sat up late, half watching the Red Sox get blown out by the Orioles. They talked some about their mother, about how sharp she seemed despite looking more and more frail. *Dwindled* was the term she used herself. Had Grace noticed how often Cinny was clearing her throat? And how soft her voice could get, especially when she was tired? That was typical of Parkinson's, Grace observed.

Brian asked about Grace's family. They were fine, she told him: Jack's law practice was thriving—estate work was a growth industry now that boomers were starting to drop off—and he'd managed to talk his partners into some *pro bono* work helping a new domestic-violence center raise funds and secure office space. He'd also just broken the twenty-thousand-dollar barrier with his watch collection.

"For the whole collection?" asked Brian, who wore a Seiko.

"For the latest Rolex," Grace replied. Jack was about to fly out to Las Vegas, she reported, to test-drive a Porsche that Paul Newman had supposedly raced. Chelsea, recently graduated from UVA like her dad, had just announced that she was in a serious relationship with a "somewhat older (but not yet on Medicare) man" whom she thought she might bring home to Westport sometime soon.

And Grace herself? Just fine, she told him. Her school was merging with another so they could offer K through 12; her SAT-prep students had been doing really well; and she and her partner had just won the doubles tournament at the Fairfield County Tennis Club.

As for Brian, things were going well at REI, where the Adventure Travel division had just hired five new staff members. Brian himself had recently returned from Croatia, where he'd scouted out hotels, routes, and general ground infrastructure for a new bicycle tour. He'd suffered a nasty fall just outside Split, badly bruised but not broken his shoulder, and learned that it was true, everything they say about codeine and disrupted bowel routines. Ella had just been named Agent of the Month at her realty company—her fourth time in a couple of years. Her daughter, Sage, had managed to stay enrolled at her high school despite her organizing a widely supported but highly controversial student strike when the food service refused to cater to vegans in the lunchroom. Sage had also just finished among the top ten women in the Tacoma City Marathon.

"How do you and Sage get along?" Grace asked.

"Better than Sage and her mom do sometimes," Brian told her.

The following days with Cinny had their ups and downs, with more and more of the latter. Grace and Brian noticed that when she reached for things, it was increasingly as though they were seeing her slipping into slow motion, watching with something between frustration and fascination as her hand inched toward whatever it was that she wanted. She joked that it was like being on a space shuttle, trying to manipulate a remote cargo arm on the other side of a thick porthole.

Some days she was remarkably chipper, others tired or even depressed. It was especially distressing when Grace brought in a perfumed candle and Cinny couldn't smell it at all. "It's a good thing I'm not eating," she quipped. "Everything would taste like cardboard. Then again, I could toot all day and never smell a thing."

Brian did better with the comment than his sister did.

One evening, Cinny dropped her hands on her chest and sighed deeply. "If I haven't gone in a few days," she said, "maybe you two should bugger off and leave me to do the job by myself." When Grace spoke with the head nurse about where things stood, she was told Cinny was "making progress." She might be a little less tired, the woman said, if she weren't scribbling away in a notebook most of the time Grace and Brian weren't around.

Brian had been there five days when the mystery of Cinny's writing project was revealed. He and Grace had grabbed a quick bowl of Cheerios and a yogurt and headed over to the nursing wing first thing in the morning.

"It's just so weird," said Grace, as they approached the nurse's station. "Here we've started our day running, showering, eating breakfast—the regular routine. And Mom will just have been lying there waiting. For us, and then for…not us, I guess."

Brian put his arm around Grace's shoulders and gave a squeeze. "It's great you put those photos up for her, Tiger. I'm sure they're bringing back all kinds of wonderful memories."

"I hope so."

They walked up to the nurse's station to check in.

"How is she?" Grace asked the head nurse. "Okay night?"

The woman was finishing a bear claw. She licked her fingers, crumpled the pastry wrapper, and tossed it into the trash. "Fine," she mumbled, her mouth still half full. "You know. Considering."

"Did she ring for anything during the night?"

The nurse smiled and shook her head. "Your mom's a trooper. With the dehydration and all, she's got to be suffering some, but…oh, gosh. I'm sorry."

"No," said Brian. "We're up to speed."

The woman looked at him sympathetically. "So, like I was saying, she's such a trooper, your mom. Lots of folks in her situation, you know, they keep buzzing us about getting their medication. She just waits patiently 'til we come. Then she thanks us so sincerely afterwards. We're really gonna miss her."

"So are we," said Grace with a taut smile.

The woman eyed her closely, then nodded. "I was just in with her. She's awake. Go ahead down."

They walked the length of the corridor, the soles of their shoes squeaking on the gleaming floor. The pale fluorescent lighting always made Grace feel like she was trapped inside a faded Super 8 movie—as though the barren passageway itself had been doused with the bleach she smelled all around. It was a relief to get into Cinny's room with natural light flowing in through the big window. When there were fresh flowers, like there were today, it was even better.

Brian stuck his head in the doorway. "Mornin', Mom. How're ya doin'?"

Cinny was studying her raised hands, her palms facing away. She turned to the door with a smile, weary but warm. "I'm still here!"

"That's good," said Brian.

"For now, sweetie, sure. Hi, Gracie!"

"Hi, Mom." Grace walked over and bent to kiss her mother on the forehead. She caught the slight, spicy scent of no-rinse shampoo.

"I've decided," said Cinny, "I've decided I…" Her lips kept moving, but her voice trailed off inaudibly.

"Can you speak up, Mom?" asked Grace.

"Oh, sorry," said Cinny, pushing the words out more strongly. "I've decided I need all the loving I can get." She smiled more broadly.

"Good for you," said Grace.

"One of the aides just came in with a warm cloth to wipe my face and hands. When she was done, she asked if she could hug me. That's what I said to her: 'I need all the loving I can get.'"

"That's sweet, Mom." Grace went to move a couple of side chairs closer to the bed. It was a large room, clearly a double in its previous life but converted to a single for its hospice role. Grace wished it felt a little more like a cozy bedroom and a little less like a transit hall in an Eastern European airport.

Cinny coughed softly and cleared her throat. "I'd say the game's into the final period," she said. "As long as nobody adds stoppage time. That's what you call it, isn't it?" She looked at Brian, who was draping his coat over the back of one of the chairs.

"Don't look at me, Mom. Grace was the jock."

"Yes, well," said Cinny, looking at Grace and then back at Brian. "You've both been such a comfort. But I don't want to tax your patience."

"Don't be silly, Mom," said Brian. "Don't worry about us. You just do what you need to do. However you need to do it."

Cinny smiled. "Anyway. Maybe you can get me those envelopes?" She pointed toward the small bureau next to the bathroom door.

"Sure." Brian walked over and came back with the modest stack. "Here you go."

Cinny took the envelopes and set them carefully beside herself on the thin cotton cover. "Help me sit up, will you? There's a couple of extra pillows. There!"

Grace handed Brian the pillows and he stuffed them behind Cinny as she leaned forward. She settled back, picked up the envelopes, and turned to Brian and Grace with another smile. "Have a seat. Perfect. Now, are you ready for the big reveal?"

Grace grimaced slightly.

"Oh, I'm sorry, Gracie," said Cinny. "You hate it when people turn verbs into nouns, don't you?"

"That's okay, Mom. I'll forgive you this once."

Cinny chuckled hoarsely. "You're such an English major. Your father's daughter. Reveal *is a verb, not a noun,*" she said in a posh accent. "*The English language has perfectly good nouns for you to employ:* revelation, *for example. Or* revealment." She winked at her daughter.

"Way to go, Mom," Grace grinned. "Making fun of me when I can't fight back. Unless I want to look like an elder abuser." It honestly did peeve Grace when people swapped around parts of speech. She went after Jack so often on the "verb-for-noun error" that he'd fashioned a stock response: "Fuck's a verb, right?" The first time he'd said it, she'd answered, "Of course it is." "So is it ungrammatical," he'd asked, "to say my wife's a terrific fuck?" She'd waited a good five seconds, stewing silently, before she answered, "No. You're just being exceedingly coarse."

"So!" Cinny said, raising the envelopes. They quivered in her grasp like aspen leaves in a rising breeze.

"Go for it, Mom," said Brian. He slid forward in his chair. "We're all ears."

"Okay!" Cinny peered at them through narrowed eyes. "I've been thinking," she announced rather formally, "when this is over—I want you all to take a trip."

Brian looked at Grace and then back at his mother. "Okay. And?"

"I want to pay for everything. Or your dad and I will, because it should come out of the estate. We'll figure a way to get enough money out quickly, because if you wait too long, who knows? Anything could happen." She looked at them with an edge of concern.

"If you want us to take a trip for you, Mom, don't worry," said Brian. "It'll happen. But…" He looked at Grace.

"But what?" asked Cinny

"I mean, what are the details? What do you have in mind?"

"I was *getting* to that!" Her face screwed up in obvious discomfort, then relaxed. "First, I want you all to go. The two of you, Jack, Ella, Chelsea, and Sage. Everybody."

They nodded.

"You'll obviously have to find a time that works for everybody. That could be a challenge. But please do it as soon as you can. April or October might make the most sense in terms of the weather everywhere."

"Everywhere?" asked Grace.

Cinny tapped the envelopes. She peeled two off the top and handed the rest to Grace. "Go on."

Grace looked down at the top envelope. It was labeled in the cursive chicken scratch that now passed for Cinny's handwriting: *Christchurch*. She looked at her mother, who grinned like a schoolgirl presenting a straight-A report card.

"Read it out loud," said Cinny.

"Christchurch," Grace read, turning to Brian. His eyes widened.

"Go on," said Cinny, gesturing with her hand.

Grace flipped to the next one. "Ko Phi Phi."

"Holy shit, Mom!" said Brian. "That's Thailand. This is going to cost a fortune. Six people?"

"There's plenty of money, sweetie. For this, and with plenty left over. Trust me. Go on, Gracie."

Grace turned to the next. "Rome."

Cinny nodded. "Go on."

"Grindelwald. Oh, Mom. What is this?"

"I'll explain in a sec," Cinny said impatiently. "Read the last one."

"Oxford." Grace dropped the final envelope on top of the others and looked back and forth between her brother and her mother. "They're all places you and Dad went. Where you spent time. Some with us."

Cinny nodded again. "We want you all to go to the spots we loved. Together. I do, anyway. This is basically my idea. But I'm sure Dad would approve."

"Mom, this is really incredible," said Brian. He leaned forward to touch her hand. "I don't know what to say."

"Well, don't think it's all going to be fun and games." Cinny coughed and cleared her throat. "You're going to have to do some work along the way. I'm going to ask a lot of you, in general."

Grace and Brian turned to each other, then looked back at their mother. "Okay," said Brian. Grace nodded.

"You're going to be spreading some ashes."

"Oh, boy!" Brian lurched back in his chair. "Wow."

"What?" asked Cinny.

"Well, I don't know. It's just so…"

"Families spread ashes all the time," said his mother.

"Yeah," said Brian. "But not necessarily all over the entire globe. I mean…"

"What? What do you mean?"

"I mean I just flew here from Seattle, and they gave me major shit about having my liquids in too big a bag. I imagine they could get pretty bent out of shape if we try to run somebody's cremains through the scanning machine. Especially somewhere like Thailand."

"They won't be *somebody's* cremains, Brian. They'll be your mother's and father's cremains."

"I'm not sure that'll make much of a difference, Mom," observed Grace.

"Then I'll write them a note. I'll explain…" Her voice trailed off.

"What, Mom?" Brian slid closer.

Cinny looked annoyed. "I'll explain that this is my dying wish," she said loudly.

Grace and Brian stared at each other once more.

"You can sneak us through in your checked luggage if you have to. Dad and I won't mind a little stealth."

Brian sighed, then composed himself. "Whatever you want, Mom. We'll make it work. I promise." He smiled. "Definitely."

"That's settled, then. Thank you. So, Dad's there in the cottage on my bedside table, down on the lower level. You can't miss him. He's unfortunately in a very tacky box. And don't pay any attention to anything else down there. I'm afraid I didn't have a chance to tuck everything away."

"Mom!" exclaimed Grace.

"What?" Brian looked at his sister. "Oh! Ohhh!" he laughed loudly.

"Dad's been gone a long time," said Cinny with a wink. "And he honestly wasn't all that attentive before he left."

Grace looked at her brother with robust disbelief.

Brian grinned back. "Give her a break, Gracie. I think it's great Mom's spunkiness is still intact."

"Thank you, Brian." Cinny looked at Grace, who managed a grin herself as she shook her head. "So where was I?"

"Dad. Dad's ashes."

"Right. Dad's remains are right there, where I told you. And when mine are, you know, available—and when you've got everything else arranged—I want you to sprinkle them in those places on the envelopes. And one more place I'll tell you about at the end." She tapped one of the envelopes she'd held back. "I'm saving that as a little surprise. All I'll say right now is that it's mid-Atlantic." She grinned mischievously. "So, maybe fly to Newark when you leave England."

Brian and Grace caught eyes as they registered the mystery.

"Got it." Brian turned back to Cinny. "Newark."

"And we'll want an equal mix. Most places, anyway."

"Mix?" asked Grace, eyes agog.

"Naturally. You're going to mix us together. Like flour and baking powder. Cinny and Frank." She made a little *skosh here, skosh there* gesture.

Brian began to laugh.

"What?" asked Cinny.

"We're not going to need a sifter or anything, are we?"

"Brian!" said Grace, peeved.

"What your brother said is funny," said Cinny. "The day this family loses its sense of humor, that's the day I want to move on."

"You *already* want to move on, Mom!" said Grace.

"Even more, then."

"I give up." Grace leaned back in her chair.

"One of the places, your Dad liked a lot more than I did," Cinny continued. "And another I liked a lot more than he did. So you'll need to sort us out accordingly. It'll be a fun little math problem." She grinned. "Portioning out our bits."

Brian looked at his sister, who blinked back at him.

"All that is covered in the instructions," Cinny went on. "All the specifics. And here." She handed Brian the two last envelopes. "The one on top's the master instructions. Read them before you start. Don't read the rest until you get to the right locations." She looked at them both. "Isn't this fun?" Her eyes, sunken for weeks, twinkled brightly. "And the other one, the blank envelope—read that one after you've finished up at Oxford. But no peeking at anything early."

"Of course not," said Brian.

"Don't give me *of course not,*" Cinny shot back. "You were a royal pain in the ass at Christmastime. Poking all over the house looking for presents."

"You're confusing me with Gracie." Brian winked at his sister.

"I certainly am not," said Cinny. "You were about as trustworthy as Donald Trump in the Miss Universe dressing room."

"Well, I've gotten better," said Brian. "Ask Ella."

"I want you to promise not to peek in the last envelope. In any of them. Promise! Both of you." She managed to look remarkably stern for a dying woman.

"Promise," they said in unison.

"There might be a few surprises along the way. I have a few things to fill you in on. Things about me and Dad. Appropriate to the places you'll be, really. Okay, then!" Cinny patted the covers on either side of her diminished frame, definitively ending the session. "Make sure to pack some good measuring cups. And a bunch of rugged baggies. Now," she sighed, sinking back on her pillows as though the excitement of revealing her plans had utterly deflated her. "I wonder if my medicine is coming."

Grace and Brian knew something was changing.

The next few days brought the proof. In the middle of the second day, Cinny pointed to the vase of mixed flowers sitting next to the television. "How long will those last, do you think?" she asked.

"A few more days, I'd say," replied Brian.

She nodded. "Perfect."

She asked how Jimi was doing without his roomie. "Is he getting his wet food?" she asked. "You know how he loves his Kitty Kitchen."

Grace supposed it might not be a lie if she responded only to the statement, not to the question. "Yes, Mom."

Cinny looked thoughtfully at her daughter. She ran her tongue back and forth over her dry lips. "Animals have such truthful eyes. All I have to do is look into an animal's eyes and I see truth."

Grace felt like weeping.

The next day was the last day the essential Cinny was indisputably all there, her spunk and humor miraculously intact. She told her favorite hospice worker, "You've been so considerate. Once we're finished here, I'll make sure to recommend you to all my friends." A little later, to Dr. Patel: "Could you please have a word with Mother Nature? Tell her it's rude to keep us waiting." And just before Grace and Brian left her for the night: "Heavens, I'm nothing but skin and bones. If I ever wanted to look like Twiggy, I'd be ecstatic."

In the morning, Cinny seemed to recognize them both, but they'd evidently slipped for her into a new role altogether—no longer one for the here and now. "There they are again," she exclaimed as they walked in. "Our escorts—our precious escorts." When Grace and Brian returned from lunch at the cottage, Cinny was sitting up in bed for the first time in days. Her eyes had retreated even further back into her skull, but they sparkled like dawn light on tiny waves.

"I think I'm getting stronger," she announced. "It could be that a new bird is getting stronger. Maybe they'll have to invest in a new cage for me. I could have a new home."

"Yes, you could, Mom," said Grace, barely getting the words out.

"It *has* been a big adventure, hasn't it? It still is!"

Grace struggled to place the curious echo. "A wonderful big adventure, Mom. You've made it one for all of us." She squeezed Cinny's hand. Wait—it was Peter Pan. She remembered staring at Brian when Cinny had read that passage to them in bed one chilly night in Hanover: *To die will be an awfully big adventure!* Neither of them had known what to make of it; they'd been afraid to ask.

Cinny napped again. When she woke this time, she raised her hands in front of her the same way they'd seen her do before. "I'm just so in love with my hands," she said in a voice so soft they had to lean forward to hear her, "but they're getting so heavy. It's like I'll put them down at my side and that's the way I'll die. Will you tell Matthew?"

Grace and Brian stared at each other, hovering between confusion and shock. Then their mother said to them, "Maybe I'm drifting off now. Bye."

Lucinda Maynard Posey never spoke again.

Cinny's body made it through two more days—one more than Milt's, across the hall.

Grace and Brian spent most of their waking hours with their eerily inert mother. Brian tried to catch up on as much of his REI work as he could manage, and Grace read the texts that her junior colleagues at the school had chosen for a new compulsory junior-year class focused on diversity issues. (The course was tentatively titled, "Why Thinking That Shakespeare May Be Overrated Is Totally Okay.")

Halfway through the afternoon the day before Cinny died, the hospice harpist appeared at the door, instrument in tow. Grace and Brian had been told that their mother's hearing would be the last of her senses to shut down, so when the woman offered to play, they said they wished she would. Cinny had always loved Mozart, and when the woman played the slow movement from the Clarinet Concerto in A Major, there was no denying that Cinny smiled. Her pale lips flattened, though, when the woman broke into Pachelbel's Canon. She'd once told the chairman of the Dartmouth music department, who was sitting across from her at a dinner party, that if Baroque Germany had had elevators, Pachelbel's Canon would have been playing in every one of them. "It's as boring as *Bolero*," she'd said, "but without the big orgasm at the end."

When the woman left, Grace and Brian sat close to their mother's bed and told her how much they loved her. Brian suggested they sing the Scottish lullaby Cinny had sung to them as infants. Grace knew she'd never make it all the way through, but Brian convinced her to try. When she dissolved into heaving sobs, he carried on bravely with only the occasional stumble. It emerged later that they'd both hoped it would bring another smile to Cinny's face. They'd only seen a profound calm, underscored by steady but ever-shallower breaths.

Early the next morning, Grace's phone wrenched her out of a nightmare about ruinously expensive dental procedures. At first, she was relieved to be awake, but when she looked at the screen, it read, "Hanover Hills Retirement Village." The time read 3:17. She touched the "Accept" button and raised the phone apprehensively to her ear.

"Mrs. Tingley?"

"Yes?"

"This is skilled nursing. Mary Evans? I think you should hurry over. Mrs. Posey has started to mottle. I don't think she has long now."

"I'll be right there. Thank you."

Grace threw on a robe, switched on the light in the hall, and rushed to her mother's bedroom. The door was half-open, so she pushed through without knocking.

"Brian? Brian!"

"Yeah?" Her brother sat up, squinting against the light. Next to him, Jimi raised his head in surprise. His eyes glowed like paired green sequins.

"It's Mom. I think she's going."

When they got to her room, Cinny was still alive, but her breathing was very irregular. A nurse had just taken her vital signs and looked at them with a resigned smile. "I'm glad you're here. I don't think it'll be long. I'll just leave you to it. Call us if you need anything or, you know, if you have any questions."

"Thank you," said Grace. She dropped her coat on the floor and pulled a chair up next to her mother. Cinny's eyes were open but immobile, all but unblinking. Grace wished she'd brought eye drops, as though they would make any difference.

"Oh, Mom!" she sighed. She turned to her brother, who had picked up her coat and was draping it neatly over a chair. "It's like she's looking straight through the ceiling."

Brian moved to sit on the edge of the bed, and Grace scooted her chair aside to make room. He sat down very carefully, patting the covers before he settled. "If I didn't see her feet," he said softly, "I wouldn't even know where her legs are."

They sat for a moment quietly.

"Maybe you should put some music on," suggested Grace. "Softly."

Brian squinted at her.

"I don't know," said Grace. "I feel like we should do *something*."

"Let's just be with her. Take our cue from her."

They sat that way for fifteen minutes, Grace with her hand on Cinny's knobby shoulder, Brian holding her hand. Cinny's breathing stopped completely. And then, there it was again. Twice. Both times it started back up as though she'd surfaced from a deep dive without a second to spare. Her stare remained fixed the whole while, then suddenly she blinked once, twice, and turned her head to Brian. He bent over her, his face no more than a foot and a half from hers. She locked him in her gaze as though she'd extended metal clamps from her cheeks to secure him—as though she were docking in orbit with another spacecraft.

"Hi, Mom," he choked out. "It's okay. You're doing great."

"You're doing great, Mom," repeated Grace. She reached out to touch Cinny's cheek with the back of her fingers. It was surprisingly warm.

"It's like she's in the water," said Brian, speaking to Grace but never breaking the mother-son communion. "And I'm in the boat that she wants to get into. And she wants me to pull her in."

"It's okay, Mom. Go with Brian. He'll help. He's your escort."

"Except she's leaving…for somewhere else." Brian's voice faltered. He clicked softly.

"It's okay, Mom," said Grace, standing now so she could lay her hand on her brother's shoulder—and be part of what she knew would be her mother's last sight on earth. "Just slip away now. We'll be fine, you know. We will."

The muscles around Cinny's mouth tightened. Those in her neck as well. She strained mightily for something, but it seemed less for another breath than for the will and power to rise out of herself and flash away like a pheasant breaking cover into the evening sky. She never removed her gaze from Brian until her breathing stopped for good, and her eyes—the ones that had always sparkled with wit and wisdom and a regular dose of naughtiness—had emptied.

Brian stayed bent toward his mother's still face for minutes, looking down only to watch the tears slip off his nose and soak into her covers. "I guess we should close her eyes," he said after a spell.

"Here. Let me," said Grace. Kneeling beside the bed, she reached out tentatively, then pulled her hand back. "Shit! How do you do this?"

"In the movies they just, like, sweep their hands lightly over the face and the eyes shut," Brian said.

"I think it'll take something more." Grace reached out and gently touched the outer corner of Cinny's top eyelid. She pulled down and toward the nose, and the lid closed almost all the way. When she lifted her finger, it opened halfway. "Oh, Mom," she sighed. "Can't you just cooperate?"

"Here," said Brian. "Let me try."

"Let's just call the nurse."

"Let me just try." Brian repeated what his sister had done but waited a good fifteen seconds before he lifted his finger. Cinny's eyelid remained where it was. He repeated the process with the other eye.

"Now I know why some people just put coins on them," said Grace. "Like in 'Penny Lane.' It's easier."

"That was easy enough," said Brian. "And I think you mean 'Tax Man.' Besides, Mom was never totally on board with capitalism."

"You're pretty tuned in," said Grace, "for a total college fuck-up."

Brian stood up, turned to his twin, and hugged her tightly.

Once they'd informed Nurse Evans and she came in to certify Cinny's death, she told them she'd contact the funeral home and they would be there within the hour. Then she left Grace and Brian in the room for their final farewells. They sat quietly for several minutes until Grace suggested it would be a good time to remove the photos she'd taped to Cinny's wall. It would be awkward to lean over the occupied bed, and Brian was taller, so he said he'd reach and remove. It occurred to him he'd be impinging on his mother's personal space until he realized the absurdity of it.

Grace pulled the bits of tape off the back of the photos and stacked them, thinking it seemed like a decade ago that she'd stuck the things up. Now and then, they paused to appreciate a particular picture: the time at their grandmother's house they'd inspired one of Cinny's books by both coming down with the chicken pox the very same night; Cinny as a teenager at the beach at Cape May, tanned and smiling like a Hollywood ingenue; the time the two of them had been cast as Hansel and Gretel in their grade-school drama pageant and Brian had misplaced the chicken bone that was the crucial prop and substituted half a roll of Necco Wafers; their parents cutting the cake at their wedding; their first, and best loved, family dog. Halfway through the process, Grace stopped to kiss her mother's hand. It was cool but not cold. By the time they were done, that had changed.

It was an hour they'd long remember, and they told each other how glad they were to be sharing it.

Eventually, Nurse Evans came back in to tell them the funeral director would be there in ten minutes. It was time to say goodbye. Grace went first. She sat on the edge of the bed, leaning over and down until she could hug her mother's dwindled frame. There was very little there but skin and bone, but Grace held them tightly, surprised by a trace of warmth lingering under the shoulders as she kissed her mother's cold cheek. She whispered something Brian couldn't catch into Cinny's ear and then stood aside for him. Brian held Cinny's hand up to his cheek, kissed it, and then arranged it with her other on top of the white covers. He bent to kiss her on the forehead and sweep back a lock of silver hair, remembering how he'd massaged away the headaches. Then he stood and took Grace's hand and they walked slowly out of the room.

"Thank you so much," Grace said to Nurse Evans as they passed the nurses' station.

"You're so welcome," replied the woman, with a gentle smile. "It was a good goodbye?"

"It was," said Grace. "So moving. And so right, I guess."

Nurse Evans nodded. "I'm glad. Now the men from Tuttle's will be here soon. They'll give you a call tomorrow to set up an appointment for you to come in. But don't worry. They'll take wonderful care of your mom."

"I know," said Grace, suddenly feeling as though she'd just left Chelsea for her first morning at daycare instead of saying goodbye forever to the person who had loved her and cared for her and regularly pissed her off for the whole of her life. She looked at Brian. He put his arm around her shoulder and squeezed.

"It was so good to know your mother," said Nurse Evans. "And you. And, if only very briefly, your uncle."

"Our uncle?" Brian turned to Grace.

"Oh! I don't know! Michael? Or Matthew, I think his name was. It began with M." She shook her head and shrugged. "He looked like your mother's age, so I assumed he was her brother or brother-in-law or something."

"Really?" said Brian.

Nurse Evans nodded. "He was in to visit maybe four, five days ago, very early in the morning. He said he couldn't stay long. Maybe he was a cousin."

"Hmmm," said Brian. "I don't know of any Uncle Matthew or Cousin Matthew, either. Or Michael. Do you?"

Grace shook her head.

"Well," said the nurse, "I guess it's a good thing we don't have to do a full background check every time somebody comes in. Not yet anyway!"

WESTPORT

"Welcome home," said Jack Tingley, as Grace stepped into the kitchen. He was wearing a white UVA polo shirt, a little too tight for his burgeoning belly, and light blue cotton boxers.

"Damn it, Jack! You scared me!"

"What? You weren't expecting to run into your husband in your own house?"

"Not standing right in front of the door, for God's sake. Like an elevator operator or something. In his underwear!"

"I heard the garage door opening." Jack leaned forward to kiss her on the cheek.

Grace pulled her head back. "Drinking already?"

Jack checked his watch. "Hmmm. 3:40." Grace had married an undeniably handsome man—tall and vaguely lupine, with his shaggy unibrow and Sean Connery grin. It was all she could do not to giggle whenever, as now, his wolfish assurance melted into a sheepish grin. "Maybe I had a tough day?"

"Tell me about it." Grace set her bags down on the pale hardwood floor. "Maybe you could take those to the bedroom? And I think I'll join you in midday inebriation."

"That's my girl!"

As Jack reached for the bags, Grace pointed to his left wrist. "That the new one?"

He straightened up and extended his arm, rotating it so she could see a sizeable, glinting, bi-color timepiece. "What do you think?"

Grace craned closer. "*Trés* bling!"

"Sea-Dweller. Rolex."

"Obviously."

"Solid gold and oyster steel." He swung his arm back and peered down in boyish admiration. "Waterproof down to 1200 meters. That's 4000 feet." He looked at Grace as though he'd done a standing double backflip.

"I guess it'll be safe for the bathtub, then. Or maybe you plan to dive on the *Titanic*?"

Jack smiled, swept up Grace's bags, and started toward their bedroom. "'We *are* royalty, Rose,'" he whispered as he passed.

"Fill me in," said Jack, as they settled onto the couch in the den. Beyond the French doors, a flagstone patio gave way to a gently rolling lawn and a line of evergreens fifty yards away. A trio of goldfinches fluttered around a birdfeeder hanging from the eaves. Jack shoved a *Golf Digest* and *Runner's World* aside on the coffee table and set his glass on a coaster, one of a set featuring classic Scottish links. He turned to his wife. "How was the drive?"

Grace sighed and peered into her tumbler, swirling the whiskey and ice. "Fine. Considering. But I've got to head back up at the end of the week."

"Really? Why?"

"To get Mom's ashes." She chuckled. "They won't be 'available'—her term—for three or four days. Dad's in the car, though. Oh, damn! Jimi!"

Jack leaned forward in alarm. "What?"

"He's still in the car. Mom's cat. He was so quiet I forgot he was there."

Grace leaped up and ran through the kitchen. A minute later, she was back with a medium-sized cat-carrier. She set it on the floor, knelt beside it, and unfastened the door. "There he is. There's Jimi. C'mon out, sweetie. It's okay." She turned to Jack with a look of dismay. "What the hell was I thinking? He could have been out there all night. We'd never have heard him."

"I'm sure he would have been just fine."

"God, I can be such a ditz sometimes."

"Give yourself a break, Gracie. Your mother just died."

"I guess." Grace peered into the carrier again, adjusting herself on her knees. "C'mon, Jimi. C'mon, kitty."

"He'll come out when he's ready," said Jack. "Give him some space. He's probably freaked out."

"Probably." Grace returned to the couch. She grabbed her glass and took another swig of bourbon.

"So," said Jack with a quick sniff. "We're going to have a cat now?"

"Don't worry. I stopped at CVS for some Claritin."

"O…kay?"

"And Chelsea's going to adopt him."

"Phew! Great!" He picked up his drink and sat back.

"It *is* great. Jimi will stay with family. And Chel gets to hold onto a little bit of her nana."

"Perfect." Jack wriggled in his seat, tugging down on the legs of his boxers. He was curiously sensitive about anyone seeing his upper thighs. Even Grace—unless he was completely naked, when he'd tease her about getting a tattoo on the smooth skin just down from his groin. She half expected he'd come home from a drunken golf trip one day with his fraternity letters inked there next to his willy. Or maybe something golf-related like *Titleist* or *Big Bertha*. He cleared his throat, then cleared it again.

"What?" asked Grace.

"Is it okay if I ask when Chelsea's actually going to come get him?"

"Please, Jack!"

He raised his hands defensively. "Forget I asked."

"Sorry, hon. That's just not a top priority for me right now." Grace stood up and walked over to the French doors. She put her hands on her hips and gazed out at the flitting birds. "I guess they're pretty much ready for spring. I sure as hell am."

"Me too," replied Jack. "Time to get the bikes tuned up."

Grace turned and walked back to the couch. "I didn't tell you, did I? Mom apparently had a visitor a few mornings before she died."

"Who was it?"

"Brian and I didn't see him. Somebody Mom's age, the nurse said." She folded her arms.

"Maybe the old girl had a boyfriend down the hall," quipped Jack. "Wasn't she on L-dopa?"

Grace snorted. "Not for long."

"I've heard folks can get a little crazy in those retirement places. Like they're on some kind of last-chance singles cruise or something."

"Sorry to rain on your geriatric fantasy, hon. None of the nurses ever saw the guy before. So the mystery remains."

They chatted for several minutes about a tricky estate Jack was working on and about the partners' ongoing effort to get the Long Island Sound Domestic Violence Center up and running. Jack had in fact had some great news just that morning about provisional state funding.

"And that explains the early happy hour," he said, winking.

"Right," Grace smirked. "How was the Porsche you flew all that way to see?"

"It was gorgeous! Spectacular! 1957 Super Speedster. Jet-black with red leather buckets and only 65,000 miles."

"And they're asking…?"

"Just under $300K."

Grace set her glass down abruptly, missing the coaster by a good two inches. "Come again?"

"That's actually a steal," said Jack. "Given its history. You know. Paul Newman?"

"Jesus, Jack! That's like four years at—I don't know—Bennington or something."

"Chelsea's done with college, no?" Jack studied her expression. "Maybe that's not your point."

"Maybe not." Grace sighed.

Jack put his hand on her knee. "I don't have to buy it if you think it's a stupid idea. I mean it!"

Grace sat for moment before she smiled and patted his hand. "No. I'm sorry. If you want it, go for it."

"Well, I don't—"

"Really, Jack. It's not like you don't have the money."

A rustle came from the cat carrier.

"Jimi!" Grace leaned forward and peered at the open door. There was no further sound. "Proof of life!" She settled back.

"He'll be out." Jack set down his glass and rubbed his hands together. "But, man, I can't tell you how much fun that little sucker was to drive."

Grace nodded distractedly and stared out into the yard. The goldfinches were gone, probably scared away by a blue jay that was pulling sunflower seeds out of the feeder and tossing them aside like wrong-sized items in a flash-sale bargain bin.

"What's the matter, Honey Pot? You don't seem very excited."

"No," said Grace, looking back at him. "I *am* excited for you. I am. I know you've wanted a vintage Porsche forever."

"But?"

Grace turned to face him. She picked up his hand and held it, grabbing his ring finger and twisting the wedding band one way and then the other. She couldn't remember when she'd first developed this particular fidget. It had become a dependable outlet, though, for simultaneous feelings of solicitude and impatience, troublesome regulars these days in her emotional inventory. "It's just that I come home from Mom and everything. And she's about to go into this little box, just like Dad. And this all…" She shrugged.

Jack nodded. "Okay, H.P. I hear you."

Grace let go of his hand to straighten the hem of her skirt. "Here you are, all excited about a sexy new car—which is great!—and I just think about how crazy it is that there are these two parts of my life. And one is about saying goodbye to someone who has loved me, basically, forever—and the other is this stupid race for, you know, fucking *things*. And...oh God, Jack!" She slumped against him, resting her head on his shoulder.

Jack twisted around so he could see her face. "Are you crying?"

"No."

"I'm worried you're thinking I'm shallow and petty."

Grace sat up and eyed him, her brows drawn into a firm line. "Of course not. No more than I am half the time. We're just obviously not in the same space right now, is all." She squeezed his hand again and summoned up a smile. "But that's okay."

"I *am* sad about Cinny, you know? I really am. She was a terrific person. And she raised a terrific daughter."

"I know." Grace reached up to pull a stray thread off his shoulder. She rolled it between her fingers and flicked it onto the floor. She could vacuum it up later. "And I'm honestly so glad to come home to normalcy. You know. After everything. Life is short."

Jack nodded. "Thanks."

"What for?"

"Well—"

"Ooh! There's Jimi!"

The cat had poked his head out of the carrier, his eyes so wide open they looked like they might pop out on stalks like a lobster's. His nostrils flared as he slunk out, creeping almost imperceptibly, through the small portal. He peered from side to side, back over his right shoulder, then back over his left, sniffing all the while.

"Good boy," cooed Grace. She bent forward. "Good boy, Jimi. You just check the place all out. When you're ready, I'll get you some food. Nice *wet* food." She looked over at Jack and smiled. "But right now, I'm getting *you* that Claritin."

Before they'd said goodbye in Hanover, Grace and Brian had settled on a division of labor for the coming months. Cinny had long ago named Grace as the primary executor of her will. Brian assumed that, like everything else in their lives, the choice followed from his sister's edging him out by a length in the Transvaginal Sweepstakes. ("You were always Mom's special first-born," he'd once told Grace. "When I popped out, she just saw somebody doubling her diaper load.") Grace assumed that Cinny had just been wise enough not to leave her affairs to someone who'd taken a half dozen years to make it through a consensus backwater college. Grace being married to an estate lawyer made her the obvious choice; living in Westport also meant she was the natural to close up the Hanover Hills cottage and sell or distribute all of Cinny's earthly goods and chattels. Jack could help Grace research the legalities and procedures of transporting human remains by air, getting them into a foreign country, and spreading them on foreign soil. Meanwhile, Brian being a global travel professional, he'd book all the flights and accommodations as soon as he'd coordinated a workable set of dates.

As it happened, Brian called the morning after Grace returned to Westport. He said he knew the cremains-related research fell to her, but he'd had a chance to stop at the Delta counter at SeaTac before Ella picked him up. The agent assured him that human ashes were transportable on Delta—and, she presumed, on most airlines—in either checked or carry-on luggage. The containers they were in, though, had to be "clearable" by X-ray: wooden, plastic, or cardboard containers were fine; metal, ceramic, and stone urns or boxes were not. Did Tuttle's Funeral Home know, Brian asked, that Cinny was going to be flying? Not unless she'd pinned a note to her nightgown after they'd left, said Grace. What about Dad? What was he in? Crappy-looking metal, Grace answered. Didn't Brian remember? Brian laughed and asked Grace if she'd requisitioned Cinny's vibrator when she'd picked up Frank's ashes; Grace told her brother to fuck off.

"Tuttle's Funeral Home," said the woman who picked up. "Always ready, always respectful. Megan speaking."

"Hello, Megan. This is Grace Tingley." Grace fought the urge to point out how tacky it was for a mortician to boast being "always ready." How medieval, basically! "Cinny Posey's...well, *Lucinda* Posey's daughter?"

"Yes, Ms. Tingley?"

"It's about my mother."

"Your mother? She's here?"

Grace hesitated. "I certainly hope so."

"Let me see." Grace heard shuffling papers. "Ah, yes," said Megan. "Here she is."

Grace had a fleeting vision of Megan standing in a large room with shrouded bodies scattered over a variety of surfaces, like rising loaves of bread.

"Silly me. It says it right here. 'Posey, Lucinda. Hanover Hills. 4 March 2019.'"

"That's her."

"How can I help you then, Ms. Tingley? Aside from saying how very sorry we are that your mother has passed."

"Well, I'm calling because we'll be transporting my mother's remains via airplane, and I wanted to make sure she was packed...well, you know, that her ashes were in an appropriate container."

"Ah! For the scanner at the airport!"

"Right."

"Well, what did you request by way of an urn?"

"I honestly don't recall," confessed Grace. "There were so many details to attend to." Their appointment with Bradford Tuttle, the stereotypically oleaginous funeral director, had struck Grace and Brian as easily lasting longer than the average college final exam—lengthened even more by the fact that almost every utterance the man voiced involved increasingly wearing references to *your dear departed loved one.* Grace didn't feel the least bit guilty about forgetting a detail or two.

"Well, most people this month have chosen the Sidereal Ewer," observed Megan. "It's on special—at a forty-percent markdown. Twice-glazed ceramic with a screw-down lid."

"I honestly don't recall," Grace repeated.

"Let me just check our firing log here. Yes. Lucinda Posey. She's in a Sidereal Ewer. Cozy as can be."

Grace took a moment to re-process what she'd just heard. "What do you mean she's '*in*' it?"

"Well, the cremains, of course. When the procedure is complete, all the remains are carefully transported to the chosen container. In this case, the Sidereal Ewer. I think you'll love it, by the way. It's gorgeous. One of our most tasteful models."

"Wait a minute!" said Grace. "Are you telling me Mom has been cremated?"

"Well, yes," Megan answered. "She was supposed to be, wasn't she?" Grace heard an additional rustling of papers, more frenzied this time.

"Of course!" Grace heaved a great sigh. "It's just…you're telling me the cremation has already been completed."

"Very much so." Megan paused. "Is there a problem?"

"Only that I was told it wouldn't be for a few more days yet."

"Ah! No. The boys must have found things went quicker than expected. You know. All the processing."

"Okay," said Grace. "Got it. Mom's done. But she's evidently in the wrong kind of container to fly."

"Oh, goodness. Thank you for pointing that out. You're absolutely right."

"And can we change that?"

"Well, I don't see why not," said Megan. "I'll have to check with Mr. Tuttle for final clearance, but I'm sure something can be arranged."

"Perfect. What are the options?"

"Well, let me see. Scanner-friendly…TSA approved…" The woman made a little *tsk* noise with her tongue. It reminded Grace of Brian. "There's the Vermont Maple Haven—that's wood, obviously. *Genuine machine-carved, in relief*, it says here, *with beloved scenes derived from the unforgettable poetic musings of Robert Frost.*"

"Right. And…"

"And the Champlain Chalice, with a lovely embossed High Country lakeside landscape. Oh, and the Green Mountain Grail. *Perfect resting spot after life's long trail.* Those are both plastic. Very tasteful, though. Thick. Solid." Grace heard the sound of knuckles rapping on a desk.

"Mom was a real believer in sustainability. Do you have anything in a recycled paper product?"

"I do believe we do. Let's see. Why, yes. You're in luck!" Megan sounded delighted. "There's the World Love Mini-Casket. It's… recycled cardboard…with a potato-starch glaze. Very earth-friendly. I believe a lot of the eco-loonies over at Dartmouth choose it."

"The eco-loonies?"

"Oh, gosh," said Megan. "Excuse me. I shouldn't have said that." She tittered nervously. "It's just a little joke we have down here in White River."

"No worries," said Grace, relieved to be presented with an obvious choice. Given Cinny's sojourn at Yasgur's Farm, something called the World Love Casket seemed the perfect receptacle for her, Mini or no. "So can you just have Mom's ashes transferred to the World Love thing?"

"Of course. I'm certain Mr. Tuttle will approve."

"And will there be an additional charge? Or maybe, if it's cardboard, we'd even get a little money back?" Grace smiled.

"Well," said Megan, "I'm afraid the World Love Mini-Casket is still two hundred and forty-nine dollars. It's a very specialized item."

"Oh. Naturally," said Grace, sliding an additional notch toward exasperation. "I expect the glaze is made from the finest organic Idaho baking potatoes."

"Pardon?"

"Nothing. Forget it. We'll pay for the World Love thing. Whatever."

"And, of course, we'll still have to charge you for the Sidereal Ewer."

"Really? Why?"

"Well, we can't reuse it once your mother has been vacated. I don't think anyone else would want to go in there, do you? No offense to your mother."

"I don't suppose you've thought of cleaning it out," said Grace, perhaps a little too loudly. "Reverently?"

"And what would we do with the bits of your mother that were in the wash water? No, I'm afraid we can't reuse an urn that's already contained a loved one. But we will be very happy to give you the Sidereal Ewer to use in any way you see fit."

"Well, that's just wonderful," said Grace. "I'm sure we're eternally grateful."

"You're very welcome."

Grace took a moment to gather herself. "So. I was planning on driving up in three days. Can you have everything ready by then?"

"We'll do the very best we can," said Megan. "Like Mr. Tuttle always says, eternity's too long to get things wrong."

"My sentiments exactly, Megan. Thank you so much."

Three days later, Grace headed north before dawn, hoping to avoid the morning traffic south of Hartford. As it happened, she hit a major accident just short of the city and was caught up in a good forty-five minutes' worth of stop-and-go before she made it past the I-84 split and got back up to speed. Fortunately, *Morning Edition* featured some interesting segments to help pass the time, including a *StoryCorps* account from an octogenarian whose father was thought to have died in the 1930s going over Niagara Falls in a beer barrel—only to turn up decades later as the millionaire proprietor of a Nevada brothel. It was especially comical that the old fellow had recorded the story with his eight-year-old great-grandson, whose education clearly hadn't exposed him to all the relevant vocabulary.

Grace considered stopping along the way for breakfast, but she'd grabbed a bagel at home, and she had her heart set on a short stack of buttermilk pancakes at Lou's in Hanover before her eleven o'clock appointment with Bradford Tuttle. As she raced through Springfield and Holyoke, narrowly escaping a State Police speed trap, she had the curious but overpowering feeling that she was driving to college to pick Chelsea up for spring break, instead of driving to a funeral home to retrieve her mother's last earthly remains. She remembered Cinny telling Frank, shortly before they moved into Hanover Hills, that the transition would be more or less like going off to Oberlin again—except now he'd have a roomie with benefits, with no need for probationary dating. Frank had joked about resurrecting the naked banquet thing in a senior setting, but he clearly wasn't keen about their change in domestic circumstances. While Cinny had joined every social and craft group Hanover Hills had to offer, Frank had turned even more inwards than he had been back in town. It reinforced the general family feeling that he'd never really recovered from the Shelley biography debacle.

Grace got to Hanover at 9:30 to find Lou's packed to the gills. She'd never been particularly fond of the place, decorated throughout with huge photos of mid-twentieth-century Dartmouth men looking odiously self-satisfied in their pomaded hair, V-necked tennis sweaters, and tweed jackets. It had been one of her father's favorite eateries, though, and the buttermilk pancakes struck Grace as the closest American diner cuisine came to plating heavenly manna. When, after a long wait, the cakes arrived at her tiny table, one of three or four orders balanced precariously up the arm of the stress-sweating waitress, they didn't disappoint.

Grace's later meeting with Bradford Tuttle went largely as expected, except that the mortician was suffering from a horrendous head cold. His sallow complexion was contrasted today by a highly inflamed nose, the tip of which glowed from repeated blowings with the crimson gloss of a baboon's derriere. He refused to shake her hand—to spare her any infection, he said—extending his forearm for a bump instead. Grace wondered offhandedly if he'd picked the move up from watching the Dartmouth men's lacrosse team in an unavailing bid to seem hip. In any case, Tuttle's earlier odious references to Grace's *dear departed loved one* now gave way to equally odious references to her *dear, depotted lubbed wud*.

After five minutes of polite but congested chatter, the man stood up and walked to the credenza next to his desk. With the flourish of a magician pulling a rabbit from a top hat, he produced the mortal remains of Lucinda Posey, modestly but hermetically ensconced in her

World Love Mini-Casket. "And here," he announced dramatically as he placed the tan six-by-six-by-nine-inch box on the corner of the desk, "is your dear buther."

Grace waited for a moment, unsure of what came next. When she finally reached out and picked the container up, its weight surprised her. She'd expected something with the heft of a modest-sized vacuum cleaner bag filled with household dust and lint. This was more like a sizeable box full of sugar.

When she stood to leave, Tuttle stepped up and reached out assertively. "Doh! Please! Allow *be*!" Grace assured him she could carry the ashes—that she in fact preferred to carry the ashes—but the man mumbled something about official services, levered the box from her hands, and strode from the room like a royal functionary bearing a crown to a coronation. And so they proceeded past Megan at the reception desk, out the front door, down the imposing front steps (flanked by life-size concrete statues of mournful maidens draped in classical attire), and across the parking lot to Grace's car. As they walked, Grace caught a flash of refracted sunlight glinting beneath Mr. Tuttle's nose and took a sudden and absurd notion she'd been swept back in time into the thick of a Charles Dickens novel, tended to by some oily cousin of Uriah Heep who was prey to a chronic respiratory infection. Thaddeus Pilch, he might have been called, or something similarly excretory. *Please, God,* she said to herself, *don't let that fall on Mom.* A few more ceremonial strides, though, and the trembling drop broke its surface tension and fell harmlessly between Mr. Tuttle's outstretched arms.

Whether oblivious to this nasal indelicacy or stoically ignoring it, Bradford Tuttle stopped next to the passenger-side door, turned, and suggested, with a nod of his head, that she open it. This she quickly did, keeping her arm as far as possible from the drip zone. The man laid the box carefully on the passenger seat, turned to bump Grace's forearm, and with a little dip of the head, assured her that, should the need ever arise again, he was "always ready" to assist her. For now, he wished her and the rest of the family all the best during this "spell of tender bourning."

"Oh, by goodness!" he suddenly exclaimed, reaching up to cover his mouth. "We've forgotted your vacated Sidereal Ewer, have'd we? And you wanted to take that alog! Doh?"

Grace thanked him energetically, but insisted she really had no use for the thing. Perhaps Megan could use it for a planter, she suggested. Or as a bean pot at her next church supper. Before she could take in the man's expression, she leaped into the driver's seat and slammed the door. As she squealed out of the lot with her mother's remains sitting beside her, she fought the powerful urge to stop, reach over, and buckle Cinny into her seat.

A week later, Chelsea drove up from Charlottesville to adopt Cinny's cat. In the meantime, Grace had been back at her school for a full week. She'd suffered through a painful three-hour meeting in which the English department decided (by a split vote) that *Romeo and Juliet* could remain in the freshman curriculum for at least one more year, but that two other Shakespeare regulars would be tossed into the literary dustbin. Grace couldn't decide whether it was more upsetting to lose *Julius Caesar* and *Twelfth Night* or to witness the criteria her fellow instructors floated for retaining *Romeo*. Her most senior colleague, an otherwise sweet old gent with one foot set firmly in the drama program and the other sadly but undeniably slipping toward memory care, reminded them that next year's musical was slated to be *West Side Story*. Now, he wasn't sure, of course, that everyone knew the show was based on Shakespeare's play. Didn't everybody think, though, that it might be a novel idea to compare and contrast the source and its adaptation? Meanwhile, two of Grace's younger colleagues opined that Leonardo DiCaprio and Claire Danes had even better chemistry in the movie than Ryan Gosling and Rachel McAdams in *The Notebook*. Moreover, both teachers had come to depend on their annual mini-break from lesson-planning when they screened the film over four consecutive class periods. Didn't everyone agree teachers there were criminally overworked? Grace had met, too, with the parents of a boy who hadn't felt adequately cautioned that there would be vivid evocations of feeding sharks in *The Old Man and the Sea*. Where was the trigger warning? they'd demanded. Poor Billy thought the story was going to be something like *Cocoon*—hydrotherapy for seniors. Not another *Jaws*, for heaven's sake.

Chelsea arrived around 11:30 Friday night, after nine hours on the road. Grace had asked to be awakened when Chelsea got in, because she knew she'd never get to sleep otherwise; as it happened, she'd just been up to pee and laid down again when she spied Chelsea's figure in the doorway. As her daughter bent to say hello and kiss her on the cheek, Grace caught the scent of cigarettes. She managed not to be riled and thanked Chelsea for letting her know she'd arrived safely—she'd see her in the morning whenever, no rush.

Meanwhile, Jack slept on. As Grace closed her eyes, the rasp of his breathing bowed before the deep sense of wholeness she always felt when her sole chick was safely back in the roost. She slipped away nearly instantly.

"It's so weird how they keep milking!" said Chelsea. "The adults." She sat in the parlor across the coffee table from Grace, who was working on her third mug of Peet's. Jimi lay next to his new mother, haunches on the couch but elbows on her thigh, rhythmically kneading her jeans with his oversized paws. His rolling purr would have been audible two rooms away. "Sweet, but weird!"

"Is he getting you with his claws?"

Chelsea looked up and smiled. "Nope. Jimi loves me. He's always loved me. How old is he, anyway? Do we even know?"

"I don't. He was a rescue. I think about eight, though."

"Assuming cat and dog years are the same, he's like, what?" asked Chelsea. "Fifty-four? And still into vicarious breastfeeding?"

Grace laughed. "How old do you think the average Hooters patron is?"

"I'm happy not to know," grinned Chelsea.

They sat for a moment in silence, listening to the cat's loud reverberations.

"Thanks for the French toast," said Chelsea.

"Of course."

"Yours is the best, you know. I've conducted a scientific study."

"Thanks."

"Grant loves French toast. I can't wait for him to try yours."

Grace had no reason to think Chelsea was laying a trap, but the apparently innocuous statement dropped on her with no warning. She took long enough to respond that she knew she was making it an issue, whether she meant to or not. "Well…that would be really nice, Chel. When were you thinking that might happen?"

Chelsea gently moved Jimi off her leg, her look finding the line between exasperation and hurt. "You still don't feel good about it, do you?" she asked.

"Oh, honey."

"I don't suppose it matters to you that I love him."

"Of course it matters, sweetheart. But that doesn't change…you know…"

"That I'm in my twenties and he's in his forties?"

"Well—"

"You don't think we've talked about that?"

"Of course you've talked about it," said Grace. "You're a smart girl. And I'm sure he's a smart man."

"Thanks for that." Chelsea sighed heavily. "I could always have ended up with an idiot."

The *ended up* hit Grace again in the gut, but she resolved not to show it. "Look, honey. The difference in age is one thing. And I know there are all kinds of marriages where the man and the woman aren't anything like the same age."

Chelsea narrowed her eyes. "I don't remember saying anything about marriage, Mom."

"Well, we just assumed."

"Please don't assume." Chelsea looked off into the middle distance.

"C'mon, honey. I'm sure you know Dad and I want more than

anything for you to be happy. And it may take us a while to understand what you need. What you feel you need."

"You can always ask me."

"Look," said Grace, leaning forward. "As I said, the age difference is only one thing, and I'm not saying it's anything insurmountable. Dad and I…we just worry more, honestly, about that fact that Grant's wife—I'm sorry. What was her name?"

"Adria."

"That Adria passed away so recently. Not that this is a ricochet romance, or anything. But Grant can't possibly have come to terms with his loss yet. Especially with two children to look after."

Chelsea stared at her mother. "I hope you're not saying that he doesn't really love me. That he just needs me to, you know, distract him from his grief? And take care of his kids? Like I'm some kind of nanny?"

Grace was surprised to feel tears coming. "I don't know, Chel. I don't know what I'm saying. I'm just worried, is all. I just want you to be happy. Dad just wants you to be happy."

Chelsea studied her mother's face intently. She patted Jimi's head as though she were testing his fur for softness, then got up, crossed the room, and sat down next to Grace. She took her mother's hands into her own and leaned forward until their foreheads nearly touched. Grace smelled cigarettes again.

"I *am* happy, Mom. I don't think I've *ever* been happier."

Grace looked at her, drinking in the openness and honesty in her only child's face. For some reason, her thoughts raced back to the hospice room at Hanover Hills, where Cinny had locked Brian in her gaze with something like the same intensity—and, now that she thought of it, candor.

"Okay, honey. Okay," she said at last. "Let's get Grant up here as soon as we can. To taste my world-beating French toast."

Chelsea wasn't heading south again until Monday, so they spent the weekend lounging around the house. Jack surprised Chelsea by asking her to join him for a run Saturday morning. "It's not like you, Dad," she said. "Moving through space without burning any fossil fuels."

"My doctor told me I'd better start burning this fuel," he quipped, grabbing two handfuls of belly. That afternoon, they watched Wales stuff Italy in their Six Nations rugby match in Cardiff. Jack had played fly-half at UVA and law school, and his passion for the game ran close behind his love for luxury watches and interesting cars—basically anything mechanical. When Grace had first met him, he was sporting two black eyes from a slightly misjudged but game-saving tackle earlier that day. When she said she hadn't thought many Yale law students went around looking like raccoons, he'd said it was all "perfectly honorable," but that he wouldn't tell her how it happened unless she went out with him the following weekend. She'd been curious enough to find out that she'd gone along with the amorous ploy—and one thing led to another.

When the match was over Jack stood up, stretched, and announced sententiously that Italians should stick to soccer and opera. But they might have perfected the art of cookery, he allowed, and proposed that the three of them drive into town for dinner at their favorite Tuscan eatery. Chelsea was partway into a mild rebuke about cultural stereotyping when something impish around Jack's eyes suggested he was baiting her. She laughed and went to get her coat.

Chelsea had adored Rizzuto's ever since she was a tiny girl, when she'd dubbed her favored dessert, tiramisu, "teary measles." Teary measles it had remained ever since. Their dinner was thoroughly enjoyable, save for the overly solicitous attentions of a busboy who seemed to believe that the lustful ogling of younger female diners was part of his job. Jack suggested that his studied proximity to Chelsea proved two things: first, that the place was authentically Italian and, second, that his daughter was clearly attractive to men of *all* ages. Grace had warned Jack earlier that any mention of Chelsea's January-May relationship was off-limits for the night, and his glib remark earned him a quick and robust kick in the shins.

As the *primi piatti* gave way to the *secondi*, Jack went on to say that Chelsea was rumored to be smoking again. She'd managed to avoid cigarettes for months, she replied, but the grueling drive up from Virginia had been her undoing. "Well," observed Jack (a good way into their second bottle of high-end Barolo), "unless they've started handing out Winstons at the toll booths along with the change, you must have stopped to buy a pack or two, no?"

Chelsea was just explaining that Grant had left some in her car when Grace steered Jack away from this awkward subject, too, with an even swifter kick in the shins. Jack flinched, re-settled, belched loudly enough to attract the notice of the diners at the next table, and slid the car keys across the table to Grace.

Grace and Chelsea were up early the next morning and chatted over fresh bagels and coffee in the sunny breakfast nook off the kitchen. Grace had brought down Cinny's envelopes for the big trip.

"Wow!" exclaimed Chelsea, shaking the stack in both hands. "I can't believe this. It's going to cost a fortune!"

Grace shrugged. "That's what your dad said. He's worried there won't be anything left from Nana's estate to fuel his crass materialism. According to Nana, though, there's more than enough to cover everything—with plenty to spare."

"Pop Pop's family was pretty well off, huh?"

"Well enough. The payout on his life insurance didn't hurt either."

"He still had a policy at his age?"

"A big one."

Chelsea nodded as she patted the pile. "Can we peek inside?"

"Nana said definitely not. Except those—the General Instructions."

Chelsea studied the inscription on the topmost envelope. "I can hardly read it." She grimaced. "She must have been really affected. With the tremor and all."

Grace gave a pained nod, then turned. "Oh! Hello, kitty."

Jimi had come into the kitchen and began twining around their legs in sinuous figure-eights. He was making a sharp little noise, a kind of severely abbreviated meow—*Meck! Meck!*

"I think he's hungry," said Chelsea, reaching down to rub his head.

"Right over there, sweetie." Grace pointed to a rubber mat next to the garage door. "Kitty Kitchen. All the chunks broken up. Your favorite."

The cat sat down, sneezed, scratched vigorously under his chin, then got up and walked languorously into the dining room.

"I hope he doesn't have fleas," sighed Grace. "Dad will kill me if he has fleas. He's already awash in Claritin."

"Maybe that's why he got so polluted last night." Chelsea's look was pointed.

"Maybe."

"Is he okay? Dad?"

"Of course he is. Same as ever." Grace smiled wistfully.

"Well, just so you know, Grant's not the only old man I worry about."

"We can probably leave it there. But thanks." Grace sniffed and pinched her nose. She sat up and smiled brightly. "I'm so glad you're going to be coming along."

"Me too, Mom."

When Chelsea had first learned about Cinny's plans, she'd inadvertently crushed Grace by suggesting she might not be able to go. Grant was still dealing with the impact of his wife's long battle with cancer, and she felt strongly that, wherever their relationship was headed, to be away from him and his children for more than three weeks would be cruel and damaging. It was actually Grant who'd insisted that Cinny's last wishes be respected by the entire family, saying that if Chelsea missed out on a once-in-a-lifetime experience just because of him, he could never live with himself. Despite their ongoing reservations about their only child pitching in with a man twenty years her senior, Grace and Jack were moved by Grant's emotional generosity. Once Chelsea had been convinced it really would be best for her to go, she'd gotten increasingly excited about the prospect.

"What has to get done before it all happens?" she asked Grace now. "And how can I help?"

"Thanks, but everything's pretty much under control. Uncle Brian is handling all the travel arrangements. And the hotels."

"Figures. And you?"

"I'm the new family expert on the global transport of human remains."

Chelsea laughed. "Great! How's that been going?"

Grace recounted getting Cinny into the right kind of box and out of the obsequious, virus-ridden hands of Bradford Tuttle. His assistant was contacting funeral professionals in the target countries to clarify rules and regulations on entry and dispersal, but having certificates of death and lawful cremation in hand would likely see them through most jams.

Chelsea thought it was charming, romantic even, that Nana and Pop Pop wanted to be intermingled and proportionally distributed. The thought, though, of her grandparents packed into ordinary sandwich bags gave her pause. Grace agreed and confessed she'd actually dreamed twice about Cinny and Frank's Ziploc-ed ashes getting confiscated at some backwater customs counter under suspicion of being drugs. "There're plenty of stories out there," she said. "Families trying to fly under the radar packing their loved ones in thermos bottles and talcum-powder tins."

"Sounds sketchy," said Chelsea. She suddenly broke into a giggle. "Can you imagine some poor woman carrying her mother's ashes in a Vagisil shaker? And her daughter, traveling with her, doesn't know?"

"Okay, honey! Curb your imagination."

"*Honest, Mom. I had no idea. I was just freshening up before breakfast!*"

Grace scowled playfully. "Whose granddaughter are you again?"

"Or imagine old Uncle Mario getting smuggled into Rome in a parmesan shaker. Somebody sprinkles him on their linguine and gets arrested for cannibalism."

Grace laughed. "That reminds me—"

A toilet flushed upstairs.

Chelsea looked up at the ceiling. "Dad must be awake."

"He's alive, at least. More coffee?"

"No thanks. I already feel like I'm plugged into the wall."

Grace leaned forward and smiled. "Let me just go up and see how Dad's doing. I don't want to have to think about funneling *his* ashes into a bourbon bottle to get him back to Florida."

"Ouch!"

"Oh, and remind me to tell you the weirdest ash story I came across when we come down."

Grace walked into the bedroom to find Jack sprawled flat on his stomach with his arms and legs extended, like Leonardo's Vitruvian Man seen from behind. He was wearing nothing but his boxers, the unadorned cotton sort he bought by the half dozen at Brooks Brothers' annual post-holiday sale. Grace had tried for years to get him into something more adventurous—maybe plaids, or arresting primary colors, or geometric patterns—but he resolutely resisted. "A man is known by his underwear," he'd once declared when she was failing to make a successful case for an Italian silk bikini.

"So, do you and your colleagues routinely flash your undies at partner's meetings?" she'd asked. "To keep tabs on each other's manliness?"

Jack had explained that athletes like him saw each other undressing and dressing a lot in locker rooms and couldn't help but notice—and draw certain conclusions from—each other's undergarments. "A guy wears tighty whiteys, he flashes way too much upper thigh. And his junk is all trussed up there in front."

"Be still my heart!" Grace had exclaimed.

"And if he wears something shiny and slick," Jack had gone on, "he might as well be saying, 'C'mon boys. I got the soap. Let's all jump in the shower and get slippery.'"

It was times like these Grace could wonder exactly why she'd married him.

The present moment, frankly, was another. Jack had likely been farting all night, but unless the noise had wakened her, Grace would have become accustomed to it. Walking back into the room was something else altogether. It took her back to those awkward Princeton Sunday mornings after those wild Princeton Saturday nights, when she'd wake up next to someone who wasn't exactly a stranger but whose name didn't spring quickly to mind. She'd grab a robe and go off to relieve her bursting bladder, then come back to her room and (lo!) simply reel at the unmistakable miasma of male body—sweaty from dancing, stinky from sex, and leaking the gaseous issue of intestinal fermentation. It was certainly something *Romeo and Juliet* failed to capture and foretell for Grace's ninth-graders. Maybe the omission was reason enough to dump that play, too, from the future curriculum.

Grace walked over to the windows, pulled back the drapes, and raised a sash.

"What are you doing?" came a muffled voice from behind her. She turned to see Jack, his head raised like a turtle's, one side of his face a tangled map of sheet marks.

"What does it look like I'm doing?"

Jack snorted. "Opening the window, damn it! You're freezing me."

"Creating a livable environment in here, actually. You've got this place smelling like a fumarole."

"Sorry."

"Are you okay?" asked Grace.

"Sure. Why wouldn't I be?"

"You had a lot to drink last night."

Jack rolled over and rubbed his eyes. "Did I?" His penis was sticking partway out of his boxers.

"Want to put that away?" Grace gestured toward his crotch. "Or did you have something else in mind?"

Jack sat partway up and looked down. "*Possum Come a-Knockin'.*" It was the title of a book they'd read to Chelsea as an infant. "You wanna help?" He flashed the grin that, for Grace, had always been solidly on the positive side of the marital ledger.

"Not at the moment. I think it has something to do with the primordial stench in here."

Jack shook his head and swung his feet over onto the floor. "Is Chel up?"

"Yup!" Grace walked over and kissed her husband on his tousled hair. "You stink, but I love you. I said, are you going to put that away?"

Jack looked down and tucked himself back into his shorts. "Oh, my." He sniffed and rubbed his eyes again with his knuckles. "Have you guys eaten?"

"Just coffee and bagels. We were kind of waiting for you."

"Thanks. Let me just grab a shower and I'll be right down."

"Sounds good." Grace reached out to fluff the hair on the left side of his head. "Oh, just so you're not surprised if she says something, you should know Chel thought you had a lot to drink last night, too."

"No more than usual. Do you think?" His eyes widened as he looked up at her. They were noticeably bloodshot.

"I don't know. But she doesn't remember you not being able to drive home before."

"It wasn't that I wasn't able to drive. I was just being sensible."

"I know. I'll see you down there. Enjoy your shower." She turned to leave, then looked back. "And if you play with yourself, think of me."

"Always do!"

Grace and Chelsea split an omelet while Jack devoured his own, added two bagels, and downed a pint glass of orange juice. When Grace got up to wash the dishes, he waved her back down and said he'd take care of them.

"Turning over a new leaf, Dad?" Chelsea grinned at her mother.

"I beg your pardon," replied Jack. "I do the dishes every night. Ask your mom." Grace nodded. "And I wash the sheets every Sunday, whether they need it or not. And I cleaned Jimi's litter box two whole times before I was hospitalized with allergic seizures."

"You're such a liar," chuckled Chelsea. "Is that because you're a Republican?"

"I was a Republican before lying was required. I'd like to claim they learned the art of prevarication from me. But that would be a lie, too."

Jack popped the rinsed dishes and glasses into the dishwasher, then turned to the pans.

"You up for another run today?" asked Chelsea.

"You want to?"

"Sure. I want to reinforce this virtuous behavior of yours. I'm proud of you, Dad."

"I'm tryin'." He slapped a little drum roll on his stomach. "Ohh! Wet hands!"

"And I'm *really* proud of what you've been doing with the Domestic Violence Center. How'd you ever convince your partners to get off their butts and do something for people who make less than seven figures?"

"You fight fire with fire. I got Mom to organize their wives and threaten *them* with domestic violence if they didn't step up."

"I'm not sure that's funny, Dad."

"Probably not."

"Oh!" said Grace, remembering. "I was going to tell Chelsea about this weird stuff I found out about Thailand. You're not going to believe this." She fetched her MacBook from her office and sat back down at the table, flipping the laptop open and typing in a Google search. She waited for a second and then scrolled down. "Here it is. Honey, I don't think I read this to you. It's nuts!"

"I'm all ears." Jack placed the scrubbed pans in the open dishrack to drip, wiped his hands, and sat back down across from Chelsea.

"*The latest craze in a small town northeast of Chiang Mai,*" Grace read, "*is drinking a concoction of a recently cremated person's ashes with the extract from leaves of the kratom tree. The beverage is made by boiling the leaves, then adding ashes taken from recent funeral pyres following cremation ceremonies.*"

"Holy shit!" exclaimed Chelsea, glancing at her father. "Is that for real?"

"It's in a legit British travel journal," Grace replied. "Right in there with the new carry-on policies at Ryanair. Listen. *Local youths reportedly drive around looking for funerals. When the cremation is complete, they sneak in to steal the leftover ashes. The person imbibing allegedly experiences a mild high, but the belief is that the mixture confers physical strength as well as spiritual protection from the ghost of the person whose ashes were drunk."*

Jack laughed. "We used to take our dates to the cemetery in Clearwater. Drink beer, maybe knock over a tombstone or two. But that's just crazy!"

"It is said by some who have engaged in the practice that the drink has an indescribably amazing taste, and that anybody who tries it becomes instantly addicted." Grace set the computer down and stared at Chelsea and Jack.

"Well, you're right," said Chelsea. "That really is incredible."

"It can't be true," said Jack. "Nobody could do that. Steal somebody's ashes and make tea out of them. What do they call the stuff? 'Ghoul Aid'?" He sat back and folded his arms.

Chelsea stared at her father with delight. "Now *that* was funny, Dad. Really funny!"

Jack snorted. "Maybe you figured you English-major types have a monopoly on funny."

"Never," responded Grace. "And that's 'monopoly on *humor*.' Or 'monopoly on *the* funny.'"

"Fuck's a verb, right?" replied Brian.

"Man!" said Chelsea. "You guys sure haven't lost it. How do you keep your marriage so fresh?"

"Are you awake?"

Grace was tugged away from a dream in which she was trying to figure out how to contact Jack from a Thai jail cell where she was being held for peddling Cinny's ashes outside a grade school. She raised her head with difficulty from the pillow.

"Hey. Are you awake?" asked Jack, more loudly.

"I am now."

"I've decided not to get the Porsche."

"What?"

"I said, I've decided not to get the Porsche."

"I heard you the first time," sighed Grace. "Why are you telling me in the middle of the night?"

"I just decided. I thought you'd like to know."

Grace turned over and sat up, propping her pillows behind her. "What time is it?"

"Around four."

"God, Jack. I swear—"

"All this talk about the trip—you know, with your parents' ashes? It somehow got me thinking that we have enough cars for now."

"Four? You think? Only two apiece?"

"The MG doesn't count. It's an antique you can't drive in bad weather. And the Range Rover is basically just a stuff-hauler, so that leaves us with just the Beemer for me and the Audi for you."

"And a new garage the size of Madison Square Garden."

Jack sniffed. "I think it looks terrific. It makes the whole place look better. More...I don't know."

"You're absolutely right," said Grace. "Perfectly expressed."

"I also thought," Jack continued, "that when we're travelling, we're going to see all kinds of stuff we might want to pick up. You know?"

"Like a flock of sheep in New Zealand? Maybe a Bentley in London?"

Jack laughed. "No, actually, like maybe a watch or something in Zürich."

"Really?"

"I'm a collector, Gracie. Don't think of them as, like, lawn mowers you only need one of. Do you think the Guggenheim gets questioned every time they decide to buy a Picasso?"

Grace broke out laughing.

"What?"

"I love you, Jack. And I forgive you for waking me up in the middle of the night to keep me posted on the status of your collections. Present and future."

"Now you're making fun of me."

"No, I'm not."

"Yes, you are."

Grace paused then giggled. "Okay. I am."

"But you do love me?"

"I do. Heaven help me."

"Good," said Jack. "I feel better. Now, why don't you try to get some sleep?"

SEATTLE

Brian was watching *CNN* when Ella came into the house, loaded down with groceries.

"Hey, Ells," he called out over the various pundits decrying the sclerosis of the American body politic. "Need any help?"

"I've got it, thanks." She crossed the kitchen and plunked the bags down. One tipped over and spilled its contents onto the granite countertop. "Damn it!"

Brian jumped up and ran over. "Anything break?"

"I don't think so." Ella turned toward him and shook her head. She pulled a runaway strand of blond hair back from her eye and tucked it behind her ear. The gesture always reminded Brian of Daryl Hannah. Ella could have been the actress's younger sister, he'd thought from the start.

"Tough day?"

She mimed projectile vomiting. "Let me grab some wine and I'll fill you in. I'll just put this away first."

"You go change, sweetness. I'll put things away."

Ella smiled. "I guess you've been around long enough to know where the tofu lives."

"Want me to keep anything out for dinner?"

"That depends. What are you cooking?"

Brian's squint turned into a grin. "Right! Got it. You want the pinot grigio?"

"Perfect. *Big* pour."

Ella came back five minutes later in yoga pants and a baggy Smith sweatshirt. Brian was pouring wine for the two of them. She walked over, grabbed him by the cheeks, and kissed him playfully on the mouth.

"Mmm!" he purred. "The old lizard tongue! D'you miss me?"

"When don't I? What's for supper?"

"I thought I'd just do the tortellini with some pesto. And a salad."

"Perfect!" Ella grabbed her glass. "Cheers!" They clinked. "So, Sage is at Tokiko's?"

"So she says," replied Brian. "Studying for their French exam."

"Too bad Paris isn't on our itinerary. She could have used her French. *Pardonnez moi. Est-ce que vous avez du Grey Poupon?*"

Brian laughed. "Who needs Sage? Take a load off. Tell me about your day."

Ella had spent more than a week now with a new-hire executive at Boeing. She had shown them easily two dozen properties, and every day their criteria seemed to change. After five days of searching, they'd found a gorgeous waterside mansion in Madison Park that Ella considered a steal at $3.5 million. The couple, though, insisted on putting in an insanely low bid. Ella had heard back in minutes from the listing agent, telling her she was "fucking crazy" to let her clients insult his clients that way.

Ella promptly drained half her glass and scooped Brian on the latest. The pair had texted that morning to say they thought it might be fun to buy on Bainbridge Island and maybe get a *pied-à-terre* downtown for him to crash on work nights. The three of them took a late-morning ferry across to the island, where Ella showed them two properties. The woman loved the second one ("We'll be just like Tom and Daisy Buchanan, with the tennis court *and* the pool!"), and the couple agreed to put in what Ella thought was a remarkably reasonable bid, given their track record. Two hours later, they called her to say they'd decided to rent for a year and use the time to sort out what neighborhood would really be best for them.

Brian reached over to give Ella's knee a consolatory squeeze. "Where's the rocket launcher when you need it?"

"I swear. I've never felt more like ripping somebody's nuts off. Both of them."

"The lady had nuts?" Ella slapped his hand. "So, they really going to rent, you think?"

"Who knows? Tomorrow, they'll probably be looking at houseboats. Can you rub my feet, boo?" She looked at him imploringly.

"Sure," said Brian, after a beat. "Pop 'em up." He patted his lap.

Ella adjusted the pillows and twisted herself into position. "Ooh!" she sighed, as he kneaded his fist into her right arch. "I'm so glad I stole you away from Kingsley."

"Mmm."

"I ran into him today, you know."

"Yeah?"

"Yeah." She paused. "At the grocery." She looked at him intently, but he kept his eyes on the task at hand. "Are you clicking?"

"What?"

"Are you clicking your tongue?"

"Probably," said Brian.

"Don't you want to know if we talked?"

Brian looked up blankly. "Did you talk?"

Ella squinted at him. "We did, in fact."

"And?" He stopped the kneading and started fiddling with her toes.

"He seemed good."

"Good," said Brian. A shallow sigh turned into a snort. "This little piggy went to Trader Joe's," he chanted, wiggling Ella's big toe. The nail, like the others, was painted a vibrant tropical aqua. "This little piggy stayed home."

Ella laughed and punched his shoulder. "God, you can be so obtuse sometimes."

"Sorry."

"Don't you want to know if there was anyone with him?"

"Not really."

"His mom is sick, you know."

Brian stopped massaging and looked at Ella with a pained expression. "I knew she was battling cancer. Has been for a couple of years."

"He just got back from Kingston. They're trying some experimental treatment, but he says it's a last-gasp deal. He had to come back to work, but he says he could get the call from his brother any time."

"Shit," said Brian. He started to rub again.

"I know," said Ella. "I think it's so weird, you know? That both of your mothers should have gotten sick. At the same time, basically."

Brian stopped again and turned toward her. "Did you tell him about Cinny?"

"I did." She paused. "Should I not have?"

Brian sighed again. "No, Ells, it's fine. I'm sure it was awkward and all."

Ella shrugged. "You don't think he told me about his mom just to make you feel—I don't know—guilty or something? Play on your feelings?"

"Kingsley's not like that." Brian nibbled briefly at a thumbnail. "I'm sure he was just filling the conversational void."

"I guess."

"Did he say anything when he heard about Mom?"

"He said he was really sorry to hear the news. He said he'd really liked her. She'd been so kind. He sent his condolences."

"Thanks." Brian started with the other foot.

"Oh, and he's excited for you about the trip. For us. He remembers when you guys—"

"I know."

They sat for a moment in silence. Ella was the first to speak again. "You don't need to keep doing that, you know?"

"No, I want to. If it feels good."

"It feels great. Thanks. I've almost forgotten about Bobby Boeing and his bitch spouse from hell."

Brian laughed. "Good. Fuck 'em."

They sat quietly for another five minutes, Ella with her eyes closed, Brian nodding slightly with each contraction of his hands.

"Would you mind if I gave him a call?" he asked at last.

"Not at all, darling. Why would I?"

"I don't know."

"I think it would be a sweet gesture," said Ella. "Really sweet."

"Yeah." He stopped his rubbing with one powerful last squeeze. "So, is that enough?"

"Until later." She winked suggestively.

"Let's see about some tortellini."

Brian had met Kingsley Shaw at a Portland wedding four years earlier. He'd driven down with a colleague from REI, a lovely woman named Sharon who worked in the same department as the bride. She'd been part of a lively crowd he ran with—bar-to-bar in Ballard, lift-to-lift up at Snoqualmie—and looked like she'd stepped out of a Patagonia catalogue. She knew from a few inebriated conversations that Brian was into women and men both, and although he'd been dating guys most of the time they'd known each other, he suspected she harbored some romantic interests in him. As the wedding approached, he'd complained about how expensive the rooms at the destination resort were going to be, and she'd laughingly suggested he could stay with her. She said it would keep her from hooking up with some random dude she'd never see again anyway. Brian surprised himself by saying yes.

The band at the reception had been wonderful, complete with five horns and choreographed back-up singers. The dancing went on for four hours, powered as much by the open bar as by the solid tunes, and the ad hoc REI roomies left the dance floor only to take on or offload fluids. Brian had to admit that Sharon's capacity to boogie with sinuous abandon, holding a brimming margarita in her hand, wasn't without erotic charm. More alluring by half, though, was the tall, slender fellow dancing right next to them, his dreadlocks swinging like palm fronds around his chiseled face. He was smiling beatifically enough at his partner, a willowy blonde twenty-something in a gauzy dress, but he had a sly way of sliding his eyes over toward Brian in an unmistakably message-laden way. He disappeared when the band took a break, but when they took the stage again, the dreadlocked stranger was right up there with them, now in his shirtsleeves and with his tie loosened and askew. He grinned coolly as he surveyed the room, but his eyes brightened when they found Brian's.

"We want to start off the next set," drawled the lead singer, "with a guest number from our friend Kingsley here."

The crowd erupted in applause. Kingsley was evidently well known and loved on the groom's side of the aisle.

"We've even rehearsed. One whole time! This is gonna kick ass."

More applause. Somebody yelled, "Kingsley's my daddy!"

"But first, let's get Denny and Meredith up here, because Kingsley wants to sing this for *them*. In fact, he says it's one part of his wedding present."

Oohs and ahhs filled the room as the couple made their way through the crowd and up onto the stage.

"By the way, Kingsley," said the singer, "what's the other part?"

Kingsley leaned into the mike with a smile. "My attorney has advised me not to reveal that information." His husky radio baritone made Brian imagine whispered endearments.

"Well, can you at least tell me this, then? Is it from Jamaica, this gift?"

Kingsley laughed, head back. "Maybe!"

"Animal, vegetable, or mineral?"

"Vegetable!"

More cheers and catcalls. "Aieee! Ganja!" yelled a tipsy female voice, spurring widespread laughter.

"'Nuff said," smirked the singer. "So, Denny and Meredith, this one's for you—from all of us, and especially from your dear friend Kingsley here."

He'd handed the mic to Kingsley, who had taken it as though it were the most natural thing in the world to stand in front of a drunken crowd of hundreds and launch into a song you've rehearsed only once.

"My very special friends," he'd said, as he turned to the bride and groom with a graceful sweep of the hand. "As you set off together on life's long journey, I and everybody else here who loves you, we want you always to remember, whether you're happy or sad, richer or poorer, younger or older—whether you always remember where you left your car keys, or whether you just called the cops to report an intruder after you spotted your wasted self in the bathroom mirror—always remember, just like Cousin Bobby said, *Ev'ry little thing…gonna be all right!*"

The drummer pounded out the four-pulse downbeat of the reggae classic and, for five full minutes, Kingsley Shaw owned the room and every man and woman in it—except, perhaps, for the bride's wasted uncle from New Jersey, who for some time had been intent on dropping fresh raspberries into every inviting cleavage he could find. Kingsley's voice was richer than Bob Marley's, and he bobbed and swayed as though the music were the blood in his veins.

Sharon squeezed Brian's arm as they stood there grinning like crazy people. "Man, is he hot!" she whispered in his ear.

Brian looked at her and nodded.

"Guess my chances of seducing you tonight just took a nosedive." She giggled drunkenly. "Too bad, but hey!"

Kingsley had sidled up to Brian forty minutes later, when Sharon was in the ladies' room. If he'd traded, even a little, on what he and everyone else knew had been a star performance up there on the stage, Brian wouldn't have given him the time of day. It was the combination of cool and talent, modesty and gentleness, that did him in. They'd be together for four years. Sharon had joked afterwards that when the bride tossed her bouquet over her shoulder, Brian caught it in his teeth.

Brian and Kingsley had dated regularly for the next year. Being from Jamaica, Kingsley had never learned to ski, but he was happy to take up one of Brian's lifelong passions, and was soon keeping up with him on all but the most extreme black diamonds. His impeccable sense of style extended to ski apparel, and while Brian was happy donning whatever functional outerwear REI gave him the best deal on, Kingsley opted, even as a beginner, for designer ski kit from Bogner or Kjus. Their first big trip together was up to Whistler, where, soaking dreamily on their last night in a snow-drifted outdoor spa under a nearly full moon, Kingsley told Brian he thought he loved him. Brian just managed to choke something out about how happy it made him to hear Kingsley say what he'd said. The arrival of another couple spared him any further calculation or articulation of his precise feelings.

They moved in together a year into the relationship. Kingsley had a generous housing allowance from Microsoft, where he was on a meteoric track in the business division, and his apartment was twice the size and four times the showplace that Brian's was. That Christmas they flew down to Kingston to meet Kingsley's mother, brother, and two sisters. During the summer, they flew east to spend a week in Westport with Grace and Jack and then drove up to New Hampshire, where Cinny had rented a cottage on Squam Lake. Jack had been his usual squirrely self around gay men—radically overplaying his acceptance—but Cinny had absolutely loved Kingsley, and declared at the dinner table the first night that if he ever got tired of Brian, he should come live with her. Grace's response had been somewhere in between.

Just short of four years into their relationship, Kingsley had told Brian that he'd been doing a lot of thinking, and they were basically throwing their money away by continuing to rent. It would make so much more sense, he said, if they bought something together—maybe a loft in SoDo, close to their go-to brewpubs and distilleries, where they'd have plenty of space for entertaining. It wouldn't necessarily lock them into a lifetime commitment—though Kingsley couldn't think of anything he'd like more. There would be ways of keeping their investments separate and very much dissolvable, if the need ever arose. Maybe brother-in-law Jack, he thought, could help with the arrangements. Jack was an estate lawyer, Brian had pointed out, and didn't necessarily know anything about, well, pre-nuptial agreements. Kingsley had laughed and asked who'd said anything about nuptials. Brian replied that was sort of how it all sounded to him: quite pre-nuptial, in fact. Kingsley laughed again and claimed he knew a good realtor. "You'll love her," he said. "She's in my yoga group. She's a single mom with a challenging daughter. Mid-to-late teen, you know? Feisty girl. I'd love to throw some business the mom's way. What do you say, Bri?"

"How could it hurt?" Brian had replied, without taxing his imagination.

So that was how Brian met Ella Bachman, née DiGregorio. She worked for a big Seattle realty company associated with Christie's, and she had a sixteen-year-old daughter by a long-gone marriage. Ella had grown up in Providence, where her father owned a construction company and—Rhode Island being Rhode Island—was therefore widely suspected of being a Mafia kingpin. She'd gone to Smith to get away from boys for a spell after a romantically tempestuous high-school career. Her senior yearbook had portentously dubbed her "The girl most likely to inspire a biopic in which she's played by Britney Spears," a prediction that captured her lively spirit and general appearance but not necessarily her keen intellect. Four relatively quiet years in Northampton fulfilled their stabilizing purpose, and she graduated *magna cum laude* with a double major in economics and women's studies. When her senior thesis, entitled "'Love Your Little Cocktail Dress!'; The Fashion Industry as Drug Cartel," earned her honors in both majors, she thought about graduate school. After hearing a few lurid narratives from older Smithies, however, about fainting at PhD orals and incontinence at dissertation defenses, she'd concluded that she'd logged as many hours in classrooms and libraries as she cared to.

She'd worked for three months in her father's office, then moved in with her Smith roommate in Queens to look for a job in the city. Within a month—before she'd found anything more than sporadic work with a temp agency—she was doing a happy hour at a beer-and-pickle place on Amsterdam Avenue and met an intriguing man named Fred, a handsome co-pilot with Alaska Airlines, and suffered a relapse into her infatuation-prone high-school ways. He was gorgeous, he was funny, he was a snappy dresser (though not, she thought, actually addicted to Calvin Klein), he seemed to be a good listener, and he was fabulous in bed. Within a month she'd followed him out to Seattle, where he and his flight crew were based. They were married the following fall, and ten months later she gave birth to Sage Maria Bachman—*Bachman* because that was Fred's surname, *Maria* after Ella's favorite grandmother, and *Sage* because it sounded unaffectedly hip. Ella had secretly hoped that a name synonymous with "wise" might endow her girl child with the tranquil stability she'd struggled to achieve for herself.

For five or six years, Ella would have said the marriage was going well. Motherhood suited her better than she could have predicted while in the thick of progressive readings in college. She'd found herself more intrigued than daunted by the physical changes and challenges of pregnancy, her labor and delivery were breath-takingly swift (Fred complained that it was easier flying a 757 through a thunderstorm than keeping track of the birthing stages she had him racing through), and nursing Sage left her feeling a deep and settled peace she'd never known. She likened it, with a certain countercultural aptness, to being a flesh-and-blood bong that harbored deeply tender feelings for its smoker.

Sage was a spirited child to be sure, given to climbing out of her crib in the middle of the night and showing up at Ella's bedside, *Goodnight Moon* in hand, to insist on an encore rendition. But she was as funny as her father and as smart as her mother, and from pre-school on, her teachers had described her with phrases like *inventive* and *bold* and *precociously independent*. When Sage went off to kindergarten, Ella followed the lead of one of her girlfriends and signed up for a course in real estate. Ten weeks later, she had her license and a job with a reputable company.

It was hard having Fred away during the week, but he was home most weekends, and he did get vacation time. He and Ella had enjoyed being close to the mountains, spending as much time hiking and skiing as work and childcare allowed. When Sage was six, Ella's father had a serious cardiac event, and she flew back to Rhode Island to be with him.

He'd recovered quickly, but when she got back to Seattle and asked Sage, that first bedtime, how she'd gotten along without her mommy, Sage cheerily allowed that she and her daddy had been having so much fun with "those other ladies." And who were "those other ladies"? Sage didn't really know, but they wore the same uniform as Daddy, and they cooked really good scrambled eggs for breakfast. When Ella followed up with Fred, he laughed and explained that one of his cousins had been in town with a friend and they'd all hung out together a couple of nights. Was it a cousin, Ella asked craftily, who'd been at their wedding? No, he said, one who couldn't make it. And what about the uniform "just like Daddy's"? Oh, she worked for Alaska Air, too. Ella commented on the remarkable coincidence but didn't have the heart to get into the scrambled eggs.

From there, things had gone nowhere but downhill: credit-card statements recording suspiciously large restaurant checks, curious delays in getting home after flights, phone calls and messages unanswered. Fred had denied everything, claiming he was terribly upset by her lack of trust. He'd agreed, though, to go with Ella to marriage counseling, and they tried that for four or five months. At one point, Ella thought things might have changed; Fred seemed more attentive, his hours more regular. In her heart, though, she suspected he was just getting shrewder about his infidelities.

The *coup de grace* had come, ironically, when Ella took Sage in for a fluoride treatment. Sitting in the dentist's waiting room, Ella had picked up a copy of *Seattle* magazine featuring a story about twin sisters who'd been cheerleaders at the U. and then gone on to become flight attendants for Alaska Airlines. There were multiple pictures: one with the pair standing in uniform by the landing gear of a plane, posing in a subtly suggestive way with one of the ground men who direct taxiing planes with those orange wands that look like a cross between a light saber and a dildo; one with them, in matching white mini-shorts and red-and-blue halter tops, standing in the sun next to a sailboat down in the harbor; and one, in uniform again, in an upscale bar with some untagged companions from their flight crew. One of the men had his head turned and was holding a hand up next to his cheek, but Ella could tell from his physique and carriage that it was Fred. *Gayle and Lee,* read the copy, *absolutely love being single and sometimes enjoy the fun of 'switching up with a guy who doesn't know there are two of us.'* Ella had ripped the piece out of the magazine and jammed it into her purse as though she were drowning a rat she'd caught biting a baby.

That night, she'd confronted Fred once she'd gotten Sage down. At first, he'd denied everything yet again.

"So I suppose this guy's *your* twin," she'd scoffed, jabbing at the man in the picture. "Separated at birth. What a coincidence *he* flies for Alaska, too."

Ultimately, she'd worn him down. The air crew, he confessed, had been staying at the Hyatt in Orlando and the captain—Lars Something—had offered to stand Fred and the twins a round of drinks after dinner at the local steak house. One thing just led to another, he explained. Lee and Gayle had a bottle of gin in their room and, before anyone knew what was happening, they'd gotten into a riotous four-way that earned them two visits from the night manager and the threat of police intervention before they managed to settle down.

Beyond general rage, Ella remembered feeling two things with sur-prising intensity. First, a sick kind of relief that she hadn't been wrong about Fred and that he was finally telling her the truth, as implausible and upsetting as it was. Second, that he was recounting his tale of com-pound infidelity with something close to relish—and with almost por-nographic detail. It was as though he were filling in a fraternity brother about an orgiastic Lauderdale spring break, and not very subtly at that. When Ella remarked on this, Fred looked vaguely cowed. And when she said she'd already cut him as much slack as she possibly could—that she was leaving him if he didn't break off the "relationship" immediately and return to marital counseling for a full year—he said he felt he was already getting things under better control.

"In what way?" she'd asked.

"Well," Fred had said, "we're not having four-ways anymore. We all decided Lars is an opportunistic asshole. It's just the three of us now."

For the first time in her life, Ella had slapped a man. Then she'd rung up the local Marriott, booked a room in Fred's name, and told him to get the hell out.

Two days later, at nine in the evening, Ella's phone had rung. She could see the call was from Fred, and thought about ignoring it. Sage was already in bed, though, and it seemed like as good a time as any for a trenchant conversation.

"Yes?" she'd answered, with the civility and warmth of a Borgia interrupted in the middle of a poisoning.

"Hi!"

Ella listened for stripper music in the background, but Fred was in a quiet room somewhere. "What do you want?"

"I've been thinking," said Fred.

"And?"

"Gayle and Lee and I have been thinking and talking, and we're going to move in together."

"Are you fucking kidding me?"

"No," replied Fred, sounding offended.

"So," said Ella. "You want to start paying rent, and buying groceries, and doing laundry, and getting driven home from your colonoscopies by a couple of blonde bimbos who think life is all about tag-team orgasms?"

"Look," said Fred after a pause. "We don't have to talk if you're going to be a bitch about it!"

Once again, Ella had been speechless. Oh, for an iPhone that could send high-voltage shocks as readily as high-resolution photos! *Hey, Siri! Fry this fuckwad!*

"I just thought you should know," said Fred.

"What about Sage?"

"She can stay with you. I'll start sending you money to help out."

"No, Fred. What the hell am I supposed to *tell* Sage? That her father is having a premature midlife crisis and has started playing house with the Olsen twins?"

"I don't know, Ella." He sighed loudly. "Just…just tell her whatever you want."

Maybe curiously, that was when Ella had realized that she didn't want to have anything to do with Fred ever again. It wasn't his infidelity; lots of men cheated and their wives gave them another chance. It wasn't his naïve stupidity, thinking that a household founded on kinky sex would hold together for more than a few months before jealousy or the taste for novel titillation tore it apart. It was Fred's saying that Ella could tell Sage whatever she wanted. Letting her tell their little girl the simple truth would be enough to break her heart—but implying that he'd be okay with Ella making up some virulent, embittered lie if she wanted to and then passing *that* along to Sage, without caring up front about what impact it might have? That was shocking, all-revealing, and unforgivable.

"I'll just tell her you don't want to live with me anymore," she'd said after a long pause. "I'll leave it to you to tell her anything else. But I want a divorce as quickly as possible."

"Ella—"

"That's it, Fred. *Finito!*"

For the next eight years, Ella had steered remarkably clear of romantic involvements. She'd dated now and again, sometimes in a mildly sustained way, but she focused the vast bulk of her emotional energy on Sage. There was a surgeon from Seattle Children's who was genuinely fun to be with, and who clearly wanted something more than their casual relationship. But (as she felt awful judging him for) he sweated her bed into a clammy swamp every time they had sex. For her, every amorous encounter turned into a race between reaching orgasm and leaping out of a bed for a towel.

That had also been around the time Sage was nearly tossed out of second grade for laughing at the Pledge of Allegiance—because, as she loudly proclaimed one day to teacher and classmates alike, "God is totally made up…just like Santa Claus and Winnie the Pooh." Ella had decided she needed to spend a little more time with her daughter—and also that (despite being totally comfortable with physiological realities like flatulence, menstruation, and armpit hair) she didn't necessarily need to be wallowing in the bedroom equivalent of a sun-warmed kiddie pool in order to achieve sexual release.

And so Ella had remained the stylish, hard-working, constitutionally fun-loving but vaguely monastic realtor, holding an adolescent tiger by the tail.

Brian had first met Ella at a sandwich shop in SoDo after lunch on a Thursday. He and Kingsley had grabbed a bite and were nursing coffees when Ella walked in, dressed in a long, cool, flowy outfit that Brian thought Kristin Scott Thomas might have worn in *The English Patient*. Her handshake was firm and her eyes were warm, and he knew right away he was going to like her. She patted her shoulder bag, told them, with a huge smile, that she had a bunch of interesting listings in the area, and led them out of the establishment with the same easy verve she'd come in with. They spent the next three hours exploring local purchase options, all of them lofts with enough square footage, Ella joked, to turn them into roller rinks if they ever decided to move somewhere else. Deciding nothing quite suited them, they agreed to get together again on Saturday to look further afield.

"Isn't she great?" asked Kingsley as they headed back uptown to their apartment.

"I love her," replied Brian.

"You ought to see her in yoga pants!" Kingsley gushed. "It's enough to steal a boy's heart away from Lady Gaga."

They'd met again a couple of days later in Pioneer Square, having told Ella they were drifting away from the loft-renovation idea. The prospect of relocating as soon as Kingsley's lease expired, without needing to hire an architect or contractor or to choose kitchen appliances and bathroom fixtures, was really appealing. She showed them two modern but stylish apartments—roomy, bright, and airy, with views out onto tree-lined streets, both of them move-in properties. When they decided, over gelati, that the one place with a balcony was more their cup of tea, Ella asked if they wanted to put in an offer.

Kingsley had shrugged and looked at Brian. "It's early days. But what do you think?" He reached across the table and put his hand on top of Brian's. "It was love at first sight when I saw you, too!"

Brian was somewhat surprised when no words came.

"What?" laughed Kingsley. "Gelato got your tongue?" He looked at Ella, who smiled warily.

"Well," said Brian at last, "I liked it and all." He looked back and forth between Kingsley and Ella, as though they were lifeguards at a pool he was floundering in and he wondered which one might be willing to pull him out. "But we *have* only been looking for two days. Is it even, like, *legal* to find something this quickly?"

Ella laughed. "It's a nice place. Right size. Right price. Although I think we can save a little with a shrewd bid—*if* you want to go for it."

"No pressure," said Kingsley.

"Not at all. Pressure's for tires," laughed Ella. "I love hanging out with you guys. I'll show you places for the next three months if you like." She winked at Kingsley. "The important thing, obviously, is for you to end up with something you really like." She looked at Brian and drew her mouth into a prim smile. If she'd twisted her shoulders a little and crossed one hand over the other, he mused, she might look like a hip, blonde Mona Lisa rocking an Anthropologie maxi dress.

Brian looked from Ella over to Kingsley. "I suddenly feel like an idiot."

Kingsley shook his head. "No way, man. You need to feel comfortable."

"You don't think we'd be settling? Finding the right place is supposed to take forever."

Kingsley and Ella laughed in unison. "Sometimes it happens real fast," she said.

Brian took a sip of water and turned to Kingsley. "What would you say about talking it over tonight and tomorrow? And getting back to Ella, say, Monday?"

Kingsley shrugged. "Sure!"

Brian looked apologetically at Ella. "You think it'll still be available Monday?"

"It's been listed for fifteen weeks. Nobody's going to see it tomorrow. I think you'll be fine."

Brian had felt strangely like he was back in his Little League days and his mother had just told him he could have his whole team over for a sleepover…and she'd make them both nachos and mac and cheese. There was something about Ella's expression that reminded him of Cinny—but not as though they were actual relatives or anything. As though they were visitors from the same distant but wonderful planet and they'd come here, very simply, to spread laughter and love. That Kingsley had informed him Ella was a prodigious smoker of weed did nothing to challenge the perception.

He'd turned back to Kingsley. "What do you say? Get back to Ella Monday?"

"Sure." Kingsley tossed his dreads and nodded. "Sure."

Brian had faced challenges with commitment for a long time. Likely forever. He sometimes joked that Grace's getting herself born first was a function of her assertiveness, a kind of intrauterine feminism that might have tempted her to tie a knot in his umbilical cord when he wasn't looking so he'd be yanked up short in the race to the birth canal. In truth, though, even if she had courteously floated back to wave him through, he might very well have hesitated, choosing to linger indecisively in the warm and familiar darkness rather than stick his head into an impossibly small fleshy aperture with no guarantee there was anything on the other side that would make the torturous transit worthwhile. Naturally, memory didn't go back that far, but he'd long had vivid semi-nightmares that he was sure were related to the birth trauma. He would dream he was away at summer camp, for example, living in an amazingly cool private cabin, complete with flat-screen television, hot tub, and a wall-mounted French-fry dispenser. But in order to get in or out, he'd have to negotiate an entrance hall roughly the diameter of a donut hole. Or, having loved flying movies as a boy, he would dream he was the tail-gunner in *Memphis Belle*, but the only way in or out of the turret was a twenty-foot metal tube that he could barely slither through greased and naked, let alone encased in a heavy sheepskin flying suit. The only poem he'd ever fully related to in his sole college literature class was William Blake's *Book of Thel*, which was about a yet-to-be-embodied spirit who stands on the threshold of incarnation and, when she's prepped on the myriad trials and tribulations of mortality, flees screaming in the opposite direction. No, commitment was not generally Brian's thing—and the weekend's charge of deciding about buying an apartment with Kingsley wasn't one he readily embraced.

Kingsley, as always, had been kindness personified. He'd told Brian Saturday night that there was no hurry. The place they liked seemed perfect, but if it didn't feel right to Brian, then they should pass and keep looking. Was there anything he could do to help Brian decide? Brian said he didn't know. Was it that Brian had some other sort of place in mind? Brian said he couldn't really say what sort of place he wanted. Should they keep looking until something just seemed right, magically or otherwise? Brian shrugged. Was it possible, sadly, that Brian was wary of making this kind of commitment with Kingsley in particular? Not at all, answered Brian, only partly telling the truth. Kingsley suggested they take the matter up again on Sunday.

Brian had awoken with the sun, and as Kingsley lay there next to him, snoring lightly, he'd found himself awash in guilt and doubt. Kingsley had in fact been pretty much on target when he'd asked if he were having second thoughts about a joint real-estate purchase. It vexed Brian that he'd swept that complicating bit of emotional truth under the conversational rug. He felt awful about it. Kingsley deserved a partner as honest as he was. At the same time, especially at emotionally charged moments like these, Kingsley's virtue *itself* could be irksome. His patience and understanding could seem limitless, leaving Brian to wonder what was wrong with the man. Brian knew himself well enough to realize he was capable of being a feckless jerk—as at present—and the fact that Kingsley never came anywhere close to uttering the same judgment either spoke poorly for his perceptiveness or suggested a saintly tolerance that, to Brian, looked a lot like gullibility. What it came down to, Brian had concluded just as Kingsley began to wake up, was very close to Groucho Marx's famous observation about club memberships: it was hard to respect anyone who could love someone like Brian Posey with unruffled patience.

Given the point Brian had just reached in sorting through his relationship with Kingsley—and, just as importantly, given the point he *hadn't* yet reached in the decision to buy or not buy the property in question—it was surprising how Sunday unfolded. Once they'd had their coffee in bed, and showered, and breakfasted on the croissants and honeydew melon they'd bought on their way home from their time with Ella, Kingsley asked Brian how he was feeling about the possible purchase. Brian confessed he still wasn't sure. "Well," Kingsley had said with a measured calm, "if you don't feel ready to pull the trigger, then maybe I will."

"What does that mean?" asked Brian, slightly taken aback.

It meant, Kingsley said, that he would simply make the purchase himself. He was sure the bank would consider him a good risk, and Brian could join him in their new digs without any formal encumbrances, legal or financial. Kingsley assumed he'd split the cost of utilities and maybe kick in some on the mortgage payments in lieu of rent. Beyond that, though, Brian could put all the past day's worry and stress behind him and they could get on with their lives in what would be, for both of them, a more financially savvy way.

Once again, Brian had been all but stunned by Kingsley's patience and generosity. For the moment, though, he found that his strong feeling that Kingsley was being a fool was trumped by an even stronger feeling that he himself would be a total cad if he let his partner do what he was proposing. And so Brian chose, himself, to do the noble thing that would soon turn out not to be the noble thing at all. "Fuck it!" he said, grabbing Kingsley by the ears and kissing him full on the lips. "Let's just do it."

"Seriously?"

"Absolutely."

They'd called Ella first thing Monday and said they wanted to make an offer. "Seriously?" "Absolutely!" They met her at lunchtime near her office and came up with a figure. She'd tendered it immediately, and within an hour they'd received a counter. They countered the counter, and by five o'clock their offer had been accepted. Ella asked if they had supper plans. Not really, they said. Then they should join her for a celebratory nosh at this great little tapas place in Ballard.

They'd met her at seven, and by nine all of them were three sheets to the wind on sangria and two bottles of Tempranillo. Ella was drunk enough that she felt Brian and Kingsley needed to hear all the details of her husband's long-ago *ménage à trois*. Kingsley was drunk enough to say that, speaking of *ménages à trois*, it was too bad he and Brian were gay, because Ella's booty was the unquestioned highlight of yoga class—by general acclamation, "enough to make angels weep." Brian was sober enough to worry that Ella would take offense, but she hooted at the feigned come-on and said if they ever wanted to switch teams, either for a quick match or a whole season, they should just let her know. Kingsley had laughed it off, but Brian felt a curious rising just under his diaphragm, and when she said it was time to head home to her daughter, he'd felt strangely deflated.

Brian was too wasted to dream that night. Come morning, he was frankly surprised to feel no incipient buyer's remorse. As he sat across the breakfast table from Kingsley, it seemed entirely plausible that they could move into their new home together and sit, just so, for the next twenty or thirty or forty years in complete contentment. Just that night, however, Brian had one of his stranger birth-canal revisitations. He was on a ski trip with Kingsley—it must have been to Zermatt, because the Matterhorn loomed terrifyingly over the scene like the giant winged devil in *Fantasia*. They'd just finished their last run of the day and were walking through the snowy streets back to their hotel, skis over their shoulders, when the space between the busy shops narrowed and they were suddenly crawling on their hands and knees.

"Ditch your skis," Brian told Kingsley. "We can come back for them later."

"No, we have to take them," replied Kingsley. "The rental place will charge us a fortune if we don't."

Suddenly the snow they'd been crawling on turned into mud. "Go in there," said Kingsley, pointing to a kind of cat door in the side of a building.

"I can't possibly fit," said Brian.

"You have to," replied Kingsley.

"Why?"

"That's where we live."

Brian stuck his head in and was scrunching his shoulders to try to get them in as well when he was overwhelmed by, of all things, the reek of garlic. He tried to back up, but Kingsley had already started in after him and blocked the way. The temperature soared, and Brian was desperate to take off his heavy parka, but the space was too constrained. Sweat trickled off his temples and into his eyes. A hot wind blew through the darkness toward him, increasing in force until its roar became a trembling and then a shaking and the tunnel collapsed on him, forcing the air from his lungs.

He'd awakened with his face buried in his pillow. As he lifted his head, he could feel drool cooling on his lips, and it came to him bleakly that he had just made a dreadful life decision. Kingsley dozed on next to him, serenely oblivious to the cataclysm. Hot breath gusted from his open mouth into Brian's face. The lingering evidence of last night's turbocharged garlic-and-black-pepper shrimp was inescapable.

It had made perfect sense to Brian when Kingsley told him *he* had to be the one to break the bad news to Ella. It was Brian, after all, who'd gotten cold feet. They were still inside the review period for the condominium contract, so even if they walked away totally, it was unlikely they'd lose their earnest money. Kingsley had decided, though, that he'd try to revert to his earlier proposal and buy the property himself, provided the financing could be shifted over to him alone. There wasn't any reason to think it couldn't be. Nevertheless, Brian's total reverse of field had finally overwhelmed Kingsley's unflappable Jamaican placidity. "You might have fucking well thought about this a bit harder back when I offered to buy the place myself," Kingsley had said.

Interestingly, Kingsley's long-deferred pique did have the effect of making him seem ever-so-much-more-human than he'd sometimes seemed before—and honestly, that much more worthy of respect, as someone who could actually see Brian's faults for what they were. At that particular moment, though, Brian hadn't especially *wanted* Kingsley to rise in his estimation—and he'd felt so totally awful about what he was doing that he would have relished a little more of that erstwhile supportive understanding.

In any case, he rang up Ella first thing the next morning and asked if she was busy for lunch. She wasn't; what was up?

They agreed to meet at a Panera downtown.

Brian arrived at the restaurant ten minutes early, ordered a green tea, and grabbed a table by a window. The couple next to him was planning a wedding—the pinnacle of irony, Brian thought. Ella breezed in right on time, dressed with her usual casual élan.

"Hi," she said as she sauntered up to the table. "Pleasure before business?" She motioned toward the counter.

"Sure."

They'd ordered soup with baguettes and walked back to the table, Brian toting the obligatory electronic hockey puck.

"So," she said with a broad smile. "What's cookin'?"

Brian sighed deeply. "I might as well just come out and say it." He was most of the way through his discommoding update when the buzzer started clattering on the tabletop like a convulsing turtle. He jumped up, got their platters, silverware, and butter, and came back to find Ella looking at her cell phone.

"I'll call the listing agent as soon as we're done. Like you said, you're still in the grace period. I think we're okay with the hand money. And as I understand it, the loan was going to depend mostly on Kingsley's resources, right?" She picked up her mini baguette, tore off a chunk, and buttered it with uncharacteristic daintiness. She'd struck Brian as more of a free-wheeling eater.

"Right," he confirmed. "He was thinking earlier, remember, about buying it solo. He got a preliminary thumbs-up. Nothing official. Just their best guess."

"Good." Ella nodded as she chewed. The motion of her jaws accentuated her high cheekbones in a way Brian found very pleasing. "So, how's Kingsley taking all of this?"

Brian wiped his lips with his napkin. "So-so, I guess. I mean, he's fine, but I could tell he was kind of pissed."

"No surprise," observed Ella. "I'd be livid." She pulled a wry smile and dipped into her soup. "This is just real-estate phobia, I assume? You're not breaking up the household or anything?"

"No," replied Brian. "Not really."

Ella put her spoon down and studied him closely. "Now, there's a ringing endorsement of domestic bliss!"

Brian surprised himself by blushing. He wiped his lips again and stared toward the entrance, his tongue clicking softly.

"I'm sorry," said Ella. "That was shitty of me. It's none of my business."

"No, it's okay." Brian took a sip of iced tea. "It's good to talk."

"Well, I'm happy to talk," replied Ella. She leaned forward. "Really. Anytime."

"Thanks."

"I have to confess," she went on, "ever since my old shitstorm with Fred? It's been hard for me to look at any relationship and not, you know, be hyper tuned-in to potential warning signs. Little frictions. Tensions. Whatever."

"I get it."

"Misery loves company, I guess."

Brian had laughed.

"What?" She eyed him expectantly.

"I'm so glad I'm fulfilling your needs."

The loan had gone through, Kingsley bought the condo, and even though he'd assured Brian, true to form, that moving in with him would imply no lasting commitment, Brian decided that the handwriting was on the wall. Not that it was easy for him to pull the plug. In favor of the domestic status quo were Brian's inherent reluctance to make big changes, coupled with a true affection for Kingsley. Kingsley was sweet, he was handsome, he was funny, he was smart, and he was much closer to being rich than Brian thought he himself would ever be. But the Zermatt birth-canal dream had distilled a number of things Brian had been struggling with for some time. Kingsley was unremittingly sure of himself and, even though he'd always gone out of his way to consult with Brian on matters affecting them both, he'd always somehow seemed to have two votes to Brian's one. It reminded him, annoyingly, of his childhood relationship with Grace, and maybe of their adult relationship, too. Also, being in a steady male-male relationship had begun to seem restraining in ways that the prospect of buying property together brought to a head. The time he was spending with Ella frankly reminded Brian that, even though his dating life had recently favored other men, he'd always loved and lusted after certain women as well. Maybe the jokes about Ella's booty had suggested Kingsley was actually willing to explore a three-way relationship. There would be an irony: Ella falling into what was virtually a mirror image of her husband's infidelity.

But Brian realized a ménage wasn't at all what he wanted. Ultimately, he wanted stability with one person, and that person pretty clearly wasn't Kingsley Shaw. Harder to disencumber was whether his reluctance to move into the new place was a reaction against Kingsley in particular, or homosexual domesticity in general. But in any case, Brian had stood firm. He wished Kingsley well, told him their time together had been something he would not for the life of him have traded away, and said he hoped they could part friends. Kingsley almost broke his heart with his reply: of course they would remain friends, and if Brian ever needed him for anything, he should just be in touch, no strings attached.

Coming from someone else, the last bit might have sounded like a calculated effort to kill with kindness. Coming from Kingsley, it had been genuine, breathtaking, and heart-rending.

Brian had walked away feeling both a lesser man and absolutely reborn.

The stages of Brian's involvement with Ella were gradual.

First, she'd helped him find an apartment. She didn't usually handle rentals, but was happy to take the task on, given she felt "centrally involved," as she put it, in his sudden homelessness. After several days of searching, rained-on and soggy-footed, they found a thousand-square-foot, one-bedroom place in Ballard that wouldn't break the bank and promised a spectacular view of the Olympics once the weather cleared. The bulk of the furniture in Brian's previous digs had been Kingsley's, so Ella took on the decorating as well. When Brian kidded her that it was consummate hubris for a woman to wrest interior-design choices from a gay male, she'd replied that she could tell he wasn't as gay as he thought. She only needed to look at what she joked was his "Klondike couture" wardrobe for confirmation. In any case, she knew three or four consignment shops with great selection and reasonable prices, and she guided Brian through his modest purchases with the solicitude of a mother helping a child set up his first home away from home. There was nothing maternal, though, about her general demeanor—or about the way she insisted on trying out the beds and mattresses she felt would best suit his coalescing décor. Her unselfconscious laughter as she struck off one odalisque pose after another echoed for days in Brian's ears and imagination.

The weekend after he'd moved in, Brian invited Ella over for wine and fondue, a recipe Cinny often prepared for anniversary dinners with Frank, especially later in life. Brian had already bought the cheese and bread when he recalled, with mild shock, that it was his own go-to meal for romantic evenings. Ella arrived with a bottle of Gevrey-Chambertin as a housewarming gift, and by the time they were done breaking bread and dipping—and Brian had forgotten to blow out the Sterno and the room had filled with the acrid scent of burnt Gruyère and Emmentaler—they'd made their way through that bottle and another, too, and were feeling relaxed and jovial.

Ella asked if Brian liked Sam Cooke. Brian replied that everyone liked Sam Cooke. "Then let's bring it on home with Sam," she declared. She cued up *Ain't That Good News* on her iPhone, stood up, adjusted her skirt, walked around the table to Brian, laid her hand on his shoulder, and leaned down to his ear.

"I wanna dance," she whispered.

And so they did. And at the end of the evening, Brian found himself kissing Ella with full lingual involvement and his hands cupped tightly over her fabled derrière. "Do I hear angels weeping?" she asked softly.

"You remember that?" Brian chuckled.

"How could a girl forget?"

Ella had flown East with her daughter the next weekend for her parents' fortieth anniversary. The following Saturday, she'd invited Brian over to her place for a swim and casual supper. She was eager for him to meet Sage, but her daughter was going to be at a friend's house for the night, so he'd have to wait for that pleasure. Brian said he looked forward to it. It was sunny and warm when he got to Ella's place, and she met him at the door in a flowing delft-blue swim cover-up that matched her eyes with eerie precision. She showed him to the guest room to change and asked if he wanted a mojito. He said sure, and she said she'd meet him by the pool.

One mojito had followed another. Brian observed that he drank more with her than with anyone else he knew. She asked if he needed an intervention. He replied that he thought that's what she'd been doing all along. Then he showed her he could do a handstand on the tip of the diving board—or at least attempt one. When he toppled over into the water with a kidney-smashing splash, she leaped in, wrapped her arms and legs tightly around him, and said it had been way too long since she'd fucked a fool.

They saw each other steadily after that. Brian met Sage and liked her from the start, although she had a precocious ability to make him feel self-conscious. Her intense, judging gaze, he thought, was a dead ringer for Kirsten Dunst's piercing pre-teen stare in *Interview with the Vampire*. When he mentioned it off-handedly to Ella, she laughed and said Sage was just extremely protective of her mother. When Brian said Sage's mother didn't seem like the type that needed much protection, Ella laughed again and told him that looks could be deceiving.

And so the relationships had developed. Ella made no effort to hide the fact that she and Brian were sleeping together, and Sage made it clearer by the day that everything Brian had ever thought about the limits and proclivities of the adolescent brain fell woefully short of the mark, at least in her case. How many of Sage's idiosyncrasies she might owe to the THC her mother shared with her from time to time, he had no way of knowing.

Ella often asked Brian how he was doing. Was he happy with her? Did he miss Kingsley? He was supremely happy, he assured her—discreetly omitting any mention of his ongoing mystification by Sage. Ella confessed she sometimes felt like she'd broken up a beautiful relationship between Brian and Kingsley. Especially considering what the Bimbo Twins had done to her marriage to Fred, she worried she might still be protecting herself from hurt and disappointment via manipulative indifference and self-gratification. But Brian reassured her there, too. He thought of her as having cast him not a baited hook, but a lifeline. Even if he hadn't ended up with her, he said, he was still well out of his former ties, warm and wonderful as he invariably insisted Kingsley had been.

Multiple weeks into their budding partnership, Ella confessed she thought Brian was a wonder, given how well he continued to speak of his former live-in. Was there a chance he still thought so well of Kingsley that he might want to slide back into his orbit? No way, Brian had replied, demonstrating his sincerity by kissing her and grabbing her butt. Then what, she asked through a giggle, would he think about proving it by moving in with her?

"Sure," said Brian after a beat. "I like your furniture a lot better than that shit you made me buy."

Five months later, they were married. Cinny had flown west with Grace, Jack, and Chelsea. It was the first leg of the last earthly journey of her life. She'd liked Ella immediately, especially after they shared a joint before the rehearsal dinner. When Brian drove her back to her hotel afterwards, Cinny did confess her surprise that he was marrying a woman so soon after breaking up with Kingsley. Brian laughed and told her the world was a strange place. He felt, though, that Ella was just the right person for him. Cinny had nodded and sat silently for a minute or two, gazing out the window at the buildings they were passing by. Then she'd turned back to him and put her hand lightly on his knee.

"She's not a tranny, is she, sweetie?"

Brian laughed so hard he nearly swerved into an oncoming bus. "No, Mom. She's not a tranny."

"Have you checked? Sage doesn't look much like her, you know."

"Yes, Mom. I've checked. Do you want to check, too?"

"That's okay, sweetie. I trust you."

A few days after the Boeing executive house-hunting debacle, Ella came home from work one day to find Sage hunched over her computer. She'd just gotten back from a run and was sitting, legs crossed, on the sofa. A glass half-full of orange juice and tonic sat on the coffee table in front of her—her go-to rehydration drink

"Hi, Mom," she chirped, setting her laptop aside and dropping her feet to the floor.

"Hi, honey. Good run?"

"It was, thanks. Ten-point-three miles. Six-thirty pace."

"Great! Cute running shorts. Are those new?"

"To me." Sage stood up and spun around. She looked back coyly over her shoulder, spun back around, and did a shallow plié. "Tokiko gave them to me. She said they made her look like a Hooters waitress."

"Right color, anyway. And really tight! They'd be even tighter on her."

"Hey! No body shaming!"

"Far be it from me to shame anybody," said Ella. "Not with this frontal annex I've been working on." She patted the hint of a belly under the front panel of her skirt.

"Shut up. Mom! You look great." Sage dropped back onto the couch and re-crossed her legs. She pulled off her running socks and tossed them onto the coffee table. "Don't worry. I'll get rid of those before Brian gets home."

"Good idea." Ella walked over to the refrigerator and pulled out a bottle of wine. She grabbed a glass from the cabinet, filled it, and sat down on one of the stools in front of the counter. "What were you looking at?" She gestured toward the laptop.

"Nothing much. Just doing a little research."

"On?"

"Bisexuality."

"Oh," laughed Ella. "Just bisexuality."

"Just that," answered Sage, with a deadpan gaze.

"Well?" Ella ventured after a beat or two.

"Well, what?"

"Is, like, bisexuality something you're…researching…for any particular reason?"

"Oh, you know." Sage adjusted the straps of her black running tank. At sixteen, her breasts had begun to fill out, but her arms were thin and toned from all her running and frequent visits to the gym.

"No, I don't," said Ella, her neck craning forward. "I don't know at all. What's *up* with you? No shitting around, okay?"

"Don't stress, Mom. I just want to be sure Brian's really into you. And not, you know, just going through a phase."

"A phase?" Ella stared incredulously. "What the fuck?"

"Language, Mom."

"Like I said. What the fuck?"

"It's not like I want to make a federal case, or anything. But when Brian called Kingsley the other day—"

"Yes?"

"He told you he called, right?"

Ella nodded coldly.

"Well, it's not like he was all lovey-dovey or anything. But you could tell he still had really warm feelings for the dude."

"Did he know you were listening?"

"I don't think so. But I really couldn't help it. I was in here and he was in the office with the door open."

"And?"

"Well, like I said. Brian just seemed very…well…warm and friendly." She shrugged matter-of-factly.

"Good!" exclaimed Ella after a pause. She reached for the bottle to top up her glass. "That's good. That speaks well for him. Kingsley was very important to Brian for years, and Kingsley's poor mother is dying. Think how awful it would be if Brian just shut him out of his life. Like he was a dead fish."

"No worries about that." Sage pulled her knees up in front of her chest and hugged them. "There was nothing *dead fish* about it."

Ella set her glass down again. "What are you saying? Are you saying you heard something I should know about?"

Sage looked at her mother with a pained expression. "No. Not really. I guess."

"You guess?"

"No. Not really. You're probably right. He just sounded…nice. And even affectionate. Appropriately affectionate, I guess."

"How about Kingsley?" asked Ella. "Could you hear him? Did Brian have him on speakerphone?"

"No. I couldn't tell about Kingsley. You're probably right, though, Mom. It was probably just Brian trying to be a good person." Sage leaned back and clasped her hands behind her head.

"Brian *is* a good person."

"Yeah," replied Sage. "Want to do a bong?"

"I'm happy with wine for now, thanks," replied Ella. "Want a sip?"

Sage hopped up and skipped over to her mother. She took the glass by the base and tipped back a substantial gulp. "Nice! Fruity, wouldn't you say?"

"Sure."

"*With a hint of ripe melon,* Sage intoned, *yielding to blackberry and mango.*" Ella laughed and took the glass from her. "Wine labels are so full of shit," declared Sage. "Grown-up, capitalistic bullshit. Beer labels, too."

"So young, and yet so wise."

"Well, look who I have for a mother!"

"Thanks, hon." Ella reached up to stroke Sage's cheek before she went back to the couch.

Sage sat there for a minute, looking at Ella with her bright, long-lashed eyes. "When you and Brain are having sex—'making love'—do you feel like he really gets into it?'"

Ella's head snapped back, but she laughed. "Yes, he does. And how many mothers do you think would let their daughters ask them a question like that?"

"Not enough." Sage sat quietly for another minute, looking at her nails—one hand, then the other. "Has he ever asked you to peg him or anything?"

Ella's eyes widened in disbelief. "*Peg* him?"

"You, know. Like dildo his ass?"

"Sage Bachman. Where in hell did you ever learn terminology like that?"

"I'm in high school, Mom."

"Jesus Christ! Jesus *Christ*! But no. Brian's never asked me to peg him."

"That's probably good." She was silent for a beat. "And does he ever, you know, ask *you* for anal?"

"My God! Sage! I don't believe you! But, *no*! And why am I even telling you that?"

Sage nodded calmly. "Sorry, Mom. I didn't mean to embarrass you."

Ella looked at her daughter, exhaled deeply, and shook her head. "You didn't embarrass me, honey. You *shocked* me."

"Well," replied Sage, "sorry for that, too. It's just that I love you. And I want you to be safe and happy. Really."

Ella sighed. "I know, Sage, honey. I know you do."

"It's you and me, Mom. You know that."

"I do," said Ella with a nod. "You and me and Brian."

"And Brian," added Sage.

When Brian got back from Hanover, he wrapped up the last details on the Croatian bicycle tour and started looking for dates when the family could jet off on Cinny's memorial odyssey. The coming fall was out, but it looked like there was a workable window the following April. Grace's colleagues said they could cover for her, and Sage's principal had practically danced with glee when Ella asked if Sage's spring break could be extended by two weeks. Brian thought they could all leave for New Zealand on the tenth, return to the New York area May fourth, and have the fifth to take care of whatever Cinny had in mind in the mysterious last envelope. Everyone could then get home on the sixth.

"Woo-hoo!" said Grace when he called with the news. "Good job, little brother!"

"Yeah. Anyway. If that seems good to you, I'll go ahead and look into flights."

"Great," said Grace. "Any idea what it's likely to cost? Best guess?"

"Economy, maybe three or four grand per person."

"How about business?"

"That would be more."

Grace laughed. "Damn! 'More.' Brilliant! I can't believe how lucky we are to have a travel professional working for us!" She heard Brian snort at the other end. "Are you flipping me off?"

"Worse. I wish we were FaceTiming."

Grace laughed again. "So, how much more? In numbers, please. No nouns or adjectives."

"Remind me what an adjective is."

"Come on, Brian."

"Maybe nine thousand apiece? Nine to twelve?"

"Hmmm."

"Then there's accommodations," said Brian. "Speaking of which, Sage is all hot to stay at the hotel in Rome that Beck stays at."

"It's probably pretty nice," said Grace.

"So she says. You have any idea what the estate is worth? Total?"

"Well, Jack was amazed. You could see his eyes light up with visions of vintage Duesenbergs and sexy new chronometers. Chronographs. Whatever you call them. You know. Watches."

Brian chuckled. "But the estate. Roughly—?"

"Roughly six million."

"Holy shit! Who knew writing about dead poets brought in that kind of cash?"

"Maybe you should have majored in English, too," Grace scoffed. "Look what it's done for me."

"You've got a great life, Gracie."

"I know. I do. Anyway. Remember Dad came into a bunch of money when Manu died. And he turned out to have a huge life-insurance policy, considering."

"At his age?"

"Like I said, Jack was shocked. Especially given the rest of his assets."

"I'm with Jack. I wonder what he was thinking?"

"I don't know. Maybe about paying for this trip."

"Maybe," said Brian. "So I guess we go with business class, then. No question. At least for the long hauls."

"Sounds good. It's all going to be exhausting enough as it is."

"I'll get right on it. Anything else?"

"Not really. Oh! Except I was going through some photos today, and I found this great picture I wonder if you remember."

"Of?"

"I'll send it. But it's a slight but gorgeous woman standing in the woods in her bra."

"Mom?"

"Yup."

Brian laughed. "We were, like, what? Eleven? Heading up to Madison Hut. The week before school started."

"Bingo!" said Grace. "It was so hot Mom was absolutely miserable, so she finally says, 'The hell with it!' and whips off her shirt."

"Dad joked she thought she was back at Woodstock," recalled Brian. "Mom said if she were, she wouldn't stop with her shirt."

"It left me scarred to this day," said Grace. "Speaking of which, I remember you had to sleep in the ladies' bunk room because the men's was fully booked."

"Shit, yes. And I had to get in bed early before any of the ladies came in and changed. I felt like a three-year-old."

"I went with you, didn't I?" said Grace. "I could have been a total bitch."

"Yeah, thanks. I was supposed to keep my head under the blanket so that I couldn't see anyone else in her bra. Or less."

"I forget what you did," said Grace. "Did you peek?"

"Of *course* I peeked."

"I'm surprised."

"Why?"

"I thought you'd only gotten into women recently. I mean *really* into them."

"Fuck you, Grace. You're never going to let that go, are you?"

"Should I?"

"Yeah, you should."

"Really? You fucked me over, Brian. On a lark." She was pretty sure she heard clicking from Seattle. "Anyway."

"I made a mistake," said Brian, quietly. "It's not like I never admitted it."

"Yeah. Whatever."

There was a good five- or six-second silence. "I'm gonna go now."

"Okay," said Grace.

"Okay."

"Thanks for looking into the flights," said Grace.

"You're welcome. Say hi to Jack."

"I will. And tell Sage I'm up for getting Beck's autograph with her. If he's there."

"If he's there. We'll see."

IN TRANSIT

Grace and Jack sat across from each other at a small table at the Hyatt rooftop bar, high above the still-busy Hudson. It was just after nine o'clock p.m., and One World Trade Center and the buildings clustered around it sparkled against the eastern skyline like an electrified bar graph. Sightseeing boats and small ferries still scurried here and there, reduced by the setting to the scale of toys, as though they were part of a nighttime shoot for *Theodore Tugboat*.

The Hyatt House at Exchange Place was a long way from the airport, but Jack had insisted on staying there. The building once housed the First National Bank of New Jersey, his grandfather's first employer out of Rutgers. William "Brother" Tingley had been the first Tingley to earn a college degree.

Grace was used to her husband going on at socially insensitive lengths about his various material and technological enthusiasms—expounding, say, at a Sunday brunch on the superiority of fuel injectors over carburetors, or explaining to their reading group why automatic watches are preferable to quartz, even if they keep less accurate time. For more of their train ride down to the city than Grace would have thought possible, however, Jack had gone on about the renovation of the building where they'd be spending the night. The developers had put nearly $100 million into the project, hiring the best designers and engineers and sparing no structural or decorative expense, including the novel retractable roof under which they currently sat—or didn't sit, actually, given that it was now pulled all the way back to reveal a stunning starscape. Grace had nodded dutifully as her husband jabbered on, looking up at appropriate intervals from the novel she'd picked up for the trip on Chelsea's (and thus, quite likely, on Grant Collier's) recommendation.

"Check it out, H.P.," said Jack, pointing toward Manhattan. A near-half moon peeked up over the eastern skyline. Closer to hand, a gentle breeze wafted down the river, enough to kick up some texture on the water and set a million reflections dancing like liquid fire. "Beautiful!"

"I still can't believe you booked all three of us into the same room," said Grace, shaking her head again. "Chelsea's twenty-four, for God's sake. She deserves her privacy. So do I."

"Look, Honey Pot," Jack replied. "A place like this, they don't give the rooms away. Besides, it's greener for us to share."

"How's that?" asked Grace, pouring herself more Perrier.

"Well, they won't have to wash as many sheets."

"Really? So, Chelsea's sharing a bed with us, too?"

"Oh, right!" said Jack. "I guess we'd be using two beds either way."

"Maybe though, dear, you two can double up on a bath towel. What do you think?"

"Okay, okay. I'm an idiot. I just hate shelling out six hundred bucks when we don't have to."

"Maybe you forgot, Mom's paying," observed Grace. "And Dad."

"I know." Jack pulled at his ear, a reflex he showed when he felt outpaced by his wife. "It's just that whatever we're getting that we don't spend now, we'll have later."

"To *spend* later, you mean?"

"Whatever."

Grace took a settling breath. "Do me a favor, dear." She leaned toward him with a taut smile. "For the next three weeks, please try to put your parsimonious banker-grandfather on paid leave. Let the rest of us enjoy the trip of a lifetime."

The two of them had gone around for decades about what Grace considered the ill fit between Jack's small economies and his obsession with luxury watches, high-end automobiles, and (most recently) a showy new garage in which to park the latter. *Carriage house* was actually the phrase he used to describe it, and damned if he hadn't put a racehorse weathervane on top of the cupola of the thirty-five-foot addition. She routinely pointed out to him that, whatever Grandfather Tingley had been obliged to do during the Depression to assure his family's future, Jack himself was two generations removed from appreciable financial peril. At the salary he pulled down at his law firm, he was more than assuring their own comfortable future, and undoubtedly Chelsea's as well. Quite probably the future of any children Chelsea ended up having, too—assuming her new partner's sperm weren't desiccated beyond any hope of potency.

"Stressing over a single night's room rate is like your dad straightening and reusing nails, don't you think?" Grace reached for a peanut. "Are you going to turn into a nail-straightener, too, dear?"

"Okay. *Touché!*" Jack looked at Grace with a blend of vexation and amusement. "I'll do my best. But if I slip up, just help me out by rolling your eyes that way you do, okay?"

"Deal," laughed Grace.

Chelsea walked briskly up to the table. "Here you go, Mom." She handed over a light cardigan. She'd just flown up from Charlottesville and made it to the hotel in time to join Grace and Jack for dinner. She turned to her father before sitting down. "Sure you're warm enough? I can go back."

"I'm just fine, honey. Thanks for getting that for Mom."

"I was chilly, too." She sat down and smoothed her skirt.

"Mom's a little peeved we're all sharing a room," Jack volunteered. "My bad."

"No, no," Chelsea said. "It's all good. It'll be cozy. Like we're all, you know, tentmates at camp or something."

Jack chuckled. "I hope not too many dads slept over with you all."

"Cool it, Jack!" exclaimed Grace.

"That's okay, Mom. I can take it."

"Well, I can't. Your father acts like he's in middle school sometimes, I swear."

"Easy, Mom," said Chelsea. "You chose him, right?"

Grace smiled resignedly. "God help me."

"Well," said Jack, sunnily. "I have to say, this is quite a view." He smirked at Chelsea.

"It is. And I really don't mind sharing. I love you guys."

"We love you too, honey," replied Jack. "You want something?"

"Maybe a Kentucky Coffee?"

Jack looked vaguely surprised. "Bourbon you're into?"

"Grant turned me on to them," said Chelsea.

"Ah, Grant!" Jack looked meaningfully at Grace. She smiled at no one in particular, her foot bobbing threateningly inches from Jack's shin.

Jack motioned to the waitress, who ambled over, leading with her hips as though she were practicing for the fashion runway. Her pixie-cut hair was as black as her uniform—clearly dyed.

"A Kentucky Coffee for the lady, please." He nodded toward Chelsea. "Need to see her I.D.?"

"Call me a sucker," said the woman, "but she looks okay."

Chelsea leaned back in her chair and grinned at Jack and Grace in turn. "What do you bet she comes back and tells me they're out of bourbon?"

Earlier, they'd Googled for somewhere to eat and settled on a self-styled "upscale gastropub" that boasted "exotic, pirate-ship décor" and scores of craft brews. It turned out half of their kegs had kicked over the weekend, and the Tingleys all ended up with third or fourth choices. Given the beverage challenges they'd hesitated to order food, but none of them felt like tracking down another place to eat. Grace and Chelsea's fish and chips were surprisingly good, but Jack's Welsh rarebit was essentially curdled cheese soup, and it dripped thinly off the bread cubes like rheum from an old man's nose. Only their Caribbean waiter's unflappably sunny demeanor convinced Jack to leave any tip at all.

"They've gotta have their shit together better here," said Jack, staring out over the river.

"I hope so," replied Chelsea. "That was like something out of *Mr. Bean*."

Grace nodded. "It was almost like Jack's old fraternity brothers had blown into town for a forty-eight-hour bash—leaving nothing behind but a bunch of deflowered maidens and a sticky floor."

"No way!" chuckled Jack. "If it was them, it's the Rolling Rock would have kicked. Not the Dogfish Head."

"If it *were* them," observed Grace.

Jack grinned. "Fuck's a verb, right?"

The waitress sidled up behind Jack, a tray perched jauntily on her fingertips. She bent to drop a black cocktail napkin on the table and set Chelsea's drink on top. "One Kentucky Coffee, hon. No dancing with any strangers, now!"

"Only on Sundays," said Chelsea. She raised her mug to her mother and father. "Cheers!"

Grace and Jack climbed into bed after changing in the bathroom. Grace heard the shower start up, lowered her book, and turned to Jack. "Hey," she said.

"Hey what?" He looked up from checking the Knicks' score on his phone.

"Sorry if I was a little hard on you tonight."

"Hard?"

"Sarcastic. Bitchy."

"No worries. Nothing beyond the ordinary."

Grace squinted at him.

"Nothing I didn't deserve," said Jack.

Grace paused for a beat, then sighed. "Maybe. I just don't like being a bitch to you when Chelsea's around. Ever, actually."

"That's okay."

"This trip has me all worked up. You know?"

"I know." Jack reached over and patted her leg.

"All the planning. All the details. And…God, Jack! Look at them!" She pointed across the room to the desk. The last remains of Frank and Cinny Posey sat there tidily in their respective containers, next to the "Life's Good" flatscreen—Frank in the glossy, scan-able Vermont maple box he'd recently been transferred to at Brian's insistence, Cinny in her potato-starch-and-cardboard World Love Mini-Casket. "It's weird, but sometimes I feel like they're really inside there. You know? Miniature versions, maybe."

Jack nodded tentatively.

"I can almost convince myself they can see out and hear us and everything."

"Like Alexa?"

"Seriously, Jack. We're taking off on this really exciting trip—and it's like they're all excited, too, that I'm really, finally making this whole family thing happen. Like they always used to do for me and Brian."

Jack nodded. "I can imagine."

"And then it dawns on me that all that's in there…if you really think about it? Ash! You know? And clinkers. That's what it's all boiled down to. Love. Jobs. Degrees. Dad's books. Mom's volunteer work. Birthdays and Christmases. Everything!" She slumped against Jack's shoulder, swiping with her knuckle at a misting eye.

"Don't worry, H.P.," said Jack softly. "They know." She turned her head to look at him. He was close enough that it hurt her eyes to focus. "They know you love them. But you're ready to let them go."

Grace dreamed that night that she was standing on a remote tropical beach—nowhere she recognized—maybe what she'd imagined Ko Phi Phi would be like. She stood in the shallows with waves surging around her knees. There was a boat a hundred yards out, rising and falling on the swells—a kind of canoe, it looked like, but big. Someone was standing in it, facing the shore, but too far away to make out the features.

Slowly the figure turned and another stood to join it, both of them looking out to sea, where a huge, coral sun dropped toward the horizon.

Grace raised her hand and hailed them. If they turned toward shore, she'd be able to see their faces. They stood motionless as tree trunks as the boat drifted further from shore, spinning slowly around until she could only see it end-on. She heard a sigh behind her and the light touch of a hand on her shoulder, but when she turned, no one was there. She reached up to where the hand had rested, its touch lingering like a ghost, but all she felt was the naked bone of her shoulder, as though her skin had been peeled away.

She awoke with the anguished thought that she was alone in the room. But as she took stock, she felt Jack's knee against the back of her leg and she could see Chelsea's face just across the gap between the beds, serene in the blue-green glow of the digital clock.

Three time zones west, Ella and Brian sat propped against a bank of pillows in their king bed, drinking the Sleepytime tea Brian had just brought in. It was something he did nearly every night, and it was high on Ella's list of things that made him a boon companion on life's journey. They were listening to Fleetwood Mac on Ella's phone when a knock came at the door.

"Come in," called Ella. She tugged the covers up over both of them.

Sage popped through the door, dressed in a cropped tanktop and boyshorts. Ella had told her soon after Brian moved in that she might consider dressing a little more thoroughly now that he was around. "We're all going to be family now," Sage had countered. "If you're worried Brian's not going to observe the incest taboo, you shouldn't have married him, right?" Ella replied that, naturally, she wasn't worried that anything would actually happen. It was just important, she said, for everyone to feel comfortable around the house. "That's exactly the point," Sage had replied "If me being comfortable makes Brian feel uncomfortable—in any kind of way—then that says something, doesn't it?" From then on, an uneasy truce had prevailed. No one said anything else about the topic, and Sage never pushed the sartorial envelope (or non-envelope) any further.

"Good news," chirped Sage, jumping up onto the foot of the bed and crossing her legs. "Tokiko's not pregnant. She's done three tests, all negative."

"That *is* good news," responded Ella. She looked over at Brian, who nodded in an out-of-the-loop sort of way.

"So, I can *go!*"

Two days earlier, Ella had come home from work to find Sage on the phone with her best friend, clearly trying to talk her down off some kind of ledge. "You don't have to tell them yet," she said, looking at Ella and shaking her head. "I'm here for you, Toke. We'll sort it out together." Ella could hear a frantic voice at the other end of the connection, but she couldn't make out the words. "No," Sage went on. "There's no age limit. Anyone can buy them over the counter." More frantic babbling. "CVS. Walgreen's. Anywhere. Just look in the Feminine Care section. If you can't find them, ask somebody. Nobody's going to arrest you, Toke." Sage looked again at Ella, who nodded with understanding. "Read the directions. They're all a little different. But you just pee on the stick. No! Sitting on the *toilet*! Right. And then wait for the results." The indecipherable jabber had then become more composed. "No. Minutes, not hours. Do one today and maybe a couple more tomorrow and then we'll see." Sage looked plangently at Ella. "And remember, I'm here for you, Toke. We'll get through this. I promise. Love you, too. Call me whenever."

Ella had predictably been full of questions and fired them at her daughter like a nail gun. How long had Tokiko been sexually active? Who was the boy? Was Sage having sex already, too? How did she know so much about pregnancy tests? What did she know about protection? Sage answered each query with precocious calm, like a veteran 911 operator. Tokiko had been having intercourse for just over a year. She'd had a steady boyfriend that whole time. Ella had actually met the boy. Didn't she remember? They'd always used condoms, so Tokiko suspected it was someone she'd been with when she was drunk who might have gotten her pregnant. Who was that? Ella had asked. Just another guy, replied Sage. "And how about you and sex?" asked Ella, with some trepidation. Sage allowed she'd given a few hand jobs, but she said she didn't want to go all the way for the first time with an idiot, and most of the boys she knew were idiots. She'd done some quick internet research on pregnancy tests, and anybody in high school who didn't know about protected intercourse had to have slept through almost as many hours of sex-ed as they'd spent in school, total. All things considered—and recalling only too well her own tumultuous adolescence—Ella felt relieved by what she heard.

That said, Sage had announced in no uncertain terms that, if Tokiko were actually pregnant, she'd have to stay back from the upcoming trip to look after her friend. "But we're leaving in three days!" Ella had reminded her.

"Like I could forget," Sage had replied, "the way you keep filling and emptying your suitcase? Just choose a few damn outfits, why don't you?"

"Tokiko's parents can take care of her," Ella had asserted.

"Tokiko's parents will kill her if they find out," responded Sage. "They grounded her for a month when she got oral herpes."

"This is unbelievable!" declared Ella. "The trip of a lifetime. It's *so* important to Brian."

"Like it's not important to Tokiko?" countered Sage. "Having a baby at sixteen? If she can't get an abortion?"

"What about the guy?" Ella had asked. "Can't he take care of it?"

"The guy's a total asshole," replied Sage. "He doesn't give a shit. Neither does…"

"Neither does who?" demanded Ella.

"You don't want to know," Sage had replied. "Believe me."

And they'd left it at that. Ella resolved not to force the issue until it became absolutely necessary. Luckily, it hadn't.

"That's such a relief, Sage, honey!" sighed Ella. "Obviously for Tokiko, but for us, too."

"I'll say," agreed Brian, setting his tea on the nightstand.

"I wouldn't have gone, you know." Sage looked her mother straight in the eye.

"Well, we'd have seen about that," said Ella.

"Yeah, we would've. And I wouldn't have gone. Tokiko's more important than spending a hundred thousand dollars polluting the planet with jet exhaust. Just so we can deposit dead people's ashes…" Sage stopped and looked at Brian, who was clicking quietly to himself. "Sorry, Brian. I mean, I know how important this is to you."

"That's okay," said Brian. "You're right. If you can't look after your friends when they need you, what's the point?"

"Right!" Sage peered at Ella again.

"Okay," said Ella. "It's all moot. Tokiko's not pregnant, and we leave tomorrow. Are you packed?" She'd tried to make the question sound spontaneous, but she suspected it conveyed more than a hint of impatience.

"I'm not taking much," answered Sage.

"We'll be gone for three weeks."

"Three or four tops. A couple pairs of shorts. Some pants. A dress."

"I guess," Ella responded.

"I don't have to look like you look every day of the week," Sage added. "All *Vogue* and everything."

"No." Ella rolled her eyes despite herself. "You don't."

"I love the way your mom looks," offered Brian, after a beat.

"Good," replied Sage. "Keep it up."

The Tingleys Ubered to Newark Airport to catch the 8:56 a.m. flight to L.A.

They had bags to check, so their first stop was the United counter in the departure concourse. The line was short, given the hour, and they quickly moved to the front, greeted there by a young black woman in a smart uniform.

"Good morning," she said. "Checking bags?"

"Two," said Jack. He reached into his jacket pocket for the boarding pass Grace had printed up at the hotel's business center.

"Flight 703?" volunteered Chelsea, over Jack's shoulder. "L.A."

"Right," said the young woman.

"And we're connecting on to Auckland," Chelsea added.

The woman nodded. "Passports, please?"

"All of them?" asked Grace.

"If you all plan on flying today, yes."

Jack looked back over his shoulder at Grace and smirked.

Once their bags were tagged and on the conveyor belt and they'd been handed the claim checks, Grace stepped around Jack, up to the counter. "Hi," she said. "Thanks. I just want to double-check something."

"Of course," said the woman.

"We have my mother and father in these bags." Grace raised her carry-on and nudged Jack to do the same. "Their ashes, I mean. They were cremated."

"And not just super small," Jack quipped to Chelsea as he slipped his travel papers back into his pockets.

"Thanks for clarifying, dear," said Grace. She turned again to the woman. "And here's documentation from the funeral directors." She extended a stack of papers to the woman, who looked at them casually and handed them back.

"I'm sure everything's in order," she said. "We see this all the time. My condolences, by the way."

"Oh," said Grace, "they've been gone a long time. But thanks." She began to file the papers back in her purse.

"You may want to have those convenient for TSA at security," the woman advised. "You've made sure the containers will clear the scan? Right materials?"

"Check," replied Jack. "No cast iron. No Ming vases." He smiled expectantly.

"Perfect," said the woman. "Have a nice flight."

All three of them were TSA Pre-checked, so they waltzed through a short line while the un-credentialed masses teemed off to the side like Black Friday shoppers waiting for the mall to open. A man who could have passed for Groucho Marx checked their passports and boarding passes and waved them through. When Grace told him they were carrying human remains, the man wrinkled his nose to inch his glasses a little higher. "Documents?"

"Yes," replied Grace, reaching for her purse.

"That's okay," said the man, waving his hand. "Just put the containers in their own bin."

"Thank you." Grace stepped by and walked over to the steel table that fed the conveyor belt. She opened her bag, removed the World Love Mini-Casket, and placed her mother's mortal remains in a dreary, gray plastic bin that wouldn't have been out of place in a military field hospital as a temporary repository for amputated limbs. She looked back at Jack, who was doing the same with Frank's wooden box. They caught eyes and grimaced.

Grace noticed a little boy—maybe six or seven—who had stepped up behind them and was watching the proceedings with wide-eyed curiosity. He was wearing a cowboy-style suede jacket that reminded Grace of one Brian had coveted at that same age. Brian had peddled lemonade for weeks at a street-side stand so he could buy the jacket at Penney's in West Lebanon. She turned and placed her carry-on, purse, and cell phone in another bin and stepped up to the electro-magnetic portal, waiting for the high sign to proceed. A disaffected woman with too-red lipstick looked up at some kind of dial as the person in front of Grace passed through. She turned to Grace and waved her on as well.

Grace always feared that, thorough as she was at removing all traces of metal from her clothing and body—short of her dental fillings—she'd someday set off an alarm, and scores of uniformed and murderous-looking officials, accompanied by a pack of equally murderous-looking Rottweilers, would descend on her and whisk her off to some dark federal facility without benefit of Miranda warning or phone call to legal counsel. As it happened, nothing happened—yet again—and she marched dutifully past the glum agent without a hint of acknowledgment.

Grace was waiting for Cinny and the rest of her possessions to emerge from the scanner's maw when she heard a thud behind her and the sound of Jack cursing. He'd stumbled walking through the magnetic gate, nearly falling into the unwelcoming arms of the ruby-lipped TSA agent.

"Sorry," said Jack as he registered her sneer. He stepped around her and walked toward Grace, shaking his head as they caught eyes. Suddenly, he spun around to look behind him and glanced hurriedly down at his left wrist. "Shit!" he said, loud enough that the frosty agent turned to look at him. "Damn it!"

"What is it?" asked Grace, alarmed but at a complete loss.

"I banged against the magnetic thingy, I just realized. Right up against it. When I tripped."

"And?"

"I hit it with my watch! My watch was right up against it."

The little boy and his father had come through the portal and stood behind Jack, waiting to move on.

"Come on, Jack," said Grace, motioning him toward the end of the conveyor, out of which Frank's box and Jack's carry-on had just emerged.

Jack hobbled toward her, holding his left wrist close to his face, staring at the shiny timepiece. "Well, the crystal's not scratched, I guess." He twisted his arm to get a better look.

"Jack," said Grace, "come on. You're holding everyone up."

Jack absently picked up Frank's box, dropped it into his carry-on, and followed Grace out past the benches where passengers who'd had to remove their shoes and belts were putting themselves back together.

"Damn it!" said Jack again as they rejoined Chelsea, who'd come through the other line.

"What, Jack?" asked Grace. "What is it?"

"Magnetic fields can really fuck up a timepiece." He looked at Grace with something approaching despair in his eyes. "That fucking security gate! And fucking clumsy me!" he moaned, looking at his wrist. "This gained less than a second a day. And now?"

"Now?"

"Who knows? Fuck!"

The waiting area had begun to fill up by the time they got to their gate, and it took a minute to find a row that had room.

"This okay?" asked Chelsea, turning to her parents.

"As good as anything," Grace replied. "Is this okay, honey?"

"Huh?" Jack looked around as he caught up with Grace's question. "Sure." He set his carryon on a seat and plunked down next to it.

"Well, we're here in plenty of time," said Grace, cheerily. "I always feel better not having to rush."

"Me too," Chelsea said. She rummaged through her bag, pulled out some lip balm and applied it, and held the little cylinder up to Grace. "Want some?"

"No thanks. You know, Dad has this friend who absolutely hates spending time waiting anywhere. For anything. Jack says that he almost left his own wedding when the bride was three minutes late coming down the aisle."

"Sweet!" said Chelsea. "They still married?"

"Good question. I don't know. But he always gets to the airport at the last possible minute, doesn't he, dear?"

Jack had his cell phone out and was resetting his Rolex in synchrony with the little clock on the screen. He didn't seem to have heard Grace.

"Who's your friend, Jack? The guy who's always running through airports?"

"Huh? O. J. Simpson?"

Grace snorted. She looked up and noticed the little boy in the cowboy jacket sitting across the aisle. He was looking at her with something like shy expectation. He turned and whispered something to his father, then stared at Grace again. She smiled, but the little fellow's expression remained unchanged, as though it were painted on. He whispered to his father again, and the man extended his hand in Grace's direction. "Go ahead. Ask her. I'm sure she won't mind."

"Does he want to ask me a question?" asked Grace. The man nodded.

Grace leaned forward, putting on her warmest maternal smile. "Sure. C'mon over, honey. Ask away."

The little boy stood up and walked halfway across the aisle, then paused and looked back at his father. The man smiled and nodded, waving him forward.

The boy turned back toward Grace. "What's in the box?"

"This one?" Grace unzipped the bag and peeled back a side, exposing Cinny's cardboard container.

The boy shook his head. "The shiny. The wood."

Grace turned to Jack, who'd put his phone away and was sitting there, hands folded, looking out of sorts. "Show him Pop Pop's box, dear." She nodded toward the boy.

Jack looked mystified. Grace nodded again insistently. He turned to his bag, unzipped it, and lifted the glossy maple container clear.

"That one?" asked Grace.

The boy nodded, his sober expression changing not a whit.

"Wow!" said the boy's father. "That looks so much like your treasure box."

The boy nodded again.

"Tell the lady what you keep in it, Marco. Tell the lady what you keep in your treasure box."

The boy looked at his father, then back at Grace. "My favorite things," he said softly, straightening him arms as he shoved his hands deep into his pants pockets.

Grace could hear Chelsea, next to her, responding with a universal, trans-cultural "Aw!"

"Well," said Grace, turning back to the boy. "That's kind of what we have in our boxes, too."

The boy nodded. "Like what?"

Grace turned to Chelsea, who smiled poignantly and shrugged.

"Well." Grace's thoughts churned. "Memories, I guess. Good ones, you know? Of Christmastime. Birthdays. Picnics in the mountains. People making us feel happy and safe."

The boy's father looked across at Grace. She wondered if he knew what was in the boxes. "Thank the lady, Marco," he said after a long pause. "We don't want to take up too much of her time."

"No, no," replied Grace. "It's all good." She smiled again at the boy.

Marco stared back. "How do you keep memories in a box? How do you put them in?"

Grace felt her eyes welling. She looked at Chelsea, who put her hand softly on her mother's arm.

It was Jack who leaned forward to answer. "You put them in with your heart," he said with a smile. "It's magic."

"Should I know who Tom Bradley was?" Sage spun her hair around her forefinger, one way then the other, winding it up, winding it back. "Or *is*?"

"Why don't you Google him and find out?" Ella was doing her best to ignore the hair-fidget she knew Sage knew pissed her off. Once, when her daughter was fourteen, Ella had been so exasperated at it that she'd blurted out that it was sort of like masturbating in public. "I know," Sage had replied. "You should try it sometime."

Sage scanned the general clientele at the Bradley International Terminal's Vino Volo. "I'd rather tap the knowledge of my elders," she said. "It establishes inter-generational trust." She flashed Ella a smug photo smile.

Their waiter arrived with a tray full of drinks. "Here you are," he said, setting the containers and glasses on the table with the officious awkwardness of Basil Fawlty. "I'll have your food in a moment."

"Thanks," said Brian, biting back an impulsive, "*Ever so kind of you!*" He filled his glass half-full of San Pellegrino and raised it up. "Here's to Frank and Cinny!" Everyone clinked.

"Not bad," said Jack, sampling his Marlborough pinot gris. "Maybe not as good as what we'll have once we get down there."

"Or even tonight," replied Ella. "Air New Zealand is famous for their wines. Quality *and* quantity."

"Count me in!" Jack grinned.

Sage eyed him quizzically. "You're the only one having wine, Jack," she observed.

"I guess I am," Jack replied.

"Mom said we could count on you to drink a lot."

"Sage!" exclaimed Ella. She looked at Brian in exasperation.

"No, that's perfectly okay," said Jack. "It's true. No secrets. We shouldn't have any secrets on a trip like this." He raised his glass again and winked at Ella.

"So," said Brian, leaning back in his chair. "Did you guys make it out to Santa Monica? On the *Big Blue Bus*?" He said it as though the name were part of a *Sesame Street* alphabet lesson.

"We did," replied Chelsea. "It was so much fun."

"What'd you do?" asked Ella. She tapped at the rim of her Coke glass with the tip of an elegantly painted nail. "Did you go to the pier?"

"Of course," replied Grace.

"Mom and I rode the Ferris wheel," Chelsea added. "I hadn't been on a Ferris wheel for a thousand years."

"I've never been on a Ferris wheel," declared Sage. "I guess that's what happens when you're the product of a broken marriage. You can forget about any chance at a normal childhood."

"Thanks for that, sweetie," said Ella. "But I like to think we can still make it up to you."

"I'm always open to the possibility," replied Sage.

Brian smiled at his stepdaughter. "So, Jack. Chelsea and Grace did the Ferris wheel. What about you?"

"Jack took a run," volunteered Grace.

"Good for you, Jack," said Brian. "Where'd you go?"

"Just down to Muscle Beach."

"There's a Muscle Beach for real?" asked Ella. "I always thought it was like a made-up place. Like Easy Street. Or Shit Creek."

"There definitely is," replied Jack. "I thought it was in Santa Monica. The original one *was*, I guess—the one with Vic Tranny and all."

"I think that's Vic *Tanny*," said Grace.

"I think Dad might be joking," said Chelsea, glancing at her father. "Right?"

"Maybe," smiled Jack. "Anyway, they moved it down to Venice. It's called Venice Muscle Beach now. Nice little run. Maybe two, two and a half miles each way. Twenty-five minutes, just cruising."

"Sounds great." Ella turned to Sage. "Maybe Jack would like to run with you some time."

"Sure," said Sage coolly. "If he wants."

Jack laughed. "I think Sage is out of my league. Marathons and all? I'm basically in it for weight control." He tapped his stomach and grinned. "She'd leave me in the dust."

"I could always take it easy on you, Jack," said Sage with a thin smile. "No need to make it a battle of the sexes or anything."

"No, I wasn't..." Jack's response got drowned out by an overloud public service announcement about unattended luggage. "Well, whatever," he smiled. "I'd love to join you sometime. If you'd have me."

"Cool," said Sage, staring at the ceiling.

"So anyway, Jack," said Brian. "Muscle Beach. Were there lots of muscular dudes down there?" Sage looked at Ella, eyebrow raised. "Any female Governators?"

Jack shook his head. "Nothing that unusual. Some guys. A few gals. Weights. Parallel bars. That sort of thing. Lots of oily skin. Lots of sand."

"I'd totally be into weights if I didn't run," offered Sage after a pause. "Buff chicks are fuckin' hot."

"Language, sweetie!" exclaimed Ella. She looked at Grace, who shrugged.

"Thanks for your patience," said the angular waiter as he delivered two wooden platters overflowing with meats, cheeses, small bowls of olives and pickles, and crusty bread. "Can I bring you anything else?"

Jack pointed to his already empty glass. "Another pinot gris?"

"Of course. Anyone else?"

"I'll risk another ginger ale," said Sage, smiling at the man. "Jack's the designated driver, right?" She looked at Ella, who frowned as covertly as she could manage.

"Okay!" Grace jumped in breezily. "Anybody need to use the little girls' room?" She looked around the table. "No? Be right back then." She grabbed her purse, stood up, and walked briskly away.

Sage watched her go then turned to the others. "Does Grace always call it *the little girls' room?*"

Chelsea looked at Sage and shook her head. "Never. I've never heard her say that. Dad?"

"Nope. New to me."

"I think this trip has Mom kind of discombobulated," said Chelsea. "The whole last year has been tough."

"Amen," said Ella.

"What do you guys think about unisex bathrooms?" asked Sage. Jack chuckled. "What?" asked Sage.

"Nothing," replied Jack. "Grace told me you were an activist."

"So?"

"That's good. Activism is good." He looked around the table for confirmation.

"I'm all for unisex bathrooms," Chelsea declared. "There's one in the store. Grant had a sign made that just says, *People.*"

"I've seen that—just *People,*" chuckled Ella. "Or *Humans.*"

"That's okay for one-holers," said Jack. "But what about when there's a mess of toilets in one room? And urinals. Maybe that's a little different."

"Why?" asked Sage.

"Well—"

"Stalls have doors, right?" Sage continued. "Nobody's dropping their drawers out in the open. Unless they're pervs."

"True," replied Jack with a tug at his ear.

"And guys peeing at urinals shouldn't be spinning around and waving it in everyone's face, right?"

"Sage, sweetie," said Ella. She reached over to touch her daughter's shoulder. "There's no need to be graphic."

"At school this year," Sage continued, studiously ignoring her mother, "there was this big brouhaha over whether girls should ever have to be in the same room when the football jocks are in there taking a major dump. And then, of course, the guys ask the girls if they think their own shit doesn't stink. It can't be about the *principle* of the thing, right? No frickin' way. It was ridiculous."

"I guess bathrooms on planes have been unisex forever," said Jack.

Chelsea scoffed. "With constantly wet toilet seats from guys leaving them down and bucking around in the turbulence as they go. There should be a law: either you flip the seat up or you have to sit down."

"No guy sits down to pee," said Brian. "Right, Jack?"

"Never. Not unless he's got the whirlies."

"Why?" asked Chelsea. "Is it some kind of manliness thing?"

"Not at all," grinned Brian. "It's because toilet seats are always drenched with the last guy's pee. Especially on planes."

Grace sashayed back to the table. "Did I miss anything?"

Once Chelsea explained how apt Grace's word choice had been, Grace said there'd been a woman in the ladies' room trying to remove her Invisalign braces. "She was standing in front of the mirror," said Grace, "sticking her finger into her mouth trying to unhook the things so she could eat. But it looked like she was trying to make herself vomit."

"Ew! Mom!" said Chelsea. "We're eating."

"Then," Grace chuckled, "one of her rubber bands popped out and stuck on the mirror."

"Ew! *Mom*!" said Chelsea, laughing now.

"My friend Tokiko has Invisalign," offered Sage. "They stick these little bumps all over your teeth to hold the clear plastic thingies on? And when you pull them out, she says, it feels like somebody tucked a pretzel inside your lips."

"Sounds charming," said Ella. "I had braces as a kid. Hated them. Train tracks."

"So did Brian," replied Grace. "No expense spared for Brian!" Brian frowned at his sister. "Of course, I had an overbite, too," Grace went on. "But guess who got the braces."

"Your teeth were just fine," replied Brian. "You always said Jimmy Lamont told you your baby bucks made you look like Carly Simon."

Grace shot her brother a filthy glance.

Ella broke a substantial pause in conversation. "We offered to get braces for Sage, but she said we should just give the money to the World Wildlife Fund." She smiled at her daughter, who smiled back.

"It's not like I'm deformed or anything," said Sage. "In fact, I think my teeth have character." She pulled her lips back like a chimpanzee, baring some admittedly long canines. "What do you think? Do I look like a vampire?"

NZ Flight 5 to Auckland boarded on time and left the gate with just a slight delay to offload the baggage of a no-show. Grace and Jack had just chosen their welcome-aboard glass of wine to accompany their welcome-aboard bowl of warmed macadamia nuts when Jack turned to her. "Man. That Sage is a pistol!" he declared. "I know Brian talks about her all the time, but I wasn't half prepared for her."

Grace laughed. "I know. You really couldn't get much of a feel for it at the wedding."

"How about that crack about my drinking? And about me being the designated driver. Half of the junior partners down at the firm wouldn't have the balls to go after me like that."

Grace turned to look at him. "I don't know I'd say she was going after you. She's just pretty direct with her thoughts."

Jack guffawed. "Direct? I'll say. If she was any more direct, she'd... she'd..."

"She'd what?"

"Hell! I don't know." He swept up the little cocktail napkin with the fern on it and dabbed at his lips.

"We know her father's an asshole, right? Maybe you're a surrogate or something."

"Lucky me," Jack scoffed. "Do you think she's on the spectrum or something?"

"The spectrum?"

"Yeah, the spectrum. You know. Autistic. Asperger's. Like Greta from Sweden. The ones that have trouble reading social cues."

"Like how to hold themselves back from telling powerful white men they're destroying the planet with their arrogance and greed?"

"Yeah," replied Jack, chuckling. "Like that."

"I don't think so," said Grace. "I just think Sage is a smart, independent girl who's been knocked around a little by life. And who hasn't always gotten the structure she needs."

Jack turned toward Grace again. "Like from a mother whose default response to life's challenges is to fire up a bong?"

"Or a stepfather who grabs it out of her hands as fast as he can?"

Jack laughed and shook his head.

"But no," said Grace, "we're not being fair. Ella and Brian do the best they can. And Brian says Sage is really sweet when you get to know her. Just, like you said, direct."

"Sweet and direct," scoffed Jack. "Like a peppermint suppository."

"Jack Tingley!" exclaimed Grace. "Where on God's earth did you ever come up with that?"

"You like it?"

"What do you mean, do I like it?"

"The imagery," replied Jack. "Do you like the image? Is it shocking but creative? All at the same time?"

"What the—"

"Does it make you see the world anew?"

"You're just so full of it sometimes, Jack. I don't know where to start."

"Ah, yes. But there's poetry in me." He took out the handset for the entertainment system and switched on the screen. "More than you know."

Grace laughed. "It's not poetry you're full of, dear heart."

Jack turned back to her, grinning. "What is it then?"

"You know damn well what it is. But just give Sage some time. There's something about her I really like."

"I guess," said Jack. "Sure."

Ella looked up at Brian from her seat next to the window. "So's your dad all tucked in?" she asked.

Brian closed the lid of the overhead bin and nodded. Jack had passed Frank off to Brian at Vino Volo, saying with a grin that he wanted to facilitate some good father-son time. Rather than repack his carryon, Brian had just toted the box onboard out in the open, wondering in the process if his father had ever carried him onto a plane in his arms, just so. He couldn't remotely remember. "He's all buckled in," he declared as he sat down and kicked off his shoes.

"They say you're supposed to leave those on until we take off, Boo."

"Why?"

"In case there's some major mishap and we have to run for our lives through pools of flaming jet fuel."

Brian laughed. "Didn't I ever tell you I was on the fire-running team at Littleton State? Swami Brian, they called me. Only pussies wore shoes."

"So Grace wasn't the only athlete in the family."

"No. She really was," said Brian. "But only boring shit. Soccer. Field hockey. Kundalini yoga."

"There's nothing boring about Kundalini yoga. When's the last time you had an orgasm walking on hot coals?"

"It's been way too long," sighed Brian.

A flight attendant stepped up with a tray. "Warm nuts?" she asked.

Brian exploded into laughter.

"Sorry," Ella explained to the woman. "When you said that about the nuts, we were just talking about sex."

The woman nodded calmly. "Well, let's restrict it to conversation until the lights go down. There are children present." *Pree*sent, she pronounced it. The Kiwi accent immediately struck Brian as charming.

"May I fetch you some bubbly?"

"Please," said Ella.

"Sir?"

"Me, too, please. "

"I'll be right back. But you two behave while I'm gone."

"That went well, considering." Ella reached over and wiggled Brian's pinkie. "So," she said, after a pause. "I never knew Grace had a problem with your having braces."

Brian snorted. "Less of a problem with me having them than with her not having them. It's always been competition with her. I love her and all, but…"

"It's funny. When I met her at the wedding, I didn't think there was anything unusual about her teeth."

"I don't think there is," said Brian.

"Still, if she felt there was an issue, I think she should have done something about it. She still could. It's important to feel good about your smile. People don't smile enough."

"You do."

"Maybe." Ella giggled. "It helps that I laugh at you so often."

Brian was reaching to tickle her in the ribs when the flight attendant came back with two flutes of sparkling wine. "How're the lovebirds?" she asked as she set the glasses down on the wide armrests.

"Just fine, thanks," replied Brian. "Patiently biding our time."

"Doesn't look like it!" The woman smirked. "We'll be taking off soon."

"Great," said Brian. He turned back to Ella. "Seriously, about Gracie. I don't know how much she does smile these days."

Ella tore the little complimentary blanket out of its plastic bag and spread it over her lap.

"I don't know," Brian continued. "I just think she and Jack have a kind of strained relationship."

"You think?" Ella snorted. "Seems like she's on him pretty often."

"Really."

"He takes it pretty well, though. Laughs it off."

"Yeah, I know." Brian took a long sip of wine. "I do think they love each other. Basically. Still, I was really surprised she ended up with a jock from UVA. A guy from Florida into the bargain."

"How'd they meet?"

"At a rock show in New Haven. She was a grad student at Yale. You know. In English. And he was at the law school. She'd just broken up with this other guy, like her second serious boyfriend ever. They'd been together three years, I think, at Princeton. Gracie's smart as hell, but this guy was a super genius. He actually got a Rhodes, and she was only nominated. But he ended up running off with this other superstar he met at a conference somewhere."

"Ouch!"

"So she and Jack meet at this concert in this little club and he's this kind of flashy guy from UVA—total opposite of her Princeton dude—with a boss car and all, and she just basically flips from one extreme to the other. She sells out and goes for Joe Rugby with some bucks and a tolerable dose of Southern charm."

"That's a little harsh."

"Probably," said Brian. "Definitely. But he's done really well for himself. And I'm glad Gracie has the security."

"Jack's a good guy," said Ella. "I like him. For a redneck." She laughed and kicked off her shoes.

"Ready to join me fire-running?" quipped Brian.

"We're taxiing," Ella replied. "And I'm hopeful we'll make it off the tarmac."

"That's why I love you, kid. Ever the optimist."

"Who else would take on a bisexual grab-bag like you?"

"Anyway," said Brian. "Then Chelsea came along, with all those complications, and Grace basically gave up everything she'd been aiming for, for decades almost, and traded in her Ivy League aspirations for motherhood. And a job at the second-best private school in Fairfield County."

"And it was Jack's fault?"

"Enough, it was," said Brian. "I mean, she's got a pretty good life—with Chelsea, and with Jack raking it in as a hotshot lawyer, and the school job and tennis club and everything."

"Yeah?"

"But I think Dad's life, working at Dartmouth and writing a few important and really influential books? I think that's what Gracie really wanted."

"And never got," said Ella.

"Right." Brian looked at Ella. "So, if you were her, would you smile a lot?"

Ella hesitated only a second. "Yeah. I would."

"Why?"

"Because I'd have a sister-in-law who could teach me all about toe-curling yogasms."

Sage and Chelsea had the two seats in the center of the airplane, between Grace and Jack on their left, and Brian and Ella on their right.

Chelsea watched as her uncle placed the box holding her grandfather's ashes into the overhead bin.

Sage followed Chelsea's gaze. "Did you know him very well?"

Chelsea snapped back from her reverie. "Yeah. I did. I was eighteen when he died."

Sage nodded. She reached up and began to put her hair up into a bun.

"I was his only grandchild. He kind of doted on me, I guess."

"That makes sense," said Sage. "My grandfathers are both still alive. I only ever see one, though. Back East. The other one… Well, when my mom divorced my scumbag dad, she kind of divorced his family, too."

"That's too bad."

Sage shrugged. "Maybe. We do okay, though."

"I'm sure you do."

Sage finished with her bun and dropped her hands into her lap. "I hear you're really serious about this older dude."

Chelsea laughed. "Who told you that?"

"Brian."

"Brian, huh? What'd he say?" Chelsea twisted in her seat to face Sage.

"Not much. Just that you were seeing him. That he's older. And he looks like Ralph Fiennes, Grace says."

Chelsea laughed. "I don't know. People say that sometimes, though. He gets a kick out of it."

"Like Voldemort Ralph Fiennes?"

Chelsea laughed again. "No, thank God. More like M."

"He's got kids?"

"Two of them."

"How old?"

"Nine and twelve. Both girls."

"And how old is he?" asked Sage

"Forty-eight."

"And you're, like, twenty-three?"

"Twenty-four."

"So he's twice your age."

Chelsea nodded. "Good math!"

"Sorry," said Sage. "I didn't mean to sound shocked. Did I sound shocked?"

"No," answered Chelsea. "That's just the facts. Plain and simple."

"So was he divorced or something?"

"No. His wife died. A little over a year ago. Cancer. It was really awful. Long and awful."

"Shit!" said Sage.

"Yeah."

"So do you think you'll get married?"

"I don't know," answered Chelsea, stretching her arms out in front of her. "We're kind of taking it one day at a time."

Sage nodded. "How'd you meet him?"

"He owns a bookshop in Charlottesville. I started working there third year. Junior year at UVA."

"It wasn't creepy or anything, was it? At the start."

"No, it wasn't creepy. We just really liked each other. And when his wife got sick, he felt really comfortable talking to me. It all happened from there."

"Man, that sounds intense."

"It was," said Chelsea. "It still kind of is. He still hasn't gotten over the whole cancer thing, and his kids really miss their mom."

Sage sighed. "I'm glad it wasn't creepy. I'm okay with people all ages getting together. Whatever. Nobody's business but theirs. But some older dudes? Man! They lock in on a young chick and something in their brain just shorts out and all they can think about is fucking her brains out."

Chelsea turned again and leaned toward Sage. "I hope you're not speaking from experience."

"No," replied Sage. "Not me. But some friends."

"Want to talk about it?"

"Sometime, maybe. If you can be cool about it."

Chelsea looked at her with concern. "What do you mean?"

"Let's just skip it for now. But thanks."

CHRISTCHURCH

Jack held up the large brown paper cup to examine it. His eyes were bloodshot. He needed a shave. "Remind me?" he said to Grace. The two of them were sitting in the garden of their motel at the south end of Papanui Road, just north of downtown Christchurch. It was 1:45 in the afternoon. Bright sunshine warmed their backs as they sipped their coffee and watched a half-dozen sparrows scrumming over breadcrumbs under the adjacent table. Chelsea and the rest were going to join them at two for a read-through of Cinny's first set of marching orders.

"It's a flat white," replied Grace. She had walked to the shops up the road from the motel for barista coffees while Jack checked in with his office via Skype.

"Really good! Can you get anything like this back home?"

"Starbucks has sold flat whites for years, Jack."

"Shows how much I get out." He sipped again with obvious relish.

"Glad you like it. They take their coffee seriously down here."

"I might like Kiwi land," said Jack, as though Grace wouldn't already know a country where good wine is cheap and rugby is the national religion would be something close to heaven for her husband. "Provided this *Look Right* shit doesn't turn *me* into a flat white."

Jack hadn't needed to come anywhere near a bungee-jump to log a New Zealand near-death experience. He'd barely slept a wink on the twelve-hour flight from L.A. and, assuming a walk from the international to the domestic terminal in Auckland would be more reviving than a shuttle ride, he'd looked the wrong way at a busy road crossing. Grace had just managed to yank him out of the path of a speeding panel van.

"Hah!" Grace snorted. "That's pretty funny, dear."

"It just popped out. It's not racist, is it?"

"I don't think so. You're white. You get run over, you might be flat. No harm, no foul.'"

"It's hard for some of us to tell these days. You know?"

"Yeah!" said Grace.

"Are those Southern Alps?" Jack pointed to an undulating line of blue hills on the far side of downtown. Flying down from Auckland, they'd enjoyed breath-taking views of the South Island's icy spine, hundreds of miles of the snowy peaks that inspired early Pacific mariners to dub the country *Aotearoa*, "land of the long white cloud." Just before they'd crossed over Cook Strait, the rising sun had begun to paint the cone of Mt. Taranaki in pale pink alpenglow, and by the time they flew past Kaikoura, the lower peaks and snow-dusted foothills of the South Island were ablaze with the fiery dawn. Jack had been transfixed.

"You're full of questions, for someone who hasn't slept for forty hours."

"That's the only way I made it through UVA, Honey Pot. Party all night and then grill the professor before he can grill you. It's called defensive curiosity."

Grace shook her head with amusement. "Those are just the Port Hills. The deep-water port—Lyttelton—is just on the other side."

Jack nodded.

"The Southern Alps are over there." Grace pointed back past the motel entrance. "West of us."

Jack looked confused. "That's not *east*? The sun's behind us. So if that's south…"

Grace laughed. "It's not, Jack. It's north. I had the same problem back when we first came down. But the sun passes north of us. It starts there and it sets over there."

"Well, shit!" said Jack. "Better not count on me for navigation."

"You'll be fine, dear. Speaking of navigation, how's the old magnetized chronometer? Is it telling you it's yesterday?"

"Very funny." He looked down at his wrist. "Okay so far, I guess. Thank you so much for asking." He made a sad-clown face.

"Hey!" Chelsea strolled up and sat down across from them. She had on a floppy, broad-brimmed hat and sunglasses. Grant had warned her about the hole in the ozone layer.

"Hi, honey," said Grace. "How was Cathedral Square?" Chelsea and Sage had set off exploring shortly after they'd arrived from the airport. Brian and Ella had opted for a shower and a nap.

"Really hopping. Dozens of buskers. Two dudes playing chess with a huge chess set and all sorts of people watching. An old Dumbledore type announcing the end of the world or something. That sort of stuff. But the cathedral's still fenced off. And it's surrounded by shoulder-high weeds."

"The earthquakes were when?" Jack peered into the cup and drained the last swallow.

"Early '11, the big one," said Grace. "February?"

Jack's eyes narrowed. "They still haven't cleaned up?" He started to peel back the cup's rolled rim.

"There are only five million people in the whole country, dear. Not a big revenue base for major recovery operations."

"I guess you're right. All the more amazing the All Blacks are world-beaters."

"And all the more happy I am," said Chelsea, "to inject some tourist dollars into their economy."

Jack smirked. "Mom and I were actually worried Ella would be injecting some tourist dollars into their legal system."

"What do you mean?"

"We were thinking she might have hidden marijuana in her luggage," said Grace.

"Oh my God!" exclaimed Chelsea.

Jack nodded. "When that cop walked up at the baggage claim with the German Shepherd, we figured the dog wasn't looking for a place to lift his leg." Jack was halfway around the rim of the cup, leaving an uneven flange that looked like the top of a cupcake liner.

"Come on, Dad. Ella wouldn't be that careless. Especially on a family trip like this."

Jack shrugged. "Pot can make you pretty stupid. Especially considering how much THC is in it these days."

"Really, Dad," scoffed Chelsea. "Ella's a grown-up. And a mother."

"A mother who shares bong hits with her daughter, I hear." Jack turned to Grace for corroboration.

"I don't know," said Chelsea. "If you're really worried, I can ask Sage tonight."

"You think she'd tell you the truth?" asked Jack.

"I do. I think she's incredibly open. And honest. Especially for someone her age."

"Whatever," said Jack. "Ask her if you want. It's no biggie to me."

Grace's eyebrows rose. "Being able to finish the trip is no biggie to you? That's interesting news."

"I didn't mean it that way."

"By the way," said Grace. "You're driving me crazy picking at that cup."

Jack leered at her playfully, then set the cup on the table. "I just mean, Chel doesn't need to go sleuthing around to find out if Ella is moonlighting as a drug kingpin."

"Speaking of whom," Grace announced loudly, "look who's risen from the arms of Morpheus!" She waved to Brian and Ella, who were just descending the outside stairs from their room. Sage trailed closely behind.

"Hey, guys," said Ella. "Here we are. All refreshed and ready to go." She reached up to straighten Brian's collar and looked at Chelsea. "Sage said you had a nice walkabout."

"We did. Cleared the cobwebs."

The three pulled up chairs and sat down. Sage drew her legs up into the lotus position.

"It's gorgeous out here," said Brian. "Perfect weather for April. The air's a little crisp already."

"Right!" said Jack. "April is *fall* down here, isn't it?"

Sage smiled and looked across at Grace. "Remind me when you all were down here?"

"We were here for Dad's—Frank's—sabbatical in '94. We lived just up the road. For nine months."

"Sounds exciting!" said Ella.

"It was. Life-changing in lots of ways."

"That's the year Frank wrote the Tit Book?" asked Sage.

Grace laughed. "It was. Who told you that?"

"Chelsea."

Chelsea grinned. "I figured I'd just get it out in the open."

"Or maybe off your chest," smirked Jack.

Chelsea looked at her mother and shook her head.

"Anyway," said Grace, turning back to Sage. "Dad's Captain Cook year. And Mom and Dad had been down here on their honeymoon in '70, it would have been. They loved it so much they always wanted to come back. Dad's project was partly just to have an excuse for coming, I think."

"It's a cool country," said Sage. "They're having a referendum on legalizing pot. They had big signs down at the Square. People handing out leaflets."

Jack looked pointedly from Grace to Chelsea. Chelsea rolled her eyes.

"What?" Sage had tracked Jack's gaze and stared at him intently.

"Nothing," replied Jack. "Family joke."

Sage settled back in her chair with a sigh.

Grace cleared her throat. "So, speaking of Mom, are we all ready to hear from her?" She reached into her bag and pulled out an envelope.

"Absolutely," said Ella. "This is so exciting!" She looked around at the group. "Before we get started, though, can I just say thank you?"

"For what?" asked Grace.

"For including me. And Sage. This means so much to us." She looked over at her daughter, who was pressing down on her knees to stretch.

Sage smiled and folded her hands in her lap. "I can't even think of the last time I got to take an around-the-world trip." Her smile dimmed under her mother's hawkish glare. "Seriously, though. This is really great. Mom's right."

Grace smiled then took a deep breath. "All right, then. *The envelope, please.*" She stuck a forefinger under the flap and ran it along the top, tearing a jagged opening. She pulled out what looked like three or four sheets of notebook paper, covered with scratchy handwriting. She paused, sniffed once, unfolded the sheets, and sat back in her chair. "Ready?"

"Still ready," nodded Jack.

"*First of all,*" read Grace in as strong a voice as she could muster, "*it makes me so happy to think of all of you down there in New Zealand. Frank and I never encountered any people who were more open and…and emergent?*"

She held the sheet out to Chelsea.

"*Energetic,* I think."

"Wow!" said Grace, shaking her head. "*…more open and energetic and resourceful than the Kiwis. We were weathering some marital challenges when we got there, and it felt like the whole country welcomed us in with a broad smile and a big old 'Good on ya!' It really helped to set us back on our feet.*"

Grace turned inquisitively to Brian. He looked at a loss. Grace turned back to the papers.

"*Our year down there with the pair of you, too. How wonderful that was! Both of you walking off together every morning in your Papanui High School uniforms (Grace's long kilt and you in your shorts and knee socks, Brian, looking like a teenage Christopher Robin); going down to Lancaster Park Saturdays for the rugby—sitting in the rain that one afternoon for hours; Stone Grill at the Brewer's Arms with Dad going on the way he did about Speight's beer being the 'Pride of the South!' (trying hard to get the Kiwi accent but sounding more like a lisping Cockney); buying you two those wetsuits for your surfing lessons out at New Brighton Beach! Were we ever closer as a family, I wonder? Or happier?*" Grace paused for another big breath. *"Just pulling up stakes and 'boldly going.' You were both so brave. I treasure the memories. I hope being down there again brings you…scones?"*

Chelsea looked over her mother's shoulder. *"Scores."*

Grace laughed. *"Scores of your own memories winging back. And the rest of you—Jack, Chelsea, Ella, and Sage—I hope, in the short time you're there, you begin to see why we loved that spunky little country so very much."*

"I'm already halfway there," confessed Ella, smiling at Brian.

"Me too." Jack raised his tattered cup, which he'd started worrying once again.

"But to get down to it," Grace read on, *"Dad and I want you to scatter our ashes on Quail Island."* Grace looked at Brian. He nodded knowingly and waved her on. *"We want you to bury them near poor Ivon Skelton's grave. Frank and I always felt he must be terribly lonely out there, taken by leprosy and lying all by himself behind that little picket fence, so far from his home and family. We want to give him some company, and also be close to where the four of us had those wonderful, silly picnics, overlooking the shipwrecks. I'm sure you remember the little rounds of cheese we bought and the L&P sodas and the crackers from Australia. And, of course, the chocolate-covered biscuits. Brian, you got so pissed off when Gracie carried them and broke a few."*

"Wait a minute!" Mock animus flared in Grace's misting eyes. *"You* always carried the damn knapsack." She grinned at the others. "It was Brian that smashed the damn cookies."

"Whatever," laughed Brian.

"Whatever," echoed Grace. *"I'm looking right now at a picture on the wall, Gracie, of one of those picnics. You're wearing that turtleneck sweater we bought for you at Ballantynes that you had forever. And Brian, we should never have let you get a mullet."*

Ella looked sharply at Brian. "Really?"

Brian shrugged again.

"Bless you," Grace continued, *"for putting up that gallery of memories to remind me how lucky we've been. They've meant the world through all this. Anyway, go out to the island. Give our love to Ivon. Tell the others*

all about him and then leave us there together—one part Frank to one part Cinny!—'Under the wide and starry sky.'" Grace sighed and looked wistfully at Brian.

Brian nodded. He turned to the others. "That's from a poem on Stevenson's grave. On Robert Louis Stevenson's grave in Samoa."

"Dad dragged us up a huge mountain to see it," added Grace, "on a miserably hot day. Mud and bugs everywhere. And lizards!" She laughed to remember it. "Dad got these notions, you know—usually about some famous writer or other—and there was no stopping him." She smiled at Brian.

"You guys were lucky," said Sage softly.

"We were," said Brian.

Grace flipped the sheet over. "So, Mom's not done."

"We're all ears, H. P.," said Jack.

"Now here's a little trigger warning (I think that's the expression) about a few things you need to know." Grace lifted her head and peered at Brian, who looked back uncertainly.

"Whoa!" Ella leaned forward. "Hang on a minute, Grace! This sounds like it might be meant for just the two of you."

Jack nodded.

Ella turned back to Grace. "Maybe you guys should share this part. Just you."

Grace looked at Brian. "Kiddo?"

Brian took a deep breath. "I don't know. But Mom knew everybody would be here with us. She wanted the trip to be for everybody, right? I don't see any reason why we should hold anything back. I mean, it's not like *she* ever did." His eyes twinkled.

Grace looked at the others. No one spoke up or seemed about to leave. Only Ella still seemed tentative.

"Here we go, then," said Grace. *"You go through life with these things. Blunders. Regrets. Everybody does, I guess. But I don't want to be carrying them all alone as I go to the next stop. More importantly, I want to pass along to the ones I love lessons I've learned about how easy it is to stumble but also about how, with luck and love, we can get back on our feet and move on. I couldn't ever talk to a priest or a minister, you know, not being a true believer. And I never did go for therapy and all that B.S. either. So let me share a few things with you about where the two of us were when we first went to New Zealand. I'll share more as we move on.*" Grace peered at Brian. He looked like he'd just been handed a registered letter from the district attorney. "*Our honeymoon trip down to that part of the world was incredibly generous of the Poseys to foot. For your father and me, though, it wasn't as much a way to begin our marriage as a chance to get past something that shouldn't ever have happened. A fresh start, or a shot at one, was how we thought about it. After a little episode of temporary insanity on my part.*"

"Oh, God," Chelsea burst out. "What did Nana do?"

"I don't know, honey." Grace looked again at Brian, who smiled grimly. "*Frank was wonderful. I'd say he was a saint, if I believed in them. Your father, with his love and his resilient trust, turned a nightmare into something completely different. When we got back home, it was as though we were in an entirely new place—remade, redeemed. That language isn't all that far-fetched. I've been more lucky than I deserved—in this and everything else that came after. Not least in the blessings that you, Gracie and Brian, brought to both of us. Now just keep in mind there's more to come—some unfortunate nitty-gritty in the middle of two otherwise incredibly fortunate lives. I want to ease you into it, though. Baby steps. For now, enjoy every moment in that best of all places. Pavlovas on me at the Brewer's Arms tonight! For everybody! And if anybody was thinking about dieting, screw it!*"

In the hush that followed, Grace re-folded the paper and slipped it back into the envelope. "Well…" She looked around the group. They stared back at her.

"I am totally wrung out," sighed Chelsea. "Just from that little bit. I sure wasn't expecting anything like that."

"No," said Grace.

Sage spun her hair slowly around her finger. "Sounds, maybe, like she had some kind of an affair?"

"Sage!" exclaimed Ella. She looked at Brian to gauge his response.

"Well, it does, doesn't it?" insisted Sage. "Something about her 'little episode of insanity'? That they had to get past?"

"Let's not leap to conclusions," said Ella. "Seems, though, like this all might be a little more intense than we expected."

"You think?" asked Grace. She clasped her arms tightly over her chest.

"Well, I think Nana knows what's she's doing," Chelsea declared softly. "I trust her. I trust all of us, too, to see this through."

"Thanks, honey," said Grace after a pause. "I appreciate the optimism."

"Is Sage right, d'you think?" asked Brian. "That Mom had some kind of affair?"

He sat across from Grace at the kitchenette counter in her room. Cinny's World Love Mini-Casket and Frank's Vermont Maple Haven rested there, side by side, bathed in the bright sunlight that flowed in through the open window. Jack and Sage were off on a run. She'd suggested it in a sincere enough way that Jack had felt comfortable saying yes—as long as she promised to go on without him if he had to stop and summon an ambulance. While Ella and Chelsea headed off to buy sunscreen, Grace and Brian were readying the ashes for the next day's trip out to Quail Island. When they were done, they'd grab a cab and pick up the minivan they'd booked.

"It might explain Matthew."

"Sure would!" Brian sat silently for a few seconds, recalling his mother's mysterious visitor. "But whatever it was she did, it had to be before their honeymoon, right? And this Matthew guy went to see her at the very end. Could they still have been…?"

Grace shook her head. "You know what? Let's not get ahead of ourselves. Let's just try not to think about it."

Brian scoffed. "Good luck!"

"I know. But let's try."

"You're not tempted to open more of the envelopes? Binge-read?" He grinned guiltily.

"Naturally. We're just not going to. Right?"

Brian stared at her for a moment and then nodded. "Right. Let's do this ash thing." He rubbed his hands together half-heartedly.

"Okay!" Grace loosened her shoulders as though she were back on a soccer pitch setting up for a long throw-in. "I guess we just open them up and transfer them into six baggies, yes? Here, Thailand, Rome, Grindelwald, Oxford," she counted on her fingers, "and number six for wherever Mom has in mind in New Jersey."

"I still don't have a clue why New Jersey. Do you?"

Grace shook her head. "Nope."

"Shit!" sighed Brian. "This is so…I don't know…Coen Brothers." He gestured to the array of supplies. Seeing Grace's eyes beginning to fill, he got up, stepped around the counter, and bent to hug her. "C'mon, Tiger. We can do this."

"I guess." Grace dabbed at her eyes then reached out and pulled the containers toward her. "So! Process! We fill the baggies, and then I guess we find some tasteful and reverent way to dispose of these." She tapped both boxes.

Brian bobbed his head in affirmation. "Baggies'll be easier to pack from here on, anyway. We got enough to double up?" Grace had shared a gruesome story she came across on the web about tumbling carry-ons and escaping cremains on a turbulent Air India flight over the Himalayas. The pilot had deployed the oxygen masks to keep passengers from choking on the cloud of ash.

"We're good." Grace reached for the baggie box and counted out an even dozen. "There you go. Twelve."

Brian's face suddenly scrunched doubtfully. "Hang on!"

"What?"

"Mom said fifty-fifty, her and dad, right? For here?"

"Right."

"But she said there'd be other ratios other places."

Grace nodded.

"So…" Brian spun his hand as though to say, *You're following me, aren't you?*

"What?" Grace looked mildly annoyed.

"We can't really do any pre-mixing and bagging unless we open all of the envelopes and read all of the directions. With all the proportions. Right now, I mean."

"Which we...shit!"

"We're just going to have to keep them in separate containers until the very end. Until Oxford, anyway."

"Seriously?"

"If you want to do it how Mom wanted."

Grace exhaled loudly. She reached out and turned Cinny's box slowly on the counter. "Do you suppose this is re-sealable?"

"Let's give it a try. Got a knife? Or scissors?"

Grace stood up and walked over past the sink. She opened a drawer under the counter and extracted a knife with an eight-inch blade.

"We're not cleaning fish, Gracie. Anything shorter?"

Grace went back to look. "Just this." She held up a serrated butter spreader.

"Okay." Brian reached for the knife, then took the box and rotated it. "There's a little seam. Let me just..." He stuck the blade in along one edge, pushed it in a little farther, and then sawed carefully along the seam.

"Progress!" said Grace. She bent closer.

Brian worked along one side, carefully rounded the corner, worked his way gently to the next, and then completed the final leg. He lifted the freed flap, lifted the one opposite, and parted a pair underneath. He looked at Grace, then peered into the box. A bag of transparent plastic lay exposed, gathered and secured with a heavy-duty twist tie. Through the bag, they could see a mottled gray powder, dotted with bits of something solid.

"Hi, Mom," peeped Grace in a tiny voice. Her shoulders began to shudder.

Brian sat, clicking softly. "It's tough," he sighed. "It's okay though, Gracie. It's okay."

Grace sniffed and swiped at her eyes once more. "I'm okay. Just give me a minute."

"Well," she said after a beat, "it looks like we could reseal that one if we have to."

"We could. If we get a good roll of tape."

Grace nodded. "How about the other?"

"Let's see."

Frank's Maple Haven was harder to open. Brian nearly sliced off a couple of fingers in the effort. He finally succeeded in breaking the knife and cracking the lid into three separate pieces. "Wasn't this supposed to be 'genuine Vermont maple?'" He pointed to a thin veneer of hardwood, underlain by a half-inch of mealy plywood. "Vermont! I bet this shit is from China."

"I bet it is, too," said Grace. She wondered in passing if the things Bradford Tuttle was "Always Ready" for included vengeful lawsuits from irate customers. The little flare of anger settled her surprisingly.

"Man," said Brian, lifting the plastic liner bag a few inches out of the box. "Dad's a lot bonier than Mom." There were considerably more solid bits in Frank's bag than in Cinny's, a number of them the size of fractured cinnamon sticks.

"Maybe it's a gender thing," said Grace. "Otherwise, I would have said Dad was always the more refined of the two. He certainly embarrassed me a hell of lot less often."

"Look," said Brian. "This thing is useless." He tapped the side of the box with the broken knife handle. "We can maybe leave Mom in her box. If it falls apart, there'll still be the inner bag. Dad, though, we'll just have to carry in this." He touched the plastic pouch. "It feels pretty rugged."

Grace looked uncertain.

"Or maybe we should just ditch both boxes?" suggested Brian. "Go with just the bags?"

"You know what worries me?" asked Grace.

"What?"

"A couple things. First, if we carry on all the way with them just, you know, in the plastic liners…is that treating them with enough respect?"

"Well, they're going into baggies for the scattering bit anyway, no?"

"They are," replied Grace. "But while they've been in their boxes, I've been able to think of them like—I don't know—valuable stuff. Being shipped by special international courier. If we just carry them in their liner bags, they'll be more like potato chips or something. Tucked in with a boxed lunch." Memories flooded back to Grace of the hundreds of school meals Cinny had packed for the two of them. It had been Fritos more often than potato chips, but the tireless caterer to the Posey family now sat, herself, on a kitchen counter—in a container that might just as well be holding salty junk food.

"I get it."

"And seriously," Grace continued, "how are airline and security and customs people going to feel about human ashes coming through in plastic sacks? I can already imagine some smarmy British matron in a starched brown uniform asking me at Heathrow, 'What kind of daughter are you, carrying your mum around in a polythene bag? Like she was a bloody leftover kipper?'"

They resolved to go out and buy the most elegant, tightly re-closeable pasta or grain containers they could find. Returning with the rented car, they stopped at a pricey home-goods boutique in Merivale, where they found what they thought would fill the bill perfectly—two cobalt blue, three-liter, screw-top plastic canisters, appropriately (they felt) "Guaranteed for the Life of the Original Purchaser." To Grace's eye, they were exactly the same blue as a sapphire ring Frank had bought Cinny for their twenty-fifth wedding anniversary, a ring she'd recently passed along to Chelsea. It all seemed meant to be. They drove back to the motel to begin the sorting alchemy.

"Alrighty," said Grace, as she reached out for a pint plastic measuring cup. "I guess we scoop them into this to calculate their total volume, each of them. And then we divide by six to get our rough estimate for each location. We can fine-tune up or down from there."

"No wonder you were nearly a Rhodie. Talk about an Ivy education setting you up for anything life throws your way."

Grace flipped her brother off. "I'm just trying not to fall apart here, kiddo. Losing myself in the task at hand."

"I get it."

"I do wish we had a scale. Seems like that would be a lot easier. Just weigh them and divide by six."

"You'd still have to do a bunch of scooping."

"True. Okay." Grace pushed up her sleeves. "Mom or Dad first?"

"Dad. He always hated having to wait for Mom."

"Okay. Can you grab the box and tip him in?"

"Sure. Say when."

Grace looked up at her brother. "This is *so* fucking weird. Like you're just pouring out a bowlful of Cap'n Crunch or something."

Brian looked like he'd bitten into a lemon.

"All right," said Grace. "Wait! Let me put something down. In case we spill." She walked past the sink again, tore off a few paper towels, and made a little nest under the measuring cup. "Okay. Fill it up. Two cups."

Brian tipped the box, then tipped it further. Nothing happened. "Dad's acting like ketchup," he said with a hitch in his voice.

"Tap it," said Grace. "Tap the side."

Brian tapped. The ashes and bits of bone began to tumble into the measuring cup, kicking up a slight cloud of dust. "This is so ghoulish!" he said.

"No, it's not," said Grace. "It's our dad. What would be ghoulish is if it were a total stranger."

"Okay. There. Two cups."

Grace bent over to check the level. A slender piece of bone stuck up from the cup like a half-burned birthday candle. It made her squeamish to see it. "Two cups. Now into the blue canister."

They repeated the process five more times, filling the measuring cup all the way until the last tip, when the cup was just half full.

"So, let's call that eleven cups of Dad," said Grace, stopping to wipe her brow. "That's just under two cups per location, except when the ratios are off."

Brian pointed to her forehead.

"What?"

"Dad! You look like it's Ash Wednesday."

Grace grabbed a paper towel and swiped at her brow.

"A little to the left."

She wiped again and looked over.

Brian's nod turned into a frown. "I don't know if I feel more like crying, laughing, or being sick." His face was a picture of dismay.

"I hear you. Just don't sneeze." Grace grimaced. "Now for Mom." She removed the tie from Cinny's plastic sac and lifted it free of the box. She handed the bag to Brian and placed the measuring cup in the center of the nest of towels. "It's a little like their wedding," she said with a wistful smile. "Dad's waiting at the altar, and here comes Mom."

"*Dearly beloved*," Brian chanted vacantly.

Four times they filled the cup with Cinny's ashes, with only a tiny bit left over. "That's just over eight cups," said Grace. "So Mom, on average, goes into every bag with about one and a third cups."

"How'd you figure that out so quickly?"

"I don't know," replied Grace. "I just did."

"You really are smart, you know? For all I've called you an elitist moron."

Grace smiled at her brother. Rare as moments like these were, they made it a little easier to downplay the ructions and resentments of the past. Not forget them, but certainly play them down. "Thanks, kiddo."

"Hand me a baggie," said Brian. "Two cups of Dad, minus a little, and one and a third of Mom?"

Grace nodded. "Recipe of the Day. Straight from the Oberlin College Naked Co-op Kitchen."

That night, Sage looked out the floor-length window at ten or so ducks paddling around the narrow pool that flanked the south wall of The Brewer's Arms like a moat. "They're so cute. Mallards, aren't they?"

"Looks like it," replied Brian. "Just like back home."

They'd just sat down in an alcove off the main dining area and bar, both of which were teeming with throngs of blustery Kiwi gents. Brian had booked his parents' favorite table, the one at which they'd hosted a farewell dinner for their closest Christchurch friends the night before they flew the family back to the States. The low slope of the shed roof overhead lent the nook a particular coziness.

"Do you think there were always mallards down here?" asked Ella. "Or did the first Europeans bring them down?"

"Good question," said Grace. "I know they brought cats. And rats. Every sailing ship had rats by the hundreds."

"They brought rabbits to Australia," said Brian. "And they totally overran the continent. No native predators."

"We read about that in Biology," offered Sage. "When they couldn't trap them all, they exposed them to this disease that gave them skin tumors. And made them blind. Lovely, no?" She looked at Chelsea, who frowned obligingly.

"So, Brian," said Jack with a grin. "You said this is an exotic meat place. Do they serve rabbit? Or rat?"

Sage turned to Jack with a cocked eyebrow. "Is it okay if I call you Uncle Jack?"

"Sure." He smiled at Grace. "Please do."

"Great. So, if you order rabbit, Uncle Jack, I'm never running with you again."

Jack laughed. "That may be the only way I survive. You almost killed me out there this afternoon."

A waiter came to take their drink order, suavely dispensing with an order pad. As he stepped away, a fellow server swept by carrying two rectangular wooden platters, each with a bowl of fried potato wedges at one end and a small tossed salad at the other. In between, smoking delicately on an eight-by-six-by-one-inch slab of gray stone, sat fist-sized, purple-red fillets, hissing like sizzle cymbals. The scent of grilling beef trailed enticingly in their wake. Jack and Ella craned their necks to follow the aroma.

"That's the beef fillet," Brian said. "Definitely recommended. Then there's everything else: chicken, venison, crocodile, ostrich.'"

"How much of what they serve is legal?" Jack winked at his brother-in-law.

"All of it," replied Brian. "As far as I know. It's farmed."

"Which, of course, makes it perfectly okay to kill it and eat it," scowled Sage.

"Oh, right," said Jack. "You're vegan!"

"I am. I prey on helpless legumes and root vegetables."

Jack chuckled. "Wasn't there some kind of flap at your school you were in the middle of? I think Grace was telling me."

"Guilty as charged," said Sage.

"Sage got her principal to convince the school board to offer vegan meals at the cafeteria." Ella reached up to take the wine the waiter had brought. "We're so proud of her." She looked at Brian, who nodded.

"That's great." Jack smiled at Sage. "What are you going to order, sweetheart? Even without the rabbit, the menu sounds pretty meat-heavy."

"I'll be fine," Sage replied coolly. "And how would you feel about a timeout on the *sweethearts*?"

Jack looked at Grace, his eyes widened. "Sure, Sage. Fine. Sorry."

"No worries," replied Sage. "Just laying down some parameters."

Grace broke the awkward silence. "Jack thrives on parameters. They're like lines on a tennis court. Or out-of-bounds on a golf course. Right, Jack?"

"Right." Jack leaned to the side as the waiter set down his wine. "You don't know where to aim until you know where not to aim. Now I know where not to aim." He smiled at Sage. "Thanks!"

When the waiter had served them all, Grace raised her glass. "Here's to our *deah depotted Poseys*!"

Chelsea finished up in the bathroom and found Sage already in bed, covers pulled up to her chin. "I sleep naked," Sage declared. "Is that okay?"

"Sure!" replied Chelsea after a brief hesitation.

"I didn't want you to freak out if you saw me get up and go to the bathroom or something."

"No. That's cool."

"It's part of the whole Circadian rhythm thing. You cool off faster naked. And when you cool off faster, that helps you get to sleep."

"Whatever works for you," said Chelsea, climbing into bed. "Shall I turn off the light?"

"Sure."

They lay for a minute in silence. A car hummed by on Papanui Road, its lights sweeping across the darkened wall.

"Does Grant wear pajamas?" asked Sage.

Chelsea laughed. "Yeah. He does."

"And do you wear a nightgown or something when you're with him?"

"I do."

"I don't mean to pry," said Sage. "It's so funny that we talk about bed*clothes*—you know? Like, *The maid came in and tidied the bedclothes*. And so many people still wear other clothes *under* their bedclothes."

"That is strange. I never thought about the words that way."

"And when you turn over, you get all twisted up and shit."

"Yeah."

They were silent for another minute.

"Can I ask you one more question?"

"Sure," replied Chelsea. "Maybe we can make it the last one, though. I'm exhausted."

"I promise!"

"Okay. Ask away."

"Why does Jack call your mom *H.P.?*"

Chelsea laughed.

"What? Why?"

"It's short for Honey Pot."

"Honey Pot?"

"Yup. He calls her Honey Pot at home. When they're out, though, it's almost always H.P."

"Like he's embarrassed? Or it's a secret or something?"

"I don't know. Or Mom or someone else will give him shit."

"I guess you don't think it's a Winnie-the-Pooh honey-pot kind of thing. Do you?"

"Nope."

"More like Sugar Pussy?"

Chelsea laughed again. "I guess."

"So does she call him, like, Love Pole or anything?"

Chelsea laughed more loudly. "Nope."

"That's good," said Sage. "'Good night, Chel.'"

When Brian got up to pee at two a.m., the wind was up, and he could hear rain slapping against the bathroom window. By dawn, the skies had cleared to a pure, unblemished blue. He dressed quickly and went out to the garden, leaving Ella to grab a little more sleep. Unbeknownst to Grace and Jack, Ella had decided not to risk traveling with marijuana and was suffering some of the headaches and insomnia that could come with withdrawal. The last time she'd gone cold turkey, she told Brian—the months she'd been pregnant with Sage—she'd experienced such world-class mood swings that Fred, her ex, had started calling her *Yo-yo Ma-ma-to-Be*. That she was currently free of similar bipolarity made her think the problem back then might have had something to do with the fact that an alien creature was actively colonizing her uterus. She'd still been awake when Brian got up at two, so he was reluctant to disturb her. He wrote a note telling her where he was going, closed the door quietly, and went out to watch the pink wash of dawn creep down the flanks of the Port Hills.

Just after eight, he went back to the room to find Ella in the shower. He stood in the bathroom door, looking at her form through the steamy glass of the stall. As she bent over to lather her calves and ankles, her right buttock brushed up against the glass, clearing a small window in the fog of condensation. Brian smiled as he recalled one of their early evenings skinny-dipping in her pool in Seattle. She'd grabbed a replica *Titanic* life-ring one of her friends had given her for her birthday and positioned it so that her stylishly groomed pubic area was framed by the hole. "Like what you *don't* see?" she'd asked playfully.

"I do," Brian had replied, with comfortingly uncomplicated sincerity.

She'd looked down his torso and giggled: "I guess so!"

"Is that you?" asked Ella as she straightened up in the stall.

"Sorry, lady," replied Brian in the voice he'd used for reading Chelsea *Billy Goats Gruff* when she was little. "It's the mad voyeur of Christchurch. Come to steal your virtue."

"Too late," piped Ella. "Hugh Jackman stole my virtue last Tuesday."

"Hugh Jackman?" Brian asked in his own voice. "I didn't know you were into Hugh Jackman."

"Oh, yes," said Ella, shutting off the water. "Mostly because you look like brothers." She pulled her towel down from the door and started to dry off.

"You really think so?"

"I do. So does Sage."

"Really?"

"That's the first thing she said about you."

"Poor deluded girl."

Ella laughed. "She said I didn't deserve anyone as handsome as you."

"It's a miracle you put up with that sharp little minx."

"It is." Ella opened the door and stepped out, her towel wrapped around her like a sarong. She stood on her toes to kiss Brian on the lips and then slid over to the sink. "What time are we supposed to leave?"

"8:30," said Brian. "Want some coffee?"

"Love some. Caffeine's the only way this sorry wench is going to make it through the day."

"Tough night, huh?" asked Brian once she was dressed. He watched her take her first sip of coffee. She sat across from him in a sporty cornflower jump suit that matched her eyes, which were currently a little puffy. Even if the rain had kept up, it would have been a day for sunglasses.

"Yeah."

"Was your mind racing or anything?"

"Not really."

"You could have asked me for a back rub," said Brian. "That usually helps."

"Or a front rub," joked Ella.

"That too."

"I actually got up for a bit. Just after midnight. You didn't notice?"

"Sleep of the dead!" said Brian.

"Funny you should say that."

"Why?"

"Because when I was up, I Googled the poor guy Cinny was talking about," explained Ella. "The one buried out at the island?"

"Ivon. Ivon Skelton. The only burial out there, I guess…behind his little picket fence."

"Well, that's the thing," said Ella. She set her coffee down. "He's not. Apparently."

"Not what?"

"Not the only one buried out there."

"What do you mean?" asked Brian.

"I found this article online about another guy—a Maori named Sam something. He died out there too. Another leprosy patient. He apparently tried to organize a strike against the crappy conditions at the colony, but he didn't have much luck. They weren't working or anything, so they didn't have much leverage. Anyway, he was apparently a *persona* not very *grata*. And when he died, they buried him somewhere, but nobody knows where."

"Interesting. I never heard that."

"Well," said Ella. "I guess it's a recent discovery. There's a book by some professor that just came out. The newspapers back then mentioned somebody died and got buried, but they didn't give his name."

"Hmm."

"Wait a sec. I can find it again." Ella picked up her iPad and typed in a search. "Here it is. *Sam Te Iringa*. That was his name. But this is what the paper said. *One of the leper patients at Quail Island, an elderly Maori, died on a Friday night and was buried the next afternoon.* Just *an elderly Maori*. That's it. *Father Patrick Cooney, the priest at St Joseph's Catholic Church in Lyttelton, conducted the service.* That's all she wrote."

Brian nodded sadly. "We know who gets to write history."

Ella set the iPad down. "This would set Sage right off."

"It would."

"I don't think I'm going to tell her. I don't want to upset the whole keeping-Ivon-company thing by playing the politically correct amateur historian."

"That's probably smart," said Brian. "Disingenuous, but smart."

"It's just so sweet that Cinny wants to be out there with poor old Ivon. Poor *young* Ivon. I guess he died when he was twenty-five."

"Man," said Brian. "When I was twenty-five, I'd barely finished college."

They were late getting away from the motel. Jack thought he'd misplaced his wallet, and it took him a while to remember that his new travel jacket had an exclusive secret pocket in the small of the back. Brian managed, nonetheless, to speed them through the harbor tunnel and down into Lyttelton in time to park the car, get tickets at the ferry office, and follow the track of painted footprints down to the wharf with ten minutes to spare. While they waited to board the big diesel catamaran that sat idling next to the wharf, Brian pointed out their destination. Quail Island lay a mile or two out past the stone breakwater protecting the inner harbor, out in the middle of the vast, ocean-breached caldera at the core of the Banks Peninsula. The layered magma cliffs of the island's north flank looked like a concrete gun emplacement, Brian always thought. Farther to the west, the bluffs dropped more gently to the shore, and you could see rolling fields of wind-swept tussock grass, dotted here and there by the occasional tree.

"I'm sorry we didn't have time to come via the high road instead of the tunnel," said Brian. The wind tossed his hair as he pointed back toward the city. "I remember Dad driving us over the top, like our second day in town. We were totally in the clouds, then they suddenly opened up and you could see down into this incredible ring of hills. And the bay, the water there, set inside like—I don't know—a huge golden punchbowl filled with an ocean of Bombay Sapphire."

"Jack's kind of scenery," quipped Grace. "By the way! Where is the old tippler?"

Chelsea pointed to where Jack was standing next to the gangplank, talking with a handsome teenager in a Black Cat Ferry T-shirt. He gestured toward the boat, nodded, and walked back toward the group. "Baby's brand-new," he announced as he pulled up. "Twin five-hundred-horsepower diesels, the kid says. I bet she flies."

"I guess we'll see," said Grace. She grinned at Chelsea.

The big catamaran burbled away from the pier right on time, three-quarters full of Kiwi families primed for a Saturday outing—"chilly bin" coolers, beach umbrellas, folding chairs, and boogie boards—together with a handful of camera-toting Asian tourists. The Posey group sat on the rear deck, braving the salt spray cast up by the twin hulls and sucked back toward them as they sped through the rising chop. Windsurfers were already out in force, slapping over the waves at frightening speeds, their boards vaulting into the air for seconds at a time. Fifteen minutes later, the ferry reached the pier on the island, where the helmsman spun the big craft into the wind and docked it with careless ease, despite the potent southwesterly.

Half an hour's walk took them past the decaying wooden pier where the Scott expedition had re-embarked its quarantined ponies and dogs prior to its doomed voyage south; past the busy swimming and waterskiing beaches; and up to the long, narrow plateau where the island's leper colony had stood. Grace asked them to gather around so she could give them a little historical background. For two decades prior to 1925, she explained, a dozen or so men had been consigned to the island after being diagnosed with leprosy. There'd been a number of large buildings there for administration and staff—now demolished but well-documented in photographs they'd see in an information hut a bit later. The patients themselves had lived in small cabins built on the hillside, one of which had recently been reconstructed by local schoolchildren and their teachers. The leprosarium had closed shortly after Ivon Skelton died, with the remaining patients transferred to one of the islands in the Fiji group. Only Ivon remained, Grace reminded them, buried in a solitary spot on the high ground northwest of where they stood. Brian caught Ella's eye, but he kept mum.

They clung to the southern shore, their path snaking in and out as it traversed a series of rocky arêtes that dropped down to the water. The track underfoot was red with pine needles, fallen from a big stand of mature trees. After a short trudge uphill, they filed through the shade of a gigantic oak and arrived at a grassy half-acre clearing, in the middle of which stood a patch of high grass and bracken, enclosed by an uneven picket fence. In the center of the tangle of mixed vegetation stood a simple wooden cross.

"This is it," said Grace. She was breathing heavily as she turned to the others.

"It's so lovely," said Ella, working, too, at catching her breath. "And wild."

"I was imagining, you know, this tidy little plot," said Chelsea. "Fence freshly painted. Fresh-cut flowers on the grave."

"It's better this way," Sage declared. "In the rough embrace of Mother Nature."

"That's so poetic," said Jack. "You kids these days are so tuned in to things we never thought about back when we were young. In Clearwater, anyway."

"Thanks," said Sage with a shrug.

Jack walked over to a small sign mounted on two stout timber posts. It was the only well-maintained human construction in sight. There were several short paragraphs of text on the left, and, on the right, an oval sepia photograph of a young man in a formal pose, wearing a dark suit, white shirt, dark tie, and a white boutonnière. He was the picture of handsome and hopeful youth, his expression open and honest but with a hint of mischief in his smile. "*Leprosy Colony Burial Ground,*" read Jack, stooping slightly to see. "*The only recorded death at the Colony is that of Ivon Crispen Skelton who died on 20 October 1923, aged 25 years.*"

"What a cool name!" said Sage. "If I ever have a son, maybe I'll name him Crispen."

"No time soon, I hope," said Ella. She noticed Brian flinch. "Sorry. That wasn't exactly in the spirit of the moment. Forgive me." She looked down at her shoes.

"*He was buried at this site on 22 October 1923,*" Jack continued. "*The burial service was conducted by the Reverend A. J. Petrie, from the Holy Trinity Church, Lyttleton. Ivon, a son of John and Emmaline (née Fruean) Skelton…*née?"

"That's French for *born,*" explained Grace. "Fruean would have been her maiden name."

"Why French?" asked Jack.

"The arrogance of the upper classes," muttered Sage.

Jack chuckled. "Got it. Anyway, *Ivon was born in Apia, Western Samoa, on 14 January 1898. He lived in Western Samoa for most of his life, but when aged 20, while visiting relatives on the West Coast of New Zealand, he was diagnosed as having leprosy. Leprosy was a disease feared to be contagious, and Ivon and his New Zealand cousin Thomas James Skelton were put in isolation. Thomas was found to be free of the disease, but Ivon continued his isolation away from his family on Quail Island until his death.*" Jack straightened up and sighed. "God, that's sad!"

"Mom always thought that last bit about his cousin was especially touching," said Grace. "They both thought they had it, so there was that consolation at least. The cousins had each other for company. But then Thomas gets cleared and Ivon has to say goodbye to his friend and face his fate all on his own." She looked at the rest of them with a grimace.

"Man!" said Chelsea.

"Dad, too," said Brian. "They were both really moved by this. When we were headed to Samoa that spring break—the time Dad dragged us up the mountain—he actually picked some wildflowers from the grave, right there, and, when we got to Apia, he dropped them between these huge rocks in the harbor jetty. He didn't want to create an ecological disaster, he said, but he still wanted to take part of Ivon back home to his family. Some of his nitrogen."

"Gosh!" exclaimed Ella, looking at Sage. "It makes me want to weep."

"It does," said Grace. "Dad wasn't much of a sentimentalist. You could barely get him to celebrate family birthdays. But there was something about Ivon that really got under his skin."

"That's perfect," said Ella. "It's just perfect that this is where they want to be. Such generosity of spirit."

Grace nodded and looked over at Brian. The rest of the group fell silent as they waited for what came next. They stood there fairly sheltered from the southwesterly winds, but an occasional gust licked into the clearing, tossing the women's hair and swaying the grass and bracken around Ivon Skelton's grave.

"Well," said Brian, swinging his backpack off his shoulder, "I guess we get on with it." He turned to Grace, who nodded soberly. Chelsea stepped closer to her mother and threw an arm around her waist. Brian opened the pack, reached in, and extracted the bagged remains. For a moment he hesitated, then he passed the bag to Grace. She reached out with both hands as though she were being handed a baby. Brian reached into the pack again and removed a small gardening trowel. "Where would be good?"

"Anywhere, I guess." Grace's voice trembled. "Outside the fence," she added more strongly, "but close, I think."

Brian nodded matter-of-factly, took a few steps forward, and knelt down a foot from the pickets. He used both hands to plunge the trowel into the turf. It took him three or four minutes to scoop away the dark soil and clear a hole eighteen inches square and a foot deep. He stuck the trowel into the pile of dirt, wiped his hands together, and stood. He looked at Grace, managed a half smile, and gestured toward the hole.

Grace took a deep breath and stepped forward out of Chelsea's embrace. "I guess we let them out of the bag now. Just like the cat." She began to giggle nervously, but when she looked at Brian, his face was a stoic mask. "Right." She moved the empty pack over to the edge of the hole and knelt. She opened the bags and looked at Brian again. He nodded. Grace grabbed the tops in her left hand. Putting her right hand under the bellied bulk of the ashes, she eased the whole package over the center of the hole and tried to tip the contents out. The bags were big enough, though, that the gray powder and ivory chips of bone slipped off to either side as she lifted, as though they were going into paired saddlebags.

"Damn!" said Grace. "I'm so sorry, everybody. Mom and Dad just aren't cooperating."

Sage stepped forward and knelt next to Grace. "Here. Just put them down with the opening right there. Over the edge. Right. Then, if you grab the two corners—"

"Got it. Thanks, honey." Grace leaned into her niece's shoulder.

"Sure." Sage stood and backed up next to Ella.

"Anybody have any words?" Grace craned her neck to look at the others.

Jack cleared his throat. "Would it be okay if I read something?"

Grace turned to him in mild surprise. "Sure!" She looked at Brian, who seemed surprised as well, but nodded.

Jack reached into his pants pocket and pulled out a folded sheet of paper. He opened it up, shifted on his feet, and began to read in a quiet and steady voice.

Do not stand at my grave and weep
I am not there; I do not sleep.
I am a thousand winds that blow,
I am the diamond glints on snow,
I am the sun on ripened grain,
I am the gentle autumn rain.

When you awaken in the morning's hush
I am the swift uplifting rush
Of quiet birds in circled flight.
I am the soft stars that shine at night.
Do not stand at my grave and cry,
I am not there; I did not die.

Chelsea broke seconds of silence. "Oh, Dad!" she said. "That was so moving. Where did you find it?"

"You liked it?"

"Of course I did. It was perfect." Chelsea looked down at her mother, who was nodding slowly as she peered into the hole.

"I found it online. You hear it pretty often, I guess. At other memorials and all."

"Well, it's new to me," said Chelsea. "And it nails it."

"The diamonds on snow bit reminded me of Cinny and Frank," Jack offered. "All those Christmastime cross-country ski tours when this Southern boy nearly froze his Clearwater heinie off." He chuckled. "But those times were great. Special." He sniffed as he returned the paper to his pocket and stepped back.

"Thanks, Jack," said Brian. He walked over to his brother-in-law. Jack smiled shyly as he let Brian hug him. "That was wonderful. Perfect. Thanks."

Jack nodded. He looked at Grace, who was smiling. She gathered herself, then raised the bottom corners of the bags. Slowly at first, and then with a rush, just under two cups of Frank Posey and a cup and a third of Lucinda Maynard Posey cascaded softly into the New Zealand soil. A ghost of gray dust rose from the hole and was whisked away by the wind. Grace shivered slightly, then pressed the baggies shut. She stood, brushed off her knees, and walked over to embrace Jack.

"Okay," said Brian. "Let's let them catch their breath and maybe start getting caught up with Ivon. Anyone care to…you know?"

"You do it, Brian," said Ella. "You should tuck them in."

They picnicked on the bluff above the Ship's Graveyard, the spot at the western end of the island where, over the years, more than half a dozen ships of all sizes and shapes had been beached once they'd reached the end of their useful lives. The hulks lay two hundred feet below them in various stages of decay, the fish-bone ribs of the sailing ship *Darra* still hinting at the long grace of her lines, the rusty boiler of the steamship *Mullogh* squatting in the shallows like a malevolent toad. It had been Cinny and Frank's favored lunch spot, and Grace and Brian had gone to some lengths to reproduce the standard Posey luncheon bill of fare: sliced ham and salami, tiny waxed rounds of cheese, cheddar crackers from Australia, digestive biscuits from England, small bottles of L&P lemon soda, and Cadbury Dairy Milk chocolate. They'd offered to buy something for Sage, but she said she'd just tap her supply of fruit, nuts, and rice crackers.

"Not a bad place to spend eternity," declared Ella. She looked out across the milky aqua waters to the wooded shoreline and grassy slopes that rose steeply to the top of the encircling ridge. "Was this a volcano or something?"

"It was," said Brian. "The whole peninsula was an offshore volcano. It wasn't even connected to the mainland until erosion washed down from the Alps and formed the Canterbury Plains. Where the city is."

Ella nodded. "It feels so—I don't know—powerful out here. It's a mystical spot. I love it that Cinny and Frank are staying."

"It is mystical," agreed Brian. "There's a Maori legend that a nasty giant used to live here. He was such a constant pain in the ass that one of their gods finally dumped dirt and rock on him until he couldn't move anymore."

"Until the earthquakes," opined Jack.

"Right," replied Brian. "I bet some people thought of that."

"Just look at the colors!" exclaimed Ella. "Turquoise water. Dark green pines over there. Golden grass. All the gray-brown rock. What a palette! You could do a whole house in this."

"We're supposed to be on vacation, Mom," said Sage, pulling the last bit of peel off a tangerine. "Time out on the interior-decorator shit."

Ella waved her hand. "I can't help it. It all feels so designed. Majestic but intimate. You know? I honestly expect a hobbit to jump out from behind a tree and snatch a cookie."

Sage rolled her eyes and asked Brian if he had any more soda. He reached into the cooler bag and pulled out another bottle.

"I can see why they shot *The Lord of the Rings* down here." Ella pulled a lock of windblown hair back from her eyes. "You've got the mountains and volcanoes, but you've also got all the cozy little green dales."

"Actually, Mom, it's totally fucked!" blurted Sage. She drew stares from everyone. "Sorry, but it's true." She took a sip and lowered her bottle from her lips with a little sucking pop. "There's this incredible, *real* history down here—with the Maori and all and their amazing legends and beliefs. Like you were saying, Brian, right? And then Peter Jackson comes along and suddenly the country is full of tourists dying to see where they built Frodo's fake house or where Orlando Bloom used to take a shit." She shook her head and kicked at a stone lying by her foot.

"Sage, honey," said Ella, "you loved those movies."

"I still do. But talk about cultural imperialism!" Sage looked around to make eye contact, but Ella was squinting at Brian. "Tolkien writes these books that come straight out of British and German legends, right? And then the movies lay them on top of a really beautiful and interesting country like this, and everybody flocks down and pretends they're visiting a fucking southern hemisphere Stonehenge or something. Meanwhile, what's the Maori standard of living? What are their statistics for child mortality?"

Chelsea nodded.

"And why don't *Maoris* get featured in Air New Zealand's pre-flight safety videos?" Sage asked. "Instead of dressing white actors up like elves and dwarves and Riders of Rohan and kidding us all into thinking we're flying back to Camelot."

"Wow!" said Jack after a pause. "That was quite a speech!"

"Well?" Sage's eyes flashed daggers.

"No. I hear you," said Jack, looking at the others. "It's funny. Strange."

"No!" said Sage. "It's sad! It's fucked! But, hey! When's the last time a Native American held high office in the U.S.?"

In the silence that followed, Brian reached out and squeezed Sage's shoulder. "I wish Mom could have heard you say all that," he said quietly.

"Shit! Well. Maybe she did," replied Sage. "Who knows how it all works?"

They were walking back toward the pier, along the mowed path through fields of tussock grass on the north side of the island, when Ella felt she could have a private word with her daughter.

"You were on quite a tear back there, honey," she said, modulating her voice so that Grace and Jack, thirty steps ahead, couldn't hear.

"Yeah," said Sage, looking less than contrite.

"Fortunately, I don't think anyone was really offended."

Sage looked quickly at her mother, then back at the ground. "Not even Jack?" She gave a little snort.

Ella chuckled. "Jack can be a little more conservative than Brian, I think. And he is from Florida. But it's not like he's Marco Rubio."

Sage snorted again. "Well, it could have been worse."

"What do you mean."

"I did a little research on Quail Island back at the motel. On Ivon Skelton?"

"And?"

"And it turns out Ivon Skelton wasn't the only leprosy patient buried out here. There was another one. He was a Maori, though, so nobody hardly even mentioned that he'd died. And nobody knows where he was buried."

"Sam Te Iringa."

Sage stopped short and turned toward her mother. "How'd you know that?"

"I read the same article, I guess. About the book somebody wrote?"

"Right." Sage turned and started walking again. They heard the horn of the ferry leaving the harbor, making for the island to pick them up.

"You knew about that when you were going on about hobbits and all."

"Yup."

"Well," said Ella after a moment. "I'm glad you didn't bring it up."

"Come on, Mom!" Sage stopped again. "Why would I want to crap on the lovely thought that the only company Ivon Skelton is going to have out here is Cinny and Frank? That would be so cruel for Grace and Brian. And Chelsea." She began walking again.

"Brian knows," said Ella, after a dozen steps. "I told him."

"Well, let's not tell the others. Let's let them keep their pretty thoughts."

"That sounds a little condescending, honey. Not the sentiment, but the way you said it."

Sage sighed. "I know. I just have a hard time, sometimes, trying to be nice and, at the same time, trying to make a difference in this shitty world."

"Well, then, *welcome* to this shitty world," said Ella. "Nothing about being a good person is easy. But I think you're doing a pretty good job."

"For a punk kid?" Sage looked over.

"At least for any daughter of mine."

Twenty steps ahead on the closely mowed track, Grace turned to Jack. "I'm glad you read that poem."

"Thanks, Honey Pot. I remembered the one your mom quoted in her note. About being buried *under the wide and starry sky?*"

"Right."

"I thought the part in mine about the soft stars really fit."

"It did." She reached out and took his hand.

"So, you don't think it was cliché?"

"Cliché*d*? The image, or the poem?"

"The poem. I'm thinking we've heard it a half dozen times."

"Maybe."

"Sure," said Jack. "I'm sure that's what Mary Brigham read at her dad's service."

"You're probably right."

"I looked at you after I read it. You were smiling, but to yourself. I thought you were probably thinking, *Nice try, Jack, but couldn't you come up with something a little fresher?*"

"Jack!" said Grace. She pulled to a halt to look at him.

"C'mon," said Jack. He tugged her along. "I don't want Ella and Sage to catch up."

"Why would you say that? That I'd be critical of your choice."

"Because you're a fancy English major and all. And I'm just a lowlife lawyer."

Grace was about to stop again, but when she looked over at him, she could see he was grinning. "You're half serious, aren't you?"

"Maybe."

"Look. When you were reading that, I started to cry. Sure, part of me said, *Here comes that that tired old poem again.* But I really started to cry."

"Really?"

"Sure, Jack. Clichés don't get to be clichés unless they really work for a lot of people."

Jack nodded and walked on. "It just seems like sometimes all you literary types go on and on about how great something is and, as soon as Joe Normal listens and gets convinced and says, *Hey! I guess I like it too!* then you all feel you have to move on to something else. Like popular acclaim is the kiss of death."

"I'm sorry, Jack, if I make you feel that way." She squeezed his hand and shook it as though she could press her sincerity through his skin.

"No, it's not just you. It's not *even* you. At least, not very often." He smiled again. "It's just this…Northeasterner thing, I guess."

Grace chuckled. "This is becoming a major indictment. I'm not sure I know what to say."

"I know," said Jack. "I'll just shut up. But I'm glad you thought what I read was right for the moment."

"I did. And you were so thoughtful to step up when us snooty Yankees didn't have anything prepared to say."

"*We* snooty Yankees?"

Grace threw her head back and guffawed.

"What's so funny," called Ella from behind.

Grace turned to her. "Jack just corrected my pronoun usage."

"You go, Jack!" called Ella. "What goes around comes around."

Ella stood in her nightgown behind Brian, waiting for him to finish cleaning his teeth.

"That was really special today," she said.

"It wush," he sputtered around his toothbrush. "I fought it wed well too." He spit into the sink and reached for the glass to rinse.

"God, it was beautiful out there."

"I told you." He turned and kissed her on the lips.

"Man, you reek of whisky."

Brian raised his hands apologetically, then reached around to grab her butt.

"Easy there, Mister," she cried, hopping backwards.

"I've been thinking about you all day. Since I watched you this morning in the shower."

"Well, you can just think a little longer," said Ella. "I won't have you interfering with my *toilette*."

"Perish the thought." Brian reached up and dotted the tip of her nose with his forefinger, belched loudly, then walked back to the bedroom and climbed into bed.

"Tell me," called Ella from the bathroom. "How did it feel leaving your mom and dad out there?" She waited a beat for the answer.

"Good, I guess."

"Good."

"I mean they're out there together, aren't they?"

"They are. With Ivon."

"With Ivon. It was really hard when Dad died, you know?" said

Brian. "Mom was in their place all on her own. I kept thinking about her having meals, and watching television, and opening a bottle of wine…all by herself."

"I know."

"No waiting lines in the bathroom. Nobody's ass to grab."

"Be serious. I'm asking you a serious question."

"I know," said Brian, readjusting his pillow. "But I'm…good. I really do feel as though they're together. And I don't have to worry about poor old Mom."

"There's a laugh," said Ella, switching off the bathroom light and walking over to the bed. "I don't imagine many people ever thought about Cinny as 'poor old' anything. She was a spirit for the ages. Tough as nails."

"She was."

Ella pulled back the covers and climbed into bed. "I wonder what bombshell she's got in store for us."

"God only knows."

"I wonder if Sage is right about an affair. I have to admit, the thought occurred to me. That's kind of the way she made it sound."

"And you?" asked Brian.

"And me, what?"

"Are you ready for *ze sex*?"

"Given how much you've had to drink, I'm the one who should be asking *you*."

"Give me your hand," said Brian.

"If I must," said Ella with a giggle.

"I never knew Uncle Brian could be so funny." Chelsea and Sage sat on the balcony of their room, looking at the nearly full moon. A few ragged clouds drifted slowly northward on the gentle southerly. "Of course, I don't know if I ever saw him drink that much."

"Yeah," said Sage. She lifted her bare feet to the railing and curled her toes over the top. She'd just painted her toenails the color of green M&Ms. "He was going shot-for-shot with your dad."

"Called up to the majors," Chelsea tittered. "It can't be easy, though, burying your parents. Or scattering their ashes."

Sage turned sharply toward her. "It would depend on the parent. Trust me!"

Chelsea floundered for a response. She looked down and pulled a cigarette from a pack in her lap. She lit it, took a long drag, and exhaled straight up into the night air.

"Moving right along, that video was hilarious." They'd all been chatting at dinner with their hip young waiter and gotten onto the subject of the New Zealand accent. He'd recommended an amusing YouTube video and Brian, a few too many sheets to the wind, insisted on watching it on the spot—at volume. It passed as an advertisement for a useful hardware product, with an earnest homeowner claiming that regular use of "Schaeffer's Deck Sealant" had given him "the most beautiful deck in town." The joke was that *deck* in Kiwi dialect is perilously close to *dick*. When the satisfied customer declares, "All the kids in the neighborhood are keen to play on my deek now, because they say it's the best deek around," Brian lost it—replaying it once and then reciting the best bits from memory. Most of their table and all of the surrounding diners indulged him cheerily, Jack being a notable exception.

"It was hilarious." Chelsea sniggered. "I still can't say for sure if it's a real ad."

"No way!" scoffed Sage. "It goes on much too long. And the guy says *deek* way too many times."

"Just like Uncle Brian."

Sage chuckled.

They sat there looking at the moon. In the distance, you could just make out a siren of some sort, either an ambulance or a police car. Chelsea looked at her half-smoked cigarette and snuffed it out forcefully on the floor. "Shit!"

"What's up?" said Sage.

"Oh, I'm trying to quit."

"Great. You should."

"I know."

"So what was with your dad?" asked Sage, after a bit.

"What do you mean?"

"He didn't seem to think it was very funny."

"He can be strange," said Chelsea. "He really likes Brian, but I think it's hard for him to accept that he's been with men and women both."

"Yeah," said Sage. "I get it. In a different way, maybe. I'm completely down with it and all, gender complexity. But sometimes I worry about Brian's commitment to my mom."

"Oh, I think he really loves her, Sage. Just the way he looks at her. And when nobody's looking. Or he doesn't think they are."

"You think?"

"I do," said Chelsea.

"I hope so. Mom and I go at it sometimes. She's a really good person, though."

"You sound like me," laughed Chelsea.

"Mothers and daughters!" sighed Sage. "Just tie my tubes."

"It was a damn joke!" said Grace. "Honestly, Jack. I don't know why you're going on."

"Well…" Jack looked unconvinced. "Consider the source. You know?"

"I've got to pee again." Grace tossed off the covers and stormed into the bathroom.

Jack listened to the impressively lengthy streaming, the briskly tugged toilet roll, some soft rustling, and then a quick flush. Grace stormed back into the room and threw herself back in bed so violently that the headboard slammed into the wall.

"Our neighbors will think we're having sex," Jack quipped.

"Fat chance!"

"Look," said Jack. "There were other people in the restaurant. Families."

"So?"

"And there's Brian, talking about his beautiful dick. And how all the children in the neighborhood have the best time playing on it. His dick."

Grace sat bolt upright. "I told you, it's a fucking joke, Jack. The stupid video was made in New Zealand for New Zealand television, for Christ's sake. Everybody's probably seen it."

"Maybe not the kids."

"I give up!" She lay back down and turned away, punching her pillow into the right position.

"Look," said Jack, leaning close. "You know I'm okay with Brian's ever-evolving sexuality. I just think tonight he was out of line."

"Probably because he was trying to keep up with you on the booze."

"Or maybe because you guys just buried your parents' ashes?"

Grace turned over and stared Jack in the face. "You say you're okay with his sexuality? Is that why you looked like you were being raped when he hugged you today?"

"What do you mean?"

"Brian came over to thank you for reading the poem, and when he hugged you, you looked as comfortable as a fence pole at a termite convention."

"What a potent image!" said Jack.

"Don't change the subject," snapped Grace.

"It's pretty ironic," said Jack after a pause. He looked for a reaction. "Really."

"What's ironic, Jack?"

"That you're okay with Brian joking about people playing with his dick, given past history."

"Don't go there, Jack. It's not the least bit helpful. Especially not now."

"Well then, maybe you can cut me some slack. Look. I can't help it. I was embarrassed being in that room with Brian going on that way, even if everybody knew it was all a joke. Maybe it's my problem. It probably *is* my problem. I'm the first one to admit I'm a work in progress when it comes to keeping an open mind. But I was embarrassed. For myself and for your brother."

"What do you say we let Brian handle his own embarrassment, okay?" Grace looked as though she might actually be calming down. "He makes his own choices. He lives with the consequences. Let's all do the same."

"I like him, Gracie. You know that. And I respect him, too."

Grace laughed. "You are so comical, Jack. When you think you're in trouble, it's always *Grace* or *Gracie*. When you're just cruising along in life, it's *Honey Pot*. Tonight, it's definitely *Gracie*."

"So I'm in trouble?"

Grace sighed. "Look. I forgive you for your gay paranoia, wherever it comes from and whoever you're worried about. I know you're trying your best."

"I am, Honey Pot." He paused. "So we're okay?"

Grace waited briefly before she responded. "Sure. We're okay."

"Do you think you'll be able to sleep?"

"I don't know."

Jack laughed.

"What?"

"Do you think it would help if we made love?"

Grace chuckled. "Who knows?"

For a moment there was silence.

"You want to?" asked Jack.

"Why not?"

SINGAPORE

The Poseys had struggled to tear themselves away from New Zealand at the end of Frank's sabbatical year. Spotting anguish on the horizon, Cinny had planned a long, fun-filled trip home as a palliative. They finished circling the globe in a westerly direction, stopping in Singapore and Dubai before boarding a well-worn cruise ship in Civitavecchia for a week-long tour of the eastern Mediterranean. After hitting Taormina in Sicily and the usual destinations in Greece, they spent another week in Rome, staying in a charming vacation rental just off the Campo di Fiore. Frank and Cinny went out each morning to walk along the Tiber and came home via the open-air market and the local *panetteria*, picking up fresh fruit and pastries for breakfast. Grace and Brian had never felt more coddled.

All these years later, leaving the South Island wasn't much easier. The biggest challenge for Grace and Brian was obviously leaving actual, physical bits of their parents behind. For a while at least, they'd still have five-sixths of Cinny and Frank's mortal remains close at hand, safely transferred into their matching cobalt blue canisters. Yet there was a deep-in-the-bone finality about turning their backs on even a small proportion of the carbon atoms that had, though in different molecular arrangements, once made up living creatures who'd loved them and cared for them and shared their joys and sufferings for dozens and dozens of years. Part of it, too, was seeing the affection their own spouses and offspring had developed for New Zealand during their short stay. And so, as they made their way to Christchurch International Airport for their own flight to Singapore, there was plenty of bona fide melancholy to go with the joyful new memories.

It was a day flight, but Brian was glad he'd booked business class for this leg as well. Sitting for ten hours with his knees mere inches from the seat in front of him would have been unbearable. Even on short hauls in Economy Plus back home, Brian suffered flare-ups of his self-diagnosed PBTSD—Post-Birth-Trauma Stress Disorder. He might, for example, be reading in the airline magazine about the most recent selection of *America's Best* (as in most publicity-conscious) *Surgeons*, or sipping contentedly on a craft IPA when something would seize up in his bones and muscles and he'd know beyond a doubt that, unless he could thrust his legs out ramrod straight and cast his arms out wide and arch his back like an Acapulco cliff diver, his seat would, any second, snap shut on him like a leather-upholstered mousetrap. He knew it was just a mental thing. But it was a mental thing he couldn't control, any more than he could will away a leg cramp or avoid weeping when he sliced onions. In his worst moments, he blamed the psychic infirmity on Grace and the crowded conditions she'd caused as co-occupant in Cinny's uterus. In his best, he took it as a challenge he might one day overcome, maybe when he finally caved to Ella's demands and joined her yoga class. For the moment, though, he raised the foot section of his business-class seat, reclined the back to a comfortable 45-degree angle, and watched *Fight Club* for the tenth or twelfth time.

Once the lunch plates and service items had been whisked away, Grace reached into her carry-on for *Atonement*. She'd been an Ian McEwan fan since *Amsterdam* won the Booker, and she'd been curiously stirred by the dark eroticism of *The Comfort of Strangers*. She was liking *Atonement* better than either, though, with its unrivalled richness of literary reference. It made her feel as though she were back in graduate school, reading another classic from the British country-house tradition of Jane Austen, Henry James, and Evelyn Waugh—but without the impending threat of a ten-page essay hanging over her head. From time to time she glanced to her left, where Jack sat immersed, first, in the Swiss-watch section of the in-flight shopping magazine and subsequently in a video replay of some rugby match or other between what must have been the All Blacks and a team in pea-green jerseys.

Four hours into the flight, the captain came on the intercom, pointing out that passengers seated on the left could see the Great Australian Bight, a huge crescent of coastline that looked as though it had been chomped from the bottom of the continent by a gargantuan shark back at the dawn of time. All Grace could see to the right was ridge upon ridge of arid red soil stretching north as far as the eye could see. It was clear there were trees down there, tiny dots strewn like poppy seeds on the vast, Mars-like expanse. She gazed down with grim fascination, imagining herself plunked down in that primal landscape with no resources except her purse and carry-on. There was nothing down there to suggest human habitation. Nothing at all.

After minutes and minutes of rapt surveillance, she thanked her good fortune that Cinny and Frank hadn't wanted to be sprinkled at Ayers Rock and returned to her reading. An hour and a half later, she looked down again and saw that nothing had changed. Nor had it, really, a half hour after that. It was clearly every bit as vast a country as the United States, and even less hospitable. Grace shuddered involuntarily and went back to her novel. The plot of false accusation was thickening nicely.

They landed in Singapore in the late afternoon, and by sunset they'd checked into the hotel Brian had booked on Clarke Quay. Their stay was largely uneventful, save for an excursion to the Long Bar at Raffles. A couple of law partners had briefed Jack on the storied history of the hotel and its signature cocktail. A visit to Singapore without a trip to the Long Bar, they'd said, was like a trip to Paris without seeing the Eiffel Tower—or a visit to Reno without driving out to see the young ladies of the Mustang Ranch. Jack insisted they start their evening with a visit.

"Holy shit!" he sputtered, after being handed the elegant leather-bound bar menu.

"What, dear?" asked Grace.

"Thirty-three dollars for a Singapore Sling! Singapore dollars. That's what, U.S.?"

"Twenty-five?" suggested Grace.

"Holy shit!" repeated Jack. "So six of them is what? A hundred and fifty American? For one round?"

"Oh, well," offered Ella. "Your partners did say a Singapore Sling at Raffles was bucket-list level, no?"

"They did," replied Jack. "That doesn't mean they thought the price should make me *kick* the damn bucket!"

Grace drew her head back and squinted. "You'd really consider just walking out?"

Jack looked undecided.

"Look, Dad." Chelsea held up the menu and pointed out that a glass of white wine would be eighteen dollars, a Manhattan twenty-five. "Anything we get, we'll pay through the nose for. And we're only doing this once, right? With Nana and Pop Pop?"

Jack sighed and looked back at Grace.

"Listen to your daughter," Grace said pointedly. "We all love you to death, Jack, but I can't believe how you can sweat the pennies. Then go out and drop twenty grand on another Rolex."

Chelsea looked stunned. "Dad's new watch cost twenty thousand dollars?"

"Okay," snapped Jack. "Let's just buy the fucking drinks."

"What if I end up wanting two?" asked Sage. "Provided I get served."

Jack replied that he couldn't think of anyone who'd deserve it more.

The drinks, once they'd arrived and been sampled, were judged worth the dollars and the family frictions, both. Sage was especially happy with hers—partly for the sheer delight of getting served. "Talk about awesome, what was in that?" she asked as she cracked open one of the Long Bar's signature peanuts. The floor all around was covered with discarded shells.

"Gin and pineapple juice," said Brian. "With a bunch of liqueurs... bitters...lime juice."

"Reminds me of Just Juice and vodka," said Sage. "My old babysitter's favorite."

"Which babysitter was that?" asked Ella.

"The one you thought Dad was fucking."

"You're going to have to be more specific."

They dined quayside among throngs of tourists and scores of brightly lit tour boats passing back and forth, blaring their spiels in half a dozen languages. Grace and Brian decided they were close enough to Thailand to dip into Cinny's next set of instructions, so once Jack settled the tab, they headed back to the Tingleys' room at the hotel. Jack fetched extra chairs from the balcony and joined Grace on the bed, where she leaned against a huge bank of pillows.

"Are we ready?" Grace herself looked apprehensive.

"No time like the present," said Ella, with a reassuring smile.

Grace opened the envelope and removed the contents. She looked around the room and cleared her throat. "*Dear loved ones.*" She cleared her throat again and adjusted herself on the bed. "*I hope your trip here was easy. Traveling in Southeast Asia can be such an adventure! If you went through Singapore, I hope you didn't go to the bar at Raffles.*" Grace's eyes narrowed. "*The tourists outnumber the roaches, and they serve better peanuts at the circus.*" She looked at Jack, who slowly shook his head. "*Ko Phi Phi was my idea on our honeymoon,*" she read on with determination. "*I'd seen pictures in* National Geographic, *and it looked like an earthly paradise. I told you Frank and I were trying to rebuild our love and trust (no thanks to me) and I thought maybe some quiet time together in a beautiful spot in Thailand could be a kind of Return to Eden, if that doesn't sound too fanciful. The island just south of the main one looked divine—this huge azure lagoon surrounded by cliffs with only a small gap to let the sea in and out. There was a gorgeous crescent beach at the bottom of the horseshoe with lush vegetation growing almost to the shoreline, and water so clear you could see the fish swimming a dozen feet down. That's where I took Dad to 'get back to the Garden.' We camped out there (illegally, I'm pretty sure), and we made love until I felt like I'd just given birth to the two of you, all over again.*" Grace stopped reading. "Jesus, Mom!"

Brian started to laugh.

Grace glared at him.

"Go on, Gracie," he said. "Sorry."

Grace raised the papers resolutely. "*I want you to take our ashes out to that lagoon—50-50 again, please. On the right side of the beach going in, as I remember, there's a stream. Walk back into the trees and scatter us wherever feels right. Mix us in gently with the sand. You'll know the right island. It's the one that looks like a giant stone shark's fin off the long beach with all the hotels. The locals will know it.*"

"Hang on," said Brian. He was thumbing his phone. "Phi Phi Leh, it's called. The island. Maya Bay. They shot *The Beach* there. Pretty crappy movie, actually."

Ella nudged Brian's knee. "Good research, boo."

"Only problem," Brian grimaced: "it says the bay is closed to tourism. Totally! It will be for two more years. *To repair ecological damage caused by excessive tourism.*"

Grace tossed the papers onto the bed. "Well, shit!"

"Okay," said Jack after a beat. "This throws us a bit of a curveball, doesn't it?"

Ella leaned forward. "Does your mom mention any plan B?"

Grace picked up the papers again, scanned the rest of the page, flipped to the next, sighed, and shook her head. "Nope. Looks like she goes on to talk about Woodstock, for some reason, and, um—"

"Woodstock?" Sage looked curious.

"I'm sure we can figure something out," said Brian. "It'll be okay."

Sage slid to the front of her seat. "So does she say anything about what screwed up their relationship and everything?" She scanned the room. "Sorry. I can't be the only one who wants to know."

"Sage, honey," said Ella. "Let's try to be respectful of the situation. Grace and Brian are hearing some challenging things for the first time. Who knows…?"

"Go ahead, Gracie," said Brian. "They stayed married. It can't be that bad. Do you want me to read it? Here." He held out his hand.

"No," Grace replied. "I'm good. Everybody good?" She looked around the room. "Okay." She squared her shoulders and started again in a measured voice. "*I hope you can forgive me for what I'm about to tell you. Forgive me for what I did, for starters, and also for telling you about it. I worry more about the latter, honestly.*" Grace paused, reaching up toward her mouth with her hand.

"Look," said Ella, adjusting her skirt. "Like I said. You guys may want to read the rest on your own. We'd be absolutely fine with that." Sage didn't seem entirely convinced.

"No," said Brian. "This is a whole-family thing. Mom clearly wanted that. Right?" He looked at his sister.

Grace drew in a deep breath, then nodded. "Okay. Where was I ? Okay.

I worry more about the latter, honestly. I can hear Dad's voice saying something about sleeping dogs. But then I can also hear your voices saying, 'When did Mom ever listen to Dad?'"

Grace looked up, grinning now. "Mom drew a smiley face there. Except, with her Parkinson's, it looks more like a bird with one eye on a stalk. Like a lobster." She held the page up for everyone to see. "Oh, Mom!" she sighed, raising the papers once more. "*As I said earlier, I don't want to leave this life with any dark secrets, especially secrets from the people I've loved the most. Frank knew from the start, because I was smart enough to know that he had to. I suppose I could have promised to be faithful to him in my wedding vows and just stood by that promise without being open about what went on before. It wouldn't have been right, though.*"

Grace paused to swallow. The rest of them stared at her fixedly. Only Sage looked elsewhere, eying Ella with an eyebrow cocked, as though to say, *I told you so.*

"*Enough of this introductory rigamarole. You remember—I'm sure I never let you forget!—your mother went to Woodstock. Loved it! A highlight of my life! Sadly, Dad couldn't go. He insisted I go without him, though, sweet man that he was. So I grabbed my friends Sally and Suzanne and we hitched up to Yasgur's Farm for all four days. We took sleeping bags and extra clothes, but we never thought to take a tent. The first night we slept under what we hoped would be the stars, but it started to rain just before midnight. It went all night and was still drizzling in the morning. All three of us were drenched. We put on dry clothes to start the day, but it was cold enough that we had to use our wet sleeping bags to try to stay warm, and that got our dry clothes wet, too. Then the sun came out that afternoon when John Sebastian was playing."*

"Should I know who John Sebastian was?" asked Sage.

"Does it matter?" asked Ella.

"I guess not," replied Sage. "Sorry."

Grace smiled and went back to reading. *"We were good until maybe 9:30, when it started raining toads. But we'd met some guys from Syracuse, and they had a tent in the woods so, about 2:00 in the morning, we went back there with them. I remember Janis Joplin was playing, and the sound of the rain on the canvas with Janis singing in the background was beyond describing—like we were in the middle of a hurricane of art or something. But, as you can imagine, these guys had a bunch of pot and we smoked a lot and when they told us we'd never get warm unless we took off our wet clothes and jumped into sleeping bags with them, it naturally made perfect sense."* Grace paused, blinked, and read on softly. *"And that's how I cheated on your dad."* She closed her eyes and clasped the pages against her chest. "Oh, Mom!"

"Okay," Brian half whispered. Ten seconds passed silently, save for the muffled clamor of the quayside throngs below. "Is that it?"

Grace shook her head.

Brian looked around the room. "Should we go on?"

"It's up to you all," said Ella.

"What do you think, Gracie?" Brian asked.

"I don't know. This..."

"What the hell!" said Brian. "It's not like any of us didn't have premarital sex, right? Mom was at Woodstock. Trying not to freeze to death. Listening to Janis Joplin, for God's sake. Mother Teresa would have done the dirty if she'd been there."

Grace sighed. "*I...was with this really cute guy with Neil Young hair and a body like Jesus.*" She paused again.

Brian shifted nervously in his seat. "'A body like Jesus.' What in hell does that mean?"

"Slender? Heavenly?" replied Grace." "I don't know. It clearly impressed Mom."

Jack patted her knee gently. "Why don't you go on, H.P.?"

Grace took a deep breath and forged on. "*It was pretty sublime, I have to say. Your dad was good enough in bed, but...okay.*" Grace handed the papers to Brian and firmly crossed her arms.

"We can stop," said Ella. She looked at Brian. "Really. This is clearly hard on Gracie."

"You think it's a walk in the park for *me*?" Brian looked from Ella to the rest of them. "This is just fucking weird, now."

Grace began to laugh, almost to herself.

"What?" asked Brian.

"All these years? All these years you made fun of me when Mom would say or do something that embarrassed me. You said I was such a squirrely prude?"

Brian stared at her, biting his lip. Then he slowly nodded. "Okay. Touché! But this is Freud squared. Right?"

"We get it," said Ella.

"Here." Grace reached out for the papers. "There's not much left. I can finish up." She smoothed the sheets and began again. "*Your dad was good enough in bed, but there was something about the whole scene that night that I could never in my wildest dreams have imagined. We finally got to sleep, I don't know what time, and when I woke up, the Incredible String Band was most of the way through their set. The last song they played was 'When You Find Out Who You Are.' And that's, really, when I did find out! Sadly, but there it is! That's not quite the whole story. I'm tired now, though, and what I'll tell you next would be better to hear about in Rome.*

I love you, and my heart leaps to think of you in that wondrous lagoon."

Grace sat wide-eyed, breathing deeply. "Well," she said, her voice quavering, "that was—"

"'Intense' doesn't quite do it, does it?" said Brian.

Grace re-folded the papers and slipped them back into the envelope.

"Almost…I don't know," said Jack. "Hippie soft-core?"

"That's really helpful, Jack." Grace re-crossed her arms.

"Your mother sounds so cool," Sage said to Brian. "Maybe that's where you get it from."

Brian looked stunned.

"She's so honest and spontaneous and, you know, sexy. Balling a stranger at Woodstock. I can't wait to tell Tokiko."

KO PHI PHI

For all of Cinny's teasing through the years, Grace could never have imagined that the Posey funereal pilgrimage would uncover intimate details of her mother's sexual adventures. One travel nightmare Grace *had* consciously dreaded, however, almost came to pass shortly after their flight touched down in Krabi.

They were slated to leave Singapore just after noon. Waiting for the flight, Jack made his rounds of the terminal's multiple luxury watch shops. He came away unscathed, save for a Montblanc rollerball he felt would nicely round out his Meisterstück collection. Ella, with Brian in tow, browsed through Gucci and Bottega Veneta before a silk chiffon baby-doll at La Perla attracted her notice. The price would have better suited a swish cocktail dress, but Brian insisted she try it on. When they agreed that even Kingsley would stand up and bark if he ever saw her wearing it, she decided at least one self-indulgent memento from such a special trip was affordable. Brian laughed and pointed out that she'd be indulging him as well. While Chelsea and Sage meandered through less tony shops, Grace bought a bottle of water and settled at their gate with her McEwan.

The flight to Krabi was largely routine, although Brian barely quelled total panic in a seat that would have been tight quarters for a stunted chimp. Fortunately, they were aloft barely long enough for the cabin crew to complete the beverage service, and he was soon deplaning with the others and marching off to Thai passport control. A pleasant woman in a green uniform asked him, Ella, and Sage how long they'd be staying in Thailand. Three nights, Brian told her. She shook her head and tutted, "Too short! Too short! Where will you be going?" When Brian mentioned Ko Phi Phi, the woman smiled and promised they'd love the island. Were they aware, though, that the "famous Maya Bay" was closed to tourism? They were, Brian told her. Sadly.

They'd just pulled their checked luggage from the carousel and were heading *en masse* through the "Nothing to Declare" exit when a skeletally thin man in what looked like a military uniform waved Brian over.

"Check luggage," he said flatly.

"I have nothing to declare," responded Brian, glancing at Grace.

"Check luggage," the man repeated, motioning toward the door to his right. "Random check."

"Damn!" said Grace, softly. She looked at the man and smiled—the Martha Stewart *I'm being gracious but don't cross me* smile she hated herself for deploying, but sometimes resorted to in stressful situations. "Do we all have to go?"

The man shook his head. "Just him." He pulled at the collar of his shirt, which was several sizes too big.

"May I go with him?" asked Ella, stepping forward. "I'm his wife, and this is our daughter." She pointed to Sage, who had locked eyes with Chelsea and was shaking her head.

"Yes," the man said glumly and waved them through.

"You go ahead in the other line," Brian told Grace. "We'll meet you on the other side."

Grace looked at her watch. "Our boat leaves in an hour and a half."

"We'll be fine," said Brian. "And if we're delayed, we can call the hotel and go over tomorrow. We've got a whole day to mess around with."

Grace nodded in resignation and set off through the other door with Jack and Chelsea.

Brian, Ella, and Sage stepped through the indicated passage and walked up to a steel table, behind which a uniformed man and woman stood with dour expressions. The man gestured to the table. Brian lifted his bag onto the shiny surface. "This, too?" he asked, holding up his carry-on.

The man nodded. He had some sort of scaly skin eruption on his cheek, maybe impetigo. Now and then he pulled his mouth to the side as though to stretch it.

"Do you have to see our things, too?" asked Ella. She looked rattled as she pointed toward Sage.

The man shook his head.

The customs woman laid her hands on Brian's big roller bag and scanned his face. "I may?"

"Sure. Whatever." He stepped back next to Ella and put his arm around her waist, clicking softly.

The woman turned the bag and reached for the zipper. She pulled it open, laid back the top, and began to search delicately through the contents. The blue rubber gloves she wore gave her the air of a surgeon pulling a stomach and intestines aside to take a good look at a pair of kidneys. After a minute of searching, she pushed all the contents back into place and zipped the bag shut. She stared at Brian and indicated he should take the bag off the table. She moved on to the carry-on, which for some reason she unzipped more carefully than the checked bag, as though she thought it might disgorge a coiled gag snake. She extracted an *Outside* magazine and a fleece, looked beneath them, and gave a little grunt. The man next to her leaned forward and looked in.

"What is this?" he asked, tipping the bag and pointing to the plastic canister holding Frank Posey's ashes.

"Those are my father's ashes," said Brian. He looked at Ella, who seemed increasingly unsettled. Sage, meanwhile, looked increasingly peeved.

"Cremation?" asked the man.

"Yes."

"Open them." The man stood back. He bent toward the woman and whispered something into her ear. She nodded and walked briskly away.

Brian reached into the bag and extracted the blue plastic canister. "Open, you say?"

"Open."

Brian held the canister in the crook of his left arm and unscrewed the top. "Here," he said, tilting the container so that the man could see inside.

The man looked carefully and then reached into his breast pocket for a retractable ballpoint pen. He handed it to Brian. "Move ashes. So I see."

Brian looked at Ella and then did as he was asked, stirring the pen through the ash and bone as the man peered in. It occurred to Brian that bits of his father were getting forced up into the barrel of the pen, perhaps to jam it when the officer next tried to use it, perhaps simply to drop out in his pocket. The thought of his father's remains staining a sweaty seam annoyed him to the brink of anger.

The woman came back with a man in a rumpled suit. He spoke to the first man in Thai and then looked into the container. Without being asked, Brian stirred the ashes again, tapped the pen against the rim of the canister, and handed it back to its owner,

"These are ashes of your father?" the man asked.

"Yes."

"What name?"

"Frank Posey. Francis Xavier Posey."

"You have papers?"

"Yes," replied Brian. He gestured toward his carry-on. When the man nodded, Brian reached in and, after a brief rummage, pulled out an envelope labeled *Dad*. He opened the loose flap and removed several sheets of paper, one of them the letter from Tuttle's Funeral Home. He handed it to the man.

The man in the suit looked at the letter carefully, turned it over to inspect the back side, and returned it to Brian. "Passport?" he asked.

"Mine?"

The man nodded.

Brian reached into his breast pocket for his passport and handed it over. The man opened it and flipped through the pages with the bored affect of someone waiting at a garage for an oil change. "Brian Posey?"

"Yes. "

"Year of birth?"

"1978."

"Place?"

"Hanover, New Hampshire. U.S.A."

The man handed the passport back. He looked up and studied Brian intently. "You have drugs?"

"No." *Click.* "No drugs." *Click.*

"You are sure?"

"Of course I'm sure." He thought he heard Sage mutter "asshole" behind him. He turned to look. Her neck was bright red.

"Why is your jar not sealed?"

"Well," said Brian, "we were just in New Zealand and we left some of his ashes there. I replaced the sealed container with this one."

"You will leave these here?" asked the man, pointing to the container.

"Some of them. Yes."

"You know you need a permit to leave ashes in Thailand?"

"No."

"I can give you one."

"I don't think so," said Brian, bracing himself for a confrontation. "I looked up the regulations. The funeral director did as well. It's all in the letter."

The man waited a moment and then smiled. "You are well prepared. Have a good stay in our country. Please spend much money." He stepped back and motioned the trio toward the exit door.

"Jesus Christ!" muttered Sage as she followed Brian and her mother out of the room and into the open hall beyond.

Grace and Chelsea were waiting for them. Jack had tracked down transport to the ferry pier. They all piled into a well-worn Toyota van—marginally revitalized by what looked like a let-the-kids-have-fun multicolored paint job. The driver informed them, with obsequious chagrin, that the air-conditioning was still waiting to be fixed by his brother-in-law. As long as they were moving, the breeze through the open windows made the afternoon heat tolerable, but when traffic stopped—which was often—six people packed into two bench seats were clearly a couple of people too many. Grace pumped Brian for the details of the bag search. She'd been smart, he said, to get Tuttle's to cite the relevant regulations in their letter. There were a few benefits to being married to a lawyer, she remarked jovially, jabbing Jack in the ribs with her elbow.

A thirty-minute drive through teeming commercial neighborhoods brought them to the ferry terminal. The driver unloaded their bags and pointed to the ticket office. While Grace and Jack walked over to secure tickets, Brian paid the driver and, with Chelsea and Sage's help, moved all the luggage to a long wooden bench in a colonnaded waiting area.

Their boat wasn't leaving for forty minutes, but the waiting area was nearly full. Half the crowd, Jack estimated, was Asian—many of them Muslim, judging from the women's apparel. Sitting on their backpacks right in front of Brian and the others were two twenty-something couples. From their looks and from what Brian could glean from their sporadic conversation, they were Scandinavian. All four were tall, blonde, deeply tanned, and liberally pierced. The men wore pastel tank tops, darkened with sweat at the chest and back, over dirty cargo shorts and sandals. The women were clearly bra-less under their loose cotton sundresses. There was an androgynous quality about all four of them, the women square-shouldered and muscled, the men indolently graceful in their posture and expression. They had the look, waiting there, of perennial wanderers. Brian envied them the un-curated beauty of their bodies and the utter placidity of their manner.

Sage seemed driven to make their acquaintance. "You going to Ko Phi Phi?' she asked as she strolled up in front of the men. She slipped her hands into the back pockets of her shorts and stood there in a casual slouch.

The man on the right looked up with the trace of a smile, then turned to the woman sitting beside him. She fixed Sage with a cool glare. "Yes," said the man, turning back to Sage.

"Where are you staying?"

The man narrowed an eye and shrugged. "No plans. We find places."

Sage nodded. "So what can you tell me about marijuana on the island?"

The man laughed and looked back at the woman, who smiled in amusement.

"Sage! For God's sake!" hissed Ella, scanning the crowd on either side.

"You're not cops, are you," Sage asked the man.

He laughed again. "We are not cops." He grinned more broadly. "Are you?"

Sage snorted.

"Why are you asking about weed?" queried the man.

"I don't know," said Sage. She looked up to the roof and then off to the side. "Just curious."

"It's everywhere," said the man. "Just wait 'til you smell it somewhere. Follow your nose. That's the only safe way."

"Thanks," said Sage. "Have a nice trip!"

"You too, little American." He looked at his companion and grinned.

"Who says I'm American. I could be Canadian."

"No, you couldn't," said the man. "Canadians don't have such balls as you."

"Okay!" announced Grace, as she walked up with Jack. She handed tickets to each of the four. "Here you go. We board in ten minutes. Right over there."

"Well, that was dumb," said Ella once she and Sage had found seats in the enclosed cabin of the ferry.

"Thanks, Mom."

"Really. Asking right out in the open like that. Who knows who was listening?"

"I wasn't asking to buy any," said Sage. "I just asked him what he knew about it."

"Yeah, it's a slippery slope. And after what Brian went through at the airport? I mean, think about it."

"I am thinking," said Sage "About you, Mom." She bent over to her bag on the floor and pulled out her iPhone.

"Yeah, right."

"How's the insomnia, anyway?"

"I'll survive."

Crossing the eastern spur of the Andaman Sea took an hour and a half. The sun was still almost straight overhead, and it beat down on the azure waters with a fierce intensity. Brian and Chelsea slapped on sunscreen and stayed out on deck with the Scandinavians, watching for the limestone hills of Ko Phi Phi to break from the horizon and rise in forested majesty into the cloudless sky. Sage joined them halfway across, leaving Grace and Ella in the air-conditioned cabin. Jack had read too many accounts of Third World ferries capsizing, with huge loss of life, to feel comfortable belowdecks. Fearless on the rugby pitch, he had an innate dread of situations over which he had no control. He stood for the full ninety minutes in the shade of the cabin entrance, wondering fretfully about what kind of safety codes allowed for cabins with only a single narrow exit.

They rounded the southeast corner of the main island just as another ferry arrived from Phuket. With two ships docking simultaneously and hundreds of people surging ashore, it was a challenge finding their transfer boat to Paradise Resort. Eventually, a graceful wooden craft approached the pier with the hotel's name blazoned colorfully on its high-stemmed prow. It nosed onto the sand and a handsome young man in a blue sarong leaped out into the shallow water to ask if they were the Posey party. Brian said they were, and he and Jack began to carry the group's bags out into the light surf. Another man on board stowed the luggage and helped everyone clamber up over the side and into the boat, where they took their seats under a ragged canvas canopy.

"Off to Paradise," announced the second fellow, flashing white teeth. As his partner heaved them clear of the beach, he grabbed the end of a long spar on which a scavenged auto engine sat at a fulcrum point above the transom. Behind it, an eight- or ten-foot shaft extended back to a naked propeller. The man pressed the starter button and the engine coughed into life, its exhaust ports spewing clouds of black smoke. He raised the handle end, lowering the prop into the water. Twisting the throttle as his partner gave a last shove seaward and hopped in, the helmsman spun the craft on its axis and headed east down the beach through shoaling waves that pitched them from side to side.

"That's quite a rig!" yelled Jack to the helmsman over the engine's roar. "I've never seen anything like it."

The man smiled.

"I hope you never hit any swimmers with that unprotected prop."

"We try no," responded the man.

They progressed down the beach, peppered now and again by spray flying in over the bow.

Brian pointed out to a huge shark fin of limestone, two or three miles off to the south. Its rightmost face looked as high and sheer as El Capitan. "Is that Phi Phi Leh?" he shouted.

The man at the engine nodded. "Very beautiful."

"But the bay is closed, yes? Maya Bay?"

The man wagged his head from side to side. "Daytime."

"What do you mean, daytime?"

"Nighttime, nobody see."

"And you go out there?"

The man wiped at his brow and smiled. "Maybe."

Brian looked at Grace, who stared back at him wide-eyed. "How do we find out?" he asked.

"Talk to me at Paradise," the man said. "All things possible."

The Paradise Resort made no pretense to luxury, although its setting went a good way toward justifying its name. It sat nestled among groves of tall and elegant palms, hard on a lush, mile-long beach offering an unimpeded view of Phi Phi Leh on the southern horizon. Brian had read that the town center, which sprawled on a low, sandy isthmus between two bays, tended to be raucous at night, with its bars and dance clubs packed with partiers. He'd looked for a place a good way from town, and Paradise Resort offered enough value for the money to take some pressure off the rest of their expeditionary budget.

Once they waded their luggage ashore and were shown to their rooms, all six of them headed to the beach. The water was on the warm side of refreshing, but it was calm enough and extraordinarily clear. Chelsea and Sage kitted up with snorkeling gear from the front desk and chased each other and small, jewel-like fish around the limestone bollards that studded the honey-colored sand of the shallows. While Grace and Jack looked on from under a beach umbrella, Ella and Brian sat chest-deep in the water, jostled forward and back by the gentle surf.

"So what did he say?" asked Ella.

"The boat guy?"

"Yeah."

"Well, that he could take us."

"Wow! That was easier than I expected."

"But," Brian added, "it's going to cost us two hundred dollars, U.S. In cash."

"We've got that, I assume."

"I assume Jack does. He told me he came equipped for any irresistible black-market bargains." Brian chuckled.

"When could he take us?"

"Tomorrow, he said. After things shut down in town but before the moon rises."

"This is starting to feel like something out of *Dr. No*," said Ella.

"Yeah." A particularly large wave swept Brian over backwards. His head went under, and he bobbed back up sputtering.

"Thought I'd lost you there," joked Ella.

"No such luck. I'm in this for the long haul."

"Good." Ella goosed him playfully.

"Help!" Brian exclaimed. "Shark!"

Ella grabbed his head and kissed him hard on the lips.

They sat on quietly, peering out at Phi Phi Leh. What must have been an osprey wheeled about high above them, its wings utterly motionless.

"It won't be the hotel's boat," explained Brian.

"Really."

"He can't risk it. But he says his cousin has a good boat. Nothing to identify it. If anybody spots us, no one will be the wiser."

"What happens if we get caught?"

"We tell them we have a note from our mother."

Ella clocked him on the bicep.

"He said it would just cost us another two hundred or so. Nobody in Thailand goes to jail over this kind of shit."

"Which, when you think about it, is really sad."

"It is," agreed Brian. "But it's not like we're going to poach baby elephant tusks. And I promise not to pee in the water. How about you?"

"Now you tell me."

They walked half a mile back toward town for dinner at a tony resort that featured live music and an elaborate waterside dining deck. The sun had dropped below the hills west of the pier, but a bright aura lingered, bathing the six of them and everything around them in a warm, coral glow. Waiting for their drinks to arrive, they listened as the waves tumbled softly just yards away and a chorus of peepers chanted in the inland trees.

"Did anyone else see that big tsunami warning?" Jack slapped at a mosquito on his arm.

Ella turned abruptly. "For tonight?"

Jack laughed. "Oh. Sorry. Just the sign by the hotel. About the sirens and how to find the routes to high ground."

Ella sighed in relief. "God, you scared me. I thought you'd gotten an alert on your phone or something."

"Sorry!" said Jack. "I didn't mean to panic anybody. It's just that I'm rarely anywhere these days where they warn you about tsunamis, is all."

"Just about rising sea levels," said Sage. "And who cares when watery disaster creeps in over several decades."

"Sage, sweetie," said Ella. "We're trying to enjoy ourselves right now."

"That's what they all say," replied Sage. "You and Exxon and everybody else."

"There *was* a big tsunami a while back," said Jack. "A thousand people drowned, I read. Another thousand missing. Never found them."

"Jeez!" said Chelsea.

"But this wouldn't be such a bad place to cash it in," said Jack. "In a setting like this. Doing what you love."

"Provided what you love involves getting smashed against a concrete wall by a twenty-foot wave," said Grace.

"Gracie can be such a buzzkill," said Brian. "But then she's had years of practice."

Grace was about to flip her brother off when the waitress came back with their drinks. She passed them around, and Jack raised a toast to Cinny and Frank.

"Anyway," said Grace, setting her glass down on a napkin. "When it comes to local danger, I think we're more likely to be arrested for trespassing out in Maya Bay than to get swept away by a tidal wave. Don't you think?"

Jack nodded. "I wonder how likely it is that they patrol out there. And what happens if they catch you going into the bay?"

"Maybe we shouldn't be talking about this in public," said Chelsea. She glanced warily at the other tables.

"Maybe you're right," said Grace.

"We're scouting out the town after we eat," said Chelsea, looking at Sage. "We'll see if anybody has any useful info on the local constabulary."

"*The local constabulary,*" snorted Jack. "I swear you and Mom talk like you sleep with a thesaurus under your pillow. Just be careful in town."

"We'll be the souls of discretion," said Chelsea. "Won't we, Sage?"

"I know *you* will," replied Sage. "But science tells me my prefrontal lobe is still the size of a walnut."

Lubricated by a meal's worth of drinks and two shared bottles of Prosecco to wrap the evening up, Brian got back to the room and insisted Ella model her scandalously expensive new nightwear for him. She was happy to oblige and pranced gaily around the room and over the bed, back and forth and back again, as Brian chased her with her discarded bra clenched in his teeth. He caught her just outside the bathroom door, grabbed her around the waist, and heaved her giggling onto the bed. "Omigod, the drapes are totally open!" she cried. "All the better to see you with, my dear," he replied, commencing an amorous onslaught that moved by degrees from comic to climactic.

Two doors down, Grace tried reading some more McEwan, only to discover that, as hard as she tried to make sense of the lines and characters that were clearly visible *right there on the page*, her level of intoxication kept her totally flummoxed.

Jack quickly showered and, just as quickly, fell asleep. He dreamed he was sitting at his desk in his office in Westport when he heard a distant siren wind up into an ear-piercing wail. His executive assistant ran down the hall yelling, *Tsunami!* No sooner had she voiced the warning than the window behind Jack blew in with a crush of water and he found himself whirled away by the flood, twisted this way and that, struggling to determine which way was up. He looked down at his wrist, no doubt to consult his beloved Sea-Dweller in order to calculate how long he might survive without a revitalizing breath, but it was gone—nothing there but a ghostly gap in his tan! He spun around and saw his senior partner, Knight Phillips, sinking into the depths with a smile on his lips and waving at Jack with his right hand—a kind of *toodle-oo* flutter of the fingers. Chained to Knight's left wrist, pulling him strongly down, was a huge, glowing jeweler's display case filled with an array of elegant timepieces, with what looked like Jack's Rolex among them. Jack watched his partner vanish below him, tiny bubbles leaking from his mouth, then kicked out with his feet and pulled with his arms and made desperately for the surface.

"Stop thrashing, for God's sake," called Grace from the darkness beside him. "It's like I'm in bed with an epileptic cheerleader!"

"Sorry," said Jack. He groped for and finally found his watch on the nightstand next to him. "I was having a horrible dream."

Chelsea and Sage wandered into town to check out the local nightlife. They needn't have worried about the Thai drinking age being twenty; prominent signs outside the first two bars they walked past declared, *We Do Not I.D.* They entered the third, a moderately crowded place with a huge bar in the center of the covered pavilion. They found a pair of open barstools, climbed up, and ordered two glasses of white wine. Chelsea took a pack of cigarettes out of her purse, laid it on the bar, looked at it, and popped it back in her purse just as the bartender brought the drinks. They'd hardly had a chance to clink and start scanning the clientele when a heavyset man in his late thirties or early forties stumbled into Sage, pushing her against the front of the bar. His breath reeked of hard spirits, and she thought she heard him make a kissy noise as his cheek scraped past her ear.

"Oh. Sorry, sweetie," he said, straightening up with a lewd grin.

Sage looked at Chelsea, then coolly took another sip of wine.

"I said I'm sorry, sweetie," the man said more loudly, pushing at Sage's shoulder with his fist. From his accent, he was North American.

Sage turned toward him with a steely gaze. "I heard you the first time."

"So?"

"You did that on purpose."

"Maybe." The man's tongue flicked obscenely at the corner of his mouth.

"Get lost. You're fucking drunk."

"Whoa!" cried the man, wobbling slightly. "Aren't you the feisty little bitch!"

Chelsea leaned over to Sage. "Come on. Let's split." She reached into her purse for cash to leave for the tab.

"I got this," said Sage. She turned back to the man, who was steadying himself on the edge of the bar. "Why don't you go home to bed while you can still find your way?"

"Man, oh man, you're a hot little shit!" The man swiped at his nose with a forefinger. "Speaking of bed, my buddy over there can take care of your friend and I'll just saddle you up and ride all night. *All* night!"

"I'm sixteen, asshole."

"Well," said the man, tipping his head back to leer down his nose, "last I heard, fifteen's legal around here. So how about it?"

Sage squared up to stare the man straight in the eye. "Where are you from?"

"Ah," he said, grinning toothily. "Gettin' a little more friendly. Good to see, sweetie."

"I said, where are you from?"

"Missouri. Kansas City, Missouri."

"And do you get to fuck sixteen-year-olds in Kansas City?"

"Well, you *can,* but—"

"You're fucking pitiful." Sage turned to Chelsea. "Okay. Let's go."

The man grabbed Sage's shoulder. "Wait a minute. Where you goin'? We're just gettin' acquainted."

"Look!" Sage slid off the stool, pushing him back a step with her forearms. "You may come to Thailand and think it's okay to pork every chick you can lay your hands on, but—"

"Like this?" The man reached out and grabbed her breasts.

Sage clasped her hands together and shot her arms upwards, elbows spread. The man's wrists flew apart and he staggered backwards, not so far that Sage couldn't whip her knee upward and deal him a glancing blow to the groin. Chelsea pulled Sage toward the door, but the man lurched after them, stumbling over Sage's stool but gaining momentum. He'd almost grabbed Sage when he suddenly spun around and fell back against a neighboring table. Grasping his elbow was the wiry young man Sage had spoken with at the ferry terminal. At his shoulder was one of the lanky women. She brandished a full wine bottle like a club.

"Should we say good night?" the younger man asked him. "You've had your fun, I think."

"What the—?"

"Look, now. You've upset my little sister, haven't you?" He turned to Sage, who nodded blankly.

The blonde woman moved closer, gazing down at the bottle like a duelist checking a pistol.

"Okay," said the older man, collecting himself. "Okay." A blob of spittle clung to his lower lip. He wiped it away with his wrist. "I don't need any trouble."

"Perhaps you should apologize," said the woman.

"No thanks," said Sage. "Just get him out of here."

The couple pulled the man toward the door, but he wrenched an arm free and pointed to a table on the other side of the bar. The three exchanged inaudible words, and the man walked unsteadily across the floor to rejoin the group he'd been with—two middle-aged men and a worn-looking woman. As Sage's molester approached them, one man stood up and slapped his fellow on the back, tossing his head with laughter.

Sage looked back at the blond couple. "Thanks," she said softly. "That was helpful."

"Oh my God!" said Chelsea. "Thank you both so much."

"You're welcome," said the man. "These assholes are everywhere in Thailand."

"Sex tourists," spat the woman, huskily. "Fucking pigs."

"Right," said Sage. "Well, it's time we get back to our hotel." She looked at Chelsea, who nodded. "Thanks! Really!"

"You are walking?" asked the man. "You know the way?"

"Of course," answered Sage.

"Before you go. You asked about marijuana?"

Sage snorted. "Yeah. I guess."

"Come with us," he said with a Mona Lisa smile. "I think tonight we are your lucky stars."

Grace and Chelsea woke the next morning before anyone else and carried their coffees out to beach chairs close to the water. The sun was just off the horizon and cast their shadows a dozen yards down the sand.

"You're obviously spending a lot of time with Sage," said Grace, once they'd settled in. "How's it going?"

"Fine. I really like her."

"Dad and I do, too. We just wondered how it is, spending so much time with a teenager. Rooming with her. On the flights and all."

"Yeah. Well, I'm used to hanging out with Grant's daughters. Sage is a hell of a lot more grown up than they are."

Grace laughed. "You could say that. It's good of you, though. Kind. How was the trip into town last night?"

Chelsea scoffed. "Interesting."

Grace set her cup on the table between them and turned toward her daughter. "How so? Anybody try to serve you Thai corpse tea?"

Chelsea laughed. "Nothing *quite* so weird."

Chelsea recounted the adventure, as Grace sat back in her chair, shaking her head now and again. "God, that's so frightening," she said once Chelsea was done.

"I know," Chelsea nodded. "The guy, for starters. But then Sage, and the way she went off on him so fast. Not just verbally. Physically, too. And he towered over her."

"I'm glad I didn't see it," sighed Grace. "It would have scared the bejesus out of me."

"I've never been through anything like that. I never want to again."

Grace picked up her cup. "Brian says they really have their hands full with her sometimes."

"That's pretty clear."

"She's almost gotten thrown out of school a half dozen times. Ella says the principal calls her the love child of Joan of Arc and She-Hulk."

Chelsea laughed.

"Brian says she's got a real thing about older men taking advantage of young women. Her dad was apparently a real jerk. *Is* a real jerk. He dumped Ella and took up with a couple of bimbos. Twins."

"Not that there's anything wrong with twins." Chelsea winked.

"Well, I'd say the jury's still out."

Chelsea smiled and gazed out over the gentle surf. "Sage asked me about Grant."

"She did?"

"Yeah. She asked if there was anything creepy about him. As I got to know him. I obviously said there wasn't."

"Obviously." Grace looked over with an eyebrow slightly raised.

"Mom!"

"I know. Grant's a great guy."

"He is. I wouldn't be with him otherwise."

"I know," sighed Grace. "We know. We raised you to be smart."

They spent a gorgeous morning lingering over the buffet, swimming in the shallow water off the beach, and reading in the shade as the breeze coursed gently through the palms. Around four, they rode into town with Dusit, the boatman Brian had contracted for that evening's trip out to Maya Bay. The last ferries hadn't left for Krabi and Phuket, and the shops and bars were still jammed with day tourists. Riding back to Paradise Resort, Dusit confirmed that he and his cousin would be at the beach to pick them up shortly after one a.m.

Brian knocked on Grace and Jack's door at 12:20 to say that the boat was there. Dusit and his cousin had seen that the town was winding down early and decided to take advantage of the extra time. Within five minutes, everyone was gathered on the cement patio between the breakfast cabana and the beach. Lamps at either end of the hotel bar lit the scene faintly. Overhead, a million stars shone unblinking in the crystalline air.

Brian touched Grace on the shoulder. "Got the ashes?"

"Fucking hell!" said Grace. She and Brian had done their sorting that afternoon. Grace had put the bags on the table right next to the door so she couldn't possibly forget them. She'd forgotten them.

Three minutes later, Grace was back and the six of them left the patio and crossed the beach. A boat smaller than the hotel's was nosed up onto the sand. Dusit stood there with his hand resting on the high prow.

"Sawasdee," he said, with a toothy smile. "Good evening, you say?"

"Yes," said Chelsea. "Good evening. Sawasdee."

Dusit gestured toward a youth grinning at them from the boat. "This is Cousin Chati." The young man waved shyly.

"The boat looks small," said Brian. "Will we all fit?"

"Oh, yes." Dusit nodded energetically. "All fit."

"Is it big enough to go all the way out there? In the big waves?"

"Oh, yes. All fit just fine." He motioned for everyone to wade out and climb aboard.

One after another they strode into the water, put their hands on the gunwale, and jumped up, swinging one leg in after the other. As Sage boarded, Chati grinned at her in that insipid, aroused-dog way males will in the company of attractive females. Sage rolled her eyes as she moved on to the middle bench, with Chelsea close behind. Jack took a seat near the engine, next to Grace. He adjusted himself on the bench, wriggled again, and reached down with his hand. "Ooh!"

"What is it, dear?" asked Grace.

Jack stood up and twisted around to look at the seat of his pants. "Shine a light?"

Grace pulled her phone from her jacket pocket and switched the light on. "Looks like oil."

Jack smelled his fingers. "Shit! It *is* oil."

"Engine oil," confirmed Chati with an enthusiastic nod. "Change oil today. Spill some. All okay. Plenty in engine." He signaled to Dusit to shove them out and turned to the engine. He pressed the starter button once, twice, and the machinery coughed into life with a reassuring robustness. As Chati angled them around, the waves caught the little boat square on the beam. For a few uncomfortable seconds, they pitched violently from side to side as though they might capsize. Soon they were headed straight out from the shore, taking the moderate swells straight on the bow.

"How long to Maya Bay?" Brian asked Dusit, sitting on the bench beside him.

"Half hour, maybe. Unless Chati get lost." Brian turned toward the man. He was grinning. "No worry. Chati good sailor."

Brian looked out past the bow. He could see nothing but stars, blocked in one vertical swath by the high prow. There was no sign at all of the island that, in daylight, dominated the southern horizon. "Do we have a compass?" he asked.

"No compass. Chati good sailor."

Brian heard the rasp of a lighter behind him and turned to see Ella lighting a sizeable joint. Sage bent toward her in the glow, smiling happily.

"Your wife?" asked Dusit.

Brian nodded. Dusit slapped Brian's knee and chuckled. Suddenly, on the starboard bow, the horizon lit up with a low, pulsing flash.

"Looks like a storm," said Brian.

"No worry," said Dusit. "Far away. Probably go there." He pointed off to the right. "Phuket."

Brian felt a nudge in his back and turned to see Ella offering him the joint. He grabbed it, took a toke, and held it up to Dusit. He shook his head. "My wife smell it. Tell me I go to hell." He laughed loudly.

Brian handed the joint back to Ella. "Tell me, Dusit. Do the police ever patrol out here? After dark?"

"Sometimes."

"What if they stop us?"

"Here?"

"Yes."

"We say we go around Phi Phi Leh. No problem. Little night trip is all."

"And how about in Maya Bay?"

"That be other thing. But no worry. A fine is all, yes? You pay, no problem."

They slashed along for ten minutes with the brisk wind in their faces. Jack and Grace waved the joint away, but Chelsea joined the circle, and when Ella and Sage began to hum bits and pieces of Beatles songs, she joined in. The lightning to the southwest continued off and on, never seeming to get much closer, until one of its snakings across the horizon came up against utter blackness left of the prow. Jack squinted hard and saw that the stars, too, were blocked by something massive.

"Phi Phi Leh." Dusit pointed to the center of the mass. "Chati good. No compass? No worry."

Brian laughed. "What if he'd missed?"

"Go home and try again." Dusit turned and pointed back toward the main island, where the lights of town stretched out behind them like a sparkling necklace.

For three or four minutes, the huge wedge of the island masked more and more stars until Chati veered to the right and they began to pass along its towering flanks. When lightning flickered now, what had seemed like a hole in the heavens revealed itself to be solid rock.

"My God," said Jack. "It *is* like Yosemite. In the middle of the ocean. I just wish we could see it better."

"It's cooler that we can't," said Sage. "You can imagine anything up there. Giant bats hanging from the crags. Toruks from *Avatar*. A huge Banksy mural."

"Smoke much?" asked Brian.

Sage laughed.

Another five minutes and they'd rounded a tall headland. To the left, a U of stars dipped close to the horizon, flanked by pillars of total blackness.

"Maya Bay," said Dusit. He turned to the others. "Everybody stay down. Police see now, they shoot." He paused a second, then broke into gales of laughter. Chati joined in, their cackles reverberating eerily off the sheer wall as they passed.

"Just the way I want to meet my maker," said Jack. "Yachting with my pothead relatives, with my butt drenched in motor oil." He laughed as he leaned over to kiss Grace.

It was darker in the mouth of the bay than outside, but they could feel they were entering some kind of bowl with an uneven rim of blackness, backlit by the stars. The waves had calmed substantially, and the engine had a fuller note as its echo rebounded from the shore.

"Before," said Dusit, "when boats come every day, sometime there no place to come on shore. Tourists jump off and swim. Boats stay out here and wait."

"I've heard," said Brian. "Thousands of people a day."

"Thousands," agreed Dusit. "Millions." He laughed. "*Millions!*" he shouted, his voice bouncing back to them loudly.

Brian flinched. "C'mon, man. Quiet!"

Dusit laughed. "No one here. You hear any gun shoot? No one but us."

Chati throttled back. The bow settled, and they heard the water gurgling along the side. Another minute and everyone pitched forward as the hull grated to a halt on the sandy bottom. "Okay," said Chati as he switched off the engine.

There was an eerie silence, an absence of sound in which the clacking pistons lingered as a ghost tone. Suddenly, from behind them, came the distant rumble of thunder, rolling and sustained.

"I guess we couldn't hear that over the engine," said Brian.

"No worry," said Dusit. "Still far away." He leaped up. "Here. I jump in, pull boat up. Help you out." He was over the side in a flash.

"Ladies first," said Jack. "I'll let you all get ashore before I cast my butt oil upon the waters."

"I'd rather you gents went first and helped us out," said Grace. "Go ahead, dear. I'll leap into your arms."

"Such an offer," said Jack, as another roll of thunder swelled behind them.

"Let's hurry," said Brian, "Remember. Hold your phones high." With no further ceremony, he leaped over the side. His feet hit bottom and he found himself waist deep in the gentle waves. "Gracie, don't forget the ashes."

They were soon ashore.

"You take care of business," said Dusit. "I and Chati wait 'til you come back. Unless we hear tigers."

"Very funny," said Jack. "Remind me to tell TripAdvisor how hilarious you are."

"Hilarious?"

"Funny," said Jack.

"Ah, thank you. Thank you."

By the light of their phones, they took stock of where they were. Thirty yards inland stood a thick screen of trees that stretched as far to the right and left as they could see. The sand at their feet looked undisturbed by human traffic, marked only by a thin line of vegetative flotsam where the last tide had peaked.

"Mom said to head into the woods on the right," said Brian. "Onward and upward." He set off across the sand with the others following. They darted the lights of their phones here and there in the darkness, as though they were six of the seven dwarves heading home after a long day's work, with strong suspicions that Dwarf Number Seven was hiding along their path, ready to jump out from behind a tree. Reaching the end of the beach, they turned inland through a gap in the palms. Fifty yards on, just beyond a slight rise, they came across a stream fed by a noisy cascade farther up and to the right. Brian stepped into the water and bent to scoop some up.

"Fresh," he said, licking his lips. He turned, redirecting his beam, and pointed to a flat spot upstream where the palms were spaced such that their canopy might offer shade throughout the day. "That looks promising." He waded out of the water and loped to the spot with brisk strides. He spun around slowly, shining the light near and far. "What do you think, Gracie? Looks like the kind of place Mom and Dad might have humped their way to spiritual renewal."

"Jesus, Brian!" muttered Grace.

"What?" Brian looked nonplussed.

"You and Mom! Can you maybe give the raunchy shit a rest?" Chelsea stepped closer, but Grace waved her away. "I mean, really. If there was ever a time to give being clever a pass." She held up the bag of ashes. "Too much to ask, though, huh?"

"Jeez, Gracie," mumbled Brian. "I didn't…shit!"

"Look," said Ella quietly. "Time out. Gracie, Brian was out of tune with the gravity of the moment. We can all see that."

"I was just—"

Ella held her hand up to stop him. The sky to the southwest flickered with pale light, then flickered more brightly.

"Okay," said Brian, shoulders slumped. "I apologize. To everyone. I don't know what I was thinking. I was being a goof. But you're right. Mom and Dad…" A rumble of thunder cut him off. "Right!" he said. "Let's do this. This spot okay? Everybody?"

"I'd camp out here," said Sage. "If that's any help. Nice and flat. Nice stream." She raised her light toward the overhanging fronds. "Rockin' tree cover."

"Okay," said Brian. "How about right over here?" He took half a dozen paces toward a medium-sized boulder flanked by two palms.

"Perfect," said Chelsea.

Brian turned to Grace. "You've got the ashes?"

"Yup."

He walked over and held out his hands. "Sorry, Tiger," he said as she laid the bags into them. "Really."

Grace nodded coolly and walked back to Jack, who put his arm around her.

Brian knelt and scraped the sand away from the base of the rock, scooping out a depression the size of a large salad bowl. He opened the bags and set them down next to the hole. "Anyone want to say anything?" He twisted around to look at the others. "Jack. What you read last time was perfect. Do you have anything for now?"

"I don't think so. Thanks, but…whatever."

Chelsea edged forward and scuffed at the sand with her toe. "I just want to say how happy I am to be here with all of you. And how glad I am that Nana and Pop Pop have given us all this chance to be together and honor the life they had with each other."

"Hear, hear!" said Jack.

"If this place is the place that allowed them to go on and live the lives they were meant to live ... and to have Mom and Uncle Brian and everything else ... then this truly is a blessed spot." She bobbed her head emphatically.

Grace stepped over to embrace her. "That was perfect, sweetie. And this is a blessed place. No matter what my stupid ass brother does to muck it up." She sniggered and kicked sand in Brian's direction.

"Okay," said Brian, turning back to the depression in the sand. "Let me…" His voice wavered. "Let me take care of them." He lifted the bags and tipped them forward, spilling the ashes into the hole. He shook the bags once, shifted them some, and shook them again. "There," he said, folding the bags and slipping them into his pocket. He picked up a handful of sand and cast it in on top of the ashes. It fell on them soundlessly. He stood and turned to the others, bending to brush off his knees. "Go ahead, if you want. Mom said to mix the sand in with them. And you can say your goodbyes."

Grace followed all the rest. She spoke so softly no one could hear what she was saying, but she swayed gently from side to side in some timeless mantra of farewell. When she was finished, she reached out wide and swept the last of the sand over Cinny and Frank's ashes. A rumble of thunder surged behind them as though to signal the finality of the moment.

"Come on." Brian reached down to help Grace to her feet. "We love you, Mom and Dad. But we gotta be going."

They splashed back through the stream and hurried down the beach, where Dusit and Chati sat quietly beside a small fire.

"Ready?" asked Dusit, rising to his feet.

"Definitely," said Brian. "Looks like the storm is coming in."

Dusit looked up and shrugged. "Maybe."

They clambered aboard. As Dusit shoved the boat out into the water, Chati went to start the engine. The starter whirred and stopped. It whirred and stopped again, once more, before the engine sputtered, seemed to take life, then fell silent. Another whir. Another.

"No gas," called Dusit from the water beside the boat.

"We're out of gas?" asked Brian. "You've got to be kidding."

Dusit laughed. "I tell Chati to fill up. Chati never listen."

"What are you saying?" Jack leaped up and looked back and forth between the two boatmen. "So, we're, like, stuck out here? For the whole night? With this storm coming in?" He gestured to the sky behind him, where lightning played, as he spoke, through the bellies of towering clouds.

Dusit laughed again and said something to Chati in Thai. Chati kicked aside a piece of canvas and grabbed a jerry can from the floor of the boat. "Plenty gas," he said. "Dusit full of shit."

He uncapped the tank that fed the engine and tipped in the spout of the jerry can. The reek of gasoline enveloped the boat, but Chati didn't spill a drop. He screwed both caps back, threw the jerry can back under the tarp, and turned to the engine. One crank. Two cranks. The engine burst into life, sputtered a stroke or two, and settled into a stable rhythm. Dusit held the boat out in the deeper water while Chati spun it around and, as Dusit leaped into the bows, throttled up and got them under way toward the bay's entrance as another web of lighting spread across the southwestern sky.

By the time they reached open water, it was clear the storm would reach them before they made it back to Phi Phi Don.

"Should we just stay out here until it passes?" Brian asked Dusit.

"Everything good."

"Are you sure? Really. It looks—'

"No good to be here in morning. Everything good now."

With every flash of lightning, they could see immense clouds boiling toward them. As they rounded the headland, the lights of the distant town leaped up reassuringly in front of them, strung across the horizon like stars strewn on a tabletop. But the wind rose by the minute—a chill torrent now, instead of the warm zephyrs they'd encountered on the way out.

"What do you think?" Brian asked again, struggling to sound calm.

"All good," said Dusit out of the darkness. "No worry. Small storm.

Chati good. Boat good." He slapped the gunwale with his palm.

"If you say so." Brian turned to the others, huddled grimly behind him like prisoners riding a tumbrel to the gallows. "Dusit says everything will be just fine," he shouted over the roar of the engine and the rising wind. "They do this all the time, he says. For fun."

"I wish we'd smoked the other joint," called Ella, her hair blowing into her face.

"We'll be fine," said Brian.

"Glad you think so," shouted Jack from behind. "I had a dream last night that I was drowning."

"Were we drowning, too?" asked Brian.

"No."

"Well, there you go, then. At least *we'll* be fine."

There was a blinding flash from behind, chased instantly by a crack like the earth splitting open.

"Must have hit the island," yelled Chelsea. "Good thing we opted for yachting instead of rock climbing."

"Thanks, honey," shouted Grace. "Be of good cheer, everyone. What did Lear say in the midst of the tempest? 'Rumble thy bellyful'?"

"I can't believe it," Jack bellowed. "We're all about to die and the English majors are quoting Shakespeare." He laughed gamely.

The lights of Phi Phi Don had been clearly visible ahead of them, reassuring as runway beacons at the end of a turbulent flight. Suddenly, they winked out completely as a wall of rain swept over the boat. The drumming of thousands of fat drops striking the canvas awning was deafening, all but masking the sound of the rolling thunder. With each flash of lightning, they could see that they were surrounded as much by water as by air, as though they were sailing through a waterfall. It seemed a miracle they could breathe.

"Mom will be pissed," yelled Grace through the gale. "We weren't supposed to die doing this."

Brian felt Dusit nudge him from his right. In a flash of light, he saw the man holding out a plastic bucket. He had another in his other hand.

"We throw water out?" he yelled. "Much rain come in. Help Chati?"

Brian could feel water lapping above his ankles. "Sure. Can he even see where he's going?"

"Chati fine. Good sailor. But not if boat sink." Dusit bent over and started scooping water over the side. Brian fell to it. It was frustrating work, as the arc of the bucket rim didn't come close to matching the contours of the hull. As often as not, it hit against the ribs as Brian lifted it to the gunwale, spilling half of what he'd managed to gather. Again and again, though, he swept the thing through the water roiling at his feet while the deluge worked to fill the hull faster than it could possibly be emptied.

A mighty gust hit them from astern, stronger than anything they'd experienced and tearing a piece of the awning from its metal framework. There was a prodigious creak, as though the frame itself were being bent over and its securing screws yanked from the timbers at its base.

Brian turned back toward Ella. As the boat flashed into visibility in another bolt of lightning, he yelled, "I love you."

"I love you too, boo," she called back.

For an ungodly long run of minutes, the eight of them huddled there with the driven rain pocking their skin like birdshot and the mad press of wind all but capsizing the little craft. And then, as quickly as it had come, the squall passed on. The lightning continued to play frenetically all around, but they could see the back of the storm pulling away in front of them. Overhead, a star or two and now a dozen of them popped out of the murk, and within three minutes, the lights of Phi Phi Don winked at them from the horizon. The boat was still steering squarely for them.

"See?" Dusit turned to Brian. "Chati good sailor." He held his hand out for the bucket, and Brian gave it to him with a great sigh. "You good sailor, too."

"We don't have any alcohol, do we?" Brian stood in the door of the bathroom, toweling off after a hot shower.

"Not that I know of," answered Ella from the bed. "Unless you want to drink mouthwash."

"What flavor?"

Ella laughed. "Too bad the bar is closed. After all that, I could use a shot of something, too."

"We ought to be exhausted. I feel totally wired."

"Me too."

Brian draped his towel on a desk chair, pulled on some boxers, and climbed into bed.

"You going to hang that up?" Ella pointed at the towel.

"Yes, dear." Brian jumped up and took the wet towel into the bathroom.

"Thanks, boo."

Brian climbed back into bed and twisted around to prop up his pillows. "I guess I might have fucked up a little with Grace out there, yeah?" Ella looked over and smiled. "I guess I was a little on edge. Being out there in that tiny boat with no compass and that storm coming in. But I should have...well...not been so flip."

"We're all going to remember this for a long time," Ella said softly. "We want to do it right."

Brian nodded. "Back in high school, you know, when Grace was editing the newspaper and yearbook both—shit, basically running the whole school—I started up this satirical magazine with a couple of loser friends. We called it *The Hangover Herald*. It lasted maybe ten issues? But I managed to piss off just about every kid and teacher in the school."

"A talent you haven't entirely lost," said Ella, grinning again.

"I always told my co-editors, when you're faced with a choice between common human decency and a cheap laugh, go for the laugh."

"That may work for stand-up. Maybe not so good for meaningful family events."

Brian nodded again. "They had a real naughty streak, Mom and Dad. Mom especially. Well, you know that. Dad did things. Mom did things and then talked about them. I think I got my *let's-make-Gracie-blush* shtick from her."

"It's obviously in the genes," said Ella.

"Mom did set me up with that sore crotch bit."

"She did. That doesn't mean you had to pile on with Grace, though."

"Yeah. Well, just don't believe everything she says about me." Brian bent over and kissed the top of her head. "You smell good."

"Thanks."

Brian lay quietly for a moment. "Did you know that Dad's guy, Shelley, drowned in a thunderstorm at sea?"

"No."

"Wouldn't it have been ironic if it had happened to us?"

"Very," Ella replied. "Didn't your dad think Shelley was hunting for a mermaid or something?"

"He did. But it turned out the letter he'd discovered was a fake. Some Oxford undergraduate prank."

"So I guess there was no mermaid out there to save the guy."

"I guess not."

"I would have saved you," said Ella, reaching over to switch off the light.

"Are you a mermaid?"

Ella laughed "Feel free to check."

ROME

Your mission, Gracie and Brian, should you choose to accept it, is to take your mother's and father's ashes to the Piazza San Pietro in Rome, Italy, and, as close to the obelisk in the very center as you can manage, sprinkle them there.

I hope you're laughing. Maybe you're rolling your eyes. But you know Mission Impossible *was one of Dad's guilty pleasures, and I thought it would be fun to throw it in. Fair warning. The mission may not be impossible, but I don't think you'll be able to dig a hole. You'll have to use your imaginations, but you'll figure something out.*

Two measures of my ashes for one of Dad's, please. Being a militantly lapsed Catholic, he'll stand for being at St. Peter's only because I'll be there too. For me, though, it was a mystical place—maybe the only manmade space I've ever been in where I felt the presence of a Higher Spirit. You know I was never a churchgoer. I would have married Dad by a waterfall in the woods if I could've. Dad and I went to Rome our Oxford spring, and I was still struggling with something I'm about to tell you about. It was at dawn in the piazza. The sun was rising at my back, and the cathedral and that dome were just breathtaking as they soared up in front of me. With the colonnade embracing me like great stone arms on either side, I prayed for forgiveness to the Spirit of Everything and I finally felt like I'd been heard. To lie there with Frank will make me very happy.

I left you at Yasgur's Farm, maybe wondering why your mother was sharing what she was sharing. Gracie, you probably think I was teasing you about sex again. Maybe you're partly right. It's funny how the thought of our parents having sex is like imagining eating chicken with the feathers on. Even though our parents' making love is the very first step in our earthly journey, it's the very last thing any of us want to think about, isn't it? But I have fun with you because I love you. More importantly, as I said before, I want to move on with no secrets held back and no lessons unconveyed. If I'm going someplace where Everything Is Revealed, I won't have any secrets anyway. If there's no such place, I want to be remembered here for who I was, not who someone thought I was. So I'm sorry if I disappoint or upset you. Doing it this way may be selfish, but it's something I need to do. I do it as a gift of honesty from your mother and with great love for you both. This poor world needs more honesty.

So—my Matthew. If you'd been there, you would have felt as I did—that we really had gotten ourselves "back to the Garden." Of course, we really hadn't at all. When it all broke up, we went back to our suburban homes and our bank accounts and our annual flu shots and everything else. But while we were there it felt, much too fleetingly, like everything had changed—like we were muddy angels listening to the choirs of God. All the marijuana and LSD going around probably didn't hurt. Even though Matthew and I never made love after those two nights, sharing what we shared there bound us together in a way that's lasted all these years. I suppose you had to experience it, along with all those thousands and thousands who felt it too. How I wish it had been your father there with me instead! But Matthew and I would write, sometimes call, once a year to peek into each other's lives. He became a very successful neurosurgeon in San Francisco and had a boy and a girl, too. We met once in New York over a coffee and a walk in the Park, but I needed to be faithful to your father in the flesh, if not wholly in the heart. Matthew knew I was here at Hanover Hell, and, just two mornings ago, he came to say goodbye to his "Cinnamon Girl." He still looks like an angel, although most of the mud is gone. He brought me a picture of us early that Sunday morning, twining around each other among the throngs of drenched and smiling faces. How we laughed and wept. And then he left.

I got pregnant one of those splendorous nights. It had to be Matthew's and not Frank's, for reasons I almost forget and wouldn't bore you with even if I remembered. But there was no way I could give birth to that child and so, with sickness in my heart, I went with Suzanne and ended it. I believe to my core that women have the right to control their own bodies, as all my years at PP attest. This never spared me guilt, though, over snuffing out a life that was conceived at such a mystical and hopeful moment—or spared me the anguish of injuring your father and Matthew both. But when you lay my ashes at St. Peter's, you'll lay them in the spot where I prayed to Someone or Something for that child who never was…and, as I prayed, I finally felt I might make a measure of peace with the past. I so hope that, as you stand there too, you can be at peace with what your mother did and was. Dad will be there with me, in this and everything else a more forgiving soul than I deserved. But don't forget—not too much of him at the church because, even though he managed to believe in me, *he had his limits.*

Grace dropped the papers on the grass and flopped onto her back. "Where do I start," she moaned, as she stared through the interwoven pine boughs up to a cloudless sky.

They'd landed at Fiumicino just past eight o'clock in the morning. After they'd taken the train into Rome, checked in at the hotel, and grabbed a quick lunch, Grace thought it might be pleasant to walk up to the Borghese Gardens to get their new directives. After Cinny's Singapore bombshell, nobody expected that her next revelation would be any less unsettling. Grace merely hoped a scenic setting might soften the impact.

"Well," said Brian, once Grace had made her way through the three pages of Cinny's chicken-scratch. "At least you got through it without fainting. Or crying."

"Or throwing up?" asked Grace.

Brian clicked audibly.

Ella broke the long silence. "I know I'm a newbie here, but I was so moved." She kicked her legs out and leaned back on her hands. "I mean, the guilt she lived with, but—oh my gosh!—the love for your dad that comes through it all." She shook her head in disbelief. "And then Matthew and her have this spiritual thing all their lives, and he actually comes to say goodbye days before she dies. It's like something out of a tragic opera."

"Hmm," sighed Grace, still flat on her back.

Ella looked down at her earnestly. "She was so honest about what she did and all. Who she was. I don't know. It took my breath away."

"You're right," said Grace, sitting up. She took a huge breath and let it out. Jack reached over to sweep some pine needles off her back.

"And to think, the whole time she was writing that," Ella went on, "she was starving herself to death. Only days before she died. It's incredible!" She looked at Sage, who nodded.

There was a crunch of gravel as a young family rode by on matching rental bikes—mother, father, and two grade-school-age children, chattering happily back and forth on the lovely spring afternoon. A flock of pigeons foraging in their path flapped away noisily as they approached.

"And I thought I was joking when I said Cinny's mysterious visitor might be a love interest," said Jack.

"Guess not," sighed Grace. "At least it sounds totally platonic. For fifty years."

"I guess," said Jack.

"What do you mean you guess?" Grace stared at her husband. "You think Mom was lying when she said they never did it after Woodstock?"

"No. It's not that. It's just that there's such a thing as emotional infidelity. But I'm no expert."

"Good to know," said Grace, with a smile.

They sat for a minute with no one saying a thing. The pigeons circled back and settled in to renew their foraging.

"Would he ever reach out to you, do you think?" asked Sage. "Matthew? I mean, he had this relationship with your mom all those years. They must have talked about you and all."

"Doesn't seem likely," said Brian.

"But if he did?"

Brian shrugged.

"For me," said Grace, "it would depend on whether Dad knew they'd kept in touch. If he did, fine. The guy probably knew a side of Mom we never did."

"Given he got her pregnant," scoffed Brian.

"As I was saying," said Grace, with a moderate eye roll, "if Dad knew, fine. But if they kept it all from him, well…"

"I get it, H.P.," said Jack. "It would be like you were condoning something your mom was trying so hard to make up for. But I'm sure she told Frank. I can't believe she would have kept that a secret."

"Yeah," said Grace. "I certainly don't want to go there."

"So meanwhile," said Jack, "sounds like we've got a little logistical challenge. St. Peter's piazza is paved, no?"

"How are your masonry skills, Jack?" asked Brian.

Once back to the hotel, Jack and Sage decided to take a run. They asked Chelsea if she wanted to join them, but she was going to chat with Grant at five and wanted to grab a bath beforehand in their huge marble tub. Sage told Jack she'd found a thirty-kilometer run on the other side of the river with spectacular views of the city. When he suggested that thirty kilometers would either put him in a coma for a week or kill him outright, Sage laughed and said they'd only go as far as he wanted.

"How do you like the St. Regis?" asked Jack, once they'd crossed over the Tiber, dropped down to the pedestrian embankment, and settled into a good pace southwards.

"Mixed feelings."

"How's that?"

"It's like an effing palace," replied Sage. "Really."

"Is that good or bad?"

"It's actually pretty decadent. It must cost a fortune."

"I know," sighed Jack. "I thought you were keen on staying there, though. Somebody said it's where Beck stays when he's on tour."

"But I didn't know it would be so glitzy. It almost makes me not like him as much."

"I don't know Beck. Who's he like? Oops! *Mi scusi*." Jack had nearly run up the back of an older lady with a wheeled market basket in tow. She turned with a scowl. "Sorry! Is he like anyone an old fart like me would know?"

Sage laughed. "Beck's like nobody, really. No one person. He started in acoustic blues. Sometimes he raps. Sometimes he sounds like Prince. Every album, though, he basically reinvents himself."

Jack nodded.

"I like people who are always searching," said Sage. "Like they get the idea to do something, they do it, and then they move on. Instead of finding something—anything—everybody likes and just making a shit-ton of money but letting their creativity die."

"I hear you," said Jack. "Can you wait a second? I have to pull up my sock."

Sage jogged in place. "Speaking of shitloads of money, Jack," she said after they started up again, "what's with the watches? Chelsea says you're addicted to watches. And cars."

Jack laughed. "That diagnosis might be a little extreme."

"Maybe." Sage grinned. "Seriously, though. Do they make you happy?"

"Man, you're direct." He reached up for a quick tug at his car.

"That bothers you?"

"Well, no. I kind of find it refreshing, I guess. But challenging."

"Yeah. Well…"

"But challenges are good," said Jack. "And back to your question, watches do make me happy, yes. Interesting watches. Miniature masterpieces of engineering, I think of them as." He looked over and smiled. "I sound like a Rolex ad, don't I?"

"A little."

"You're probably thinking I'm a crass materialist or something."

"Not necessarily," Sage replied.

They swerved to either side of a couple that had stopped abruptly in the middle of the walkway to kiss.

"Look," said Sage. "It's not like I have any kind of divine insight about what matters or anything. I'm just a kid trying to figure out what to do with her life. Besides, our fucked-up culture is so into things, stuff, there's probably no way anybody is ever going to change that."

"Probably not."

"What's really sick is when people in power think they can own other people. Or do whatever they want."

"Right," said Jack. They ran for a minute without speaking as the declining sun fired the travertine walls across the river like clay in a kiln. "You were talking about figuring out what to do with your life?"

"Yeah. Not that there's a huge rush. I just don't want to waste my time dicking around."

"You should think about going into politics."

Sage laughed.

"No, really," said Jack. "You care about things. You're not afraid to speak up. You play hardball."

Sage laughed again.

"What?" asked Jack. "You don't believe me?"

"It's just how you said I play hardball."

"Well, you do."

"As opposed to softball. Which is what girls usually play."

"I guess."

"So, you're trying to say something nice about me and that I ought to go into politics. But to say it, you have to say I'm not like a girl."

"Hang on a minute. I didn't say that."

"Well, you kind of did."

Jack laughed. "I'll have to think about that a little more."

They came up behind a man toting a sizeable wooden box and what looked like a folded-up easel. He heard them approach and, turning to look back, almost swung the legs of the thing into Jack's midsection. Jack jackknifed out of the way.

"You okay?" asked Sage.

"Yup. Old rugby dodge."

Sage smiled. "There's all kinds of hidden biases in language. My friend Tokiko and I found this book that really blew our minds. Like, if you call a guy who's a selfish jerk a bastard, what do you call a woman who's a selfish jerk?"

"I don't know. A bitch?"

"Right! So a slimeball man remains a human being, even if his mother slept around. But a slimeball woman is a *dog*!"

"I don't know, Sage."

"Okay. What do you call a guy whose wife has sex with another man?"

"I guess he's a cuckold."

"And how about a woman whose husband has sex with another woman?"

Jack ran on, working on an answer. "I don't know. What?"

"Basically, just your average wife."

Jack laughed. "Maybe I was wrong about you being a politician. Maybe you should be a college professor."

"At some kind of socialist academy of feminist brainwashing?"

"Exactly," chuckled Jack.

"I'll text you the name of the book. You should read it."

"Okay," said Jack. "Maybe I'll learn something. They say it's never too late to start."

"You're an okay guy, Jack," Sage said after a beat.

"For an addict?"

Sage laughed. "Chelsea's lucky to have a good dad. Some of us aren't so lucky."

"Thanks," said Jack. "I appreciate that. Do you think maybe we should head back?"

Sage looked down at her watch. "I guess. Sure. Perfect."

Sage got back to the room to find Chelsea sitting on the ledge of an open window reading a magazine. She'd changed into a black sleeveless dress and was smoking a cigarette.

"How was the run?" asked Chelsea, half-hiding the smoke.

"Great. A little short, maybe. That's cool, though."

"You didn't kill Dad?"

"Didn't try." Sage walked into the bathroom and came out wiping her brow with a towel. "Did you talk with Grant?"

"I did."

"How is he?"

Chelsea put the magazine face-down in her lap. "Okay. As far as we know right now."

Sage sat on the edge of the bed and kicked off her shoes. "What's up?"

"Oh, just a little health thing." Chelsea dropped the half-smoked cigarette into a San Pellegrino can. It sizzled out in a burst of citrus scent.

"Little? What is it?"

"It's kind of embarrassing, I guess. He's having some trouble with his prostate."

"Jeez!" said Sage. "I knew he was older and all, but isn't prostate stuff, like, usually for guys over sixty? Like osteoporosis and cataracts?"

Chelsea smiled. "Usually. But Grant has a family history. And his uncle died of it in his fifties."

"Shit! I'm sorry, Chel."

"We don't know anything for certain yet, but he's been having symptoms. He's going in for a biopsy next week."

"Jeez! What's that mean? Needles up the butt or something?"

"Something like that. What he's most worried about, actually, is telling the girls. Whatever the doctors discover."

"Oh, man," said Sage, peeling off her running socks. "They just lost their mom, didn't they?"

"Yeah. A little over a year ago. The older one is pretty stoic. Daria. But bad news about her dad would really freak the younger one out. She's only nine."

"I get it. He's all they've got left."

Chelsea sighed. "I wish I were there."

"Have you thought about going? I mean, it would be an easy flight. Here to D.C.?"

"I have," replied Chelsea. "Grant said no way. He'll be fine, he said, and I'll be back home anyway before anything bad could happen. Even if it was going to."

Sage nodded. "Let's assume he'll be fine, and all. What happens, though, if he's not? If it's cancer?"

"Well, I guess there are a number of options."

"I've heard, when you have your prostate removed, you can't get it up. Is that true?"

"For some men, I guess," answered Chelsea.

"Man! That would be a bummer."

"You might say."

Sage sniggered.

"What?" asked Chelsea.

"The guys I hang out with? They walk up to you, say hi, and pitch a fucking tent before you can even say hi back."

Chelsea grinned. "So I recall."

"Well," said Sage, standing up, "fingers crossed. I'm gonna jump in the shower. Unless you recommend a bath."

"It was pretty memorable." Chelsea grinned again. "I used the bath salts, Valerian and chamomile."

"I don't know," said Sage. "Sounds like a sleeping potion for your vagina."

Chelsea laughed. "Like that would be a problem? With Grant three thousand miles away?"

"Sounds way too decadent," said Sage. "I don't want to end up like Marie Antoinette."

For dinner, they walked back toward the Villa Borghese and had an excellent meal at a restaurant lined with huge mural photos of Fellini stars. When the waiter cleared the last dinner plates, Grace suggested everybody consider "teary measles" for dessert.

Ella looked up from the menu. "What's teary measles?"

"That's what I called *tiramisu* when I was little," volunteered Chelsea. "It kind of stuck—basically freezing me forever at age four."

"Which," Jack added loudly, "makes her current live-in even more of a cradle robber." Encouraged and paced by Brian, Jack had downed more than enough wine to forget Grace's ongoing ban on references to Chelsea's domestic arrangements. "Ouch!" he exclaimed, as the toe of Grace's shoe crashed into his shin. "Fucking hell, Grace!"

"You know," Ella chirped brightly, ending the awkward pause in conversation, "kids' names for things are just so cute."

"Don't!" snapped Sage. She glared at her mother over tightly folded arms.

"Sage, honey!"

"I mean it, Mom. If you trot out any of my kiddie cute-isms, I'm going to go out tonight and fellate every homeless Italian dude I can find."

"And I might have to join her," said Chelsea, laughing.

"Well, okay then," responded Ella. "I'll bite my tongue."

Brian leaned against her with a tipsy wink. "Maybe I can bite it later, too."

Grace threw up her hands. "What? Is Mom writing our dialogue here?"

"She'd love it," said Brian. "And she'd probably have special instructions for serving the teary measles."

Twenty minutes on, Grace set down her fork and carefully folded her napkin. "Okay. What's the plan?"

Brian leaned forward with his elbows on the table. "Maybe we should do a little reconnaissance. Go over to St. Peter's tomorrow and check out the lay of the land."

"Sounds smart," said Grace. "I'm pretty sure the whole square's paved. I doubt there are any planters or anything, either."

"Brian shook his head. "Nope. Checked online. Nothing close to the obelisk, except a ring of stone bollards."

"So where do we put the ashes?" asked Ella.

"That's why we scout it out," replied Brian.

"Case the joint." Jack burped then slapped his wrist. "Cut it out, Jack!"

Brian grinned at his brother-in-law. "If the gaps between stones are big enough, we could take a broom or something and sweep Mom and Dad into the cracks."

"*Sweep* Nana and Pop Pop?" Chelsea's eyes bugged out. "Into the *cracks?*"

"Sure," said Jack. "Like you sweep sand in around new pavers. When you build, say, a carriage house." He looked at Grace and stifled another burp.

"I know sweeping sounds a little irreverent," Brian allowed. "But how many options do we have?"

"Listen up," said Jack, setting down his second *limoncello* with a loud smack of the lips. "We got two separate challenges, as I see it. There's the *Where-do-the-ashes-end-up* challenge. And there's the *How-do-we-get-them-onto-the-ground-in-the-first-place* challenge. Given the prying eyes of the public."

Chelsea looked at the others. "Dad's right. We can't just go over to Rome's biggest tourist attraction, open up some baggies, and empty them out onto the pavement."

"We could go at night," suggested Sage. "Like Phi Phi Leh."

"The whole place is lit up at night," said Brian. "The front of the church, and then there're these big lamps right next to the obelisk. We'd be even more conspicuous doing something weird when no tourists are around."

"So we go in the daytime," said Jack.

"Maybe," replied Brian.

"Get lost in the crowd!"

"Maybe."

"I could hold the bag up in front of my face and sneeze," suggested Jack. He slid forward in his chair. "All the ashes fly out, right? And I say, 'Sorry! Coal miner. Black lung!'" He looked around the table, inviting a grin.

"Maybe," said Brian, with a sidelong glance at Grace.

Jack snapped his fingers and sat up even straighter. "Or we could do the *Great Escape* thing!"

"What's the *Great Escape* thing?" asked Chelsea.

"The *Great Escape* thing. There's this movie about prisoners in a Nazi P.O.W camp. Steve McQueen. They want to tunnel out under their building and escape. The only problem is, they have all this dirt they have to put somewhere without the guards figuring out what they're doing."

"Okay," said Chelsea.

"So they come up with this system to sneak the dirt out, bit by bit, in their pants pockets."

"Like they just turn their pockets inside out?" asked Sage. "Wouldn't the guards see that and be suspicious?"

Jack shook his head. "I told you, they rig this system. When they get to where the dirt's going, they pull this little string and the bottom of the pocket opens up and the dirt just falls down their pantleg to the ground. Then they shake it off their shoes, smile at the guards, and go back for another pocketful."

"It is a great movie," said Brian. "I don't know though, Jack."

"I'd be so into it." Jack actually bounced in his seat. "You load me up at the hotel and I'm strolling, all cool and relaxed, up to the obelisk, and I get right to where we want the ashes and I pull the string. And…"

"And?" repeated Grace.

Jack's eyes twinkled. "Maybe I'm having trouble with the string. And I pull and I pull and nothing happens. And every time I pull, my pantleg jumps up and down." He stood up to demonstrate, yanking up on his pocket.

"Sit down, Jack," hissed Grace, scanning the room. "You're embarrassing us."

Jack sat down, but his excitement was undiminished. "Maybe there's this couple standing next to me. Maybe they're from Korea or Bosnia or something, and the guy asks, 'What's the trouble, sir?' And I say, 'Nothing, really.' And he says, 'Can I help?' And I say, 'No thanks. I'm just trying to get my mother-in-law out of my pants." Jack sat back and started to guffaw. He looked happily around the table as the others joined in.

"That's really funny, Dad," said Chelsea. "I *figured* there might be another mother-in-law joke coming. Don't forget, though, Pop Pop would be in there, too."

"Right," said Brian. "You'd have a pocketful of *Poseys*, Jack. Plural."

Jack snorted. "It's funnier with just the mother-in-law." He drained his *limoncello*. "A man's got the right to control what goes on in his own pants."

"And women don't?" asked Sage.

"Word!" said Chelsea.

They were up early the next morning and fell in the door of the Sistine Chapel when it opened. They took their time in the Vatican Museum and the basilica itself and headed out to the great piazza after the tourists had flooded in, allowing for a realistic check of the drop zone and its various logistical challenges and options.

As suspected, the central obelisk was surrounded by stone paving blocks arrayed in a geometric pattern that extended clear out to the colonnades. There were no significant gaps in their coverage. Brian knelt with Grace just inside the ring of bollards and ran his hands over the cobbles. There were in fact spaces between the stones, but Brian calculated that they'd almost have to sift Cinny and Frank's ashes to remove any but the very smallest chips of bone. Even then, they'd need to cut back substantially on the volume and sweep the ashes over a wide area. They wrote off Jack's *Great Escape* technique as being far too likely to fail—say if Jack's legs were sweaty from walking over, or if his shoes were damp with rain—but they still had to devise an alternative. Meanwhile, Sage and Chelsea would try to lay their hands on a broom while Brian and Grace bagged the day's remains.

Brian brought Frank's container up to Grace and Jack's room and set it on the marble desktop in front of the oversized mirror. He stared at his reflection and then at his sister's, wondering idly if a stranger might ever conclude they were siblings, let alone twins. Who looked older? More settled? More content with life? He noticed a flake of dried snot dangling from a nose hair and reached up to pluck it off. If Ella's frequent references to his "Christmas tree ornaments" were any indication, he was more prone than the average male to nasal danglers. He'd never noticed if Grace had a similar problem, and he'd never asked. It might be a male vs. female thing, he supposed, related to the density and hardihood of nasal cilia. "I wonder if we should have gotten a sieve," he remarked distractedly, as Grace placed Cinny's blue container on the desk next to Frank's.

Grace held up a silver spoon. "This'll do."

"Where'd you get that?"

"At breakfast." Grace winked. "It'll work fine."

"You're going to get us thrown out on our butts, you know? Brazen hussy that you are."

"No court in the world would convict us," said Grace. "Not considering what we're doing."

"What? Dumping foreigners' carbonized body parts at a world-famous cultural site?"

"Fulfilling the last wishes of our beloved parents."

As Grace spooned some of the finer ash from their mother's canister into the baggie Brian held open, she asked if he'd noticed, the day before, the way Cinny had referred to herself as Matthew's "Cinnamon Girl."

"I did," said Brian. "It really struck me. But there were a few other things grabbing my attention at the time."

"No kidding," scoffed Grace. "But what do you make of it?"

"It has to refer to the song, no?"

"It's got to. And Neil Young was there, right?" She stared at Brian. "Connect the dots."

Brian's expression sobered. "Shit, Gracie! Mom goes up to Woodstock as Lucinda/Lucy and she comes back as Lucinda/Cinny.

Dad never knew why the change. She never told him. She just laughed and said it had been a profound experience, is all."

Grace nodded him along.

"Matthew must have turned *Lucinda* into *Cinny*—as in his Cinnamon Girl—and she spends the rest of her life with a name Matthew gave her."

Grace nodded, "And how faithful was that being to Dad?"

"Shit, Gracie!" Brian felt his stomach tighten.

"Do you think there's any way Dad knew?" asked Grace.

"I don't know. He knew about the fling, Mom said. And the baby. He knew about the name. He could have put two and two together."

"But they stayed married," said Grace. "And for all we know, completely happy and committed. Until Dad died."

"Shit!" exclaimed Brian. "I don't know what to think. Should I?"

Grace shook her head. "I guess we process this for a bit."

Brian sighed.

"Although honestly," Grace added, "I really don't know what difference it would make. One way or the other."

"Well, it makes a difference how we feel about our mother, doesn't it? How we remember her? How completely we figure she wanted to put her mistake behind her?"

Grace sighed. "Let's just sit on this for a bit, okay? Even with Ella and Jack. If they notice and put things together, fine. We'll deal with it."

"Yeah. We will."

"Anyway," said Grace, after a pause. "Hold the bag. Four teaspoons of Dad?"

"I guess."

"What do you mean, you guess?"

"This is so fucked, Gracie. I almost feel guilty putting him in there with Mom now. Like we're playing him for a sucker or something."

"I know."

"Damn it!" Brian set the bag on the desk, walked over to the settee at the foot of the bed, and sat down.

Grace dropped the spoon into Frank's canister and walked over to join him. She put her arm around his shoulder. "Look. Let's remember, they stayed married and they seemed to be happy and in love. As much as married couples can be. Ones that make it past the first five years, anyway." She grinned at Brian and poked him in the ribs. "So if they didn't go their separate ways, finally, who are we to go and do it for them?"

Brian took a deep breath and let it out slowly. "Yeah. You're right."

"C'mon," said Grace, standing up and walking back to the desk. "Four teaspoons of Dad." She tipped the canister and delicately dipped the spoon.

"Nothing too big!" Brian reminded her.

Chelsea and Sage experienced some communication difficulties securing a broom. When they inquired at the hotel desk about where they could find one, the smartly dressed young woman assured them that the housekeeping staff was there to take care of all cleaning needs. What room number was theirs again? When they explained they wanted to buy a broom to use elsewhere, she apologetically directed them to a nearby hardware store. Chelsea asked if anyone at the shop was likely to speak English, since a nails-and-paint store wasn't likely to cater to many international shoppers. "Perhaps not," said the woman. "But if they don't, simply ask for *una scopa*."

Chelsea and Sage were certain, after the fact, that the woman hadn't set them up, but they walked into the store without the helpful information that *una scopa* is Italian slang for an act of sexual intercourse. It was only the solicitous assistance of an older Italian gentleman, shopping for a pack of lightbulbs, that curtailed the randy amusement of the two young men behind the counter and got Chelsea and Sage the thing they'd actually come in for. Chelsea thought it was all hilarious. Sage was slower to laugh.

Brian suggested they walk back to St. Peter's around four o'clock in the afternoon, when the piazza would still be crowded but the sun would be lower in the sky and the various guards might be relaxing their attentiveness. There must have been some sort of official pontifical address earlier in the day, because when the Posey group arrived, a team of workmen was busy disassembling and stacking hundreds of wooden crowd-control barriers. For some reason, the obelisk at the center of the vast space seemed to have attracted the greatest part of the remaining sightseers, as though it were a lightning rod for an epiphany they'd all come to this holy spot to share.

"It may be a challenge clearing some space," observed Grace.

"We'll see," replied Brian. "We can always huddle and then back up in a circle to establish some butt room."

They'd entered the ring of stone bollards close to the obelisk when they realized that most of the people standing there were parts of tour groups. As luck would have it, three of the guides finished at roughly the same time and led their people away to other locations.

Brian looked around quickly to see if there were any *carabinieri* or Vatican Guards nearby and motioned to a clear space. "You got the broom, Chel?"

Chelsea held up the now-infamous item.

"Great. Gracie?"

Grace nodded and reached into her purse, pulling out a tin she'd purchased from a sweets store. She removed the lid and was pretending to offer a candy to Jack when she let the tin drop to her feet. "Oh, goodness," she said. "How clumsy of me!"

"That's all right, H.P.," said Jack, loudly. "Let me just pick that up for you." He bent down and grabbed the container, flipping it over before he stood so that the fine gray ashes of the late Poseys—those that hadn't already tumbled from the container—poured out onto the paving stones. As he handed the tin to Grace, Chelsea stepped up with the broom and did her best to sweep the ashes into the cracks between the stones.

"How's that?" she asked, stepping back.

"Not bad," said Brian. "Maybe a little more over here."

"Sorry, Nana. Sorry, Pop Pop." Chelsea stepped gingerly across a well-swept section to another where a good dusting of ash was still visible on the cobbles. She swept lustily and stood back again.

"Great!" said Brian.

"Nope. There!" Grace pointed to a sizeable bit of solid material square in the middle of a stone. "Sorry," she said. "My bad. I thought I'd only put in powdery bits."

"What do we do?" whispered Ella. "Can we just leave it like that?"

"No way," said Brian.

"Maybe grind it around a little, it will disintegrate," suggested Jack. He demonstrated a vigorous crushing action with his shoe.

Sage stared at him in disbelief. "We've got to pick it up." She was bending to do it, but Brian waved her back.

"Thanks, Sage. I'll get it." He stooped down and picked up the shard of bone, slipping it quickly into his shirt pocket.

"Wow!" said a voice behind them.

They turned to see a rotund man in a Hawaiian shirt and sunglasses standing there. Next to him was an anorexic-looking woman in what appeared to be black silk pajamas. She had a magenta scarf draped around her neck and wore a kind of turban of a similar shade. The pair smiled pleasantly at the six of them.

"Oh, hello," said Grace. Nothing more came to her to say through the blush of embarrassment.

"Hi," said the woman.

"We don't mean to pry," said the man, "but Nancy here and me, we're really curious about what you dropped."

"Oh!" Grace looked flustered. "This?" She held up the tin. "This candy box?"

"Well, more like what was in it."

The man's wife nodded. "It looked to Bill and me kinda like ashes, you know? Human remains?"

"Not like candy?" Grace looked imploringly at Brian.

The couple shook their heads in tandem, like twin bobble-heads.

"Actually," said Grace, facing the two squarely. "You're right. It was my parents' ashes. My and my brother's parents." She pointed to Brian.

"Ah!" said Bill. "That sure explains it."

"Your parents mustn't have been very big," observed the woman. "When we scattered my Aunt Blanche—just her, mind you—there was ten times that many ashes. And Aunt Blanche, she was a rail!"

"And I only saw one piece of bone." The man looked at Brian. "In your pocket, right?"

"Do you guys have a second?" asked Brian.

When Brian finished explaining about the family's funereal odyssey, Bill thanked him for his time. He suggested to his wife that they think about doing the same thing, blushing when she reminded him that they'd just spent two thousand dollars for burial plots, not to mention locking in a deluxe embalming-and-casket package at their local funeral home. When he suggested that they could instead cremate some of his hunting trophies along with a few of her prize-winning quilts, and have their children sprinkle the ashes at Wrigley Field and the Grand Canyon, she agreed that sounded nice. Then they said that it was great running into fellow Americans and strolled away arm in arm.

"Well, that could have been worse," said Ella. "I guess."

Brian nodded, scanning the area furtively. "Anybody have any words?"

Chelsea cleared her throat. "Just that I'm grateful that Nana found some peace here. It's awful thinking she could have gone all the way through life beating herself up over something that, you know, happened over two days when she was really young."

Brian caught Grace's eye across the circle. She was biting her lip.

"I'm looking at this huge enclosure," said Ella, gesturing toward the colonnade that girdled the piazza. "I'm not particularly religious, but the thought of the Church as, you know, some kind of overarching spirit gathering humanity to its breast...all humanity...that's really moving to me. It makes me happy to think of Cinny and Frank being here with all the other pilgrims that come here year after year."

"I thought Frank hated the Church," said Sage.

"He did," said Grace. "So did Mom, essentially. But she clearly liked to think there was Something out there—maybe Some*body*—that rose above human stupidity and hypocrisy and greed."

"Well, if she found it here," said Jack, "that's something. I guess we could all learn something about rising above stupidity, hypocrisy, and greed."

"Amen," said Grace.

"So, thanks, Cinny and Frank both," Jack continued, "for pushing us a little further every day in the right direction."

"That was sweet, Dad," said Chelsea.

"Your dad's okay," said Sage. She kicked the toe of Jack's shoe. "Middling runner, but at least he's trying."

GRINDELWALD

Sage and Chelsea had their own row on the flight to Zürich. Chelsea was a fair way into the book she'd picked up at Fiumicino when a flight attendant came on the P.A. to announce that lunch service was about to begin. Sage shut off her video, pulled out her earbuds, and turned to Chelsea. "You remember back when I said I might want to talk to you some time about older guys hitting on girls?"

"I do," replied Chelsea. "I've been thinking about that a lot lately—for obvious reasons." She smiled. "I was wondering when you might bring it up."

"Yeah," said Sage. "With that bar shit, and then the hardware store, it's been totally insane. It's like I can't sit on it anymore, you know?"

"Sure."

"This a good time?"

"None better." Chelsea closed her book, stuck it in the seat pocket, and slid into the middle seat. "Shoot."

Sage took a deep breath and peered out the window. They were flying over the Alpine foothills. The higher ones had snow on their summits and northern slopes. She sighed and turned back to Chelsea. "So I have this friend, Tokiko, back home."

"You've talked about her."

"Yeah. I suppose she's my best friend. I mean, she *is* my best friend. I don't have a lot of people I'm close to. I guess I have an abrasive personality or something."

Chelsea laughed. "You just tell it like it is, is all. Dad loves you for it, by the way. He's always going on about how being with you is like being with the kid in 'The Emperor's New Clothes.'"

"That's pretty funny."

"Honestly, it makes me kind of jealous. I feel like I must be incredibly wishy-washy or something in comparison."

"Shut up, Chelsea. You're great. I think I would have gone batshit on this trip if it wasn't for you."

"Thank you. Same here, actually." She smiled with the realization. "I know it's corny to say, but you're kind of like the sister I never had. You knew Mom almost died having me, didn't you?"

"I did."

"They didn't want to chance another. I never knew anything different, but looking back, I think it was kind of lonely."

"It's tough being an only child, don't you think?" Sage twisted around and leaned back against the window. "It's like you're what your mom ended up with at Christmas, but you can't help thinking she really wanted something more."

Chelsea laughed. "Right. But what's up?"

Sage's expression sobered. "Maybe you know Tokiko thought she was pregnant before we left. It turns out she wasn't, but I wasn't going to come along if she was. And Mom was really pissed."

"No, I didn't know. But I'm glad she wasn't pregnant. For a couple of reasons. She's your age?"

"Yeah. Sweet Sixteen. Anyway, Mom and Brian were away on this business thing for her company, and Tokiko was staying with me for the weekend. Mom was worried about leaving us alone, but she told my dad they'd be away so he could be available if we needed him or anything. Not that I'd ever call him unless, you know, the world was coming to an end and he was the only one who could save the planet." Sage took a quick nibble at a nail. "And even then…"

"That bad, huh?"

"Let me know when you've got, like, a week to hear about it."

"Jeez."

"So, it's Saturday night. Mom and Brian have been away since Friday and they're coming back the next day, and at eight o'clock or something, Tokiko and I order in a pizza and we're sitting on the couch watching *Ladybird* when the doorbell rings. It's my father and this other dude, his co-pilot with Alaska or something. Dad says they're in the neighborhood having dinner and asks if they can come in to say hi. Tokiko and I are enjoying the movie, but she says what the hell, so they come in." Sage drew a deep breath.

"I'm not sure I like where this is headed," said Chelsea.

"Yeah. Well, they come in and Dad heads straight to the liquor cabinet and pulls out a bottle of something, bourbon I guess, and asks this other guy, Alec, if he wants a drink. They're both already a little wasted, but Alec says sure, and my father pours him a glass and one for himself. They ask what we're watching, and we tell them, and they sit there until it's over, pretty much making fun of everything that's happening. Dad actually said he thought the fucked-up family in it was kind of like ours."

"Nice."

"So *Ladybird* finishes and *SNL* starts up, and they ask if they can stay and watch. We were planning on watching anyway so, stupid asses that we are, we say yes. Alec asks Tokiko if she wants a drink, and she asks if there's any rum and Coke. Well, there is, and pretty soon we're all shit-faced watching *SNL,* and a little later Alec says he'll get Tokiko another drink if she'll sit in his lap, and the stupid bitch does. The rest is history."

"Jesus!" said Chelsea.

"Yeah. I went to bed before anything happened, but what a fucking moron I was to leave Tokiko there with them. Drunk. I can't believe I did that."

"I can't believe what your dad did," said Chelsea. "Bringing a guy like that over. What was he thinking?"

"He doesn't think. About anybody but himself. So, when I wake up in the morning, there's, like, a volcano erupting inside my head, and

I walk out into the living room and there's Dad on the couch asleep, with his shirt untucked and one sock off. I walk into Mom and Brian's room, and there's Tokiko and Alec, in bed in just their underwear. I start yelling, and I tell Alec to get the fuck out of the house before I call the cops. Dad tries to get me to calm down, but I tell him to get the fuck out, too, and they leave. I get Tokiko undressed and into the shower. She throws up all over the place, but I get her cleaned off and dressed and we sit down to figure out what to do."

"Jeez, Sage," said Chelsea. "Nobody should ever have to go through what you went through."

"Either of us, right? But especially her. I mean, as far as we know, she's been raped. By some kind of pussy-crazy, middle-aged frat brother. So I tell her we've got to tell somebody and she fucking freaks out! I mean, she goes off like an I.E.D. Her parents will kill her if they find out. If we call the cops, her parents will find out from them and they'll kill her even worse. They grounded her once for months when they found out she'd only kissed her boyfriend, so imagine what they'd do if they found out she'd gotten drunk with some middle-aged dude and sat in his fucking lap. Let alone that they'd ended up in bed."

"So what did you do?"

"Well, Tokiko says she's not really sure they had sex. I mean all the way. She said she really couldn't remember anything, but she woke up with her underwear on—him too, which I saw—and maybe that meant something. When I asked her if she couldn't tell if she'd been, like, penetrated, she said she couldn't. She and her boyfriend have been doing it for a year, so her cherry was already popped, and she said she couldn't really tell if the guy had been inside her."

"Oh, man."

"So we decide maybe it made sense just to wait and see what happened. Wait for her next period, and if it came, maybe just chalk it all up to experience."

"Oh, Sage. How awful!"

"I know. It totally sucked. And so she was, like, late for a week and then ten days, and really started to panic and was talking about killing herself before her parents could kill her. And that's where we were just before the trip, when she finally got her period and the heat was finally off. Sort of." She looked plangently at Chelsea.

"Yeah. Sort of."

"And then, with all the shit that's been going down in the last week…" Sage stared out the window again. They were definitely over the Alps now—huge, jagged peaks encrusted with snow and ice, as far as the eye could see. The massive summit off to the west had to be Mont Blanc. Sage entertained a fleeting thought about living up there for eternity in her own private ice cave.

"I get it," said Chelsea. "It would have gotten to anyone. Given what you went through with Tokiko, though…it made total sense you reacted the way you did."

"I was goddamn pissed!" spat Sage. "Cut-their-nuts-off pissed. My tolerance for that kind of shit was never high, but now it's goddamn zero. Two fucking places in a row!"

"I hear you." Chelsea put her hand on Sage's knee and patted it gently.

"What do I do?" Sage looked over. "I mean, Tokiko is over it. She says she is, anyway, when we text. She's good with her boyfriend and her parents don't suspect a thing. But how do I sit on this? I mean, with everything I believe about women's rights and social justice, and us being strong and not being taken advantage of by asshole men—"

"I know."

"That fucker Alec! He ought to fry, whatever he did or didn't do. But if I blow the whistle on the dude, there's no way it's not going to come down on Tokiko. And her parents really are crazy."

Chelsea shook her head.

"And I'm so pissed at Dad. Like this is the cherry on top of a whole life's worth of selfish fuck-ups." She slapped at the magazine in front of her. "But then, he's my *dad*. And if Mom ever finds out about everything, she's going to end up in jail for castrating her ex. No way she wouldn't."

"You know what?" asked Chelsea.

"What?"

"I think you should talk to *my* dad."

"Jack?"

"Yeah. He's a lawyer. Not a criminal lawyer, but he's really smart. As dumb as he acts sometimes."

Sage laughed.

"Really. He's great at seeing the big picture. How everything fits together."

"I don't know," said Sage.

"What do you mean?"

"I mean, I guess I make fun of Jack all the time. I have to nurse him along when we're out running, even." Sage laughed again.

"Yeah, well, my dad's a piece of work."

"Don't get me wrong. I really like him. He's a good guy. Funny. Kind."

"But you don't respect him?"

"No, I do," protested Sage. Chelsea had never seen her look any more earnest.

"Did you know he and his law partners basically started up a center for domestic-violence victims in our town?" Chelsea asked.

Sage stared at her, wide-eyed.

"Yeah," said Chelsea. "I think Mom had a major hand in it, but even though Dad likes to act like an idiot sometimes instead of tooting his own horn, that doesn't mean he doesn't have a few things going for him, social responsibility–wise."

"Okay."

"Then let's think about it. Let me start out by asking if he's a mandatory reporter."

"A what?"

"A mandatory reporter. Somebody—professionals, usually—who, if they hear about some kind of child abuse—or the possibility of it—they have to report it to the police."

"Ooh. No!" Sage raised her hand like a traffic cop.

"No, I get it," said Chelsea. "We don't want to start anything we can't stop. Not right now. But I can ask him, in some low-key way, what Connecticut law is. Depending on what he says, we can go from there. Sound good? Okay, at least?"

"Maybe," said Sage. "Let me think about it."

"Good. So how do you feel?"

"Besides hungry?"

"Yeah."

"Maybe better," said Sage. "At least for right now."

They caught the 11:02 train from Zürich to Interlaken. Jack had always heard that the Swiss rail system ran with unearthly precision, so he was charmed to discover that his Rolex, synced that morning with the online Atomic Clock, matched to the second the time on the Hauptbahnhof's digital display. Even more impressively, the conductor's whistle sounded at precisely 11:01:45—and at 11:02:00 on the absolute dot, the electric motors wound up into a heavy purr and the train inched smoothly into motion. When he turned his attention back into the carriage, Grace was eyeing him with amusement.

"It's true," he said with a broad grin. "What a country!"

"I'm so happy for you," said Grace, with indeterminate sincerity.

Grace had actually been hoping that the carriages would be the old *Orient Express* type—the kind with individual compartments running along one side of a narrow passageway. If they'd been able to grab an enclosure all to themselves, she could have read Cinny's next set of instructions in a novel but appropriate setting. As it happened, the car was thoroughly up to date, with clean, comfortably upholstered seats that faced each other over narrow tables on either side of a central aisle. She decided the next installment of orders could wait and settled back into her novel for the bulk of the two-hour journey.

Her chance to convey Cinny's latest directives came after they'd taken the spur railway from Interlaken up to Grindelwald and checked into the pleasant but affordable hotel that Brian had booked for some budgetary relief after the St. Regis. The Bellary was a classic, chalet-style Swiss hostelry built of weathered wood the color of railroad ties. It sat on a south-facing slope opposite the Eiger, half a mile up from the center of town. Counter to anyone's hope that they might be welcomed by a beaming, buxom fräulein in dirndl and clogs—just back, perhaps, from a regional yodeling competition—they were met at the door by a dour older woman in a gray dress who showed them unceremoniously to their rooms, each of which was airing with windows thrown open wide. It was the second half of April and the day was sunny, but winter hadn't fully released its grip on the Oberland. Word was, there was still good skiing at the higher elevations.

Once they'd freshened up, they gathered in the small garden in front of the building. Brian suggested that everyone bring a jacket or sweater, but it was warm enough to sit in shirtsleeves on the sturdy wooden lawn furniture. They arranged their chairs to face the sun and sat in a semi-circle, with Grace at the center. Below lay the town of Grindelwald, and just beyond it—soaring so high into the cloudless sky that they had to tip their heads back to see the summit—rose the massive north wall of the Eiger, still shrouded in shadow as it was for every month of the year outside of high summer. They might have imagined they were sunning themselves on a beach, about to be swept by a mile-high wave—especially Jack, who hadn't fully recovered from the signage, storms, and nightmares of Ko Phi Phi.

They might have been forgiven, too, if they'd feared Cinny's next letter would immerse them in still more troubling confessions. News, for example, that Cinny had been rendered sterile by her abortion and that Grace and Brian were actually Frank's children by their maiden Aunt Eunice, whom they'd dubbed "Aunt Cruella" after she'd been caught on a home movie kicking a chihuahua that was trying to hump her foot. It turned out Cinny had anticipated their confessional shellshock and began her next installment accordingly.

"*I suppose, after Rome,*" read Grace, shielding her eyes from the bright sun, "*you're worried now that I'm going to tell you Frank and I ran a brothel in Geneva. But no such bombshells this time.*

"*You'll be in Grindelwald now, one of the most scenic places Frank and I have ever been. I do have to say that the Eiger is one frightening mountain, but everything else about the Oberland is absolutely lovely. We were there in March the year we spent in Oxford. Frank wanted to teach me how to ski, even though I was set on going to the Côte d'Azur for a little nude sunbathing.*"

Brian chuckled. "You've got to admire Mom's spunk," he said.

"No, I don't," said Grace. "*Frank had skied all his life, but I never had. I loathed it. You lace on these awful Frankenstein boots that gouge your ankles like iron shackles and you strap them onto these huge planks that you can't walk in or turn around on, and you aim them downhill when there's clearly no way in hell of turning or stopping. I'm sure the sport was invented by medieval monks as a way of letting gravity take care of heretics. Frank tried to teach me, and it nearly destroyed our marriage. He got me lessons, and it nearly drove the poor teacher—Anton, I think his name was—out of the ski school. I was cold. I was terrified. I was a petulant bitch. All I could think about was how sublime it would be to be in San Tropez, and how Frank was an absolute Nazi for keeping me there.*

"*You might gather I didn't like skiing, so this time, please, a half a measure of me to a full measure of Frank. I did think it was beautiful up on the Jungfraujoch, so I want you to take the train up and, on the level that looks out over the glacier, dig a hole in the snow and put me in there with Frank. It might be good to find a shady spot so we stay covered. But if you can't and we don't, I imagine we'll attract enough sunlight that we'll melt our way down into the ice again. In fact, the thought of the two of us seeping together down into the snow isn't unromantic.* Nice!" Grace snorted. "Count on Mom to turn simple thermodynamics into something kinky."

Brian laughed along with the others. "Anything more?"

"Another paragraph." Grace took a breath. "*I've been worried, since I wrote the note for Rome, that I might have left you thinking that Matthew and I were more important to each other through the years than we were.*

If I had the energy and time, I might go back and rewrite that note and maybe the one before it…make it clearer that we'd simply shared a glimpse of something that was wonderful and (we could hope) world-changing, but that couldn't really ever be. He was like a charming stranger who happened to be standing next to me on the deck of a ship when Halley's Comet went by, something so rare that people who saw it side by side would always be spiritually knit together by the experience. I can't tell you how much I wish it had been Frank. It may be selfish and stupid of me to have held onto that bright, fragile moment by having someone I could turn to and ask, 'Remember when?' I don't expect you to forgive me. It was a miracle that Dad could. But I didn't love Matthew for anything more than having shared a time with me, long ago, when the heavens flashed."

No one spoke as Grace folded the paper and sat back. Brian peered over at his sister. His eyebrow was cocked.

"Well, there's some additional data," Grace declared, meeting Brian's gaze.

Ella looked at her husband and then at Grace. "How does it make you feel? Not that you have to talk about it at all."

Grace took a breath and looked up across the valley, squinting against the sun. "I guess it makes me feel better. In some ways, definitely. I mean, she said she didn't love him. In any serious way. Any more than someone she'd been on a cruise with way back when. You look dubious, kiddo."

"Not really," replied Brian. "But sleeping with someone a bunch of nights and getting pregnant is a little more momentous than stargazing in adjacent deckchairs on a Carnival cruise. Don't you think?"

"Of course it is," agreed Grace. "But she did imply Dad knew she and Matthew were keeping in touch, so he must have been okay with it. Which does make me feel better."

"I guess," said Brian. "I want to believe her."

Ella reached up to stroke the back of Brian's head. "I feel like Cinny's being honest with us, boo. Why would she be telling us *any* of this if she was only going to lie about it? She's got to be telling the truth. As she knew it, anyway."

"I'm with you, Ella," said Chelsea. "But I know it's hard, all this. I mean, I don't have a clue how I'd react if Mom ever delivered news to me like Nana just delivered to her and Uncle Brian."

"Neither do I," said Jack, smiling at Grace. "That's for damn sure."

"Are you sure you want me to stay?" asked Chelsea. Jack had just come into their room and had yet to sit down.

"I'm sure," replied Sage. "As long as Jack's okay with it."

"Fine with me," said Jack. "I think it's always wise to have a second set of ears listening. If you can."

"Okay," said Sage.

"Take the chair, Dad," said Chelsea. "I'll sit on my bed."

Jack sat down next to the gaily stenciled bureau and threw an ankle over his knee. He looked at the two of them and drummed his fingers on the heel of his shoe. "First of all, Sage," he said with a smile, "I guess Chelsea told you I'm not a mandatory reporter. Lots of professionals are, but lawyers and priests aren't. For reasons that are pretty obvious."

Sage nodded. "I guess."

"Well, I doubt you'd be talking to me right now if it was about something I'd have to report. Just asking for advice might commit you to something you didn't want to set in motion. You do want advice, right?"

"Definitely."

"And let me say upfront I don't bill hours when I'm on vacation." Jack grinned and tapped the crystal of his watch. "If I did, you'd already owe me fifty bucks."

Chelsea rolled her eyes.

"You could take it out of my trainer's fee," Sage replied distractedly. "So," she said after a moment, "Chelsea filled you in on the details?"

"I think so. Your friend woke up in bed with this guy?"

"Yes."

"And they both had their underwear on?"

"Yes."

"And she couldn't remember anything—that she'd consented to anything or not? Or that they'd even had sexual contact, either touching or intercourse?"

"Right."

"Have you communicated with her lately?"

"A little," said Sage.

"And have you talked about this situation?" Jack looked over at Chelsea, who sat on the edge of her bed with a long face.

"Yes," replied Sage.

"But she doesn't remember any more now than she did before?"

"Nope."

"How old is she?"

"Sixteen. Same as me."

Jack nodded. "And at the time of the incident?"

"Sixteen. Her birthday was, like, two months before. Her parents gave her one of those stupid parties." She looked at Chelsea. "I hope you didn't have one."

"Are you kidding?" Chelsea looked horrified.

"Okay," said Jack. "I expect you're aware that the age of consent in Washington State is sixteen. So we wouldn't be talking about statutory rape or corruption of a minor."

"It could still be rape, though, couldn't it?" asked Sage. "If she didn't consent?"

"It could," replied Jack. "If there was penetration. But you said she had no idea if there was?"

"Right. She'd been having sex with her boyfriend for a year and all."

"And there was no evidence of semen in her vagina?"

Sage shook her head.

Jack looked at Chelsea. "Sorry, honey."

"No. It's okay," said Chelsea. "Just not a lot of fun."

"I get it," said Jack.

"So, where are we?" asked Sage. She got up and walked over to the window, looking up at the mountain.

"Well, even if there had been penetration, no evidence got taken, so we couldn't really move on a rape charge even if one was warranted. And like I said, she was of legal age. What's left, then, would probably be something called indecent liberties, which in Washington would include things like non-consensual touching and exposing. But I have to be frank: unless you saw or heard something, or unless Toriko remembers something…"

"That's *Tokiko*," said Sage. "Two Ks."

"Sorry. I suck with foreign names."

"How about *international names*, Dad?" suggested Chelsea. "Or *Japanese names*?"

"I also suck at cultural sensitivity in general," said Jack. "Grace is the one in the family who handles all that stuff."

"Jeez, Dad!" said Chelsea. "You might as well say Mom does all the breathing for the family. Everybody's responsible for their own human decency."

"I know," said Jack. "It's just tough when you start life as a redneck." He smiled at Sage. "But back to Tokiko. I don't know there's anything to be done unless something else turns up."

"Well, that sucks!" said Sage.

"It does," agreed Jack. "And it's more or less sucky depending on what actually happened. Is *sucky* a real word?" He looked at Chelsea.

"It works," she said.

Jack turned back to Sage. "You say she doesn't want to follow up on this in any way?"

"No," replied Sage. "She's not pregnant, and she's scared shitless her parents will find out."

"And you've tried to help her see it from another angle?"

"I have. And I have to say, it's really frustrating. She just clams up or tries to change the subject."

Jack nodded. "Want some advice?"

"What gave you that idea?"

"I've got two pieces of it. First, if anything like this ever happens again, nip it in the bud at the very start."

"Thanks," Sage said snidely. "I already got that figured out."

"Hey, don't forget I'm not charging you for anything," said Jack, feigning indignation. "I get to say things you've already thought about if I want to. For emphasis, is how you should think about it."

"Okay," said Sage, with a little sigh. "What else you got?"

"I think you should maybe run it all by Tokiko one more time. Just to make sure she gets a last chance to consider that there may be a larger issue at stake than her relationship with her parents."

"*Is* there any larger issue for a sixteen-year-old than her relationship with her parents?" asked Chelsea. She looked at Sage, who stared back at her.

"Maybe not," said Jack. "But if I were Sage, I'd give it one more try. Just lay out the chance this guy might do something similar in the future—hell, something worse—and how she might feel for the next girl."

"I guess," said Sage. "It seems pretty hopeless, though. I've tried. And, honestly, me having a mother who's great—don't you dare tell her I said that!—and a dad who totally sucks…it's hard for me to imagine what it would be like to have two parents who are both just semi-assholes. I get what she must be feeling. But the thought of this Alec dickhead just breezing along to the next 'indecent liberty' drives me batshit."

"I understand," said Jack. "That's why I suggest you try with her one more time."

"You can say something about how this trip helped you see things from different perspectives," suggested Chelsea. "Being out in the world, seeing different cultures, watching a family bury their loved ones and talk about the whole big sweep of life. Beginning to end. We're only with our parents for a short time, really. Maybe that would help."

"Great suggestion," said Jack.

"Maybe," replied Sage. "But it just pisses the shit out of me to see bullshit like this and not be able to do a thing about it."

"I can tell," said Jack. "And if I were Ella and Brian, I'd be incredibly proud of you. Aggressive impatience and all." Jack grinned.

"Is that supposed to be a compliment?" asked Sage.

Jack laughed. "Look, Sage. Anybody can see you're a great campaigner for everything that's good. Gender equality, social justice, environmental sustainability. What have I left out?" He looked at Chelsea, who just smiled. "You've got a whole life of good works to be doing, though, and you're not doing anybody any favors if you burn yourself out before you hit twenty. And let me tell you, even when you hit fifty, like me, you'll be kicking yourself for all the things you didn't accomplish, no matter how hard you tried. So trust me. Learn how to cut yourself some breaks as soon as you can. Keep up the fight." He banged on the dresser top. "Finish the marathon. But be realistic about the number of old farts you can drag along with you to finish under three hours."

"I don't want to drag any old farts along. I just want to kill a few."

"Well, if you get caught," said Jack, "call me up. Fair warning, though: I *do* bill for homicide defenses."

Ever since Jack awakened her in the middle of the night with the news that he wasn't going to be buying the Paul Newman Porsche, Grace had assumed he'd never get all the way around the globe without making some kind of lavish compensatory purchase. It had seemed unlikely he'd spring for anything in New Zealand other than assorted rugby paraphernalia; his materialistic fancy hadn't extended—not yet at least—to foreign real estate or herds of livestock. Singapore was riskier, world-famous as it was for high-end shopping, yet he'd come away with nothing but the Montblanc roller ball of record. He'd been dangerously fascinated by the longtail boats in Ko Phi Phi, but he might just as well have purchased a baby elephant in Krabi when it came to the practicalities of shipping one home, not to mention the challenge of owning and maintaining one in Westport, Connecticut. In Rome, he'd ended up buying a handsome briefcase—stylishly designed and handmade from butter-soft leather—but it was always going to be Switzerland that offered Jack his next great opportunity in a lifelong effort to bury his Clearwater roots under a mulch of luxurious possessions.

Grace could tell that, as panicked as he'd been by the chance that the mainspring of his latest Rolex had been magnetized at Newark Airport, the watch no longer charmed him as it once had. He'd stopped putting it back into its original box every night after only three months, and within half a year, he wore it no more often than he wore his Omega Moon Watch, his IWC Portugieser, or the Rolex Submariner that Grace, with her unpracticed eye, could hardly distinguish from the Sea-Dweller anyway. The Sea-Dweller was the only watch he'd brought on the trip. She suspected, though, that it had therefore devolved in his mind into a kind of "everyday timepiece," and that its failure to excite him any longer as he strapped it on in the morning would soon lead to another, even more extravagant, purchase. She supposed she should be grateful that he seemed timelessly devoted to her personally—rather than, say, supplanting her, too, with a newer model. She *was* in fact grateful for that. But that didn't mean that, when he returned to their bedroom at the Bellary in mid-afternoon and asked if she'd be interested in walking down to the watch boutique in the center of town, she didn't have a strong feeling of *déja achetée*. Curiosity, as much as anything, drove her to accept his offer.

Grindelwald's main shopping street was crowded with pedestrians, strolling contentedly past the various boutiques in pairs and small groups. "Anything particular in mind?" she asked him.

"I've got an idea." He looked at her and smiled.

"Another Rolex?"

"I'm not sure how many Rolexes they have here, actually."

"Really? What an horological backwater!" They walked on in the warm sunshine. "Is this it?" She paused by a corner shop, its display windows topped by bright logo signs for Tissot, Swiss Military, and Swatch.

Jack chuckled. "That's just a toy store, Honey Pot."

They wove on through the crowds to what was obviously a tonier boutique, occupying the ground floor of an attractive, four-story building. A bell jangled as they walked through the door into a quietly tasteful showroom. There were a dozen or so display counters arrayed around the central space, each of them blazoned with the name of an elite Swiss watchmaker: Breguet, Patek Philippe, Vacheron Constantin, Omega, Cartier, Blancpain.

"*Guten Tag*," said a middle-aged man in a trim gray suit as he stepped out from behind a desk. He had the assured manner of a professional who knew his business and clientele well.

"Hi," said Jack. "Beautiful day!"

"It is," agreed the man. "Somewhat warm for April."

"Suits me," said Jack. "I don't ski."

"A shame. The conditions are still excellent up above, I'm told."

Grace smiled. "My brother is on the mountain right now, with his wife. They were very excited."

"Perfect," said the man. His eyes dropped to Jack's wrist, quickly taking in the Sea-Dweller. "What can I help you with this afternoon?"

"Well," said Jack, as he turned slowly to appraise the whole of the shop, "I wonder if you have something with a tourbillon escapement. Maybe a Ulysse Nardin?"

The man's eyes lit noticeably. "Of course. We have the Executive Tourbillon Free Wheel, right over here. And the Bucherer Manero as well. And we have others in our shop in Interlaken."

"Great. Can I see the Nardin, please?"

"Of course." The man walked over behind the appropriate counter, removed a key from his pocket, and opened the case. He reached in and extracted a striking gold watch. The dial was jet black, and raised above it, almost as though they were suspended there in space under an unusual raised crystal, were various wheels and cogs of the movement, delicately crafted from a gold matched to the case. The man placed it on a velvet pad inscribed with the Ulysse Nardin logo and turned to Jack. "Would you like to see it on your wrist?"

"Sure." Jack removed his Rolex, placed it on the pad, and extended his arm across the counter, palm down. In what looked to Grace almost like a ritual of homage for a mystical guild, the man draped the Nardin carefully over Jack's wrist, then reached around to buckle it loosely. Jack tucked two fingers inside the strap to hold it firm and turned to Grace.

"We don't want to bend the leather," he explained with a smile. "In case I don't end up buying it." He turned again and extended his arms to examine the watch, dipping his shoulder so Grace could see.

"It's pretty big," said Grace. "And strange-looking. Kind of steam-punk, if you ask me."

"Just my style," chuckled Jack. "It would go great with my armored blimp. Forty-five millimeters?" he asked the man.

"Forty-four. Rose gold. Manual wind, of course, but with a 170-hour reserve."

"What's that mean?" asked Grace.

"It means you only have to wind it once a week," replied Jack.

"Great. Maybe when you put out the trash?" She smiled at the clerk. "Why does it look like that?" she asked Jack. "Kind of like a Miró painting?"

"Just to be unique. Artful." Jack turned to the man. "Can we see it running?"

"Of course."

The man unbuckled the strap, rotated the watch, and gave the crown six or eight twists. The movement sprang to life, and he strapped the timepiece back onto Jack's wrist.

"Here. Look," Jack said to Grace, pointing to the six o'clock position with his thumb. "That little doohickey at the bottom? That's the tourbillon escapement."

Grace laughed again. "Meaning?"

"The escapement is what allows energy to be transferred from the mainspring to the hands, basically. It rotates back and forth, quickly, kind of like a pendulum—look!—and allows the gears to move the hands at a precise rate. You know, the *tick tock*?"

Grace nodded.

"That's the sound of the escapement. Except, in a watch this fine, you'd need a stethoscope to hear it."

The clerk nodded. "Your husband is very knowledgeable," he said to Grace.

"How do you know he's not my chauffeur?"

The man laughed. "Very sorry. I don't. But if he specializes in automobiles, I believe he also knows timepieces. Would you care to see it in a full-length mirror, sir? There's one just over here. You can see if it suits you."

Jack waved his hand in the negative. "Here," he said, holding the watch up closer for Grace to see. "There's the escapement. Look at it carefully."

Grace bent over and squinted. "The little wheel is rotating back and forth...but the whole thing is spinning, too. The mount and all. Rotating slowly."

Jack chuckled. "Right."

"Why is it doing that?"

"Well, partly because the whole thing serves as the second hand. The whole unit rotates every sixty seconds. The real reason, though, is because it's designed to keep the force of gravity from making the watch less accurate."

"You're kidding me," said Grace, shaking her head. It struck Jack that she actually looked interested. "So tell me how the rotation counteracts gravity," she said. "It's not like a magical elevator watch, is it? 'Beam me up, Scotty'?" She grinned at the clerk, who smiled back politely.

Jack laughed. "The escapement rotates every sixty seconds, so any distortion in the mechanism caused by gravity at any given time gets evened out over the course of a minute."

"Interesting. Maybe not really necessary, but I'll give you interesting."

"It *is* interesting," replied Jack. "It's a miracle of engineering, I think. To make something that precise that small."

"I get it," said Grace. "Kind of like the space program without the rockets." She looked at the clerk. "How much would something like that cost?"

The man smiled easily. "The Executive Free Wheel is 81,000 francs."

"And dollars?" asked Grace. "U.S.?"

"Roughly the same in dollars, at the current rate of exchange."

Grace's jaw dropped. She stared at Jack.

"Of course," the man continued, "when you leave the country, you can recover the Value Added Tax. Which would make it roughly twenty percent less."

"Holy mother of God," said Grace. "Maybe if it negated the effects of gravity on *me*, I could see it. But Jack…"

"Take it easy, H.P. I just wanted to look at it. Explain how it works. You know? Let you see the artistry and invention. But that's only part of why I wanted to come." He extended his wrist to the clerk to let him remove the watch.

"What's the other part?" Grace eyed him suspiciously.

Jack turned to the clerk. "I'm actually thinking of something for Madame today. Maybe something in the Cartier range. Casual to formal. No frills, necessarily, but something elegant."

"Well," said the man, turning to Grace with a twinkle. "I'm sure we can find something perfect."

Grace walked back to the hotel with the first truly nice watch she'd ever owned. It came along with her first clear inkling—perhaps even a budding understanding—of what had attracted Jack to the world of luxury timepieces. Part of the charm, she had to admit, was being served a flute of champagne and some insanely cute specialty chocolates as the clerk wrote up the sales ticket. She was also intrigued to learn that the very first wristwatches had been made for women, since women then tended not to wear the trousers and vests into which a standard pocket watch could be slipped—unless, she quipped to Jack in the giddy indulgence of the moment, they were cross-dressers. The watch she'd chosen had actually been invented by Cartier for the famous Brazilian aviation pioneer Alberto Santos-Dumont, who'd found that, in the midst of trying not to crash and burn in his finicky experimental aircraft, having to haul out a pocket watch to see how long his gasoline would last was not particularly convenient.

Grace's first instinct, once the purchase had been made, was to pop the watch back into its box and walk back to the hotel wearing her trusty Movado. When Jack and the clerk convinced her to wear the new acquisition, she found herself looking down at it every fifty strides or so, exactly as she had often made fun of Jack for doing. With every swing of her arm, she thought she might just be able to feel the rotor of the automatic movement swinging back and forth to wind the mainspring.

As they began to climb the hill to the Bellary, it occurred to her that she'd rarely heard Jack speak with the combination of knowledge and passion he'd shown that afternoon, except maybe at a rugby game. She'd begun the walk expecting to be bored almost to death in the shop and, ultimately, to end up rolling her eyes at yet another of Jack's addictive acquisitions. Instead, he'd come away with nothing more than a small Swiss Army knife the clerk had thrown in as a gift "for Monsieur." More surprisingly, she'd glimpsed the appeal of an enthusiasm she'd never considered anything but absurd. She'd also been deeply touched by Jack's generosity—of spirit and of credit card, both. In the end, he'd made the whole afternoon about her.

That night, the six of them walked back from dinner in town under a brilliant dome of stars. Overnight, as they slept the fitful sleep of stomachs overfilled with fondue and strudel, a warm front lifted further out of northern Italy than weather models had predicted. When they gathered in the dining room for breakfast, the upper half of the Eiger was completely shrouded in thick, swirling cloud. Brian checked at the desk to see if the Jungfraubahn would still be running. He was told that it would be and that they'd likely have their pick of departure times, since most tourists would hold off for a clearer day. And so, with a reminder from Brian to bring hats, gloves, plenty of warm layers, and a hearty windbreaker, they grabbed the day's bag of ashes and headed down to town to catch the train up to Kleine Scheidegg.

Sitting in the antiseptically clean, polished-wood-and-stainless-steel carriage with a large group of young Italians, equipped to ski but presently caught up in a kind of random group flirtation, Jack went on a bit of a tear about how exciting it was to be riding the celebrated cog railway up to the "Top of Europe." The line, he'd been reading and was more than willing to make known to one and all, was completed in the first years of the twentieth century—just under six miles of it, almost all of which tunneled through the solid limestone of the Eiger and the neighboring Mönch before it broke through the glacier at the Jungfraujoch itself. At over 11,000 feet, the station at the low point between the Mönch and the Jungfrau was the highest on the continent. The rolling stock itself, Jack avidly informed them, was the pinnacle of Swiss engineering: rack-driven exactly like the movement of a fine watch, it recouped on every descent over fifty percent of the electrical energy it required on the way up. He sat on the edge of his seat, gesturing energetically as he spoke, while Chelsea looked on with a grin. Once he'd reached the end of his expanded briefing, she looked expectantly at Grace.

"What's up, Mom?" she asked after a beat or two.

"What do you mean?"

"You're not going to make fun of Dad for the little techno rant?"

Grace looked at Jack, who sat there with his eyebrows raised. "I think I'll give it a pass."

Chelsea snorted. "What's up with that?"

"I don't know," shrugged Grace. "All the cheese last night must have clogged my sarcasm ducts." She caught Jack's eye as she thumbed the bracelet of her new Cartier and smiled.

They arrived at Kleine Scheidegg to find that the trains up to the Jungfraujoch hadn't yet begun to run. The winds were still strong enough that they were coursing down the tunnel with dangerous intensity. Conditions were expected to ease before noon, however, so Brian suggested they go into the big hotel uphill from the station for coffee or hot chocolate. The place had featured in the film *The Eiger Sanction*, and a photo of Clint Eastwood and George Kennedy still hung in the café. Brian shared the story of Toni Kurz, the young German soldier on whose death a portion of the film, like the novel it came from, was partially based. He had perished in 1936 while answering Hitler's call to prove the mastery of the German race by being the first to scale the Eiger's "unclimbable" North Wall. He'd frozen to death at the end of a rope, only feet from his would-be rescuers. None of the group was surprised by Sage's take on the tragedy.

An hour later, they boarded the boxy red-and-yellow carriage of the Jungfrau train, and forty minutes later, they arrived at the Jungfraujoch Station, a long, stone gallery arched like a Quonset hut, with ranks of florescent lighting, ventilation ducts, and trolley wires strung along the ceiling. They took a lift to an upper level and made for the exit to the Ice Plateau, at the far end of an angular concrete structure that looked like it had been built as a villain's lair for a James Bond movie. The current view through its southwest wall of high-impact glass was like the inside of a cotton ball. Brian, first out the door, reversed course immediately, jumping back inside with a shake of his head.

"Damn!" he said. "It's really blowing up a storm. And they said the wind was down."

"Is it safe?" asked Grace. "Should we even go out there?"

"We'll be okay," replied Brian. "But zip up, everybody. You may have to hold onto your hats. Do you have Mom and Dad ready?"

Grace held up her bag.

"Okay," said Brian. "Let's go."

They stepped out onto a widening fan of snow. The section nearest the door was black with crushed rock thrown down for traction. The wind blew fiercely from the south, upwards of thirty or thirty-five miles an hour, enough to force them into little involuntary steps even when they tried to stand still. Two rows of stout wooden pickets, strung with rope, extended out on either side of a track that disappeared into swirling cloud a hundred feet away.

"We all set?" yelled Brian. The others looked at each other and nodded as the wind whipped at their clothing. "Just stay between the ropes. The path leads up and around to the right," he called, turning and pointing. "The plateau's up there. If something happens and you can't see anyone, just stay put, and we'll find you. But we'll be fine. They wouldn't let us come out here if it was really dangerous."

"That's what Little Red Riding Hood kept telling herself," yelled Grace.

They set off along the track as the wind shoved them on. Wraiths of vapor raced past, opening up short vistas and then closing them down completely. Brian led the way, sticking close to the right-hand ropes, even though the marked track was no more than fifteen feet wide. They climbed a small rise, bent around to the right with the wind doing its best to knock them sideways, then bent around again to the left. The footing was tricky. They were off the gravel now, and the snow underfoot was icy, packed solid by hundreds of walkers. At one point Grace slipped, but Chelsea was walking by her side and managed to catch her and hold her up.

Their rapid gain in altitude on the train was painfully apparent; it was eight thousand feet from Grindelwald up to where they stood. Brian stopped several times to catch his breath, and the others did as well. Another hundred yards and they reached a level spot where the ropes flared out on either side into what looked to be a circle, perhaps forty yards in diameter. In the center stood a flagpole on which a Swiss flag snapped violently in the gale. They were the only people there, their fellow passengers having evidently opted to visit the touristy Ice Palace before they ventured out.

"What do you think?" Brian called loudly.

Grace shook her head and held her hand to her ear.

"What do you think?" Brian shouted again. "Next to the flag?"

"Why not?" shouted Grace. "No time to scout all over."

Brian took off his backpack and opened one side pocket, then the other. "Shit!" he muttered. He unzipped the main compartment and rummaged around until the wind nearly whipped the bag from his hands. "Damn it!" he yelled, looking at Grace. "I must have left the trowel at the hotel. God damn it!"

"Try using your hands," yelled Grace. She reached out and took the pack from him.

Brian knelt down and dug at the snow with his gloved hands. He scraped repeatedly to no effect. "Like concrete." He stood up and kicked at the surface with the toe of his boot, then tried hacking with his heel. "Man! I thought the snow would be softer."

"It may be when the sun's out," called Ella.

"Then see what you can do about these clouds," grinned Brian.

"Try over near the ropes," suggested Sage. "Maybe just outside, where nobody's walked."

"Good thought." Brian walked downwind past the flag, staggering as a gust caught him. The others followed, huddling close as he reached the edge of the circle. A triangular warning sign was mounted on a four-by-four post. It wobbled crazily in the wind. *Stop!* it read, in large lettering. *Hinter den Abschrankungen Bleiben: Stay behind the ropes!* Pictured in black silhouette was a man tumbling backwards into what was obviously supposed to be a crevasse. Brian lifted the rope and ducked under.

"Careful, boo!" shouted Ella. "You're not supposed to be there."

"Just getting on the other side here. Where the snow isn't compacted." He knelt and tried again to scoop the snow away. Nothing. He stood up and kicked again, with scarcely more luck. A few chips of ice spun away in the wind. "Anybody got anything to dig with?" he yelled. "I can't believe I left the fucking trowel."

"I don't suppose my cell phone would be of any use," quipped Jack.

"Not unless you call Jeff Bezos and he sends a drone up with an ice ax," laughed Brian. He knelt again and took off his gloves, holding them up to Ella.

"No, boo!" she said. "You'll get frostbite. It's freezing." The outside thermometer at the station had read -12 degrees Celsius—10 degrees Fahrenheit.

"Let me just try." Brian bent his fingers and clawed at the surface. After fifteen seconds, he shook his head, stood up, and reached for his gloves. "Shit! I should have gotten organized instead of spending yesterday skiing."

Jack looked at Grace, who was biting her lip.

"Don't beat yourself up, Uncle Brian," yelled Chelsea. "It's on all of us."

"What do you think now?" asked Jack. "Do we just let them fly off with the wind?"

"We could," responded Brian. "But that's not what Mom wanted."

"She couldn't have anticipated this," said Jack. "Under the circumstances…"

"Look over there," yelled Brian. He pointed downwind. Past the sign, visible and vanishing by turns, was a soft fold in the snow. A darker edge rose up behind it.

"What?" asked Jack.

"A crevasse. Like the sign says. A glacier drops down to the valley from here."

"And—?"

"Maybe I can crawl over to it and drop them in."

"No effing way, boo," yelled Ella, panic rising in her voice. "I mean it. Look at the sign. That's the dumbest shit I've ever heard."

"Thanks for the confidence, honey," replied Brian.

"Look," said Grace. "Let's just dump the bags, say a few words, and head back down. How would Mom feel if you fell into a crevasse?"

Brian laughed. "Sad, probably. But there's plenty of times *you* would have jumped for joy."

"This isn't one of them," shouted Grace.

"I've got an idea." Jack stepped forward. He removed a glove, reached into his pocket, and pulled out his complimentary Swiss Army knife.

"What? You're going to whittle the flagpole into a shovel?" asked Grace.

"There's an idea worthy of an Ivy Leaguer," shouted Jack. "But no. Look at all those ropes." He pointed to the pickets and the doubled strand of rope running between them.

"No way, Jack," yelled Grace, the wind whipping her hair. "That's safety equipment. They catch you destroying it, they'll lock you up for the duration. Drown you in a bowl of fondue or something."

"It *is* safety equipment. We'll just use it for Brian. And when he's done with it, we'll string it back up. No one will be the wiser."

"That's crazy," cried Grace. "I mean it." She looked at Jack, and then at the rest of them. "What do you all think?"

"I don't know," replied Chelsea. "What do you think, Uncle Brian? Would it be safe?"

"Safer than without a rope."

"There!" said Jack.

"Look," yelled Brian. "I'm not worried at all. This is the top rift in the ice, so it won't be deep. I could probably stand up in the bottom. And, if I'm on a rope, it'll be that much safer. There's no way I'm going to end up like Toni Kurz."

"You promise?' asked Ella.

"You're so cute, Mom," shouted Sage as she stepped over to give her mother a hug. "But Brian promising isn't going to make a big difference, is it?"

"Yeah, it will," said Brian. "I honestly, truly, absolutely wouldn't think of it if there was any real danger. Doing what Mom wanted is a thousand times worth the risk."

"I guess," said Grace.

"Okay," said Jack. "And I get to use my new knife!" He held it up with a grin.

"But take it easy, Jack," said Brian. "We only need about forty feet. I can tie on to one end and you can take a wrap around the sign pole to belay me. Good?"

"Got it." Jack cut the bottom rope free from the picket nearest them, walked back and un-looped it from the next support, and made another cut at the next picket. He coiled the rope with some difficulty in the wind and walked back to Brian, handing him a loose end. Brian wrapped it around his waist, tied in snugly, and turned to Grace. "Okay, Tiger," he said. "Deliver the goods."

Grace reached into her bag, pulled out the baggies, and handed them to Brian. "Be careful, kiddo!"

"I will. On belay?" He looked at Jack, who stood by the sign with the rope looped around the pole at snow level.

"Aye, aye, Captain," yelled Jack.

Brian laughed. "Wrong sport. You say, *Belay on!*"

"Belay on," called Jack.

"Perfect," yelled Brian. He ducked under the rope and walked slowly toward the edge of the crevasse.

"I thought you were going to crawl," shouted Ella, pushing up against the rope restraints.

"In a minute," yelled Brian, his voice all but muffled by the wind.

"Easy, Mom," said Sage, putting her arm around her again.

"Brian!" Ella yelled.

Brian dropped to his knees and edged toward the brink of the crevasse just as a major gust whipped over the ridge. It nearly blew him onto his side.

"Brian," Ella screamed again. "Come back. You're a stupid fuck!"

"Mom," said Sage. "Really. He's fine."

"Don't worry," called Jack, paying put out rope. "I've got him. If Brian goes, I go too."

"That's reassuring," said Grace.

Brian crawled on hands and knees to within feet of the soft fold marking the near side of the crevasse, then went down on his stomach. He wriggled forward, like an Army trainee crawling under barbed wire, and came to a halt right at the brink.

"How deep is it?" yelled Jack.

Brian turned his head and shouted something that a gust swept away.

"What did he say?" asked Jack "'Very'?"

"I think it was '*Not* very,'" said Sage.

"I thought it was 'Scary,'" offered Chelsea.

"Shit!" said Ella. "If anything happens to him…"

"Shit!" they heard Brian yell in a dip in the wind.

"What?" yelled all five of them in unison.

"Lost the bags!"

Brian wriggled around to face in the opposite direction, crawled a way, and then staggered back to them. He explained he'd managed to open the baggies and sprinkle Cinny and Frank into the crevasse. He was pretty sure most of them had fallen in, but a gust had torn the bags from his hands before he had a chance to check. As the things slapped against the far side of the crevasse and slid down into the depths, he'd had a terrible feeling that Cinny would be angry at him for littering. Grace said she was certain their mother would understand. The important thing was that Brian was safe.

"So what were you saying about how deep it was?" asked Jack.

"It was *very* deep," replied Brian. "I was totally wrong. I could see down at least twenty feet, and there was an edge there that opened onto something even deeper."

"I knew it!" cried Ella. "You really are a stupid fuck."

"But you still love me, right?" asked Brian, with an uneasy grin.

Ella paused for a moment. "God help me, but I do."

Jack turned to Grace as he organized the rope. "Get that, H. P. They're playing our song."

Grace was used to retiring along with Jack before the rest of the crew. That night, however, she found herself sitting with Brian in the hotel lounge after all the others had gone up to their rooms. The wind was still high, and the window frames rattled intermittently with the gusts. They'd returned from the mountain to find a fire crackling on the hearth. It still glowed warmly in front of them as they sat, side by side, on the massive couch.

"Well, that was another minor epic," said Brian. "Almost as good as Phi Phi Leh."

"Yeah. What is it with Mom, anyway? Is she trying to kill us?"

"You're thinking, like, radical late-term abortion?"

"That's not funny, Brian."

"Sorry. It's just so weird, though. Here we are spreading Mom and Dad's ashes in the places they loved the most, and it's turning into a dump-and-run operation. You know? Like dropping trash alongside the road and peeling out before anybody catches us."

"As though Dad's a bag of empties and Mom's a chicken carcass?"

"Jesus, Gracie!"

"Sorry. You started it."

"Doesn't it feel impersonal, though?" asked Brian after a pause. "I mean, not just when we're about to drown in a thunderstorm or get blown off a mountain. Rome, too. Really, the only time I felt like we could really say goodbye was on Quail Island. And part of that was Jack's poem."

"I know what you mean," said Grace. "But a year from now, we'll just be thinking how wonderful it is that Mom and Dad are where they want to be. We won't be thinking about having to rush off. Dump and run or whatever."

"I guess," said Brian.

They sat for a moment, listening to the soft sigh of the fire.

"Look," said Grace. "Let's think about the time we had with Mom in Hanover as our goodbye time. We told her we loved her. We hugged her and thanked her for being our mom." She reached over and patted Brian on the knee.

"You're right," replied Brian. "But Dad?"

"He knew we loved him. We had some great times his last years. Talking about trips. Talking about books. It's like he almost knew it was a time for goodbyes. And hugs."

"I guess." Brian stood up and walked over to the fire. He pulled the screen back and pitched on another log. "Have you thought any more about Mom and Matthew?"

"A little."

"And—?"

"I guess I'm okay with it," Grace replied. "It seems like Dad knew and was okay with it, too. Did you ever see *anything* to suggest Mom and Dad weren't still in love to the very end?"

"You mean except for the fact they couldn't change their sheets without screaming at each other? Or pack the car?"

Grace laughed. "Jack freaks out when I drink out of the milk carton."

"You drink out of the milk carton? Do your students know that? Does Chelsea know that?"

"Chelsea taught me."

"And to think we share the same genes." He sat back down beside her, kicked off his shoe, and reached down to pull back on his toes. "Little cramp."

"Ooh. Sorry."

"I've got to ask," said Brian, staring at her candidly.

"What?"

"Do you believe all that shit about Woodstock? That it really was as big a thing as Mom always said?"

"You don't believe her?"

"It's not that," replied Brian. "I guess if that's the way she felt about it, then that's the way it was. The dawn of a new age. Personally, I guess I'm too much of a cynic to believe anything's ever going to change the way things are in this world that much. For the better, at least."

"I hear you. Sad to say."

"So I guess it's one of those *You had to be there* things. But I've got to say, standing on the outside and believing that three days of music and rain and hooking up in a tent justifies a lifetime of emotional trickiness? That's still hard for me to get my head around."

"Maybe it's more intellectual trickiness, Brian, than emotional."

"Whatever. And when it comes to fidelity, who am I to judge, anyway?" He looked uncertainly at his sister.

"Don't get me started," said Grace. "Not tonight."

OXFORD

Brian was keenly aware that peak-hour arrivals at Heathrow meant agonizing delays at passport control, so he'd arranged a flight that got them in during a midafternoon lull. The walk from the gate to the immigration hall still went on forever—long enough for Ella to joke that the U.K. Olympic Committee probably used it to screen for the next generation of marathoners.

Once they'd taken the train into Paddington and checked into their chic little hotel opposite the station, Chelsea and Sage set out for a run down through Hyde Park. Grindelwald had offered nothing but lung-searing uphills and shin-splitting downhills, and they were eager to get out on the flat for some good chatty miles. They looped around Speakers' Corner, where a bald man with a parrot-beak nose was railing against the health dangers of latex clothing, then dropped down to the north side of the Serpentine. Scores of people, white and brown, young and old, plied the glassy waters in rented rowboats and pedalos, while hundreds more strolled or bicycled along the graveled banks—all of them clearly relishing being out and about on a warm spring evening.

A dozen or so children splashed barefoot in the Princess Diana Memorial Fountain as Sage and Chelsea ran by. Chelsea spied a girlish grin erupt on Sage's face and insisted they take a break, pull off their shoes and socks, and wade right in. For ten minutes they circumnavigated the oval of stone sluiceways, befriending in the process a pair of curly-haired and totally drenched pre-teen girls. When the girls' mothers called them away, Chelsea and Sage padded over to a stretch of lawn beside two shade trees and sat down to let their feet dry as they watched the strolling throngs.

"Wow! Thanks for that," said Sage, shaking out her hair in the soft breeze. "Sometimes I forget to be a kid."

Chelsea laughed. "I know. Growing up can be serious business. Too many of us make it a full-time job way too early in life. Girls especially."

"Beauty sells," Sage replied with a scowl. "Start 'em early."

Chelsea snorted. "You know Naomi Wolf?"

"I love Naomi Wolf. Tokiko does, too."

Chelsea nodded. "Have you been in touch?"

"Tried." Sage leaned back on her arms and crossed her ankles. "I don't think she wants to hear what I have to say."

"Maybe that's not a surprise."

"Nope. But it *is* fucking frustrating. Oh! Damn!" Sage sat back up with a start. "I wanted to ask. What did Grant find out?"

Chelsea took a breath and exhaled slowly. "Mixed results."

"Oh, Chel!"

"Three of the samples—out of twelve—came back positive. For cancer."

"Oh man." Sage put her hand on Chelsea's shoulder.

"The good news, I guess, is that it isn't very advanced. I don't understand all the numbers yet, but Grant said the urologist doesn't seem overly concerned."

"That's great!" Sage leaned back again. "How weird is that, though? They find cancer, and then they say they're not very concerned."

"I guess prostate cancer is slow-moving, usually. And, again, Grant's evidently isn't very advanced."

"So does he have to have an operation? Have it removed?"

"He doesn't know. They may decide just to wait and watch it for a bit. And I guess there are a bunch of non-operative things they can do, including radiation."

"Nuke it."

"Yeah."

Sage touched her shoulder again. "I'm so sorry, Chel. It's got to be really hard being so far away right now. And knowing about his kids. Has he told them yet?"

"Not yet."

"Shit!"

"I know," said Chelsea.

They watched as a four- or five-year-old boy staggered by on tiny rollerblades, his father running alongside him. The boy grinned insanely.

"I don't know how to say this, actually," said Sage after a minute, "but are you going to stay with him?"

Chelsea looked shocked. "Of course I am. Of course!" She took another deep breath and looked back toward the fountain.

"No offense, but I don't know if I could do that. I hope I would, you know?" Sage looked at Chelsea imploringly. "If I loved him."

"I *do* love him. And his kids, too."

"That's so cool, Chel," said Sage after a beat. "You're such a good person."

"I don't know."

"Yeah, you are." Sage wrapped her arms around her knees. "Like I said, if I were in your shoes, this little voice in the back of my head would probably be saying, *Man. I didn't sign up for this.*"

"Life's always about more than you sign up for," replied Chelsea. "I mean, who even asks to be born in the first place, right? It's all about being the kind of person you want yourself to be. What you do when the shit hits the fan."

"I guess."

Chelsea laughed. "I think, if Grant and I ever get married, I'm going to make him put that in the wedding vows. *I promise to love, honor, and cherish you—even when the shit hits the fan.* It's got a romantic ring to it, doesn't it?"

"It does. Almost Biblical. Like a reading from the Book of Excrement.'"

Chelsea laughed.

They sat quietly as the shadows lengthened. Somewhere down toward the river, a police siren did its signature European *dee-dah, dee-dah,* then faded away.

"I hope Brian sticks with my mom," said Sage at last.

"Why wouldn't he?" asked Chelsea. "They're great together. I've never seen him so happy."

"Really?"

"Really. Are you worried about anything in particular?"

"I don't know," replied Sage. "He was with Kingsley for so long. They seemed really happy, I guess. And then Brian meets my mom and, poof! He's off with her and Kingsley's just spinning in the breeze."

Chelsea sighed. "I don't know. Brian and Ella seem like they're meant for each other. That sounds corny, but they do."

"Sure," said Sage, with a shrug. "Mom's his ideal woman, maybe. Probably. But he's loved men before. And who's to say he won't fall in love with a man again?"

"You don't think he's after my dad, do you?" Chelsea tittered. "The manly, rugby type? With all the cool watches?"

Sage smiled in spite of herself.

"Look," said Chelsea. "I'll tell you something. If you promise not to talk about it with anyone. Not your mom. Not Tokiko. No one."

"Jeez, Chel!" Sage looked apprehensive. "But okay. I promise."

Chelsea slid closer, arranged her legs in a modified lotus pose, and leaned forward. "You know how Mom and Brian go at it sometimes? I mean, get after each other more than it seems like they need to?"

"They're siblings." Sage grinned. "I thought that's what siblings are supposed to do."

"I wouldn't know," said Chelsea. "Any more than you. But Mom told me years ago that when she and Brian were in high school, and she was a better student than he was and a better athlete and all-around more popular—"

"Yeah?"

"Mom was going out with the quarterback on the football team, this really hot shit named Jimmy Lamont that all the girls wanted to jump all over. A really handsome dude, and a total athletic stud."

"Sounds like he must have been an asshole."

Chelsea laughed. "Well, he and Mom were going hot and heavy, like King and Queen of the Prom and everything. And one weekend their senior year when Mom is in Boston with Nana—Cinny—looking at Harvard, Brian and Jimmy are hanging out together and they get really drunk, and Brian ends up having sex with the guy."

Sage sat bolt upright. "You're shitting me!"

"Honest to God. That's what she told me."

"And you believe her?"

"Why would she lie?" asked Chelsea. "It's not the kind of thing you make up about your own brother. Unless she really hated him."

"Damn! How'd she find out about it?"

"Jimmy was into this honesty thing."

"Wait a minute!" Sage sat up even straighter. "A macho high-school quarterback is so big into honesty he tells his girlfriend that he's had sex with her brother?"

"He went on to be the first gay Episcopal minister in the State of New Hampshire. Mom was basically the first person he came out to, and he told everyone later on that knowing he had to tell her the truth was the first step on his path to redemption. That's what he said, anyway."

"Holy shit!"

"Yeah. So, speaking of shit hitting the fan, you can imagine what happened in the Posey household. Mom confronts Uncle Brian and says he's a total fuck for having sex with her boyfriend. Was it just because he's jealous of her? He says no, but when she asks him if he's really gay and if it was attraction and not spite that made him do it, he just clams up." Chelsea uncrossed her legs and sat sideways on her hip, scooting even closer to Sage. "Nana—Cinny—finds out about it when she hears them shouting at each other, and she drags them both off to the hospital for an HIV test. They both came out negative, but it was years before Mom could really look at Brian without wanting to kick him in the balls. It was only when she had that uterine cancer and Brian came down to take care of everybody in New Haven that the rift between them started to heal. But like I said, you can still feel the aftershocks sometimes."

"Jeez," said Sage. "What a story! And you're telling me because—?"

"Because Brian's first involvement with another guy may have been at least partly about screwing his sister over."

Sage stared at Chelsea. "And Mom and I should trust him more as a result? Because he fucked a guy as part of a family feud?"

"Listen." Chelsea sat back up and tugged at the legs of her running shorts. "Maybe it was stupid to get into this. I know what you may be thinking. But Uncle Brian came clean with me once, and he said he felt incredibly guilty about what he'd done. That's the big reason he went down to New Haven—to make it up to her. And who knows? Maybe the whole time he was going out with men, it was partly his way of telling himself that he hadn't just fucked Mom over."

Sage looked at Chelsea skeptically. "I don't know. I'm not sure I buy that."

"Yeah. I guess that would be pretty extreme. You wonder how he could have stayed with Kingsley all that time."

"Exactly," said Sage. "And if it *was* true? God! What a fucked-up situation! I'd need to feel good about my mother being married to a guy who might not really be bisexual, as much as he was willing to have sex with a guy to screw his sister over."

"I get it. I wouldn't have told you, though, if I didn't think the bottom line is that Brian really wants to be with your mom and finally feels like he's sorted out his life."

"He's told you that?" asked Sage.

"Not in so many words. But I can see it."

"Yeah," said Sage. She turned and looked Chelsea square in the eye. "I'm going to have to think about this."

"Of course."

"And I may have to talk with Brian."

Chelsea hesitated. "I guess that would mean what I told you won't stay just between us. But I get it," she said. "As long as you keep an open mind, I can't imagine he'd be too pissed. Especially if he knew I was trying to reassure you he really loves your mom and wants to be with her."

"Of course I'll keep an open mind," said Sage. She looked mildly indignant. "Brian's never been anything but great with me. Better than my mom, half the time."

Chelsea laughed. "We don't have to go into that."

"But thanks," said Sage.

"I didn't fuck things up trying to make you feel better?"

"No more than I probably would have if I'd been you."

The six of them sat in the shaded garden of the Old Parsonage, a charming inn at the bottom of the Banbury Road in central Oxford. They were gathered in a quaint, hexagonal gazebo with a pointed roof and arched lattices, enjoying after-dinner coffee and tea. "You know, it's funny how we're always hearing from Nana in a garden," remarked Chelsea. "Christchurch, Rome, Grindelwald, and now this. Singapore's the only place we weren't in a garden."

"I never noticed," said Grace, with a little shrug. "I can't think I planned it. I guess when you're on the road and looking for privacy it just makes sense to step outside."

Chelsea nodded.

"Or maybe it's an Eden thing," said Grace after a pause. "I've lost a lot of innocence the last couple weeks."

"Tell me about it," said Brian.

"I think that goes for everybody," said Ella. "But it's all good."

"I hope so," said Grace.

"It is," Ella assured her.

"Okay," said Grace resignedly. She took the envelope from the table in front of her and tore it open. She pulled out several sheets of paper, arched her eyebrows reflexively, and cleared her throat. "*Welcome to Oxford. Dad and I spent one of the happiest years of our lives here. All we were missing, Gracie and Brian, was the two of you, or it would have been the very best.*" Grace looked at Brian, who smiled at her with a touch of wistfulness. "*Then again, if we'd been changing diapers the whole time, I don't think I'd have let Frank escape to the Bodleian Library all day, and he'd never have written the book that got his Shelley career started. Or, I suppose, the book that ended it either. Anyway, this is the Shelley chapter of your mother's confessions, and Oxford is the only place for you to hear it, really.*

"*Please go first off to the Shelley Memorial—I'm afraid I don't remember what college it's in, except that it's on the High—and see if you can find a little corner to stash a literal thimbleful of our ashes, 50/50. Dad was working on his dissertation that year—about Shelley's wife, Mary's, impact on his work. He must have taken me to see that bizarre statue a dozen times. Wait 'til you see it. It's pure white marble, with Shelley lying naked on a dark plinth, as though he's just washed up on shore after drowning. He's so curvaceous and supple, he looks as much like a woman as a man, we both thought. Through the years, I guess lots of Oxford boys used to pull naughty pranks so that finally they had to protect the statue with a set of bars. I heard a favorite thing was to paint his penis and balls, which are hanging right out there, you know...*" Grace resettled herself and took a measured breath. "*...so that the authorities had to scrape the paint off over and over and, as time passed, his parts got smaller and smaller. I'll let you judge for size and for the plausibility of the story, both, but they always looked a lot smaller to me than Frank's.*"

Brian looked puckishly at Grace and then over at Ella. "Thank you, Mom! Always good to hear about the dimensions of the old family tree."

Grace rolled her eyes. "*Frank and I never learned so much about homosexuality as we did at Oxford. Now, there's a segué,*" said Grace. "*Of course, the Oxford boys and dons have been doing it with each other for centuries, and there's Oscar Wilde and all. The best dancing in Oxford when we were there—by far!—was at a place called the Stage Club. The most beautiful young men would dance there until dawn and kiss and*

*laugh with each other to beat the band. We loved going. Brian, you would
have loved it, too.*"

Ella stared at Brian. Jack stared at Grace, who looked over at
Brian. Sage looked at Chelsea. Chelsea stared at Grace. "Go on, Mom,"
Chelsea said firmly.

"*Before Ella, that is. Ella's such a lovely woman. How silly I was to
think she might have been a tranny.*"

"What the fuck?" blurted Ella.

"I don't have a *clue* where that came from," said Brian.

"Damn! This really *is* a Tree of Knowledge thing, isn't it?" said Ella.

"Shall I go on?" sighed Grace.

"I guess you have to," replied Brian. "That's the deal. But I wish I'd
had a few more Pimm's cups."

"*There's a place on the Cherwell near the Parks where all the gay university men go to sunbathe naked. They used to, anyway. But Frank and
I wanted to go up and see, so we took a punt from Magdalen Bridge and
poled up the river. When we reached the place, I was supposed, being a
woman, to walk behind this modesty wall to go past, but I just stayed with
Frank in the boat and took it all in. It was a lot like Woodstock but with
even fewer clothes, and all men, and more advanced degrees.* Mom drew a
little smiley face there," noted Grace. "At least I think it is. *And instead
of smoking pot and smearing themselves with mud, they blushed and covered
up when they saw me. I felt like I was doing a* National Geographic *article
about some exotic culture, except I didn't take any pictures.* Just as well,"
said Grace. "She would have enclosed them, right? Enlarged for detail!"

"Keep going, Gracie," said Brian. "You're doing fine."

"*Well,*" Grace continued, "*it was quite a lark, and we poled by, maybe
a little slower than we should have. Frank joked that maybe we should go
ashore and consort with the natives, but I told him not to float any options
he couldn't deliver on. When we got a little further we tied up, drank a
bottle of wine, lay there in the sun, and decided it would be an even greater
lark if we made love. We did! As our friends at the Stage Club would have
said, it was positively splendid! It was maybe the second naughtiest place*

we ever had sex."

"Why do I suspect," interrupted Ella, "we'll also end up hearing about the first naughtiest place?"

"Because you're getting to know my mother," declared Grace. "*So I want you to take another equal measure of me and Frank and, on the east side of the river, maybe two hundred yards past the weir, spread us on the edge of the field that looks like it came right out of* The Wind in the Willows. *Please read something from Shelley—you choose, but something sublime—and then all of you go back to the Turf for a pint!"*

"Okay," said Brian, after a beat. "That's simple enough, I guess. No trains. No brooms. And I'll remember the trowel this time. Is that it?"

Grace shook her head and held up some additional sheets. "Any predictions?"

"I'm afraid to guess," said Ella. "But can you wait a minute, Grace? I have to go to the loo."

Grace nodded. "Anybody else?" Jack jumped up and scurried off.

When Ella and Jack were back, Grace picked up the papers once more. "Here we go! *Speaking of Frank's Shelley books, you know how crushed he was by the reviews of the big biography. He'd been working on it, night and day, heart and soul, for fifteen years, and to have one bastard from Ohio State say it was hard to tell if it was serious scholarship or intellectual parody broke your father's heart. He put on a brave face, especially with you two, and he said anybody who wasn't prepared to deal with mean, small-minded people should stay the hell out of academics. But he was so glad, Gracie, that you decided not to go on with a career in literature—and he was so amused, Brian, when you borrowed Bill Witherspoon's nail gun and nailed your copy of* David Copperfield *to a tree."*

"Did you really, Uncle Brian?" asked Chelsea, eyes agog.

"Reading that book was like trying to run through quicksand," replied Brian. "Four weeks. Eight hundred pages. It sucked the frickin' life out of our whole class. I was just doing what had to be done. But go on, Gracie."

"*You know how disappointed he was, but you can't know how very low* *it took him. For months and months, he had to drag himself into his office, peeking over his shoulder to see if his colleagues were watching him with pity as he went by or, worse than that, sniggering. He would come back from faculty meetings and tell me he'd so wanted to stand up and address some crucial issue or other, but that he was afraid no one would want to hear anything he had to say. He felt as though he'd gone from being one of Dartmouth's most celebrated professors to being an object of pity to his friends and a laughingstock to his enemies and even his best students. I came home from Planned Parenthood one day and found him sitting in the den with a half-empty bottle of whisky in one hand and a loaded pistol in the other. I didn't...*oh God, Dad!" Grace stopped, tears flowing.

Chelsea sprang up and raced over to her mother. She put her arms around her and hugged her tightly. "It's okay, Mom. It's okay."

"No, it's not," Grace sputtered. "We never had a fucking clue." She turned to Brian, who looked like he'd just seen the skin peeled off a puppy. "Did you?"

Brian shook his head. "God! Not that it got that bad. Not...like that."

"Do you want to stop?" asked Ella. She leaned forward on the bench. "Let's just stop."

Grace shook her head and sat there silently.

"Do you want me to read, then? I'd be happy to."

Grace nodded.

"Here." Ella reached out for the sheets. Grace handed them over and sagged against Chelsea.

"*I didn't know which one to grab first,*" Ella read softly, "*so I went for both. I told Frank over and over that I loved him and that I couldn't think about living on without him. He sat there like a dazed child...dossed up?...*No! Sorry! dressed *up like a college professor as I called 911 and told them to send somebody quickly. They were there in minutes and took him to Hitchcock, where they drugged him up and calmed him down.*" Ella paused, swiped at her nose, and read on. "*I know how hard this is for you to hear, so I won't go into any more details, except to say that the only thing* *that I think really brought him back was his love for his family and, most of all, his love for you two, Brian and Grace. How wonderful was that? That a man who never wanted children in the first place, whose family was so fucked up he was worried he'd be a congenital ogre, that he looked at me a month later as we sat at the breakfast table and said, 'Cinny, I don't want our kids to have a father who gave up.' That was it. He bounced back for years and taught his classes and published a few good articles and even let the English Department throw him a retirement party. I was so lucky to have walked in on him when I did. But I was luckier that I had the two of you, and that Frank did, too, and that he loved you more at that dark moment than he loved the idea of death. And, believe me, for somebody who taught English Romantic poetry, that's a shitload of luck!"*

"Thanks for stepping up, Ells," said Brian once they'd gone up to their room. He sat in front of the desk tucked into a dormer. The leaded windows were still swung open, and you could hear the hum of traffic on the Woodstock and Banbury Roads. Ella was slipping out of her clothes, getting ready for bed.

"Of course." She pulled a well-worn Smith T-shirt out of her bag, took off her bra, and pulled the tee over her head, shaking out her hair once it was on.

"Nothing sexy tonight?" he asked with a tired grin.

"I'm going for comfort."

"Got it." He kicked off his shoes, stood up, and then sat down again to pull off his socks.

"You're all efficiency tonight." She smiled and climbed into bed, fluffing the pillows behind her.

Brian snorted.

"How'd you feel about Cinny saying you'd like the gay dance club?" Ella pulled up the crisp white duvet and organized it around her hips.

"How did you?"

"I know you didn't have any secrets from your mom. It just felt like she was tweaking you a little. She usually saves that for Grace."

"Yeah," said Brian. He pulled off his pants, stumbling a little as he caught a foot, and tossed them on the chair. "I don't know whether I'd rather be off the hot seat or on it sometimes. It's that old competing-for-Mommy's-attention thing. Even when it involves catching shit."

"What *was* that bit about me being a tranny?" Ella stared at him, arms crossed.

Brian laughed awkwardly. "Didn't I ever tell you about that?"

"Nope."

"We were in the car together. It was after the rehearsal dinner, I think. I was driving her back to the hotel. She was telling me how much she liked you, but she said she was surprised I was getting married to a woman so soon after Kingsley and I split up."

"It *was* pretty quick."

"That's when she asked if you were a tranny." He pulled back the duvet and sat down, twisting around to grin at her. It was what she called his George Clooney look, and he tended to use it when he felt at a slight disadvantage.

"What did you say?"

"That I hadn't checked."

Ella punched him in the arm. "Made her think you were into wedding-night surprises, huh?"

Brian laughed, plumped his pillows, leaned back against them, and patted his bare belly. "No. I told her I'd made sure to do a little pre-flight walk-around."

Ella glared at him. "No pilot jokes, fuckhead! I mean it!"

"Okay. Sorry. I said we'd already done it so much you'd almost worn out my willy."

"Like Shelley's statue?" She reached over and tickled him. "Oooh! Wee Willie Winkie?"

"You're cruel," said Brian, writhing under her assault. "Did anyone ever tell you you're really cruel?"

"All my clients," purred Ella. "Check my reviews." She giggled and sat back up.

"Are you going to read?" Brian asked, once he'd caught his breath.
"I don't know. You?"

"I can't decide. I'm still processing tonight's news."

"I'll say. Just when you think she's run out of bombshells."

Brian shook his head. "Mom was like a munitions factory in twenty-four-seven production. Everything she did. Everything she said. Dad told us once that being married to Mom was like being a fireman. He never knew when an alarm was going to go off and he'd have to race off here to put out a fire in a grade school, or dash off there to pull a kitten out of a tree."

"Cinny was an arsonist who abused animals?"

Brian laughed. "You know what I mean."

They sat for a minute listening to the fan Brian had switched on for white noise. It was a habit he'd gotten into while living with Kingsley, who snored like a congested grizzly bear. Ella's only regular night sound was an occasional soft peep, as though she were being fondled in a public place.

Ella turned toward him and re-adjusted her pillows. "I never knew how really devastated your dad was when his book got panned."

"Not everybody panned it, but a lot of people did. I guess that's what happens when your big discovery turns out to have been forged by an Oxford prankster."

"What is it with students over here?" asked Ella. "It's like they're at the best university in the world, and all they can do is paint the penises on statues and write fake documents to fuck scholars up. I mean, get serious."

"I don't know they're any different from anywhere else. But I get it. I'll take Sage's student strikes over drunken British penis painters any day."

"Good," said Ella. She turned to her nightstand and picked up her book. She sighed and put it down again. "Cinny said she was glad Grace had gotten out of the academic rat race. Do you think Grace is?"

"Well, she hasn't really." Brian put a leg out from under the duvet.

"I know she's a teacher and everything," said Ella. "But she's not a professor at some big university who's got to publish or perish…and then when she publishes, worry about someone saying they can't tell if her work is serious or a joke."

"No. She's not."

"It all seems so cruel. And I've got to say that literary criticism, or whatever you call it, hardly seems like the most important thing anybody could be doing with their life. The thought you could get so invested in it you'd want to kill yourself when somebody dumps on something you've written…that's just weird and silly and sad."

"I know," said Brian. "And sadder that Gracie and I were clueless how bad it was. I mean, maybe we could have been there for him."

"But it sounds like you were, from what you mom says. I mean, what brought him around in the end was his love for you guys. Think how lucky you are that she's been telling you all this! Really!"

"I guess," said Brian. "But it's not the same as us knowing and helping back then. Actively."

"Who's to say?" Ella sniffed and dabbed at her nose. "Give yourself some credit for all the things you must have said and done. Even if you didn't know it at the time, those were the things that made a difference. Finally. Somebody once said the biggest tests you ever take are the ones you don't even know you're taking."

Brian huffed. "Sounds like a zen mantra for kids with a phobia about their SAT."

"I'm trying to help, asshole." Ella folded her arms again with a *harrumph*.

"I know, Ells," said Brian. He leaned over to kiss her. "I've got to confess, when Mom said what she said about Gracie and me, I started to cry."

"I was afraid to look."

"Why?"

"I was trying to make it through her damned letter."

Brian determined that the Shelley Memorial was at University College, and he walked over early the next morning to scout out ash-placement options. There was already a sizeable tour group standing in front of the poet's statue, listening to a wizened old gent whose pedantic manner reminded Brian of a professor in a Monty Python skit. Around to the left, however, was a kind of passageway, lit by leaded glass windows that opened out onto the quadrangle. Between it and the statue, a series of twin columns supported the main ceiling, each of them mounted on a stout base with ledges that might easily hold a thimbleful of Poseys.

Armed with this information, Brian walked briskly back to the hotel, where he found Ella, Grace, and Jack lingering over coffee. Jack had caught wind of an airshow featuring WWII aircraft that was being held that afternoon just up the road at Brize Norton. Grace was just making it clear he'd find himself divorced if he tried to alter their established plans. Chelsea and Sage had meanwhile gone off to a woolens shop in the covered market where, years back, Grant had bought a handsome handknit sweater vest. Chelsea hoped to find something Cotswoldy for the girls, whose birthdays were coming up in May and July. The two had promised to return to the hotel by eleven.

They were back a good bit earlier and, just after the hour, everyone set off for the memorial, with Grace carrying a pinch each of Cinny and Frank, safely sealed in a hotel envelope. It was another unusually sunny spring day, with just the hint of a breeze. As they turned down Broad Street past Blackwell's bookshop, a big clot of tourists was already milling outside the gates of Trinity College, waiting to go in. Here and there a robed don strode purposefully along, clutching a briefcase or a stack of books, while pairs or small groups of what were obviously students made their way impatiently through the throngs of sightseers.

They dropped down past the stately Radcliffe Camera and St. Mary's Church, entering the long, graceful arc of the High by Brasenose College. Traffic was already heavy—trade vans, red local buses, multi-colored tourist coaches, and flights of bicyclists cranking furiously along like caricatures of tardy scholars. As they approached a zebra crosswalk close to University College, Jack frivolously suggested they reenact the famous cover photograph of *Abbey Road*, saying he'd even take off his shoes and socks and be Paul. He was just about to step out blindly in front of a little Fiat 500 when Grace once again yanked him back from obliteration. She advised him to do a little less joking and a little more looking around, or she'd soon be sprinkling *his* ashes at various watch boutiques and golf courses around the globe.

When they got to the Shelley Memorial, another large tour group was on the way out, leaving them the space virtually to themselves. Only a tweedy old British couple stood by the windows to the left, poring over a well-worn guidebook. Brian and the others stepped up to the elaborate grillwork barrier. The statue lay centered in an oval space beneath a sky-blue dome. The dead poet was carved from brilliant white marble and lay virtually life-size on a dark marble slab, his body twisted as though the wave washing him ashore had rolled him halfway from his back onto his side. His head was tipped slightly back, resting on a tangled nest of shoulder-length hair. One ankle was tucked under the opposite calf, and his right hand rested languidly on his left forearm. Beneath the altar-like plinth, a mourning sea-nymph, cast in dark bronze, slouched in grief, flanked by a pair of griffins. Grace's mind flashed back to the statuary mourners outside Tuttle's Funeral Home in White River, a world away in distance and taste.

"Wow!" said Chelsea, leaning her head between the bars. "I can see what Nana was saying about him being curvaceous."

"And looking as much like a woman as a man," added Grace.

"He looks like a boneless chicken to me," observed Jack, with a chuckle. "Look how his shoulder sort of droops down over his chest. There's a guy who never played much rugby."

Grace laughed. "Are you *trying* to be a total Philistine, dear?"

"Not really," Jack replied. "I know you think I make a point of it. But it is a little weird, don't you think?"

"What?" asked Grace.

"Commemorating a famous alum with a naked statue? What if Notre Dame did that for Joe Montana? Or Harvard for Jack Kennedy?"

"You don't find it strangely erotic?" asked Brian. He winked at Ella.

"Not really. Are we supposed to?" Jack surveyed the others with a mystified expression.

"I think Uncle Brian is jerking you around, Dad," said Chelsea.

"You think?" said Brian.

"There's something about it, though," observed Grace. "It *is* kind of androgynous. Definitely male—look at the jaw and the calves." She pointed through the barrier. "But, you know, soft. Supersensitive."

"Poetic," said Chelsea.

Grace nodded. "He's got that Timothée Chalamet thing going on."

"What do you all think about his penis?" Sage asked loudly.

The older couple was on their way out, and the woman glared at Sage with matronly shock. The man eyed her with a twinkle and nearly tripped on his wife's heel as he passed. He caught himself by one of the columns.

"What do you mean, what do we think about it?" asked Ella.

"I don't know," Sage replied. "Does it work with the rest of the statue?"

"Do you mean, when it comes to general sculptural technique?" asked Chelsea, affecting a posh accent. "Artistic flair?"

"Indeed," said Sage, responding in kind. "Does it move you? Does it strike you, *par exemple*, as realistic? True-to-life, size-wise?"

"Sage!" exclaimed Ella. "Somebody might come in!"

Sage laughed heartily. "Come on, Mom. These days, any parent should be glad if their teenage daughter has to ask if a statue has a life-size schlong."

"Okay! Enough!" said Ella. "Brian, where were you thinking the ashes could go?"

"Right over there." Brian stepped around the line of columns and walked over to the spot where the last of them joined the corner of the curved back wall. "There's a ledge here, and—" He bent down. "Yeah, a little crack between the column and the wall."

"Perfect," said Grace. She walked around to join him and reached into her bag for the envelope. "Do you want to do the honors?"

"Sure." Brian took the envelope and tapped the small quantity of ash down into one end. He ripped off the opposite and, with a solemn glance at the others, pinched the envelope open and tilted it into the enclosed corner. He flicked his fingernail against the paper to jar the ashes loose and then flicked it again. "There. Anyone want to say anything?"

"I hope the cleaning lady isn't too thorough," said Chelsea.

Ella looked at Brian. "You'll read a poem out on the river, yes? Like Cinny wanted."

"I will," answered Brian. "Somebody will. Gracie and I picked one out."

"Okay, then," said Jack breezily. "Anybody hungry?"

Chelsea and Sage suggested they grab some lunch at Brother's Café, an Oxford landmark they'd run across in the covered market. Leaving the bright sunlight of the High, they entered a cool commercial maze that had likely changed very little since the days of Oscar Wilde. The daily lunch crowd hadn't yet overwhelmed the restaurant, and they found a table by the plate-glass window nearest the door. The place was pure early-last-century working-class quaint, with a low ceiling, rustic wooden tables and chairs, and shiny, mustard-colored walls straight off a Van Gogh palette. They had barely sat down when a sparkly young woman in a long black skirt and magenta turtleneck came and took their orders.

"I keep thinking," said Sage once the woman had left, "about that thing Jack said about celebrating men with naked statues. I think it's a great idea."

"You do?" Ella looked skeptically at Brian.

"I do. The same foods that make you fat make you stupid, right? If powerful people thought they'd be on public display for all eternity—totally bare-ass—they'd take better care of themselves, wouldn't they? And then they'd make better decisions."

Chelsea grinned. "I bet it would also totally change your local Weight Watchers' gender balance, no?" Sage nodded. "Speaking of which, I wonder if you tallied up all the naked statues in human history, what percentage would be male and what percentage would be female? Not just statues but naked ones."

"Female by a mile," opined Grace.

"You think?" countered Brian. "Even with all those classical Greek athletes and gods?"

"Well," said Grace. "All I know is that, in that famous Guerrilla Girl survey, something like eighty percent of the nudes on display in the Met in New York featured women."

"Maybe," said Brian.

"Whatever," said Sage, "But it was really interesting today that you have a statue of a naked man, and everybody thinks there's something feminine about it."

"Part of it was that he was lying down," said Chelsea. "Don't you think? You think about David in Florence—Michelangelo—he's standing. *The Thinker* is sitting. How many statues of naked men have you seen that are lying down?"

Jack glanced at Brian, who smiled.

"He reminded me," Chelsea continued, "of all those paintings, forever, of women lying naked on couches and things. That motif. Except dead. It's something about sexual availability, isn't it?"

The waitress edged up to the table with a heavily laden tray. "Who was having the cheese-and-ham ciabatta?" Ella raised her hand. The woman put the plate in front of her and quickly distributed the rest. "Can I get you anything else?"

"I think we're fine," said Jack. "We're just having a little debate about art and sexual availability."

"Of course you are," said the woman. "This is Oxford. Enjoy your meal."

As they strolled down the High toward Magdalen Bridge, Chelsea reported on the research she'd done on Parson's Pleasure. It had been an exclusive spot for nude male bathing for over three centuries before it was closed down in the early 1990s. Opinions varied as to whether the majority of men who frequented the spot were innocent naturists or went with more carnal interests. Regardless, many of Oxford's most eminent dons had been regular loungers and bathers, including C. S. Lewis, famed author of the *Narnia* books. A nearby spot, aptly called Dames' Delight, had been reserved for the use of women and children, but its rules for bathing attire were more conservative. Parson's Pleasure had always exerted a greater fascination for punters on the Cherwell.

As punters approached the notorious spot, the "modesty wall" Cinny mentioned had allowed for women to scramble out just downstream, walk discreetly past the sensitive acreage, and re-join their male companions farther upstream. Any women who chose to stay in the boat were expected to ride past the naked bathers with eyes averted. Now and again, though, a few of Cinny Posey's spiritual sisterhood opted to take everything in, which tended to discommode the bathers. One famous anecdote featured a classics professor named Cecil Bowra, internationally known for his learning and keen wit. When a punt filled with gaily chatting and mischievously ogling ladies had come slowly by one sunny afternoon, a group of dons in Bowra's company rushed to cover their privates with hats, towels, or whatever else came quickly to hand. Bowra had simply covered his head. "I don't know about you, gentlemen," he said calmly, "but in Oxford I, at least, am known by my face."

"Look!" said Chelsea when they arrived at the Magdalen Bridge boathouse. "Rowboats."

"So?" said Brian.

"Maybe we should take rowboats instead of punts."

"This is Oxford, Chel," explained Brian. "Punts are to Oxford as gondolas are to Venice. You wouldn't take a jet ski in Venice, would you? Or a PT boat?"

"It's just that I've rowed rowboats before," replied Chelsea. "I've never punted punts." She eyed a flat, scow-like wooden craft that was just shoving off from the dock. Three giggling women sat in the central seats and a bearded youth stood behind them. He gripped a very long pole in both hands and was using it to shove the punt in the opposite direction. It looked to Chelsea more or less like standing inside a big wheelbarrow and trying to propel it with an oversized broomstick.

"Life's for learning," said Brian. "It can't be that hard."

They approached the attendant, a slim young man in a white shirt and pants and a jaunty straw boater, and arranged to rent two punts for a couple of hours. As Brian paid in cash, he registered a novel pang as he noted how riveted the fellow was at the sight of Sage in her light cotton sun dress. Nothing earlier in life had prepared Brian for the visceral protectiveness that can come with fatherhood—apparently even step-fatherhood. The more time he spent with Sage, the gladder he was that she had a level, if willful, head on her shoulders. On balance, she seemed much less likely than many of her age-mates to be taken unawares by eruptions of male carnality—witness her recent experiences in Thailand. The real question was whether she'd ever get sufficiently past the caddishness of her father to a place where she could embrace a male with joyful confidence and trust. She deserved, in the end, the best possible partner, and she was a cinch to be a wonderful companion for whoever she ended up with. Whether it turned out to be a man or a woman didn't matter a whit to Brian; whether or not Ella would agree, he couldn't yet say for certain. Neither of them had broached the subject of Sage's sexuality. He wondered, in fact, if there was any reason to have done so.

"So," said Brian, dwelling on the moment. "Who's poling?"

"You, for one," volunteered Grace. "You're the one who nixed a PT boat."

Brian rolled up his sleeves and spat into his hands with cinematic flair.

"I'm game," said Chelsea, stepping to the front of the group. "Just warn me if you see any icebergs. Or white whales."

"Who's in what boat?" asked Brian.

"How about Sage and I go with Chelsea?" suggested Ella. "Girl's boat. Jack, you and Grace go with Brian."

Brian steadied the nearest punt as Grace and Jack stepped in and sat down next to each other on one of the low seats. Jack reached out to rub her knee affectionately.

"No teasing now, Gracie," said Brian. "This is my first time."

"When have I ever teased you?" asked Grace.

"I think it started in the second trimester. I remember this little voice in the dark telling me I had a fat ass."

"I think everyone would agree you've got a *great* ass," called Ella from the dock.

"Chill, Mom," said Sage, as she scrambled into the neighboring punt. "Just get in and save the courtship behavior for the hotel."

Ella boarded daintily and settled next to her daughter.

Chelsea hopped in after her. "Sage, hand me the pole there, would you?" She grinned at her uncle, who grinned back at her. "Here goes nothing!"

"That end with the metal foot obviously goes into the water," called Brian. "Then, I guess, you hold it upright like this, drop it down until it hits bottom, and then you lever it like this, until you start forward and...*push*." Brian shoved the pole back hard, hand over hand, and the punt moved out into the river. "Shit!" he yelled, as the top end of the pole slipped from his grasp and dropped into the water.

"I guess you're supposed to hold on after you finish pushing," observed Grace flatly. "That way you can use the same pole more than once."

And so they progressed up the river, weaving haphazardly from side to side like drunken turtles swimming home from a late-night binge. Twenty minutes on, the river's main channel bent to the left, around a broad swath of lawn bordered by trees and what looked like old foundations. The spot was totally deserted.

"That's got to be where Parson's Pleasure was," said Brian. "And that must be where the changing sheds were."

Sage watched him pointing from the other boat. "Why'd they need changing sheds? Wasn't the whole point just to come up here and get naked?"

"Maybe they were into grand entrances," suggested Chelsea. "You know. The shed doors swinging open for the Big Reveal. *Ta-da!* Instead of your awkward, piecemeal approach to being bare ass."

"I doubt they bothered with changing tents at Woodstock," said Sage.

"Maybe Nana will say," laughed Chelsea.

"Maybe we can leave a few stones unturned," suggested Grace.

Another bend or two and they arrived at a spot that could truly have inspired an illustration in *The Wind in the Willows*. A trio of graceful trees hung majestically over a sloping bank, pocked here and there by dark recesses that might cozily house a water rat or mole. Behind the willows stretched a lush lawn, maybe forty by eighty yards, shaded by alder, ash, and hawthorn. A handful of skylarks wheeled dizzily above.

"This has got to be it," said Brian, turning the prow of his punt toward the bank.

"Must be," agreed Grace.

"I don't suppose you see Toad's caravan parked anywhere," said Jack. *The Wind in the Willows* had been a had been a Chelsea childhood bedtime favorite, and Jack had conjured up special voices for each of the characters. It was one of the things that endeared him most to Grace—clear evidence not only that he adored his only child but also that his character hadn't been blighted by overexposure to *Uncle Remus*.

They pulled the boats as far up as they could manage, stowed the poles, and climbed up the low bank and through the feathery willow tendrils to the greenspace. Like Parson's Pleasure, it was unoccupied, save for the birds they'd seen and any other wild creatures who might have been watching from the hedgerows. Sunlight slanted in through the riverside foliage, as distant sounds of the city mixed with the sigh of a light breeze through the new leaves.

"Perfect," said Grace. "Just perfect. *I* want to stay here forever."

Ella gave Grace's shoulder a squeeze. "Could it be any more different from the Jungfrau?"

Grace laughed.

They grouped themselves spontaneously in a circle and stood there quietly.

"Well," said Grace. She unslung her bag from her shoulder and held it in her hands. "This will do just fine. Better than fine. Anybody see the perfect spot?"

Chelsea pointed toward a hawthorn set in from the back of the field. Its lower branches spread outward in a leafy umbrella, creating kind of shaded bower where it wouldn't have been a surprise to find baby hedgehogs taking a nap.

"What do you think, Brian?" Grace asked her brother.

"Yup."

"You've got the trowel, right?"

Brian pulled the small tool from a side pocket of his pack. "Fool me once…" He walked slowly over to the hawthorn, knelt down, and began to dig. He soon had a twelve-by-twelve-by-twelve-inch hole scooped out of the untrodden soil. The earth was damp and pungent, and its clean scent enveloped them. Brian stood up and walked back to his pack. He bent and picked it up, pulling a paperback from the main compartment. He turned to Grace. "You've got Mom and Dad ready?"

Grace held up the doubled baggies with a wistful smile.

"Let me read this first. Then, if you'd like to put them in, Gracie, that would be great. Or anyone else." He dropped the pack, opened the book, and thumbed through the pages, looking for his spot. "'Love's Philosophy,'" he began, "by Percy Bysshe Shelley…Dad's…" His breath caught. He cleared his throat awkwardly and squared his shoulders.

"The fountains mingle with the river
And the rivers with the ocean,
The winds of heaven mix for ever
With a sweet emotion;
Nothing in the world is single;
All things by a law divine
In one spirit meet and mingle.
Why not I with thine?—

See the mountains kiss high heaven
And the waves clasp one another;
No sister-flower would be forgiven
If it disdained its brother;
And the sunlight clasps the earth
And the moonbeams kiss the sea:
What is all this sweet work worth
If thou kiss not me?"

Brian closed the book, clasping it in front of him as he gazed down at the ground. The wind sighed through the leaves, but everything else was silent, even the birds. It was almost a half-minute before Grace walked up to Brian and hugged him. And then Ella came and hugged them both.

"Perfect," said Chelsea, as tears rolled down her cheeks. "Unbelievably perfect. I don't know, Uncle Brian. It's as though that was written for this whole trip. And for this very day. For this very spot and time. I'm…I'm…blown away."

"So am I," Sage sniffled. "And I usually hate poetry."

Jack walked over and put his hands on Brian's shoulders. He tipped his head forward until his forehead rested against Brian's—something like a Maori *hongi*. Then he stepped back, nodded, and smiled. "Thank you, brother," he said.

Brian had brought two bottles of prosecco, kept cool in a fleece, and plastic glasses. The six of them sat on a pair of tartan picnic blankets Grace had borrowed from the hotel, and they drank in the moment with the wine.

"I can't believe this is our next-to-last stop," said Chelsea. She looked pensively around the circle. "This has all been so wonderful."

Ella nodded. "I feel so lucky to have been able to share this with everyone. I don't know how else we could ever have felt so much a part of the family." She reached out for Sage's hand.

"Mom would be so happy to hear you say that, Ells," said Grace. She looked around the little meadow as though Cinny might somehow be hovering there.

"Two weeks ago," said Jack, "we were just getting to Christchurch."

Grace shook her head in disbelief.

"Two Tuesdays ago."

"Man!" said Ella. "It has gone fast!"

Grace broke a pensive silence. "I guess Mom would say the very same thing. Not necessarily this trip, but everything. Life. The two of them at Oberlin, then the two of them at Dartmouth. Brian and me. Dad's career in crisis. Parkinson's." She shook her head again. "Whoosh!"

"It's funny,' said Brian, looking into his glass. "I don't think anybody knew how to live in the moment better than Mom. Not that she couldn't plan—look at this trip she set up—but the whole Woodstock thing's a great example." He chuckled softly. "I'd say, if Mom had a motto, it was *Count me in!*"

"And *ask questions later*," added Grace with a smile.

"Still," said Brian, "there was something in her that was so sentimental and vulnerable. That just wanted to hold on and be safe. I don't know what it was. Maybe I'm…"

"No," Grace jumped in. "You're right. Remember that Christmas? We were twelve, I guess. Something like that. Eleven or twelve."

Brian nodded.

Grace looked at the others. "Mom was always so into Christmas. Not that Dad wasn't, but she always knocked herself out getting the house ready. The tree, the stockings, milk and cookies for Santa, Christmas breakfast. Everything."

"Sounds wonderful," said Ella, looking at Sage.

"It was," said Grace. "Of course, she used to orchestrate the present-opening like it was a religious ceremony. Or a court case."

"She'd be Santa," said Brian. "Down on her knees on the rug. You'd open your box, pull out the sweater or whatever, hold it up in front of you for size, and then it was on to the next person, next present. No double-dipping. No breaking the order."

Chelsea laughed. "Grant's like that. His girls call him the Christmas Bully."

"Anyway," said Grace. "This one Christmas, we walk into the room where the tree is, and it looks like New York in the middle of a garbage strike. I mean, there's a pile of presents three feet deep—in a circle maybe ten feet across." She held her arms out as wide as she could manage. "Seriously."

Brian smiled.

"We start to open the presents," Grace continued, "and it's not just sweaters and socks and long underwear for skiing, you know? It's all of these toys for Brian and me, stuff we hadn't been into for years. My third Etch-a-Sketch, I think it was, and a View-Master with pictures of all the national parks, and a stuffed Garfield doll, for God's sake! And, Brian, it was what? Hot Wheels?"

"Maybe twenty little cars. Honestly. With this huge plastic layout to race them. A big *Star Wars* figurine set, I remember, and this incredible Transformers thing that turned from an eighteen-wheeler into a giant robot that shot darts out of its eyeballs." He mimed with his forefingers.

"They just kept coming," Grace went on. "Dad would get a book or a necktie and Mom would get a subscription to *Rolling Stone* or a new apron, but it was just this...*cornucopia* of toys. A Magic 8-Ball and a *Little Mermaid* T-shirt for me. A model tank and a balsawood glider for Brian." She looked at her brother. "And a Slip 'n Slide, no?"

Brian grinned and slowly shook his head.

"It was the middle of winter, for God's sake. And we hadn't used a Slip 'n Slide for years." Grace sighed and adjusted herself on the blanket. "Mom just sat there the whole time, looking—I don't know—like she was watching a home movie while the repo man was waiting to take the projector away."

Jack sniffed. "She was trying to hold onto you."

Grace paused and dabbed at her eyes. "It was so hard. I remember looking at Brian and knowing that he knew what I was thinking. I think Dad did, too, but he was doing his stoic Dad thing. So we just played out the scene—acting really happy when, inside, we both felt like crying."

"We talked about it later," said Brian. "We came up with a plan to keep playing with the things—at least one of us every day, tag-team—until everything settled down. Somehow."

"Jeez!" said Sage.

"And then, maybe five days later," said Grace, "Mom just comes up to us out of the blue when we're watching *Full House* or something and says, 'Thank you!'"

Brian nodded again. "And we ask her, 'For what?' And she just says, 'For being my babies for just a few more days.'" He breathed in deeply.

"Then," said Grace, "she bends over, kisses us both on the head, and walks back out of the room. That's the last we ever heard of it."

"Mom's 'Whoosh!' moment," said Brian.

Just after four, they rolled up the blankets and headed back down the river. Before they left, they took a moment to walk back over to where they'd buried the ashes. Brian took out a pen and wrote a *C* on one of the prosecco corks and an *F* on the other. He placed them carefully in the grass, side by side with their rounded tops touching.

Back on the water, they were rounding the bend at Parson's Pleasure when a single airplane thundered by, low and fast. Jack nearly fell out of the punt as he leaped up to see if he could spot it. He cupped his ear, the better to catch the deep, receding purr of the engine. "That was a Spitfire! Or a Hurricane," he declared excitedly.

Grace asked, in a tone of sincere mystification, how he could possibly know what kind of plane it was. He told her that what they'd heard was a Rolls-Royce Merlin engine—there was no other engine note like it—and the only single-engine planes the British ever put it in that were still flying were Spitfires and Hurricanes. There were supposed to be several of both at the air show they'd "missed." Chelsea shook her head and told her father he was incredible. Jack said it was just stupid mechanical stuff. He just wished he'd been able to see the plane.

Their transit of the last section of the river was so leisurely that they missed their rental-return deadline by ten minutes, and the young man in the boater told them they'd need to pay an additional fifteen pounds. Brian was reaching grudgingly for his wallet when Sage walked forthrightly up to the fellow and put her hands on her hips.

"Are you really going to charge us for being ten minutes late when you have all of those empty boats sitting right there, and nobody's waiting to use them?"

The man tugged at his ear and blushed. "I'm afraid those are the rules. It says so right there." He turned and pointed to a large sign just behind him.

"I don't suppose you know what we were doing today, do you?"

"Frankly, miss, it's not my business to know." He'd recovered some of his composure and was eyeing Sage once more with a kind of goggle-eyed canine zeal.

"They were sprinkling their parents' ashes." Sage motioned toward Grace and Brian. "My aunt, there. And my dad."

Brian turned to Ella, who suddenly seemed ready to cry.

"Oh. I'm sorry," said the fellow. He took off the boater and held it over his heart, bowing his head slightly. It occurred to Grace that, like some other Oxonians they'd seen, his hair could have used a good scrub.

"Sorry enough to forget about the fifteen pounds?" Sage turned her hands so that it was her closed fists, now, that rested on her hips. She stared at the young man, unblinking.

"Of course," the fellow replied. He slipped his hat back on. "I hope it was a wonderful…sprinkling." He looked uncertainly at Brian and Grace.

"It was wonderful," said Brian. "As sprinklings go. Thank you."

The man nodded.

Sage reached out to shake his hand. "You restore our faith in the British gentleman."

"Oh," he stammered. "Good."

"What did you think of Sage with the punt guy?" asked Grace, as she leaned forward to pour Chelsea a little tea. They sat across a coffee table from each other in the cozy lounge of the Old Parsonage, lingering together after the others had retreated to their rooms for the night.

"She was great. I remember the guy in Krabi—the one that helped her out at the bar—saying she had balls."

"I guess that's a good thing," laughed Grace.

"Yeah, it is. As long as she doesn't get carried away too often."

"Right." Grace took an appreciative sip. "I didn't think I'd get into tea over here." She elevated the cup, comically extending her pinky. "Especially with milk."

"Too foofy? Too Beatrix Potter?"

"Something like that." Grace settled back into the leather couch and lifted her stockinged feet to the table edge.

"Grant loves tea," said Chelsea. "At first I thought it made him seem like an old man. Then I decided it made him seem settled."

Grace nodded with a slight reserve. "What do you hear from him?"

"Nothing more, really." Chelsea sighed. "I guess it's just wait and see. The long haul."

"Yeah." Grace shook her head in sympathy. "Has he told his girls yet?"

"Nope. Actually, he told me he wanted to wait until I could be there. He thought they'd take the news better if I were around to reassure them."

"Oh, Chel!" Grace leaned forward again, setting her cup on the saucer. She looked at her daughter, seemingly at a loss for words.

"What?"

Grace reached for the cup again. "I don't know, honey. It's just so poignant. Grant having to tell the girls he's ill—"

"But not that ill, Mom." There was a pregnant pause. "We don't know yet. Right?"

"Right. But still. And his wanting you to be there to help them get through it. To take it all in with equanimity. I guess you're pretty important to them."

"Yeah. I think so. I do."

Grace took another sip and stared at the remains of the fire glowing softly on the grate.

"Mom?" said Chelsea after a half-minute. "How are you feeling about all this? Grant and me?"

Grace's brows rose. "Me? It's not about me, really."

"Sure, it's about you," said Chelsea. She got up and walked around the table to sit next to her mother. "Tell me what you're thinking."

"I don't know, honey." Grace turned to look Chelsea in the eye. "Just that you're getting in so deep, I guess. I mean, I know how important you are to Grant—how you've helped him manage after Adria, and all. I guess I just wasn't prepared to hear how important you are to his girls."

"Because it makes it all seem so long-term?" asked Chelsea. "So permanent? 'Grown-up'?"

Grace paused for just a second. "Bingo!" Chelsea put her arm around her mother and nuzzled up against her. "Whoosh," said Grace, choking slightly on the word.

"I know," said Chelsea. She reached up to sweep a tear from Grace's cheek. "I honestly feel so lucky, though. To have met somebody I really respect and love. And to feel as though he needs me. That his family does, too."

"I'm happy for you, honey," said Grace, turning to her again. "I really am. It's just hard letting go. All I really want to do is take you out and buy you a couple of dozen American Girl dolls." She laughed and swiped at her cheek with a knuckle.

"I know." Chelsea's eyes were welling, too. "And all these goodbyes to Nana and Pop Pop just keep reopening a wound, sort of."

"I'll say." Grace sniffed, sat up straight, and squeezed Chelsea's knee. "Well, I know you know what you're doing. And it feels to me like a good thing. Enough said."

"Thanks, Mom. You're the best."

They sat silently, listening to the fire.

"So," said Chelsea. "How are you doing otherwise?"

"Me?"

"You and Dad."

"Oh," said Grace, adjusting the knees of her pants. "Fine. We're fine. Doesn't it seem like we're fine?" She turned to face Chelsea directly.

"No, it does," said Chelsea. "You seem really good lately."

Grace peered at her searchingly and then nodded.

"Has he bought you off with that nice watch or something?"

"Yeah. That's it," chuckled Grace. "Bought off with a bauble. Will you ever respect me again?"

"I'll make a special effort, Mom."

Grace laughed. "You know," she said after a beat, "this may seem totally obvious, but if I ever had to write a book about ways to get a new perspective on life, it would be about taking a trip like this."

"It's been amazing."

"It's not just, like we said, the way we've been living every day with reminders of how fast it all goes by. Or how life is so full of blessings and blunders. Or how there are so many things that can get in the way of love...but that, finally, love and forgiveness are all that matter. I know I sound like a Hallmark card. I don't know that that makes it any less true, though."

"No," said Chelsea. "You're right, Mom."

"But when we were reading that last thing Nana wrote, and she was talking about Dad sitting there with the loaded pistol in his hand..." She looked at Chelsea, who nodded encouragement. "It was like I was catapulted into a realization I never thought was there to realize."

Chelsea surprised her mother by laughing. "It's not that I don't want to hear what you have to say, Mom. But 'catapulted'? Like off an aircraft carrier?"

"Oh. Well, I guess."

"That's so completely Dad."

Grace laughed. "You're right! That's the danger of living with someone like your father. His obsessions sneak through your defenses, and suddenly you're all into Swiss watches and British fighter planes."

"I know. But sorry. What were you saying?"

"Well," Grace went on. "I'd been thinking for days about how Pop Pop's career ended, really, so cruelly for him. But it was only when I heard about Nana walking in on him with the whisky and the gun that I realized how incredibly glad I was that my life didn't finally go in that direction. If you'd asked me almost any other time in my life, I would have said I'd given up so much when I married your father and we decided his career was more important to nurture than mine."

"And when you had me, right?" Chelsea's gaze was probing.

"Oh, honey, no!" Grace turned to embrace her and, for five or six seconds, held her tightly. "You were the best thing that ever happened to me. Just the way Nana said Uncle Brian and I were the most important things in Pop Pop's life. The things that gave him the will to struggle on. But I know I've held it against your father. That part of me has resented his power and his success and all the money he can spend on cars and watches and golf—while I labor away at a second-rate school trying to teach spoiled kids what a dangling modifier is. Trying to keep my benighted colleagues from building a curriculum around *The Da Vinci Code*. And *Friends*!"

Chelsea laughed again. "I can imagine, though. It must have been hard. It must *be* hard. But you're doing such great things, Mom. You're at a *good* school. And you're one of the best teachers there. And you're sending kids off to college who can write good papers, and tell you what's tragic about *Julius Caesar,* and why Atticus Finch is a hero."

Grace sighed and nodded. "Thanks, honey. I know. But I guess I know even better now. Now that I've gone off the catapult with my, whatever it was, Rolls-Royce King Arthur engine." She chuckled. "And it makes me more appreciative of your father. Your sometimes-silly father. More ready to smile than to snipe."

"You don't really snipe, Mom. You just have Nana's sense of humor."

"No, I snipe," said Grace. "But this has been sobering. Wonderful but sobering. Wonderful *and* sobering. But effing exhausting!"

"I hear you."

"I've been drinking *way* too much," said Grace. "Dad too."

Chelsea shrugged.

"We'll be better," said Grace. "As soon as we get home. And what in *hell* do you imagine your grandmother has in mind for us in New Jersey?"

"I don't have a clue. But it's all going to wrap up in the *Garden* State now, isn't it?"

"Oh my God!" said Grace. "You're right. That's so weird!"

"It's all going to fit together, Mom. Somehow."

NEW JERSEY

Newark Immigration was packed. What looked like four or five hundred arrivals were backed up in the international passport queue—self-assured business types, golden-haired youth hostelers, families in drab clothing peering around with a mixture of exhaustion, wonder, and unease. Holders of U.S. passports were better off, and the line for the Global Entry kiosks was even shorter. Brian had urged everyone to apply for the expedited process, which they'd all managed to secure—Chelsea at the very last minute.

As they waited in line in the overheated hall, they noticed a short, elderly couple standing hesitantly just to the side. The man wore a rumpled brown wool jacket and a checked flat cap, and he clutched his and his wife's passports tightly as he stared around the room. The woman stood very close to him, fussing with the lapels of her coat. Brian, who was closest to them, could hear them whispering to each other in what sounded like an Eastern European language.

As the line for the kiosks moved along, the two of them edged along with it, looking over now and again at the much longer lines to the side. After several minutes, they came abreast of a burly immigration official in a blue uniform—the soul, it seemed, of congenital impatience. The people ahead of them in line showed him their passports and answered yes when he asked if they were cleared for Global Entry, whereupon he gestured them brusquely past. When the short couple stepped up and the old man tendered his green-covered documents, the official shook his head and pointed left toward the international line.

"Please," said the old man. "We go through?"

The stocky man shook his head again and gestured to the side.

The old man looked uncertainly at his wife and then stepped forward again, showing the passports.

"This is Global Entry," the official said loudly, "for United States citizens. You and your wife are not United States citizens. Go over there. That line." He pointed again to the international queue.

The old man shook his head. "Line is long. And we wait here." He gestured toward the queue behind them.

"Look," barked the immigration official. "You go over there. There! Hey!" he shouted to a colleague who was standing a few yards away. "Come get these bozos, will you? They can't even read English." He gestured to the sign next to him: *Global Entry Only*.

The second official came over and grabbed the woman by the arm, pulling her toward the other line. She looked back desperately at her husband, who stepped after her as quickly as he could manage. The second man delivered her to a third, someone who finally looked at the old couple with a measure of sympathy, spoke to them softly, and led them off toward the proper line.

"Jesus!" whispered Brian to Ella, as they stepped forward. "I can't believe it. Talk about ugly Americans."

"I know," Ella whispered back. "I was this far from saying something." She held up her hand with thumb and forefinger an inch apart.

"Can I help you with something?" asked the burly official, leering at them.

"Yeah." Brian looked at the man coolly. "We're Global Entry."

The man gestured them on. They paused, then stepped past.

"I'm embarrassed," came Sage's voice from behind them.

"Excuse me?" said the official.

"I'm embarrassed for my country. I'm embarrassed for America. The way you just treated those people."

"What people?"

"That old couple." Sage pointed after them. "They're guests in our country, and they obviously didn't know what was going on or where to go, and you treated them like shit."

The man's head snapped back on disbelief.

"What are they supposed to think?" Sage continued. "They're exhausted. They probably haven't slept for twenty-four hours. They come to a place they've never been, and there are these huge crowds, and they have no idea what to do, and suddenly this big dude in a uniform starts to boss them around like they're cattle or something."

"Cattle?"

"Yeah. Cattle. Like cows? Give me a break. Try to be a human being."

"Look, sweetie," said Ella, who had turned back. "Let's just go to the kiosk. Let it ride." She looked sidelong at the official and muttered "Sorry."

"Don't apologize for me," snarled Sage, her hands cocked on her hips now. "He should be apologizing to us. To them!" She pointed again.

"Look, little missy," said the man. "I've been standing here for eight fucking hours. I'm paid shit, I get a fifteen-minute break every four hours, and if I leave to pee, my supervisor looks at me like I just let Osama fucking Bin Laden into the country. And I couldn't sleep a wink last night because of this goddamned cold I picked up from some… some…'guest of our country.'" He looked at Sage as though she should reach into her wallet and pull out a sympathy twenty.

"Come on, honey,' said Ella. "Come on along with me and Brian."

"I'm sorry about your cold," Sage said to the man. "And I'm sorry this country you're working so hard to protect doesn't give enough of a shit about its workers to pay them a living wage. But, Officer Dooley," she said, staring at his laminated identification badge, "you should be ashamed of yourself. I'm ashamed of you. And by the way, call me *little missy* again and I'll report your sorry ass."

The man gaped for a second, then puffed himself up indignantly. "I could have you arrested," he said.

"Try it," said Sage, staring up like David at Goliath. "I'm traveling with a lawyer." She gestured at Jack, who looked on in amazement. When the man stared at him, Jack pulled his shoulders back and nodded.

"Okay," said Officer Dooley. "Global Entry. Right over there. Welcome back to the country, folks. Land of the free."

"And home of the brave," said Chelsea as she shuffled past.

Brian had followed Jack's lead and booked rooms at the hotel in Jersey City where the Tingleys had stayed back in April. When Chelsea asked if she'd be sharing a room with her parents again, Brian laughed and said Jack had okayed a splurge to celebrate their safe return to the U.S. She'd be rooming with Sage as usual.

It was nearing four o'clock when they gathered around a low coffee table at the Hyatt's rooftop bar, in a corner they had virtually to themselves. The sun was still well above the cloudless horizon, and it glinted off the glass facades of the Lower Manhattan skyline with the intensity of halogen lights.

"You know," said Jack, looking out across the busy Hudson. "That has to be one of the world's great views."

"It's an amazing view, Jack," said Ella. "It might look even better with a snowy volcano behind it, but it really is something."

"I wish I'd seen it before it got sold to the Dutch," said Sage. The others smiled in amusement. "You all knew I'd say that, right?"

"No, that's totally cool," said Chelsea. "What's that great line in *The Great Gatsby*? About the 'fresh, green breast of the new world?'"

"'Virgin forest.' 'Virgin territory.'" Sage sneered. "Somebody should have put up a 'No Vacancy' sign."

"Well, we are where we are," said Jack. "Let's just try to make it all as good as it can be for as long as we can."

"Amen," said Chelsea.

"Speaking of making things better," said Jack, "where's our waitress?"

Once the drinks arrived and they'd raised their glasses anew to Cinny and Frank—and to each other, for everything they'd planned, managed, and endured—Grace sat up ramrod straight, cleared her throat, and asked if everyone was ready for Cinny's last chapter. Each of them seemed to wait for someone else to answer. They looked at each other with wistfulness and a curious reserve.

"Well," Ella piped up with theatrical brightness, "we've reached the mystery moment, haven't we? New Jersey! What's it going to be? The boardwalk in Atlantic City? Frank Sinatra's boyhood home in Hoboken? Giants Stadium in…? Giants Stadium's in Jersey, right?" She looked at Brian, who shrugged.

"Mom and Dad weren't into football," said Grace. "They wouldn't let Brian play. They thought it was a recipe for brain pudding."

"How about Princeton, Tiger?" suggested Brian. "Right in front of the library where you wrote your thesis?"

"Like they'd want their ashes sprinkled at Princeton," scoffed Grace. "Mom thought Princeton was just a big finishing school for the Young Republicans. Nothing but white *a cappella* groups decked out in striped blazers singing love songs to their stockbrokers."

Brian smiled.

"Anyway," said Grace. "Everybody ready?" She suddenly looked about as ready as a mother set to drive her child to the hospital for major surgery.

There were sober nods all around.

"All right." Grace tore open the envelope, pulled out the notebook sheets, and began, resolutely, to read. "*Dear Loved Ones. It's so strange to think this may be the last time I ever put pen to paper—after all those endless years of schoolwork; after all those weekly grocery lists; after all those silly stories of mine; after all those birthday cards and Christmas labels for the three of you.*" Grace paused and sniffed. "*I suppose everything we ever do, we finally end up doing for a last time, whether we're aware that it's the last time or not. At the other end, of course, it's all about firsts: our first word, our first step, our first successful pee in the potty, our first kiss—every one of them noted and celebrated and thoroughly labeled as firsts by us and by others. At this end, it's the last Christmas, the last hour sitting out in the sun, the last breakfast, the last breath…*" Grace lowered the papers and exhaled loudly.

"What is it, Tiger?" asked Brian.

"She's found a whole new way," said Grace.

"To what?" he asked.

"To get to me."

Chelsea motioned to Sage to trade seats. She sat down next to her mother and grabbed her hand.

Grace sniffed again, raised the sheets, and read on. "…*the last breakfast, the last breath—few of them, I suppose, as clearly marked as the firsts. Do I even remember the last time Frank and I made love? We couldn't have known it was the last time, but whenever it was, it* was *the last time. I wonder if I'll know when I'm taking my last breath. Will I just think I'm tired and that all this inning and outing of air that came so mindlessly before is now a labor that I choose not to keep up…so I simply stop the effort and feel the soft blanket of nothingness drawn up over my face?*" Grace paused again, her face taut with emotion. "*Or will I struggle for my last gasp against a traitor body that smothers me like fathoms of dark water? Maybe it all ends in a sleep—like a candle flickering out in an empty room, with no one there to see. Qui sait? But even if there'll be no more Goodbyes for Bessie or Accidents for Markie, it feels right to end it all with 'Dear Loved Ones.' I have honestly loved my life, my friends, and my world—except for what's always been a liberal sprinkling of assholes.*"

Ella broke into a giggle. She looked anxiously at Brian, but he was grinning at her. "God, I wish I'd known her better," she said. "She was so strong. And honest. And my God, that's beautiful writing. It takes my breath away."

Grace nodded. "*You'll all be home now, at least this side of the Pond, as Frank used to say when he was being snooty. Thank you all for doing these last things for him and for me. It does my heart good to think of the pair of us whirling about in distant winds or leaching with the rain into the bosom of earth, bits of us now in sunlight, bits of us next 'under the wide and starry sky'—cheered by the dawn, soothed by sunsets, together. I hope your travels brought more joys than troubles, rich memories, and love for each other."* Grace looked around at the group. They sat transfixed. *"I know kids never listen to their parents, but maybe you've learned something from me through all this. Not just learned something about me. And if you older ones are past being reached, maybe Chelsea and Sage will have opened their minds a little to a grandmother. Anyway, enough twaddle! Frank always laughed at me when I got sentimental. He said it was like I was a hammer trying to be a hairbrush. I'm afraid you'll laugh at my last request, because the final place to leave our ashes won't be nearly as scenic or culturally sophisticated as your other stops. It's infinitely richer, though, in terms of how important the thing that happened there has been to us and to our lives. You'll see. First, some backstory.*

"It was just after Christmas in 1977. Frank's parents were visiting his sister in California, and my mother had an awful case of the flu, so we celebrated in Hanover with some friends. The English Department was hiring that year, and they chose Frank for the committee that went to the MLA convention in New York to interview job candidates."

"MLA?" asked Ella.

"Modern Language Association," said Grace. *"I decided to go along to visit museums during the day, when he'd be busy, and we'd take in a few shows at night. Then, when he finished up the last afternoon, we'd drive down to be with my parents in Wilmington. We got a late start from Manhattan, and by the time we got through the Holland Tunnel, it had started to snow. Really snow! We had a little red Audi then, and it was good in sloppy conditions. Unfortunately, by the time we got onto the Jersey Turnpike, snow was building up on the road faster than they could plow it away. It was almost like they hadn't invented salt. Traffic slowed, and it was just poking along at about twenty miles an hour, but we started seeing more and more wrecks as cars spun in the slippery whiteout and others piled into them. It got so bad that Frank decided we should stop at the next rest area, and we ended up pulling off at the Molly Pitcher Service Area.*

There were already hundreds of cars in the parking lot, and when we got inside the building it was a madhouse—families everywhere, filling the restaurant and spilling out into the lobby, kids chasing each other through the aisles of the shop, mothers yelling at them to calm down, babies crying, fathers lining up for the phone to call family or friends or babysitters. It was like something out of Hieronymus Bosch. It was already past seven, so we braved an endless line at the restaurant and got something to eat. I had to wait another forty-five minutes to get on a phone to let my parents know we were going to stay put until conditions improved. Afterward, Frank and I needed to escape from the crowds and get some fresh air, so we bundled up and went out into the storm and walked around under the parking-lot lights. Curtains of snow were gusting down, covering every stretch of ground and shrub and vehicle in a thick white shroud. We went back in, thinking we'd find a little corner and maybe get some sleep until the storm passed, but it was absolutely unbearable inside and we decided to sleep in the car. Frank always kept a sleeping bag and a couple of extra sweaters in the trunk for winter travel, so we broke those out, tipped the front seats back, and snuggled up. With the light coming through a layer of snow, it was actually quite romantic! As I'm sure Gracie won't be surprised to hear her mother say, we decided this was our chance to play Doctor Zhivago—*Yuri and Lara in the frosty dacha—except in a rest area on the Jersey turnpike. My diaphragm and spermicidal jelly were in my suitcase in the trunk…*well, shit!" said Grace. *I've been doing so well!…but I didn't think there was enough risk to bother getting them, and they'd be freezing cold anyway! So, Brian and Gracie, you were conceived on the night of December 31*st*, 1977, in a red Audi 80 parked next to a Peter Pan motor coach filled with the girls' gymnastics team from Ho-Ho-Kus High School."* Grace stopped reading, tipped her head back, and looked straight up into the air.

"Now, I guess," Ella said slowly, "we know the *first* naughtiest place your mom and Frank ever had sex. Especially with the girls' gymnastics team right next door."

"Jesus!" said Brian. "Jesus! We were conceived at an interstate rest area?"

"In New *Jersey!*" sighed Grace.

"It could have been worse," said Jack with a tentative grin. "It could have been in the restroom. Or under a table at the restaurant."

"I know you're trying to help, Jack," said Grace. "It's sweet of you. It really is. But how would you feel if you just found out you were conceived at a Shoney's Big Boy somewhere? Or a Waffle House?"

"I could have been," answered Jack. "Dad loved those places. The first time he ever kissed Mom was out behind a Howard Johnson's."

"I don't know," said Grace. "All I can picture now is a stork driving along the interstate in this big road-service vehicle with flashing yellow lights—and me and Brian plopped in the back with the tire pump and jumper cables."

"Look," said Brian. "Like Jack said, you've got to be conceived somewhere. Why don't you read on? Maybe Mom will have something to say that…well…puts everything in a slightly more upbeat light."

Grace looked at him skeptically. "You do know you're mixing metaphors, don't you?"

"Fuck's a verb, right?" said Jack.

Grace rolled her eyes and read on. "*The snow had basically stopped by the time we woke up, and we were on the road again by 6:30—but the two of you, Grace and Brian, you were already on your road, too. I want you to put the last of our ashes in the ground in the wooded area at the back of the parking lot. I assume there won't be any snow. I apologize for the unglamorous location, but the thought of keeping company with Molly Pitcher really appeals to me. I don't mean to embarrass anyone by choosing the spot where you got yourselves started, but as I told you last time, the fact that you did get started made my life and saved Frank's. I mean that quite literally. He hadn't ever wanted children, for reasons you already know. I honestly think that, when we found out I was pregnant, he might have wanted me to end the pregnancy if I hadn't said I'd never consider another abortion after what happened before. But he loved you as soon as he saw you, and you saved him when he was ready to slip away. How can we not thank a nor'easter, Molly Pitcher, and the Garden State for that?* Okay, Mom," said Grace quietly. "I get it. *Oh, my!*" Grace read on. "*I guess it's time to say goodbye. Well, you know I love you all. I treasured every minute I spent with you, Gracie and Brian (except for the odd messy intestinal bug, the AIDS scare, and that first time you got suspended from Littleton State, Brian). I dearly wish I could have had more minutes to spend, too, with Jack, Chelsea, Ella, and Sage. I hear Sage, especially, is a young woman worth knowing."* Grace looked up and smiled at Sage, who looked mildly stunned. *"I am so glad that Frank took out that ridiculous insurance policy. I think he was worried about me being looked after if something happened to him. But, my! Didn't it let us plan a grand trip for all of you! With something left over, I should think. Dad blessed us in many ways, not least in this. In the years to come, be healthy and happy, and smile when you think of the two of us girdling the globe now, together, and of the great goose chase we sent you on. Well, mostly me. Bless you all. Bless you. Mom."*

Grace lowered the sheets and sat in silence. The others had been hanging on every word, and now the chatter and clinking of the bar surged into their soundscape as though a radio had been switched on.

"And bless you too, Mom," said Grace after a long pause. "You and… every crazy thing about you." She looked up from the papers and over at Brian, her eyes brimming. He nodded soberly.

"Well," said Ella. "That was…something." She barely got the words out.

"That *was* something," agreed Chelsea. "It's all been something. All of this."

"I don't see the logistics being any problem," said Jack, retreating to practicalities. "We rent a big SUV or a minivan. We drive down the turnpike…how far is it?"

"Easy to check," said Brian.

"You just remember the trowel," Jack continued, grinning at Brian; "you remember the ashes," he said to Grace; "and…boom!"

"Right!" said Brian. "Boom!" He rose from his chair and walked over to stand next to Grace.

She looked up at him, blinking, then reached up to grab his hand. "That's it!" she said. "Last envelope."

Grace and Brian met in her room the next morning to sort out the final baggies. Jack had arranged for a rental car and had just gone off with Chelsea to pick it up. The plan was to drive down to the Molly Pitcher Service Area after lunch and be back in Jersey City in time for a walk or a swim in the pool and then dinner.

"It was thoughtful of Jack to get the car and drive," said Brian as he set the container of Frank's ashes on the desk next to the television.

"Jack can be a thoughtful guy," replied Grace. "He *is* a thoughtful guy. I know I wouldn't want to hassle with the turnpike today."

"Me neither," said Brian. "It's going to be hard enough. This being the last…" He looked at his sister somberly. "You know?"

"Yup!" said Grace, firming up her lips. "So everything into the one set of bags?"

Brian nodded. "Simple this time."

Grace slid Frank's container over next to Cinny's, unscrewed both lids, and set them carefully back on the desk. "This has worked out well. They're coming out really even."

"You're a mathematical genius, is all."

"Yeah, right. Just hold the baggies, will you?"

Brian grabbed the bags they'd used the last time, one still tucked inside the other. He held them open as Grace tipped Cinny in and followed up with Frank. "There you go, Mom and Dad. Go wild!" Looking at Brian, she offered up something between a chuckle and a choke.

"You know," said Brian, "I don't know why we didn't just combine them after Oxford. We could have just popped them in the baggies. Or at least left one of those behind instead of carrying it all the way back." He pointed to the empty canisters.

Grace laughed. "When you and Ella have been married a little longer, you'll understand. Marriage requires a little good separation time. 'A room of one's own.' They'll be spending eternity together in a hole in the ground, these bits. We did them a favor. Besides, I think we should hold onto the containers."

"You don't think that's a little macabre? What are we going to use them for?"

"I don't know," said Grace. "But they're a lovely blue." She held one up to the light and turned it slowly "Maybe I'll keep rice in mine."

"You can have both of them, as far as I'm concerned."

"You don't think Ella will want to keep her stash in one?" Grace was smirking.

"Oh! Good idea! And if there's any Cinny dust left in them, when Ells tokes up, she'll get the munchies like always…but she'll want to eat her potato chips off my naked six-pack."

"You don't have a six-pack. You never had a six-pack. You've always been a pudgy dork." Grace leered at him impishly.

Brian pulled up his shirt, revealing what was in fact a very well-delineated abdomen.

"Well, I'll be damned!" said Grace. "Very impressive."

"Sage makes me go to the gym."

"Good for her. Speaking of Ella toking up, how's she doing? It's been since Thailand, right?"

"Yeah."

"I'm really glad she hasn't risked traveling with anything, obviously. But it has to have been tough, no?"

"She's been okay. She says it's been good for her, actually."

"That's great," said Grace. "She's a trooper."

"Isn't she?"

Grace studied one of the containers. "There's still a little bit of Mom in there. Dusting the sides."

"That's Dad."

"Is it?" Grace looked distressed.

"I don't know," said Brian. "It's awful, isn't it?"

"What should we do?"

"What do you mean?"

"With their left-over atoms? We can't just leave them in there, can we?"

"They'll mix in with your rice," said Brian. "It will be like some kind of communion with Mom every time you have a stir fry."

"You're sick, Brian. I mean it!" Grace looked as though she did.

"Yeah. I know."

"It's like *The Hangover Herald* all over again. Anything for a laugh."

"Can you tell this is getting to me?" asked Brian.

"It's okay," said Grace. "So maybe we just fill the containers with a little water and slosh it around to pick up the ash. Then we can take them with us, one of them anyway, and dump it at the rest stop along with the ashes. We can even rinse the baggies."

"Brilliant! Do it."

"Hey. Want some coffee?"

"Sure. Thanks."

Once the coffee was ready, they retreated with their paper cups to the chairs by the window. "So, kiddo! 'The AIDS scare.'"

"Yeah," said Brian, shifting in his seat.

"Does Ella know anything about that?"

"I haven't told her. Have you?"

"No way."

"I assume Jack knows." Brian looked at her somewhat despondently. "And maybe Chelsea."

"Both," said Grace with a grimace.

"I figured. That's okay, though. I deserve it."

"Look!" said Grace, leaning forward in her chair. "That was a long time ago. I'm thinking it might be just about time to let it go."

"Yeah?" Brian sat wide-eyed. "You're shitting me."

"What do you think? I'm a complete asshole? No! Don't answer that!" She sat back in her chair but kept him fixed in her gaze. "But what? Like I'm going to go to the grave holding a grudge against the only other one in the family who's left? Just because he had the same taste in boyfriends that I did?"

"I don't know, Gracie. I'd like to say it was just, you know, the same taste in boyfriends." He suddenly grinned. "I *did* used to get excited watching him go up under center with those tight football pants and all. But if I'm going to be honest…"

"It's *time* to be honest, Brian. Life is short."

"Okay. I know. And a bunch of it was just wanting to dick you around." He paused, watching for her response.

"Of course. Of course you wanted to dick me around. I was everything you wanted to be. Brilliant. Athletic. Popular. The secret sexual partner of the school's star quarterback. If I'd been you, I would have dicked me around, too."

Brian stared at her with his mouth open.

"I'm dicking *you* around now," said Grace, with a big smile. "But it stops here, okay?"

"Okay," said Brian.

"You don't look convinced."

"You're just suddenly going to be able to forgive me for something you've been sniping at me for thirty years over. Just like that?"

"I hope so."

Brian laughed. "That's great. That's just so funny. 'I hope so.'"

"I do."

"Okay. I hope so too."

"I'll tell you what," said Grace, reaching out to give Brian's knee a horse bite. He flinched, as he always did. "Let's just assume you coming down to New Haven when Chelsea was born—when you just pulled up stakes and came down to take care of all of us like that—that meant the world to me. Even if it's taken me this long to admit it to myself."

"Wow!" said Brian, shifting again in the chair.

"All of this," said Grace, holding her hands out wide, "from Mom's dying on—all the planning, the trip, Mom's confessions and stories, everything—how could it not make a difference?" She gazed keenly at her brother.

"I don't know how it could. Couldn't. Whatever. Yeah. I hear you."

"I'm not saying I'll never drop another nasty comment about Jimmy Lamont. Or—and this is another project I'm working on—make fun of Jack around other people when it's a stupid and cruel thing to do. Or get on Chel for smoking…that or get all stressed about her hooking up with an older man with kids and prostate cancer."

"Have you seen Chel smoking lately?"

Grace sat up straight. "Oh my God! No! I don't think I have."

Brian smiled. "Sage says she's really trying to quit."

Grace heaved a great sigh. "Well. Wow! Anyway. You get what I'm saying?"

"I do."

"Dad, you know…look what he forgave Mom for. And look how she stuck with him through thick and thin, when all he wanted to do was die. And what she did for us. And Planned Parenthood, for God's sake."

"I know," said Brian. He drained the last of the coffee and put the cup on the table between them.

"How brave she was!" Grace leaned back, crossed her arms, and stuck her legs out straight. "And smart. And funny. Usually at my expense, but she was hilarious. And now she's gone! You know—"

"Know what?"

"It's all so small, so insignificant. The stupid stuff siblings do to each other. But you know what? It's Darwinism, just like Dad would say. You fucked Jimmy Lamont so that, eventually, I could be a big enough person to forgive you."

Brian chuckled. "I always wondered why I fucked him. Did he come too soon with you, too?"

"Okay, asshole," said Grace, sitting bolt upright. "I take it all back."

"Don't," said Brian. He stood up slowly, crossed in front of her, and pulled her up onto her feet. "What you just said is maybe the most beautiful thing I ever heard."

"Really?" asked Grace.

Brian's answer was close to the tightest hug Grace had ever experienced.

"Okay, Bri," she croaked after twenty seconds. "Time to let me breathe."

Google Maps had the drive to the Molly Pitcher Service Area at just under an hour, given the current traffic conditions. They left the hotel at 1:45, after a leisurely lunch. Jack was at the wheel of the midnight blue Ford Expedition. Grace sat next to him, with Brian and Ella in the second row. Chelsea and Sage sat together in the back.

"All right, everybody," called Chelsea, once they'd made their way out of city traffic and onto I-78 headed west. "According to Mom, Nana and Pop Pop always played Mad Libs with her and Uncle Brian on road trips, so…I decided to make one up for us to do today. Everybody up for it?"

"Absolutely," said Ella. "I love Mad Libs."

"You all know how it works?" asked Chelsea.

"Yep," replied Jack. "I may just need some help with the parts of speech." He looked at Grace and grinned.

"You already know *fuck* is a verb, dear," said Grace. "I'm sure you can build out from there."

"Okay," said Chelsea. "Dad, we'll start with you. Everybody remember, though: you don't have to hit it out of the park with every word. Sometimes the simplest is the funniest. Everybody got it?"

Jack turned to Grace. "I'm pretty sure she didn't get her bossiness from me."

Grace smiled. "Keep your damn eyes on the road!"

"Okay," said Chelsea. "Dad. A professional occupation."

"A professional occupation…pole dancer."

"Dad!"

"I'm sorry. That's the first thing that popped into my head."

Chelsea sighed. "All right. Pole dancer. Mom, a famous celebrity."

"Michael Jackson."

"Ella. Planet in our solar system."

"Let me see…Uranus."

"Great!" sighed Chelsea, "Everybody's really listening to me."

"You wanted simple," said Ella. "What's complicated about Uranus?"

"Plead the Fifth, Chel," called Jack from the front seat.

"Dear!" Grace gave a little huff and reached out to adjust the air-conditioning vent.

"Uncle Brian," said Chelsea forcefully. "Body-part plural noun."

"Kidneys."

"Sage. Verb."

"Menstruate. No! Wait! *Eat.*"

Chelsea laughed. "Dad. Verb. Past participle."

"What's a past participle?"

Grace slapped him on the arm.

"C'mon," cried Jack, flinching dramatically. "If I crash this American behemoth, it's all your fault!"

"Verb, Dad. Past participle."

"Pissed off."

And so it went around the car, following the Murphy's Law of the game—a general but inevitable slide toward bawdier and bawdier word choices. Once Brian had offered up the last adjective—and just as Jack was exiting onto I-95 South—Chelsea cleared her throat and read away.

"This is called, 'Moseyin' with the Posey Kin.'"

"Perfect," said Ella.

"*Once upon a time, the widow of a Dartmouth pole dancer decided that her daughter and Michael Jackson should travel around Uranus carrying her and her late husband's kidneys in special blue containers. She wanted her children to eat them in all of the foreign countries they had especially pissed off. Both of their families were excited to break wind along with them and quickly humiliated their suitcases, filling them with loose teeth. First they went to Neverland, where they spent three centuries fellating many of the popular tourist spots and sampling all the local tater tots. Next, they took a tandem bicycle to Thailand, where they almost drowned taking a trip on a tampon that got caught in a violent rainbow. Burkina Faso was next, where they left their parents' fallopian tubes right in the middle of the Louisiana Purchase. When they got to Schleswig-Holstein, Indian summer wasn't over yet, and there was still fresh white duck-liver pâté on top of all the highest fuck-me shoes. Brian almost bellowed in a crevasse. Next was Horny Olde England, where they left their testicles very close to a spot long famous for naked loathing. They also went to a quaint fake pub and drank some wonderful British milk. Finally, they got back home, where their last trip was to Mt. Rushmore. There, they left the nipples in a bra and called it a day. An annoying, yellow time was had by all. Although it was a trip that they said they would never imply, they were all upset to be home.*"

"That was absolutely, pant-peeing hilarious," declared Ella after she'd caught her breath. "I love the tampon caught in the violent rainbow."

"Here's to the humble tampon," said Chelsea. "God's sign that She'll never flood the earth again."

"Maybe we can move on to something else, now," said Grace, up front.

"Nana would have loved it, Mom," Chelsea shot back. "You know she would."

Grace paused for a moment. "You're absolutely right, honey. And I guess this is her last hurrah."

"Here's to her," said Jack. "Wonderful, naughty lady. And here we are." He switched on the blinker to signal he was pulling into the service plaza.

"Why don't you stay to the right?" said Grace, motioning with her hand. "That line of trees. I guess that's where Mom had in mind."

"Okay."

They circled around the north side of the parking lot and pulled in between an old Plymouth station wagon and a pest-control van with the image of a huge expiring cockroach painted on its side. *The Bug Man*, the written copy read. *Call us 24/7. Nobody Better to Hush 'em, Crush 'em, and Flush 'em.*

"Nice," said Brian. "I'm kind of picking up another St. Peter's sort of classical vibe here. Anybody else feel it?"

"Definitely," said Ella. "It's sublime."

"All right, everybody. This is it!" Grace's voice quavered noticeably. "Oh, I should have made sure you had your poem, Sage."

"It's on my phone."

They climbed out of the car and headed toward a grassy margin at the back of the parking area. Jack led the group along a painted walkway that bisected the lot. A big BMW approached slowly from the right as Jack came abreast of a "Stop for Pedestrians" sign. The car kept coming. Jack was just starting to step into the striped crossing when Grace called out.

"Whoa! Watch—!"

Jack managed to turn away just as the car rolled into the crossing. He semi-sat on the hood and shuffled awkwardly along to keep from going under the bumper as the BMW finally came to a halt. "What the hell?" Jack yelled, sliding back off the hood and stepping around to look in the driver's-side window.

"Yeah, what the hell?" yelled the driver as his window rolled down. "You just sat on my fucking hood!"

"Look," said Jack, pointing to the sign. "State law. Stop for pedestrians."

"I was talking to my *doctor*!" The man raised his phone angrily.

"Oh, you were talking to your *doctor*," said Jack, arms akimbo. "Booking an appointment, I hope, for the guy you were about to run over in the fucking parking lot?"

The man glared at Jack. "Just get out of my way, asshole. Hey, what the hell are you doing?"

Sage had walked around to the front of the car and was taking a picture of the front license plate. She checked the image and then walked slowly back around the car and stood next to Jack, getting a video of the driver. "Stick your head out a little farther, will you, sir?" she said brightly. "I can't quite get your comb-over."

"Fuck you!" cursed the man, and he squealed away in a cloud of burning rubber.

"Well, that was cheery," said Grace. "Everybody okay?"

"He just missed my toes," replied Jack. "Good thing I have such classically proportioned feet."

"Dad," said Chelsea, stepping up to hug him. "What it is with you and crosswalks? This is, like, the third time. In three continents!"

"Sort of like your mother and gardens, I guess," answered Jack. "This is all being scripted."

"At least you were looking the right way this time," said Grace. "I could see it all happening. I just couldn't get the words out."

"That's okay, H.P. I know you're not quite ready to get rid of me."

Grace took a second to settle herself. "Not quite," she said with a laugh. "Hope springs eternal."

They walked to the back of the lot, where a twenty-foot-wide strip of grass backed up against a line of mature hardwoods. Ten feet in from the curb, a row of small boxwoods had recently been planted. Nursery labels still hung on the lower branches, and the fresh mulch around their bases filled the air with a damp, woody scent.

Brian took the trowel out of his coat pocket. "How about back by that tree?"

"Not as idyllic as Oxford," said Grace. "But fine."

They stepped through the line of boxwoods and walked to the base of a maple tree. Brian knelt and started digging. Once he had a suitable hole excavated, he stood up and turned to his sister. "You want to do this last one, Gracie?"

Grace stood there, virtually immobile, her arms folded, her face starting to crumble. Jack moved next to her and threw his arm around her waist. She looked up at Brian. "This is it, kiddo," she sputtered. "Last dance!"

Chelsea stepped closer. "Is it okay if I put them in, Mom?" she asked quietly. Grace handed her tote to Jack and refolded her arms. He pulled out the crumpled baggies and passed them to Chelsea with a melancholy smile. Chelsea walked over to where Brian was standing and gave him a little hug. She knelt, opened the bags, and tipped them slowly into the hole. As the ash and bits of bone tumbled in, a tiny dust cloud rose and hovered in the still air.

"Damn it! The ash water," said Grace. "We left it in the car."

"I'll get it," said Brian. "Jack. Keys?"

Jack tossed them over, and Brian scurried off.

"Don't get hit!" called Grace, with the hint of a laugh.

A minute later, Brian was back with one of the blue canisters. Chelsea held the baggies open. Brian poured some water in, added a little more, and nodded. Chelsea sealed the inner bag, sloshed it around, then reopened it and poured the liquid back into the blue container. Some spilled out onto Brian's hand.

"No worries," he said. "Mom's used to me being a slob." He grinned at Grace, and she grinned bravely back. Brian held the canister over the hole and tipped the liquid in with the muffled sound of milk pouring into a bowl of flour. He held the cannister upside down until the last drops fell out, then stood and turned to Sage.

"Me?" she asked.

Brian nodded.

Sage stepped closer, taking out her phone. Her fingers danced over the screen, then she tapped an icon and turned the thing sideways. "I'm not great at poetry," she said, looking around the group with uncharacteristic shyness, "but this has meant a lot to me." She looked at Chelsea, who pinched her lips together as her chin started to tremble. "I wanted to say something, and this is what came out." She walked over to the hole, knelt where Brian had knelt, and began to read:

You can know someone your whole life and still,
When you sit with them and talk,
There's a wall there between you with no windows and no door.
Or you can meet someone once,
At a wedding, say, or in a line outside a movie,
And you begin to hear, somehow so soon,
The music they have danced to all their lives.
I met you once, and the music was more the kind
You listen to under the stars—
Not dancing but holding someone's hand,
Smiling as the moon peeks up above the willows.
Now I've followed your dreams around the world.

I've seen you hold that other hand you held,
And loved, and trusted, soothing your wounds and worries.
I've followed your path with these others,
Some known, some not so much,
But at every step of our long way,
Doors have opened, windows have been un-shuttered,
Until the walls have fallen now between us—
Now just ghosts of dust rushing down the wind
Into yesterday.
How to thank you for a life, for love, for laughter
That my weak words can never capture?
How to thank you for a family?

Before Sage could rise all the way to her feet, Chelsea rushed over and crushed her against her chest. It occurred to Jack, looking on, that he'd endured rugby tackles that were less forceful.

"I don't think I've ever known a girl quite like you," said Jack. He and Sage were returning the rental car later that afternoon. The streets were still jammed with commuter traffic, and it was raining hard enough that the wipers flipped back and forth at the highest speed. "Or even a *person* like you."

"You're not coming on to me are you, Jack? Like grabbing your last chance?"

Jack looked at her in shock.

"Shit!" said Sage. "I don't know why I said that. Of course I was kidding."

"I hope so."

"I was." She turned to him with real concern. "Totally. But it was dumb."

"I thought we trusted each other. After everything."

"We do. I do. Totally. I'm sorry, Jack. That was, like, so adolescent."

"Well, I guess you're entitled. Anybody with the weight of the world on her shoulders is going to slip up once in a while."

"Yeah. Well, it was still dumb. I won't do it again."

"Deal. Hey, buddy!" Jack honked at a beat-up minivan that was straying into their lane. "Wake up and smell the coffee!"

Sage sighed. "I'm going to miss you guys. Chelsea, and Grace, and you."

"It's been great."

"I know it's kind of corny, but I guess you're kind of like another father to me. Or a real one. Which is why it was so dumb what I said just now."

"Let's just forget about it, Sage. It's okay."

Sage sat for a moment, gazing out the window as they passed a row of shops—a convenience store, a hair salon, a Mexican grocery. Here and there, brave souls scuttled along with an umbrella or hooded raincoat. "You know what's so cool? You're kind of like a dad, but you're also kind of like a brother, too." She laughed and looked over at him. "A goofy one."

"I'm not sure how I should take that."

"I think everybody tends to be an adult and a kid at the same time," Sage went on. "Unless they never grew up at all, like my real dad. And you can be a real adult, Jack."

"High praise," said Jack. "I'm flattered."

'You've got a great daughter, too."

"I know. Grace and I are lucky."

"Well," said Sage. "You both probably had something to do with how she turned out."

"Grace did, anyway," replied Jack. "I spent most of my time at the law office. When I wasn't playing golf. Or shopping for cars I didn't need."

"Chelsea told me you used to read to her every single night. And make up stories when she was in the bathtub. About mermaids and pirates."

"Maybe. I don't really remember."

"Right!" scoffed Sage. "Tell me another one." She turned to gaze out the side window. "Have you always been into cars?"

"Everybody in Clearwater was into cars. If you didn't rebuild an engine by the time you got out of middle school, people figured you were headed for ballet school."

"That's homophobic, Jack," said Sage.

"I know it is. I probably thought that, too, for a while."

"But you got over it?"

"I guess. So what do you hear from Tokiko?"

Sage poked him in the shoulder. "Good, Jack. You remembered her real name."

"Lucky guess. Been in touch?"

"Yeah, I talked to her again from the airport in London."

"And—?"

"She doesn't want to do anything. She's afraid to. She's afraid her parents would kill her if they found out what she did."

"Would they?"

"Probably. She calls her dad the Emperor."

"That's really sad," said Jack. "On a number of levels."

"It just pisses me off." Sage cracked the window.

"Is it too hot?" Jack reached for the dash. "You want the AC?"

"I'm fine. I just wanted to smell the air. I love the smell of rain."

"Me too," said Jack. "Look, Sage," he continued after half a minute. "I mean it. I don't think I ever met another girl like you. Chelsea's wonderful, but she's somebody who works inside the system. She sees how other people are doing and finds ways of helping them."

"The world needs more people like that," said Sage. She opened the window a little farther.

"It does. But it also needs more people like you. People who shake up the system. Who don't settle for making everything work more smoothly, but who can see when things are screwed up and have the courage to say it and do something about it."

"I guess," replied Sage. "You catch a lot of shit, though."

"And you take some chances, right? Ko Phi Phi was pretty scary."

"So Chelsea says."

"It was," said Jack. "And you need to pick your battles."

"I'm hearing that a lot lately. But thanks. I have a hard time remembering sometimes."

"You know what else you need to get better at?"

"So, what? You're not being creepy, but now I've got to live through a major lecture, is that it?"

Jack looked at her quizzically. "You can just tell me to shut up."

Sage laughed. "No. Tell me. What do I have to get better at? Seriously."

Jack shook his head and looked back at the road. "At letting things go when you can't make them happen. I told you before, you've got a real fire in your belly. But you're going to burn out if you can't let it cool down sometimes. And if you can't walk away from lost causes."

"I guess."

"Listen. Tokiko's going to do—or not do—what she's finally able to. You can try to help her—you should—but, in the end, just being her friend is what's going to have the most lasting impact. The best payoff for both of you."

"It can be so hard, though. Watching somebody you care about retreat back into herself and just say, 'Fuck it!'"

"I know. But there's only so much you can do. People have to find it in themselves to change their lives, in the end."

"Yeah. I guess. Thanks, Jack."

"Flipside, I guess we've all got to be realistic about how much we can change ourselves. Or *should*."

"Okay."

"I grew up thinking Clearwater should be called Backwater," said Jack. "I mean, there was a great beach, and some terrific athletes to hang around with, and hot cars out the wazoo. But even at UVA, I always felt like I didn't measure up to the Virginia gentlemen—all the guys named Ashley and Grainger and Beauregard. Then at Yale, even at the law school, I felt like everybody's country cousin. I was smart and I was ambitious enough, but I didn't go to the Hamptons for Thanksgiving or Aspen over Christmas. I did manage to persuade the beautiful, brilliant daughter of a Dartmouth English professor to marry me, but I was still shaky on past participles and dangling modifiers. Before I knew it, I was playing up being the Southern bozo half the time just because it was safer than trying to pass, you know?" He looked over at Sage. "Pass."

"Is that where the Rolexes come in?"

Jack chuckled. "Sort of, I guess. And maybe some of the drinking. But the watches are part of the hopefulness. Letting your wrist talk when you can't remember the name of Hamlet's girlfriend."

Sage nodded.

"At least the last watch I bought was for Grace."

"That was sweet," said Sage. She sighed and rolled up the window. "You don't have to tell me all this, Jack. Besides, I think you're an amazing guy. Who gives great advice. Chelsea agrees with me, by the way."

"Chel's a sweet girl. Anyway, I'm just trying to make the point that you can drive yourself crazy if you can't let certain things go. I know I'm making things sound worse than they are. My life and everything. Funny how, when you start lecturing, you're tempted to start lying—or, if not lying, exaggerating the truth for effect. I'm happy with Grace. I really am. If I weren't, I wouldn't be saying any of this to you. But for you, me, anybody to be happy?" He paused.

"What?"

"It helps to change your great expectations into reasonable expectations."

"Is that a Dickens reference, Jack?"

"I guess it is!" He slapped the steering wheel. "Hot damn!"

They drove on in silence for a minute. The rain was still heavy, and they ran through occasional pools on the road. The car would suddenly decelerate, water whooshing in the wheel wells like thunder, while huge curtains of spray flew up to either side of them.

"Look," said Jack. "I've got an idea."

"What's that?"

"If Tokiko doesn't want to go after this guy, maybe I can write him a letter on company stationery. Tell him we suspect he's guilty of a sexual impropriety with a minor in Seattle and if we get wind of any more monkey business, we're prepared to go to the authorities."

Sage stared at him, wide-eyed. "You'd do that?"

"Sure. Would it work? Who knows? But at least it'd be something." Hearing no response, Jack turned to look at Sage. She sniffed and wiped at her eye. "Are you okay?" he asked.

"Yep," said Sage. "I think so, Jack."

Grace awoke at six o'clock the next morning to the sound of a text coming in from Brian. "*Morning,*" it read. "*Would love a few minutes with you solo before we head to the airport. Coffee in the restaurant soonish?*"

"*Be there in ten,*" she replied and eased out from under the covers.

"Very chic," said Brian, as Grace walked into the room where the breakfast buffet was setting up. He gestured toward the oversized UVA hoodie Grace had thrown on. "Calvin Klein?"

"Jack Tingley!" She sat down opposite her brother at the small table where he cradled a steaming mug.

"Wa-hoo-wa! Sleep okay?"

"Finally. It took me a while to wind down."

"Me too. I can't believe this is all over."

"Me either," said Grace. "Thanks for all the planning, Brian. It was flawless." Brian waved his hand dismissively. "I can see why REI hasn't fired your ass. Despite your challenging personality."

"Thanks for your flattering assessment."

"It's actually pretty sincere," said Grace. "Here. Let me get a cup. You okay?"

"Perfect."

A minute later she was back. "Cheers," she said, touching her cup to his.

"Thanks, too, for what you said yesterday. Really."

"Yeah," sighed Grace. "That felt good. It's been…I don't know. Like I said, life's too short to mope around with a that big a monkey on your back."

Brian nodded.

"Sage is just so great," said Grace. "You know? Wow! That poem!"

"Yeah," said Brian. "Who knew?"

Grace took a long sip, studying Brian over the rim. "You seem really happy with Ella, too."

"She's the one, Gracie. She really is."

"I can tell. I think everyone can."

"Well, I don't know." Brian moved his cup in a small circle on the tabletop. "Sometimes I worry about Sage."

"Of course she's protective, Brian. Anyone would be. With an ass- hole like that for a father? Ella was all she had."

Brian nodded.

"But now she's got you, too. I've heard her say some great things, by the way."

"Thanks."

They looked at each other a little awkwardly, as though they'd just discovered they shared a guilty pleasure.

"I have to say I've been worrying about something," said Brian at last.

"What's that?" Grace set her cup down and leaned toward him over the table.

"That big insurance policy Dad bought? The one that made it so easy for Mom to send us all on this trip?"

"Yeah?"

"And then he dies in a single-car crash, running straight into that big rock wall on 91?"

"What are you saying, Brian?"

"I'm not saying, really. Just wondering. Isn't it obvious, though? After what Mom said about finding him with the pistol in his hand."

Grace sighed and sat back in her chair. "Okay. It occurred to me, too."

"What really scares me is that what put him over the edge might have been Mom."

"You don't mean her Parkinson's."

Brian looked at her and nodded. "I do." His brow pinched with concern. "I mean, maybe he had all the suicidal thoughts under control and then, when he found out about her being sick, he just couldn't handle it."

"And ducked out on her?" There was burgeoning anger in her voice. "You really think he'd do that?"

"I don't want to," said Brian.

"Look," said Grace. "First of all, I'm almost certain Mom hadn't talked to anybody about any tremor before Dad's accident. She certainly didn't to me."

"*Almost* certain?"

"I know for sure she didn't go to the neurologist until afterward. Because the doctor told her at the first appointment that it might have been the stress of losing Dad that brought on the symptoms. At least made them worse. She told me later the chance of that really gave her hope for a while. That it might not be something worse."

"Worse than losing Dad?"

"You know what I mean." Grace found a gentle smile. "Dad would never have deserted Mom if he'd known she was getting sick."

"Even with Matthew, you think?"

"That was ancient history, Brian."

"Maybe he did know—somehow—and bought the insurance so she could get the best care. Maybe he knew we'd still be here if he died, and we could use the money to take care of her. Better than he could."

"Look, Brian. I don't know any life-insurance policies that don't have a suicide exclusion. The policies Jack and I got way back wouldn't cover a suicide for a full two years after the effective date. Mom was just fine two years before Dad died."

Brian nodded thoughtfully. "I guess you're right."

"I know I'm right, Bri. Put your mind at rest. Really."

"God, Gracie!" sighed Brian after a pause that included a click or two.

"What?"

"This whole family thing. I didn't have a clue what it was going to be like having a stepdaughter. How you go through all the awkwardness of getting to know someone—especially an adolescent. And you work through all the ground rules for getting along and being a parent at the same time—not to mention making it all work with her real mother. And then you suddenly realize that you care desperately about how they're doing and how they make it through the day, and you almost care more about their being happy and safe and feeling good about themselves than you care about yourself."

"Welcome to parenting."

"And then…" Brian shrugged. "Then you discover that, behind the familiarity and the facades and all the roles your *own* parents played in your life, they were as needy and frightened and confused as you. But you weren't smart enough to realize it. And, when you did, maybe, it was too late."

"I don't worry about Mom at all," said Grace after a bit. "I'm not sure there's ever been anyone who knew how to take care of herself any better than Mom."

"Not that she never made any mistakes."

"Of course not. But Dad? Life hurt Dad really badly. Way more than Mom ever did. Thank God she was there for him through everything."

"I just wish *I'd* been," said Brian. "This has all been like some kind of weird screenplay. All of Mom's letters put together. And we've been listening while somebody read it, taking it all in and having all these profound feelings—after the fact. But we didn't ever realize before—I didn't, anyway—that we were right in the middle of the thing all along and didn't know it. And we didn't do anything to help. I mean, enough."

"We loved them, didn't we?" Grace asked.

"Of course we did," replied Brian.

"And they knew it, didn't they?"

"I guess. I hope so."

"So it could have been a hell of a lot worse."

Brian's lip rose dismissively. "I guess I'm just not totally happy summing it all up that way."

"So you're going for total happiness?"

Brian looked at her intently and shook his head. Then he laughed. "Fat chance, with you as a sister."

Brian, Ella, Sage, and Chelsea were all flying around midday, so they opted to Uber out to the airport together. Grace and Jack waited with them in the lobby as Brian watched the car zigzag closer on his iPhone. Laughter kept pace with the tears as they said their farewells. Among the tight hugs none of them could have predicted three weeks back, Ella's embrace of Grace was especially robust. Stepping back from it, Ella slipped an envelope into Grace's hand. "Don't open it now," she said softly. "Whenever you have a quiet moment. This has just been so wonderful!"

Grace's moment came once she and Jack had settled into their seats on the train back to Westport. Jack had snagged the latest copies of *Golf Digest* and *Road & Track* at the Grand Central newsstand and was happily thumbing his way through them. It was raining as they broke out of the tunnel into daylight. Pulsing drops of water etched their way across the window past Jack's head.

Grace reached into her purse and pulled out Ella's card. She turned it slowly in her hands, recalling all the other envelopes she'd opened over the past days and weeks. When it came to scenic settings, blasting through the Bronx on an Amtrak coach was hardly on a par with lounging at the Villa Borghese or sitting across from the north face of the Eiger. Then again, the message inside wasn't likely to be as dramatic or consequential as any of Cinny's had been. Grace stuck a forefinger under the flap and ripped the envelope open.

It disgorged a humorous card. Two attractive middle-aged women were cavorting hand-in-hand in the photo on the front, as though they were models for a Breughel festival scene. "*Every time I sneeze,*" read the first speech bubble, "*I have an orgasm.*" "*Are you taking anything for it?*" asked the second. Grace turned to the inside for the response: "*Pepper!*"

Just below, Ella had crossed out, *It's your birthday. Have a great one!* and written, *Here's to my wonderful fellow traveler!* Grace tittered.

"What?" asked Jack, looking up from a review of the newest Callaway Big Bertha.

"Just from Ella," answered Grace. She showed him the card.

Jack laughed. "Great! Haven't we seen that before?"

"I think so. But it's still funny."

Jack gestured to the message inside the front. "What's she have to say?"

"I don't know yet."

Jack nodded and turned back to his magazine.

"*Dear Grace.*" Ella's stylish longhand struck Grace as exactly what Katherine Hepburn's would have looked like in a classic 1940s movie. Grace's own "cursive" was more like printing, with a few decorative barnacles. "*I apologize for the bawdiness, but this was the only card I had with me. Let's just say Cinny inspired me. You know how much this trip has meant to me and Sage. She was so bang-on when she wrote about how much you all made us feel we're part of the family. You are all so wonderful—so warm, and funny, and smart. You know how much I love Brian. I hope you know how much I love you as well. I look forward to many more terrific and enlightening times together, wonderful sister-in-law.*" Grace turned with a smile to the back of the card. "*I wanted to let you know, though, just how much Jack has meant to Sage. She says he's really helped her out with some personal issues she says she'll fill me in on sometime. Who knows what about? You know Sage! Meanwhile, she raves about what a fun and good man he is. I've never seen her do that before—maybe even with Brian—and I can't tell you how much that means to me, considering Sage's more-than-deadbeat dad. Chelsea is also one of Sage's favorites—"Like my sister," she says—but I think Chelsea's also been a kind of mother to Sage in ways I haven't managed. I don't know where things with Grant will end up, but if she stays with them, his daughters couldn't have a better influence in their lives. We'll call when we get back to Seattle, but know that we love you guys more than I can say. Ella.*"

Grace sighed and tucked the card back in the envelope.

"What'd she say?" asked Jack.

"I'll let you read it later. But it's all good."

Jack nodded.

"Time for a new set of clubs?" Grace asked brightly.

"I think I'm okay for now," Jack replied. "Actually."

CHARLOTTESVILLE

Grant met Chelsea at the airport. He was waiting in the cell lot when her flight landed, and drove to the terminal as soon as she texted to say she'd retrieved her bag.

"Over here!" he called as she came out the terminal door.

"What's with the car?" She eyed the little blue hatchback as she walked over to where he'd pulled up.

"It shrank at the car wash," he said, grabbing her and squeezing her mightily.

"Changed color, too. God, it's good to see you!" She went up on her toes and kissed him hard on the lips.

"And you too, sweetness. I missed you so much. We all missed you. Especially Jimi. Here, give me that." He grabbed Chelsea's bag and lifted it into the back of the car. "And that." He threw her carry-on in with the other bag and slammed the hatch.

"The Volvo's in the shop," he explained, slipping into the driver's seat. "What for?"

"Mice, again. I don't know how those little bastards keep getting in. I turned on the heater yesterday morning and it was like fake snow coming out the vents. All these little shreds of chewed-up fabric and that dog-foot smell, you know?"

"Maybe you should let Jimi sleep in the garage. He loves mice."

"Who'd snuggle with *you*, then?" Grant asked suggestively.

"You, I guess," laughed Chelsea. "If you could bear it."

"Done!"

"How are the girls?" Chelsea asked, as they pulled onto the airport approach road.

"They're good." Grant looked at her and smiled. "They're keen to see you."

"Me too. I picked up a few presents for them along the way."

Grant laughed. "Save them for their birthdays. You'll spoil them."

"More than *you* do? No way!" She peered out the window, marveling anew at how many Virginia houses had ochre skirts on their walls from the rainwater splashing up the red dirt. "Have you told them?"

Grant looked over again. "We were waiting for you, right?"

"Right," said Chelsea. "Maybe tomorrow?"

"Perfect."

"It's funny. Mom and Dad are getting pretty comfortable with us, I think. You and me. But when Mom heard you hadn't told the girls and were waiting until I was back, I think it kind of freaked her out."

"Oh, Chel!"

"I get it. I mean, when I was just hanging out with you, even when I moved in, I figure they thought it was all just a little post-graduate adventure. That eventually I'd meet some lacrosse bro and move to Richmond and get our pictures in the Society section every Sunday."

"You still could."

"And I could still find a copy of *Space Travel for Dummies* and become an astronaut. But when they heard we figured it would be easiest for El and Daria to handle the news if I were there too, I think that was some kind of handwriting on the wall."

Grant looked over under knit brows. "That makes what's going on here sound pretty grim, doesn't it?"

"I'm just suggesting what *they* might be thinking. Not me. I'm all for Rod Stewart–Rachel Hunter marriages."

"Did you just propose to me?" asked Grant. "Because if you did, let me pull over so we can get out and you can kneel down and pop the question properly."

Chelsea laughed. "I'll need something to drink first."

"Reach in the back. I think I've got some warm PBRs in my computer bag." Grant wriggled in his seat. Chelsea looked over in time to see a pained expression leaving his face.

"Change your mind about our relationship?" she asked.

"Never."

"What is it, Grant?"

"Just a little twinge, is all." He wriggled again. "I usually don't get it unless I'm running."

Chelsea put her hand on his leg. "What's it like, dear?"

"Oh, just a twinge, I guess. Between a twinge and a sharp pain, maybe. Fleeting. Like somebody's grabbing my prostate and wringing it out like a sponge."

"Oww!" said Chelsea. "Grant!"

"It's bearable. The doctor said it's not all that unusual." He laughed.

"What?"

"Especially after a twelve-needle biopsy. Damn!" A yellow light stopped them at one of the major intersections.

"No worries," said Chelsea. "We're not in a hurry."

Grant looked over at her, kissed the back of his hand, and held it up to her lips.

She kissed it back. "I missed you."

"Good." The light changed and they started up again. "So, any more asshole encounters for Sage after Rome?"

Chelsea shook her head. "Not really. Just a few random teachable moments. But she's so brave, Grant. And funny. It was like I was rooming with Kate McKinnon or something."

"So it wasn't a constant trial? Hanging out with an adolescent?"

"Are you kidding?" Chelsea tipped her seat back a couple of notches and pulled her knees up to her chest. "You remember about her fucked-up family life, right? Her real dad?"

"Who could forget the flying fornication twins?"

"Yeah! Well, the last place we scattered Nana and Pop Pop's ashes, she read a poem she'd written, and—my God!—it was moving, Grant. All about feeling, for the first time in her life, like she was part of a family. And it was so direct, and honest, and she seemed so vulnerable and sweet as she read it. This out of the tough girl whose principal can't decide if she's She-Hulk or Joan of Arc."

Grant chuckled. "Sounds like an incredible poem."

"I'm sure I can get a copy. You'll be amazed."

"Can't wait. And how are your mom and dad?"

"Actually, I'd say never better."

"Really?"

"It had to be everything we went through together. Full immersion, really. Everything we saw. Witnessing and celebrating and weeping over the whole arc of Nana and Pop Pop's lives. The longer the trip lasted, the more that back-and-forth, 'Jack, I love you, but you're an idiot,' and, 'What's wrong, Honey Pot? You haven't rolled your eyes at me all day' shit they do really got dialed back a notch or two."

"That's wonderful, Chel. It must have been really nice for you to see."

Chelsea nodded. "And the only watch he bought the whole time was one he bought for Mom."

"What? And I pictured him coming back from London with Big Ben."

"Sorry to disappoint."

"No. Let's hope it lasts."

"Time will tell. Hey!" Chelsea tipped her head back, sniffing around the car. "No smoke. Did you quit?"

"Sorry." Grant looked sheepish. "It's a loaner. I pay two hundred bucks if I stink it up."

"Hmm. Well, *I've* quit."

Grant looked at her with surprise. "Really?"

"Ten days and counting."

"That's great, sweetness. I'm so proud of you."

"It's for you, dear. And the girls."

SEATTLE

"Okay," called Ella from the kitchen. "I'm headed to the grocery store. I think I'll just get enough for tonight and tomorrow, but does anyone want to come along?" They'd just gotten back home from SeaTac. Brian was sorting through a big batch of mail a neighbor had taken in for them.

"No, thanks," he replied. "I think Sage wants to unpack when she's off the phone with Tokiko."

"Okay. Want anything special?"

"I don't know."

"C'mon. Help me out here."

"How about something simple and healthy?"

"You mean like pressed duck?"

Brian laughed. "Perfect!"

"I'll throw together a veggie stir-fry. Bye."

Brian moved the box of mail off his lap and onto the coffee table. He stared at it as he drummed his fingers on his knee, then got up and walked over to the refrigerator. He opened the door, surveyed the meager contents, and reached for a bottle of white wine. He was getting a stem from the cupboard when Sage walked in in her socks.

"How's Tokiko?"

"Same old Tokiko. Fine, I guess."

"You don't sound very excited about getting back in touch."

"No, she's good. It's just so challenging," Sage intoned poshly, "for seasoned world travelers such as myself to—you know—pick up the quotidian threads of a provincial past."

"You are so going to ace your SATs."

Sage huffed. "What's the wine?"

Brian chuckled.

"What?"

"You look like a hungry puppy staring at a guy with a steak."

"Shove it, Brian!"

He checked the bottle. "Kono sauvignon blanc. From Marlborough. Want some?"

"Sure."

Brian grabbed her a glass, poured in three fingers, and poured the same for himself.

"I *am* planning on drying out soon, you know?" She reached out for the glass. "But they say it's good to taper." She giggled, then pointed to the couch. "Let's sit down."

"Cheers," said Brian once they were settled in.

"Cheers."

"Great trip!"

"It was." Sage sipped the wine. "Tasty! Hint of guava?"

Brian chuckled.

"I might actually like to learn about wines, though. Someday."

"Well, there's plenty of time," said Brian. "No need to rush."

"Thanks, Dad!" she said with a scowl. "Brian?" she said after a minute. "You know I really like you, right?"

"Of course I do."

"And you don't have to say you like *me* or anything."

Brian scoffed. "I do, though, Sage. You know I do."

"I know. And that's cool. But can we talk for a little? Before Mom gets back?"

"Sure." Brian set his glass on the table.

"Cinny's letter, you know? The last one?"

"Yeah?"

"That bit about 'the AIDS scare'?"

Brian looked at her uncomfortably. After a second, he nodded. "Umm. That." He shifted on the couch. Turning to face her, he pulled a foot up under his other leg.

"You don't have to explain what it was all about. I mean, I know about Jimmy Lamont."

Brian took a breath, and his brow lowered. "Was it Chelsea? I don't think Grace would have told you. Or Ella."

"So Mom knows?"

"Of course she does."

Sage looked at him thoughtfully. "It doesn't matter who told me. It just really bothered me when I heard about it."

Brian nodded slowly. His lips parted to say something, but he stayed mum.

"I thought to myself, *Great! My mom's married to this guy who not only just broke up with Kingsley after being with him for years and almost buying a house together, but maybe his first sexual experience with another guy was getting the dude to cheat on his sister.*"

Brian took another deep breath. "I'm sorry, Sage. I don't know what to say."

"Maybe there's another angle. Maybe I just heard Aunt Grace's side of it."

"No," said Brian. "There's some truth to it. What you heard."

Sage eyed him closely.

"I mean, I had a crush on him. Jimmy was pretty hot." Brian smiled. "But I'm not sure it would have happened, necessarily, if I didn't know it would totally piss Grace off."

"I think I get it," said Sage after a beat. "I don't have any siblings. Sometimes I wish I did. But, from what I hear, they can do some pretty shitty stuff to each other."

"They can."

"I mean, look at Shakespeare's plays. You know? And Dostoevsky. And *Family Guy*."

Brian laughed. "Yeah."

"I would never judge you, Brian, for anything you did a long time ago. I'd only judge you for something you did now. To my mom."

"I love your mom."

Sage nodded. "Or something you did to me."

Brian looked mystified. "What do you mean?"

"For the first time in my life, I feel like I'm sort of in a real family. Not just you and me and Mom, but now Grace and Jack and Chelsea. Especially Chel. Even Cinny and Frank."

Brian nodded. "Your poem."

"I wake up in the middle of the night sometimes and I almost cry to think how long I've waited to be part of something I didn't have to pick apart and try to change. It's not easy being a sixteen-year-old nihilistic feminist socialist."

Brian smiled at her guardedly.

Sage stared at him. "That was supposed to be funny."

Brian broke into a laugh. "It was!"

"Sort of," said Sage. "But I mean it. Life's put a chip on my shoulder. Not that there's not a lot of good shit that motivates me to do, in terms of sticking it to the Man. The assholes. Know what I mean?"

Brian nodded.

"But if I keep being angry, someday I'm going to kill somebody. Probably somebody pretty powerful and important. Or maybe I'll get myself killed. But I've just spent three weeks getting a peek at something else. I've seen some real honesty and courage and caring. I'd say love, too, but this world is so fucked up, that sounds completely corny, doesn't it?"

"I don't know," said Brian. "I guess it can sound corny sometimes."

"Just promise me, Brian. That you love my mom and you'll never do anything bad to her. That you'll never hurt her. That you'll never fall back in love with Kingsley." She stared at Brian, her eyes wide and imploring.

"Of course I promise that. Of course I do."

Sage looked at him so intensely it felt like her gaze was boring right through his head and out the back. He reached out and grabbed both of her hands and bounced them up and down until she smiled. And then she nodded. "Tokiko says everybody is basically bisexual," she said.

Brian shrugged. "Maybe."

"That's what she says. Not that she's ever come on to me or anything."

"No." Brian stared at her earnestly. "I'm not going to argue with that, personally. But I can tell you one thing."

"What's that?" asked Sage.

"When you find someone you really love—in every way you *can* love—that's an anchor."

"Really?"

"I swear."

There was the sound of a key in the lock and the door swung open. They heard Ella call out, "I'm back!"

"Hey, Mom." Sage slid around in her seat.

"Trader Joe's was a madhouse. I just got a few things and fled for my life. What have you two been up to?"

Sage held up her glass. "I'm learning how to be a boozer."

"Brian's teaching you?"

"No. Brian says he's through with alcohol. After tonight, anyway."

"That's too bad." Ella stepped out from behind the kitchen counter. "He won't be any fun at all anymore."

"Sure he will." Sage pointed to Brian's phone, sitting there on the coffee table. "He just scored you a couple ounces of Purple Kush."

WESTPORT

Grace and Jack took an Uber from the train station back to their house. Their driver turned out to be a sixty-something Manchurian who had moved to the States two years earlier to be near his son and his family. He'd been a professor of neuroscience at Kenkoku University, and he cheerily shared with them the conclusion he'd reached, after decades of teaching and research, that humans were essentially robots. He offered this striking revelation, in animated but halting English, with the amused nonchalance of someone describing the premise of a whimsically apocalyptic Netflix series.

"Is your theory that *everyone* is a robot," asked Jack, "or just certain people?"

"Everyone is robot. Brains store memories. Bodies programmed as cell factories. Make new cells, scrap old cells. Nervous system send electric signals to control different parts of body. Binary system, too. Neurons fire or not, on or off. My wife extra robot." He laughed loudly, grinning at them in the rearview mirror.

"Hmm," said Grace. "Why do you say that?" She glanced at Jack.

"She stay married thirty-eight years. With me!" He laughed again. "Wife keep going day after day, around and around, never walk away. So many things automatic. No thought. No change. Robot!"

"I think I see what you mean." Jack looked at Grace and smiled. "I think I'm going to take it as a metaphor."

As soon as Grace walked in through the garage door, the iconic scent of the place washed over her. She was reminded of the unmistakable smell signature of the Posey house in Hanover and, therefore, of everything she wished she'd done for her parents in their final years—and at the same time, of all of the things she wished she hadn't been forced to endure growing up there. She wondered offhandedly how she might feel if she'd come home to the oily stench of Kitty Kitchen. Could that really have been eighteen months ago?

"There's a message for you from school," called Jack from the study.

"Thanks," Grace called back as she wheeled her bag to the foot of the stairs. "Probably Macey about the goddamn curriculum." She walked back into the kitchen and checked the fridge.

"Sounded like her. She gave a number to call when you get a chance."

"When I feel like wading back into the hellish breach of the culture wars."

"You and Sage. Always fighting for something. No dangling modifiers in compound sentences. No dangling penises in corporate offices."

"Absolutely not, dear," called Grace. "Sage and I are making the world a better place."

They were sitting in Jack's den when Grace's phone rang. It was Chelsea, apologizing for not calling as soon as she got back to Charlottesville. Grace told her it was okay. She and Jack had just made it home, so this one call did double duty. They spoke for three or four minutes, swapping vignettes about the rhythms of their day. Grace told her she and Jack loved her very much, that they'd had a terrific three weeks, and that she should say hello to Grant. She and Jack, she added, certainly looked forward to meeting Eloise and Daria.

"We do?" asked Jack, once Grace had signed off.

Grace stared at him incredulously. "Of course we do!"

"You're right," said Jack after a beat. "It's just that meeting his kids will seem so…committing, you know? Like investing all our savings in his bookstore."

"That's a silly analogy, Jack." She took a big sip of Perrier and put her glass on the table. "Look," she said, pointing at the bird feeder just outside the French doors. A pair of brilliant goldfinches had landed on adjacent perches and pecked busily for seeds at the access ports. "They don't miss a thing. They must have been watching from the Piersons' yard. Thanks for filling the feeder, by the way."

"Sure," said Jack. For a moment he was silent. "I know she loves him and all, but I wish I was sure Grant's the right person for Chelsea," he said. "Not too old. Not too widowed, with kids. Not too dyed-in-the-wool Democrat."

Grace smiled. "Your biases are showing, dear."

"Really, though."

"I know. I wouldn't have said a few months ago that they'd be likely to stay together. It's almost as though his cancer is sealing the deal. At least in the short run. She'd feel awful leaving him when the sledding gets tough. And now her wanting to be there when they tell the girls? It's like she wants them to know their new mom's not going to leave them in the lurch."

Jack nodded. "You know what, though?"

"What?"

"It could be worse."

"Yeah?"

"She could have fallen in love with a sick leftie widower with kids the summer she spent in Paris. Then everything would be just the same, except thirty-five hundred miles away."

"There is that," said Grace.

"You know, the more I think about it, the more I'm really proud of her."

Grace laughed. "I am, too."

"Think how we'd feel if she really had gotten in this deep and then cut and run when he got diagnosed."

"I know," said Grace. "Let's just hope it works out. I mean, that he's okay. By the way, how would it feel being emergency grandparents to his girls? Which we'd be, no question, if something happened to him."

"We'd manage," said Jack. "We've had some practice with girls."

Grace nodded. Then she sighed.

"What is it, Honey Pot?"

"I want to have *real* grandkids. At least one."

"I hear you," said Jack. "Someone to pass our watches along to."

"Precisely!" Grace looked down at her wrist. "You were so sweet to buy me this. I love it."

"It's a classic," said Jack. "Perfect start to your collection."

Grace shook her head. "Nope. This is the only one I want." She smiled at him. "Speaking of collections, you didn't wind up with much, did you?"

Jack shrugged. "No biggie. More?" he asked, holding up his glass.

Grace nodded.

Jack got up and walked to the kitchen. He came back with a half-full bottle of Perrier and poured a good measure into Grace's glass, the rest into his. "So how are you feeling about everything?" He sat down next to her again.

"Exhausted. Dutiful." She looked at him with vague melancholy in her eyes. "Like it all went too fast. Everything."

Jack nodded. "You know, aside from the fact that we were all almost killed on that boat, it went off pretty smoothly."

"You were almost killed four times, Jack!"

"Oh yeah!"

"Brian did a terrific job with logistics, though."

"He did," agreed Jack. "You'd think he was a professional or something."

"Who'd a thunk?" asked Grace. "After his myriad early fuck-ups."

"Myriad? That's the hotel chain, right?" Jack's grin turned into a laugh as she flipped him off. "I'm glad you sorted out the whole Jimmy Lamont thing."

"It was time."

"It was. Not that it was necessarily easy for you."

"Well…" Grace reached forward to flick a piece of lint off the coffee table and onto the floor. "Easier when it happened than it would have been before the trip."

Jack nodded and put his hand on her thigh.

"It was so funny in the Uber just now," said Grace. She put her hand on top of his and gave it a squeeze. "*Humans all robots.*"

"What a character!" said Jack.

"You were right, though. If you take it as a metaphor, it's pretty apt. It's so easy to get into ruts. Reflexive put-downs. Tired quips. Assuming people never change."

"Maybe mindless materialism?"

Grace smiled again. "We read this French philosopher at Yale who says comedy is all about living people acting like they're machines. Like Wimpy in *Popeye* cartoons, salivating every time he sees a hamburger."

"Or Joey Tribiani, every time he sees a sexy girl? 'How *you* doin'?'"

Grace sighed again. "I guess there really is nothing like travel to shake things up," she said, "especially if it's one long *memento mori*, with your mother and father as Yorick's skull."

"That's pretty morbid, Grace."

"I guess. Still…"

"I tell you what, Honey Pot." Jack bounced his fist on her knee. "Let's just run down to Rizzuto's to get a bite. We can pick up some breakfast stuff on the way home and save the grocery store for tomorrow."

"You want to?"

"I do. Come on. We can have teary measles for dessert."

Grace seemed to freeze. "Oh, Jack!" She turned to him. There were tears in her eyes.

"What is it, Gracie?"

"She's just so grown-up. Look at what she's doing! Look at her life! Where did it all go?"

"Maybe it went right where it should have," replied Jack. "Maybe she's found her place. Her moment."

"You think? Honestly?"

Jack nodded. "I do. Trust me?"

Grace looked at him searchingly. "Well," she said, her eyes beginning to twinkle, "since you know so much about watches and things—"

Jack smiled. He was used to Grace teasing him. He'd come to depend on her quips and gibes, really. They were the bunkers and water traps that were always out there on the course and, honestly, made the game that much more fun. But he wasn't sure he'd ever fully appreciated—when she was at it—just how much she looked like her mother.

ABOUT THE AUTHOR

Thomas Reed taught literature, film, and writing at Dickinson College for thirty years. His first novel, *Seeking Hyde*, grew out of courses he taught on Robert Louis Stevenson's celebrated novel and was named Finalist in the 2018 Foreword INDIES Book of the Year Award for Historical Fiction. *Pocketful of Poseys* draws more broadly on his experience growing up in an academic family; his education at Yale, the University of Virginia, and Oxford; years spent living in Rome and Christchurch, N.Z.; circum-global travels with his wife and children; and courageous decisions made by his mother-in-law as she faced her death. He and wife Dottie now split their year between Sarasota, Florida, and Camp Pemigewassett, a summer camp for boys in New Hampshire.

ACKNOWLEDGMENTS

My first debt is to Claudia Stuart Grant, my late mother-in-law, whose resolved and brave farewell to life gave me Cinny and her behest for a memorializing family trip... "gave me" only basically, as she and her fictional avatar are very different ladies in many (perhaps most) ways. As a result, I owe almost as much to her children, David and Jim Grant and Dottie Grant Reed, for giving their blessing to this rather fanciful variation on their mother's story.

John Peck, a great friend who took care of both my father and mother towards the end of their days, contributed more to the overall slant and tone of the book than he apparently remembers. It was definitely John who, over a beer, listened to my embryonic sketch of the "Great Escape" scenario at St. Peter's in Rome and came up with the line about Jack trying to get his mother-in-law out of his pants.

Jeryl Schriever and Alex Huppé generously read an intermediate draft of *Pocketful of Poseys* and offered many suggestions for improvement; Jack especially is a better character (and man) for their observations. At Beaufort Books, Olivia Fish's giving the project an enthusiastic green light didn't mean that she didn't call for crucial reworkings as well. My publisher at Beaufort, Eric Kampmann, and editorial director, Megan Trank, continue to be a pleasure to work with. And, as with an earlier book, James Carpenter gave the manuscript a meticulous copy editing, saving me from countless embarrassing missteps and offering more substantive insights as well.

It is a truism that writing is a lonely pursuit, but I have always enjoyed the support of fellow writers, foremost among them Susan Perabo, Robert Olmstead, and Virginia Pye. Many sincere thanks to all three for being out there to consult and commiserate.

Finally, boundless thanks to my family: Abby, Dan, and Dottie. All of them listened with something well beyond dutiful tolerance as I read to them portions of the book along the way, and all of them made their way through the entire manuscript at least once—always with broadly sensitive eyes that yielded wise and practicable advice. I'm not sure if Abby and Dan have guessed that Dottie might set them the same task that Cinny sets Grace and Brian after we've both given up the ghost, but I have no doubt that they would dispatch their charge with the same love and competence as the Posey kids. And finally, Dottie, this book is dedicated to you because you are Claudia's daughter and because you supported me unstintingly through all the months and years that *Pocketful of Poseys* filled more of my days than it probably should have. I hope that the finished project allays any fears you might have had that I was just sitting at the desk in the living room interminably typing "All work and no play makes Tom a dull boy."